Praise for
The Mercy of the Tide

"Keith Rosson's fearless and genre-bending debut novel, *The Mercy of the Tide*, is harrowing, haunting, and hypnotic. This is nightmare material of the first order, at once exhilarating and profoundly disturbing. It'll leave you breathless. Riptide, Oregon, is a forbidding landscape of shattered lives and broken dreams, and it's a scarier place than the world you're living in. Pour yourself a bracing drink, settle into your comfy chair. Once you begin this book, you won't be going anywhere. What talent, what nerve, what an astonishing first novel."

—John Dufresne, author of *I DON'T LIKE WHERE THIS IS GOING*

"An astonishing debut soaked with suspense. Rosson brings his characters to life with surefooted precision. The town of Riptide, Oregon, may be cursed with rain, but it will be scorched into your memory. Outlandishly excellent."

—Jim Ruland, author of *FOREST OF FORTUNE*

"This story of a community of wounded souls takes some gutsy turns off the main roads to stake its own unforgettable territory. With grit and empathy, Rosson tells a story of heartache and grief unlike any I've ever read."

—James Boice, author of *THE SHOOTING* and *MVP*

"A dark thrill ride."

—Kyle Minor, author of *PRAYING DRUNK*

THE MERCY OF THE TIDE

A NOVEL

KEITH ROSSON

Meerkat Press
Atlanta

ISBN-13 978-0-9966262-4-8 (Paperback)
ISBN-13 978-0-9966262-5-5 (eBook)

Library of Congress Control Number: 2016955723

This is a work of fiction. Names, characters, businesses, places, events and incidents are either the products of the author's imagination or used in a fictitious manner. Any resemblance to actual persons, living or dead, or actual events is purely coincidental.

CRETIN HOP. Words and Music by Jeffrey Hyman, John Cummings, Douglas Colvin and Thomas Erdelyi © 1977 (Renewed) WB Music Corp., Taco Tunes, Inc. and Evergreen Copyrights, Inc. All Rights on behalf of itself and Taco Tunes, Inc. Administered by WB Music Corp. All Rights Reserved. Used by permission of Alfred Music.

Cover design by Keith Rosson
Book design by Tricia Reeks
Author photo by Lindsay Beaumont

Printed in the United States of America

Published in the United States of America by
Meerkat Press, LLC, Atlanta, Georgia
www.meerkatpress.com

It is less a question of their loyalty to the way of the white man than their simple unwillingness to learn. Many of them have done well to learn the language and adopt the notions of civilized man—subjugation to God, cultivation of crops, a care for appearance, desire for individual comforts—but some of them will, I fear, forevermore view reservation life as a lessened version of their earlier, savage ways. These are the ones who stubbornly cling to their old myths, and there is no teaching them otherwise.

—DAVID E. MUYNER, Indian Agent of the Tumquala Reservation in a letter to LUKE LEA, Commissioner of the Office of Indian Affairs, 1851

If we have to start over again with another Adam and Eve, then I want them to be Americans and not Russians, and I want them on this continent and not in Europe.

—RICHARD B. RUSSELL, Chairman of the Armed Services Committee during a Senate debate, 1968

There's no stoppin' the cretins from hoppin'.

—THE RAMONES, "Cretin Hop," 1977

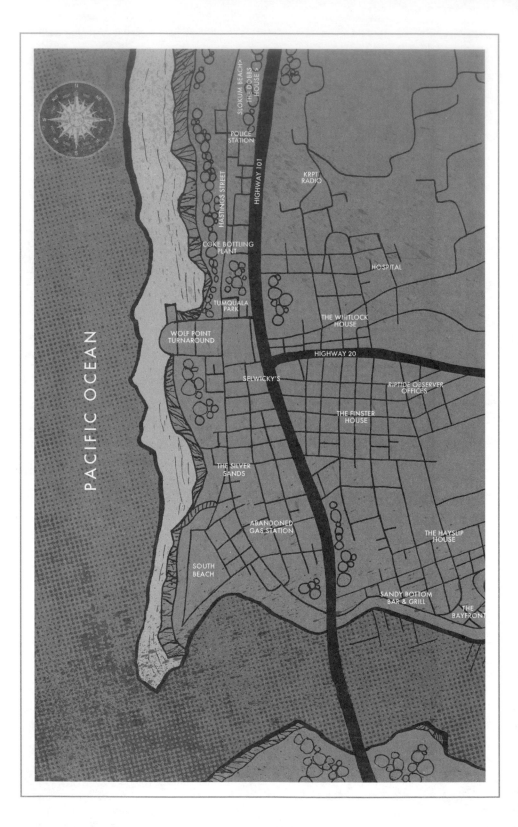

RIPTIDE, OREGON

November–December 1983

ONE

DAVE DOBBS

If there was a catalyst to it all, it was most likely when Joe Lyley, the sallow evangelical man who ran the town's bed and breakfast, was led into Dobbs's office one rain-lashed Monday morning carrying a paper sack that rattled with sand.

Dobbs had been seated in his chair for a grand total of seven minutes or so—just enough time to look over the upcoming day's patrol roster and the previous evening's meager arrests, enough for a few sips of sad, scorched Yuban in a Styrofoam cup, for the slivered ache in his heart to be quelled slightly with the familiarity of the morning's routine—when one of his deputies, Nick Hayslip, rapped his knuckles on the open door. It was just past eight in the morning and rain flew in ugly little spats against the windows; in the station room beyond his office, Dobbs could hear the morning shift slowly coming to life—the ringing phones, the sudden and brittle screech of the fax machine, the hushed tones of the station's dispatcher.

Hayslip leaned his head in, his hat in his hand, and said quietly, "Got a Joe Lyley hoping to have a word, Dave."

Dobbs, his mouth to his coffee cup, motioned him in. Hayslip, frowning and clean-shaven, and in keeping with his recent shift to a tight-assed, deadly seriousness, nodded and wordlessly motioned for someone out in the hall to step inside. Which was when Joe Lyley walked into Dobbs's office carrying about him a familiar air—it wasn't entitlement exactly, the way many of Riptide's citizens walked in, but it was close to it. Call it a sense of barely quelled righteousness, then. A strident little show tune, Dobbs thought, that should be called "I Am the Taxpayer and You Work for Me." Lyley himself was pale and thin, with a little caterpillar of a mustache and owlish glasses that sat huge on his face. He wore his chinos practically hiked to his tits and was holding a wrinkled paper sack to his chest. While they'd never traded words, Dobbs recognized him immediately as a face at town hall meetings. Now as then the man emanated a kind of uneasy, scattershot psychic effluvia that was immediately recognizable: *Religious nut,* Dobbs thought. With some people it was easy to call: it just sang out, like a tuning fork set to thrumming. The kind of man that made people nervous. The paper bag was rolled tight at the top, like a little kid's lunch.

"Sheriff," Hayslip said, still worrying the brim of his hat, "I believe Mr. Lyley here wanted to talk to you about some happenings down at the beach."

"That right?"

"Yes sir," Hayslip said.

Dobbs rose, leaned over his desk, and held out his hand. Joe Lyley, with obvious reluctance, shook it. The man's grip was limp and tepid. Dobbs heard the rattle of sand in the bag and an inkling arose that whatever was in there, no good was going to come from it. He had been a cop for a long time and early on had understood that some men carried calamity on them like a bad cologne.

Dobbs said, "Mr. Lyley, you don't mind if my deputy sits in on our conversation, do you?"

"No, I do not," Lyley said. He sat in the single chair facing Dobbs's desk and crossed his legs, showing a pale stretch of calf between sock and cuff. "A whole lot of trouble might be saved, actually," he said, "if more of your deputies were paying attention to the town's goings-on. Or any attention at all, really." Hayslip took station in front of Dobbs's bookshelf, a dented metal affair full of battered binders and incident logs, cardboard boxes of old paperwork. The rain spat sudden and hard against the window, and Lyley flinched and uncrossed his legs, pressing his knees together, the bag in his lap.

Dobbs leaned back in his chair and nodded. "Okay. Well, let's see if we can't change your mind about that, Mr. Lyley. What is it we can do for you?"

"Well, for starters, there's the matter of the beach down there at the turnaround," he said.

"Down at Wolf Point?"

"Indeed," Lyley said. The word was drawn out, rich with contempt.

Dobbs felt the first distant stirrings of anger. Wished yet again he could call his wife after they were done here, pushed the thought away.

"Alright then," he said. "What about the turnaround?"

Lyley cleared his throat. "Well, beyond anything else I might have to say, there are vandals running around down there. Were you aware? Teenagers.

Most likely fornicating, and I'm positive alcohol is involved. Narcotics, too, I assume, why not? Lord only knows what else goes on down there."

"That is unfortunate," Dobbs agreed. Hayslip stood by the bookshelf, his hands behind his back as he frowned down at his boots. "Though we regularly send patrols to the beach at the Wolf Point turnaround, Mr. Lyley."

"Fornication!" Lyley said as if Dobbs hadn't spoken. "I see bonfires down there at all hours. All hours. You go down there and it's like a—like a hobo encampment. Empty alcohol containers. Trash everywhere." He suddenly lurched forward, eyes dark and gleeful behind his lenses. *"Multiple rubbers of the used variety, Sheriff."*

Hayslip, at the bookshelf, coughed, turned his head and squinted toward the window.

"I'm starting to connect the dots here," Dobbs said, pointing at the man and smiling. "Mr. Lyley, you're the owner of the Surf and Sand, right there on Hastings Street, isn't that right? The nice little bed and breakfast there?"

Lyley's shoulders rose. "It's the *Silver* Sands, Sheriff. But yes, that's correct. My wife and I."

"My sisters-in-law spent a weekend there when they visited here this summer, and they loved your place. Said it was just gorgeous." Lyley stared back at him, unsatisfied. "Well," Dobbs said, resigned to the fact that there were some folks who came to his office determined to remain unhappy. He fell somewhat deeper into the familiar patois when he said, "We do take citizen concerns very seriously, especially when they're small business owners, like yourself, who contribute so much to the community. Our deputies patrol all the beach access points here in town. Every one of them. That's just part of their routes. *Especially* at night, I can assure you. Deputy Hayslip can attest to that."

Hayslip was on point. He dutifully raised his head. "Yes, sir," he said. "That's very true. Absolutely."

Lyley's smile was acerbic, wry, a man used to people trying to pull the wool over his eyes. Some shift took place inside him, the man's fussy little frown replaced with a smile that showcased a mouthful of truly unfortunate orthodontia. "I know you *say* that, Sheriff, but it's quite clear that no one's doing much of *anything* down there. As far as the turnaround goes, or Slokum Beach, or anywhere that I can see. Indecency abounds. Half-dressed children running wild. It's *winter*, Sheriff, good lord. It flies in the face of decency." As if to punctuate his point, Lyley rattled his paper sack again. Hayslip and Dobbs shared a glance, there and gone.

"I really am sorry you feel that way, Mr. Lyley. And I can assure you this isn't just lip service. Do you mind if I ask, what *specifically* is your issue of concern? If it's just our general lack of patrols on the beaches, I will definitely address that with all my deputies."

Lyley tilted his head; Dobbs was reminded of a dog, curious. The overhead light caught one of the lenses of the man's glasses, turning it a gleaming white. "I've never been a huge fan of sarcasm, Sheriff Dobbs."

Hayslip coughed again, fist to his mouth.

"I'm not being sarcastic, sir," Dobbs said. He leaned forward, put his red-knuckled hands on his desk, suddenly tired of the day. Just like that. Already weary with it. Any humor or interest he may have taken from Lyley's strangeness was gone. He had no more use for anecdotes, which is what this interaction with Lyley, at best, would become. Some story that would get passed around the station during the day's breaks. He wanted to spin his chair around, look at the gray wash of the rain in the parking lot, the cruisers slotted neatly in their spots, the sky the color of iron shavings. Get this nutjob and his unerringly solemn deputy out of his office. Simmer in the luxury of his own grief. Didn't he at least deserve that, goddamn it? When he spoke again, his voice was edged in flint. "I'll ask you once more, Mr. Lyley. Is there something specifically you would like to talk about?"

Lyley clucked his tongue and began to primly unroll the paper sack in his lap. A dry, serpentine hiss of paper, one of his hands cradling the sack's bottom. "These are unlovely times," Lyley said, and he spoke with the air of a showman now. "Fornication abounds. Selfishness, greed. Lust. Holy institutions are mocked. We face a *dismantling*, Sheriff."

Ah, here we go, Dobbs thought. He sighed. *We have arrived.*

"Heretics abound. Our leaders moored in godlessness. Countless perversions on television." The speech seemed prepared. Lyley leaned forward and tilted the open mouth of the sack toward Dobbs.

Dobbs, almost relieved that the depth of the man's instability had presented itself this quickly, rose and leaned over his desk and peered into the bag. Hayslip even elbowed himself from the bookshelf and, arms crossed, leaned over to take a look as well.

The contents were at first unidentifiable. Something white and gray, a whiff of salt and then, like an afterthought, the sharp tang of decay. Like a Rorschach, the image fell into place, and he couldn't *unsee* it: the downy wing, the rich butter-yellow of a beak. Lyley rattled the bag—again the rasp of sand—and more was revealed: the seagull was in *pieces*, Dobbs saw, a desiccated body, the two pieces halved and stacked on top of each other. The feet ridged, almost insectile. Lyley stared at him openmouthed now, the merry light of madness brazen in his eyes. A man given over to it entirely.

Hayslip saw the bag's contents and let out a cry, almost sounding disappointed, like a man losing a bet. He recoiled and Lyley's lips suddenly split into a grin as he looked back and forth between them.

"Proof. Proof that a divine judgment walks the earth. It won't be long now." His voice loud in the room, almost musical, bright and reverberating. Gleeful. He was unhinged, absolutely, and his voice seemed ageless and mad. His face behind those glasses wore the grim righteous joy of the soothsayer.

Dobbs took one step around his desk, awake now, fury singing up his arms and ratcheting up his spine like electricity. It happened like this since June's death: his heart's velocity leaned only toward anger. How he spent entire days almost asleep, ensconced in a quiet despair, and then leapt toward anger like a drowning child at a life raft. He caught himself as he stepped toward Lyley, physically caught himself, hooked his hand around the edge of his desk to slow himself. A man swept up in a current. His own voice throbbed in his ears. "Do you have a mental condition, sir? Do you need medication?"

"Judgment," Lyley crowed, rattling the bag above his head with the flair of a conquistador, his wrists knobby and huge above the cuffs of his shirt.

Hayslip pulled his handcuffs from his belt, held them in a fist, looked at Dobbs over Lyley's shoulder.

"Proof!" Lyley cried. His teeth were small, yellow, tilted things beneath his mustache. "The wages of our sins. A divine retribution."

"For Christ's sake," Hayslip muttered.

Lyley lowered the sack. Almost conversationally, he said, "This isn't the first animal I've found on the beach, Sheriff. The first bird." And then he screamed, the cords in his neck suddenly leaping like wires, "'Therefore shall the land mourn, and everyone that dwelleth therein shall languish! With the beasts of the field and with the fowls of heaven!'"

Dobbs could see heads craned outside his office door. For a moment, everything—his office, the station floor, even the great sad cave of his own head—was silent. And then Lyley whispered hoarsely: "What happens when it's no longer birds, Sheriff? Beyond the beasts of the field? What then? What price then?"

Lyley upended the bag with a flourish, and the halved pieces of gull tumbled out onto his desk in a wash of grit and sand, its eye sockets hollowed cups, the few tendrils of organs in the body hanging loose, tough as strings. The scent of rot heavier now, exposed. Hayslip grabbed Lyley by one freckled arm and spun him against the bookshelf. The paper sack tumbled to the floor. There was the ratchet of cuffs; Hayslip hiked Lyley's arms up toward his shoulder blades and the man cried out. Outside Dobbs's office, his staff members were all standing at their desks, openmouthed and still as paintings.

"Harassment of a law enforcement officer," Hayslip growled into Lyley's ear. He knuckled something from his eye, put his hand back on Lyley's neck. "At the very least. That's county time right there. Sound good to you, Mr. Lyley, a harassment charge? You've got to be out of your fucking mind, you know that?"

In seconds the day had turned into a caricature. A cartoon. A thread of a headache knotted itself inside Dobbs's skull. "Just get him out of here. Walk him out. And you are on my list, Mr. Lyley."

Lyley's laugh was high and reedy. He seemed to be enjoying himself. "We're all on *His* list, Sheriff. Yes? You agree? That the Great Redeemer puts his mark upon all of us?"

"Enough with the horseshit," Hayslip said.

"You're not to set foot in this station for ninety days, Mr. Lyley. Is that understood?"

Lyley's glasses fell to the ground and Hayslip, cursing, stooped to pick them up. He put them folded in the man's shirt pocket. "Ninety days?" Lyley said, craning his neck to lay a fierce eye on Dobbs. That fey, yellow-toothed grin. "The world's great cessation may well have come and gone by then, Sheriff."

"Well," Dobbs said, looking sourly at the shipwreck of his desk, "in case it doesn't, I don't want to see or hear word one from you."

Hayslip frogmarched Lyley out of the office and Dobbs could still hear the man's proclamations as they made their way out of the station, a radio signal fading out. Dobbs grimaced and pushed the pieces of the torn gull into his wastebasket with the end of his pen and then, after a moment, threw the pen in the basket as well. He cinched the garbage bag shut and stepped out onto the main floor, all eyes on him, and headed out to the garbage bins at the back of the station. Some fool's dog gets too exuberant with the corpse of a bird and zealots like Lyley see an apocalypse in it: a story June would've tsk-tsked over. Hell, their own dog would've done the same thing when she was a pup. He'd need to sanitize the everliving shit out of his desk.

NICK HAYSLIP

They walked down the hall, Lyley's wrists fragile, breakable things in their bracelets. It crossed his mind, that fragility.

Hayslip's work schedule: four days on, three days off. Twelve-hour shifts.

With work came focus, came intention, a distraction. The days off were the ones to struggle through.

Work was the only thing saving him. Everything else was stunted and slow-moving and moored in an unspeakable guilt that skirted darkly at the edges of his life. But at work, even with the weight of the belt on his hips growing heavier as the day progressed (pistol, baton, flashlight, cuffs, radio), there was a lightness to it all. He could lose himself in it. His life before the accident (those carefree days, practically gilded in shimmering light and soft-focus camera work when he thought about it now) had seemed something malleable. Not an endurance test, but something to actually be enjoyed. Something he had some modicum of control over. Now? Now a day had become something to be trod through, each hour a solid object to rally against, to exert his will against. But he was grateful for it: memory was the enemy, not movement. He would start his shift and feel the demands of all that goddamned *free time* roll off his shoulders like stones.

As they walked out of the station he hiked the cuff chain up toward Lyley's shoulder blades every couple steps, not minding at all the way the man hissed in pain. Their footsteps echoed on the marble floor. They stepped out the glass doors together into a warm morning rain and Hayslip unlocked Lyley's cuffs only once they were on the sidewalk. They looked at each other then, rainwater darkening their shoulders in seconds. Lyley rubbed his wrists and then took great care in putting his eyeglasses back on. A passing car slowed to watch them, throwing up a sluicing fantail of water in its passage.

"Ninety days, Mr. Lyley," Hayslip said. He put his cuffs back on his belt and nodded, standing with his arms folded before the glassed doors. "I'll go ahead and tell you—you're very lucky the Sheriff didn't decide to arrest you."

"The scales are being weighed," Lyley said, his shoulders hunched up against the rain. Bright red coins on his cheeks, hair curling dark on his forehead. That little mustache. He had come to the police station with pieces of a dead bird in a paper sack but hadn't thought to bring a jacket. "Make no mistake, sir."

"I think you need to talk to somebody. A professional."

"I don't—"

Hayslip held up a hand. "I'm not going to argue with you," he said, stepping into the lobby. And yet he couldn't resist: he leaned out of the doorway and said, "Even think about talking to someone in your church. I don't know. I'm sure you go to church, right? Because what you did in there? That's not healthy. That's the opposite of healthy."

Lyley sniffed and said, "The church we frequented was shown to be full of sycophants and atheists." He managed, rain-drenched and coatless, to sound haughty.

Hayslip laughed. "Of course they were. Well, you show up here in the next ninety days without a dire, life-threatening emergency, I'll arrest you myself." A pause. "And you may very well fall down a few times during processing. I hope we understand each other."

Before the accident he had spent his days using the few piecemeal currencies afforded him: booze, running, the rib-rattle of the jukebox in the Sandy Bottom. Briefly, Melissa. And always his job. He hadn't drank since her death, hadn't lifted a glass. The job was the focus now. He shrank time into lumber-sized pieces—an hour, a mile—and ran it through the saw-wheel of his will. He did the thing in front of him until there was nothing left of it, and then he found something else. Since Melissa's death, sleep had become, mostly against his will, a disdainful thing. Just a salve that danced in front of him with only a ghost of its old sweetness, its old simplicity.

"It'll all end in doom and ruination," Lyley called out, his arms spread wide, water running from the sleeves of his shirt.

Hayslip made a shooing gesture with his hand. "Just get out of here, okay? I'm trying to give you a break. For Christ's sake, guy."

Lyley seemed poised to say something more and Hayslip shook his head, reached for the cuffs on his belt again and took a step forward. Lyley slunk away then, his hands balled into fists against his legs, shoulders hunched up.

Rain suddenly began falling so hard Hayslip could see the jumping static of it on the man's shoulders, his skull, the pavement at his feet. It was only a matter of time, he thought, before some internal, vital mechanism inside the man locked up and he wound up doing something truly shithouse crazy. If Hayslip heard that Joe Lyley had taken it upon himself to one day eat his wife and run around Slokum Beach in a loincloth holding her severed head aloft while shouting misquoted Bible verses, would he be surprised? No. Not hardly. There were people like that in the world these days and he could picture, all too easily, the pale scarecrow of Joe Lyley bounding nude and bloody down 101 in some downpour. The man just had that cut about him.

Lyley turned the corner without a look back.

Twelve-hour shifts. Grateful for the work. For the focus of it like a magnifying glass, excluding all on the periphery.

You just do the thing in front of you.

• • •

He came back into Dobbs's office to find the sheriff leaning over his desk with a rag and a spray bottle. He wiped the top of the desk in quick, irritated swipes, his mouth curled.

"Goddamn lunatic," Dobbs said.

"Yeah, he had that air about him for sure."

"My own dog finds a dead possum, she'll roll in that shit like it's a bubble bath. Loves it. Animals are rough on each other."

"I hear you."

Dobbs stood up, sighed, looked around the room as if assessing what else had been soiled by Lyley's visit. "I tell you what," he said, "why don't you add a few extra stops today down at Wolf Point so that Mr. Lyley can't say we didn't hear him out."

"I mean, we all hit up Wolf Point every day—"

Dobbs flapped his rag and sighed again, looking down at his desk. "I know it. But let's just cover our asses, Nick."

• • •

He got into a cruiser and spent a number of hours patrolling 101. Up and down the backbone of this little coastal town he'd grown up in, a place he'd lived his whole life save for basic training and his eleven-month tour of South Vietnam. 101: A stretch of highway as familiar as his own hand, as familiar as the smooth grip of the cruiser's steering wheel worn dark with use. Up and down those four windswept lanes, Riptide's shops tiled on each side, stoic little buildings cinched up tight against the weather, tiny wind-lashed things, their neon OPEN signs glowing bravely in the windows, parents hustling children inside homes, battling keys and front door and sacks of groceries. The cruiser's wipers clacked furiously across the glass. He often felt a fierce love for the town when patrolling the highway. Love, or something close to it. Loyalty, maybe, to the worn little town's bravado. Loyalty or love to the things given voice in the murmur and static of the radio, the purr and burnt-wool stink of the heater, the intractable weight of the gun on his hip. The ticking off of the town's waypoints beyond the windshield—Slokum Beach, Selwicky's Grocery, the junction where 101 met Highway 20, the Wolf Point turnaround, the bayfront, sad little Tumquala Park, South Beach, finally the bridge that crossed the bay—all of it marked off internally. Low-hanging sky and flaking paint, rainwater gurgling in the gutters. And then across the green expanse of the bridge at South Beach, only to turn around and head back the way he came. He took occasional side sojourns onto less traveled streets. At one point he passed the shuttered gas station and thought of Melissa Finster and June Dobbs and ignored the way his heart juddered in his throat.

A day was a day. Cut and section it. Avoid the wide-angle lens of your life. Do the thing in front of you.

He pulled a few people over. He issued some tickets. A Failure to Yield, a Failure to Signal. He issued a beefy fisherman with heartbreaking psoriasis a Speeding in a School Zone. He pulled over a man for suspicion of DUI, but Hayslip was disappointed when the guy passed the field sobriety test. But dispatch came back with a warrant for Failure to Appear, and Hayslip took meager solace in handcuffing him, the one tow truck in Riptide taking his car to impound. At lunch Hayslip stopped at Selwicky's and stared for a number of minutes at the cold cuts and sandwiches and soups in the deli section. Long enough for his uniform and blank-faced concentration to unnerve the woman behind the glass counter. Hunger was still a ghost that eluded him; he kept expecting that to change but it didn't. He settled on a Coke and drank it in his cruiser in the parking lot of the Slokum Beach State Park, smiling ruefully at the fogged glass as he listened to the news, the sky almost indiscernible where it met the sea, that near-invisible line. The day jockey on the local station, KRPT, was calling Reagan to the carpet for selling his autobiography for three million dollars. "I love the man, but please, Mr. President, *share the wealth,* pal," the DJ said. Hayslip laughed with his mouth open, sipped his bottle of Coke. "We got decorated veterans on the street hustling for change, no place to live, eating food out of garbage cans. These are decorated veterans, people. Homeless, handicapped, starving. And this guy goes and sells his *ghost-written* book for three mil? Three *million?* That's the President of the United States. Like he needs it. But that's America today, folks, am I right? I'm a Republican born and bred but *sheesh.* Anyway, my two cents. We'll be back with sports scores after the break." He turned the radio off and wiped fog from the windshield. A gull stood motionless and regal on the wooden fencepost in front of him, seemingly pinning him in place with that one black eye. He thought of the bird on Dobbs's desk, halved, sand-salted. That one shriveled eye.

And then like a gift: a peal of static and dispatch sent him on a Domestic Disturbance call down toward the center of town, near where 101 and 20 intersected. It only took a few minutes to get there. It was a short, dead-end clay road with a half-dozen salt-ravaged shacks on one side and a thin stand of scrub pines on the other. The houses were small and boxy, the paint long faded and blistered with age. Each little house was separated by a chain link fence, each with its own tiny, mudded yard. In one, a child's pink Big Wheel lay on its back. The windows of many were milked over with sheets of stapled-up plastic or with yellowed newspaper. Hayslip parked around the corner, out of sight of the houses.

Mark Fitzhugh arrived a minute later and pulled up next to him, the driver's-side windows of their cruisers facing each other. Fitzhugh was a redheaded, slab-armed cop who'd been a decent fullback when they were in high school together. He'd been in Nam as well, a year before Hayslip, and they frequently shared beers together at the Bottom, trying, mostly unsuccessfully, to pick up women. He was the only man on earth that could call Hayslip *Nicky* with impunity. Hayslip didn't have a lot of friends, but Fitzhugh was one of them.

"Neighbors called it in," Fitzhugh said now. "These two have got into it before. We come and tell them to knock it off, they're quiet for another couple months."

Hayslip nodded. He sucked his teeth and touched the scar tissue on his neck. "So it's a regular thing then."

"Same old, same old, apparently."

"You been out here before?"

"Not me personally, no."

"Well, we'll just drop in," Hayslip said.

Fitzhugh smiled and drummed his fingers on the door of the cruiser. "Totally. Just say hi. See how things are going."

"Which house is it?"

Fitzhugh pointed. "Second to the last one. Baby-shit brown one there."

It was still raining. Fitzhugh pulled in behind him and they walked down the road, the mud squelching and pulling at their boots. Both men walking carefully with their hands on their gun belts. The gate opened with a squeal and it was only a few steps to a pair of rusted handrails that marked each side of the moss-furred cement steps leading up to the door. Fitzhugh stood to one side, his eyes to the road and the thin slash of woods beyond it, while Hayslip rapped on the door with his knuckles. "Sheriff's Deputy," he said loudly. "Open the door, please."

Silence. A beat, two. Shuffling, then another pause. Muffled by the door, a man's voice: "Ah, well, there's no problem here, officer."

"Sir, we've got a complaint. I need you to open the door, please."

"We're not doing anything in here. We're fine in here."

"Sir, I need you to open the door."

The door opened half a foot. A wedge of dim light. The man standing before him wore a pair of turquoise surf shorts and a yellowed t-shirt mounded tight at the gut. Stocky, maybe mid-fifties, grizzled gray hair curling out of the shirt collar. Pores on his nose big as pencil lead. Behind him, Hayslip saw dirty, threadbare carpet worn to the nub, a scarred hutch against the wall stacked high with junk mail. The bleach-sting of cat piss wafted out, sharp and acrid, and a white cat meowed and twined himself around Hayslip's feet. The television played loudly in the other room.

"We're not doing nothing here, officers," the man said plaintively. His voice was surprisingly high considering his size. His eyes pinballed between the two of them.

"We've had a complaint, sir, about the noise." Hayslip said. "Everything okay here?"

"Everything's fine," the man said. "I'm telling you."

"Is your wife or girlfriend at home right now? Someone called and said they heard quite a bit of yelling coming from your residence. Can we speak to her?"

"She left," he said, and started to close the door. His smile was a frozen thing. "There's nothing's happening here. This is me telling you that."

"Blood on his t-shirt there, Nick," Fitzhugh said calmly, like a passenger telling someone to take a left here, and time slowed in that devilishly tricky way it always did when shit started to happen. Hayslip fell into it with relish. Fitzhugh was right: dottings of blood on his undershirt, near his gut, new and fire engine-red. Hayslip got a foot in the door and the guy leaned on it from the other side, and he heard a groan come from deeper inside the house. In his peripheral he saw Fitzhugh unholster his sidearm. Ah, the world and its maddening provision of details: the mossy cement and how the doorbell had no bell, just an empty socket where a button would go. He put his hand on the doorknob and pushed against the door with his shoulder and the man stopped leaning against it at the same moment, instead turning and running further into the house, and the door cracked open, smacked against the interior wall and came back at Hayslip as he stumbled inside. The guy tore down the hallway, elbows pumping, quick the way some big men are quick, the soles of his socks a filthy gray.

And in the entrance of the house, that chemical stink of piss in his nose, his mouth sour with adrenaline, Hayslip froze. Just stood there.

Fitzhugh, his face gone red to the roots of his flattop, gave Hayslip a searching, incredulous look—*Go! Go!*—and stepped around him, his revolver cupped in both hands. Hayslip followed, pulling free his own weapon, the same Smith & Wesson Model 66 that Fitzhugh carried. At the end of the hallway he could see a kitchen—a dirty yellow grid of linoleum, a counter clotted with dishes—and off to the immediate left a living room where the television blared. From this room came another scream. Fitzhugh went through the kitchen and Hayslip, his legs seemingly full of half-set cement, entered the living room. Across from him he saw a woman sitting on the floor with her back against the couch. Her hands were cuffed around a heavy marble coffee table topped with bowls and plates congealed with food. Mounded ashtrays. A fly buzzed past his ear. The woman was gray-haired and potbellied and nude from the waist down. A constellation of black-red cigarette burns salted her shins, her marbled thighs. She wore a pink t-shirt and her face was a patchwork of bruises. It had been like this sometimes in firefights in Nam, too: this kind of freeze-up. This distancing. Fitzhugh from the kitchen bellowed, *"He's coming around!"* as the man burst through the doorway. He jumped over the coffee table and slammed into Hayslip full-tilt. Hayslip was slow, deathly slow, not even raising his pistol. When it happened in Nam, when you froze like this, you either died or you hunkered down until someone pulled you up and screamed at you and then you lifted your rifle and started firing blindly into the jungle, into a mountain. It had never happened to him before as a cop. Never once.

He bounced off the wall, knocked the television to the floor. Fell to his knees. The man kept going, Fitzhugh storming after him. Another scream from the woman cuffed to the table but she was looking out the window when she did it. Like she was doing it by rote, totally disconnected to what was happening now and this terrified Hayslip more than anything else, more even than her appearance. In the hallway Fitzhugh slammed into the man, they dug a divot in the wall, a puff of buckled plaster and lathe. Still the television blared from the floor, the maddening laugh track. Hayslip rose to his feet, his pistol still hanging from his fist. Fitzhugh and the man did a crazed grunting dance out the front door where one of the metal railings gave way with a sickening twang. They fell into the muddy yard, the man landing soundly on top. Hayslip stepped out onto the stoop, saw the man push himself up on top of Fitzhugh, saw the backs of his bone-white thighs. Fitzhugh lay unmoving beneath him. His pistol lay near the fence.

Hayslip stood frozen on the stoop. That same frozen part of him murmured that Fitzhugh probably had a few broken ribs, and that yes, definitely, the man was reaching for Fitz's pistol.

"Fuck, Nick," Fitzhugh gasped, working a hand around the man's throat. The man mud-covered and leaning, his crotch on Fitzhugh's chest, one hand splayed over Fitzhugh's face, pressing him into the mud as his other hand reached for the revolver.

Hayslip with his own gun at his thigh. In some way marveling at the colossal nature of his own fuck up. Fitzhugh was going to lose his gun to this guy, and Hayslip was going to stand here and watch it happen. You heard grim my-buddy-knows-this-guy stories about it happening to other cops all the time but now it was happening to him, and if it wasn't guilt that was seizing him up right now then what the hell was it?

As if on cue another scream came from the house. Fitzhugh groaned again as the man put a finger in his eye and his free hand searched blindly for the baton on his belt. With a heaving effort he pushed the man off and leaned over on one elbow and brought his baton down on the back of the man's neck. Reared up onto his knees and brought it down on his skull. A hollow *thwock,* and the man fell face-first into the mud like a destringed marionette. Quick as that.

A movement caught his eye, and Hayslip saw an old woman in a bathrobe standing on the stoop of the house next door, fifteen feet away, a tall boy of

Hamm's in her hand. Mute and blank-faced and witnessing, hoisting her can of beer to her lips. All he could think was *Jesus Christ, lady, it's one in the afternoon. I don't even drink at one in the afternoon.* Fitzhugh now with one arm curled around his ribs, the other bringing the baton down on the man, over and over. Grunting with the effort, cursing with each blow. One of the man's socked feet spasming and twitching, dreamlike.

"Fitzhugh," he said, his own voice in his ears like something underwater. "Fitzy, stop."

And Fitzhugh didn't stop. He didn't. Not until Hayslip finally walked down the steps—Oh, *now* he could move! Now that the danger was passed! Fucking perfect!—and wrestled the baton from his hand. The three of them like some terrible frieze of life in that muddy, fenced yard: one man standing, one kneeling, one lying still.

SAM FINSTER

Wolf Point turnaround on a school day, where he and Toad hid from the wind beneath the circular concrete wall of the parking lot, down where the sand was wet and filthy from a runoff pipe; the pipe today dribbled a thin gruel of green, nearly phosphorescent water every few minutes, water that would then fan out in a thinly-carved channel that wended slowly, patiently, toward the tide line. The turnaround stank here, no bones; but there were sand fleas in the dunes, and it was too goddamned windy on either the beach or the turnaround itself, impossible to smoke. When summertime arrived, even this place, this noxious section of beach near the pipe, would be crowded with families. Big-hipped parents in golf-visors and neon-colored windbreakers, disappointed in the unending blustery gales. Their children disappointed in the cold, cold water, the brittle tang of salt in their mouths. The tide bringing with it not fistfuls of decorative seashells but rather the distended membranes of dead jellyfish washed ashore. There would be teenagers wearing Walkmans, trying fervently to distance themselves from their parents, and sand everywhere, gritty in everyone's mouths, crystalline between the folds of everyone's fingers, their toes. Taffy bought at the bayfront would pull out an errant tooth here and there. Motel beds were found at night to have grown malicious with springs and strange lumps, and there was always, always the ceaseless cawing of the gulls outside. Shower floors of beachside motels were rough with grit and always the hint of mold, and the summer traffic on 101, sweet Jesus. Finally was the odd accumulation of the town's innumerable stray dogs, the constant rip and snarl of random dogfights drifting up and down the lonely beachfront, packs of these half-feral dogs warring to the teeth over scraps of trash left by the tourists, or by the high schoolers that used the hidden coves of the beaches to party. You lived here and it became familiar. You lived here and you didn't even see these things anymore. You were local, after all. This was your life.

But for now it was winter and the beach was empty. The dogs, like the tourists, were mostly gone, though unlike the tourists they still made the occasional appearance on the off-season, these half-starved revenants seen trotting down along the surf at night or in the mist of a brushed-steel dawn, snouts pressed to the ground in search of some elusive scent, the ghost of old gustatory riches. Sam sat down on a log next to the runoff pipe and the wind shirred the bursts of crabgrass that topped the dunes around them. He tucked his chin into his shoulder and lit a Newport. He was smoking a lady's cigarette. More specifically, his mother's. He'd prided himself a Camel man before the wreck, but now: Newports, exclusively. A connection thin as a hair, maybe, but still a tangible remnant. Toad stood nearby absently drawing gigantic penises in the sand with a crooked branch of driftwood.

"It was a mess," Sam said.

"What was?"

"The thing with Jordana. What have I been talking about the past ten minutes, Toad?"

"Fuck if I know," Toad said. He reared back and threw the driftwood like a javelin and they watched it wobble through the air before it disappeared behind a dune. The sky was the color of cotton batting and dense with mist, and Toad hiked his collar up around his neck. "Can I have one of those?"

He took a smoke from the pack and Sam handed him the lighter. Toad, with a grunt, hunkered down next to him as Sam dug a divot in the sand with his heel. Toad tried to light his smoke in the wind; the lighter sparked and sparked and failed to catch and he scissored two fingers in front of him. Sam handed him his cigarette.

"So," Toad said. "Jordana Benedict. You asked her out." The side of his head where he shaved it had grown out dark and pebbly.

Sam winced. "Kind of. I mean, I talked to her."

Toad did this kind of huffing thing with his mouth, subdued laughter that sent out little puffs of smoke to be torn apart by the wind. "You talked to her. Jesus Christ, Sam. I thought your heart was all a-flutter and shit. You didn't even ask her out?"

"I would have. But it wasn't a good situation, like, straight away."

Toad handed Sam's cigarette back to him. "I swear," he said, frowning down at his own smoke, "your dad smokes old lady cigarettes. What *are* these? Virginia Slims or something? I quiver just thinking about the ancient dust that puffs out of your dad's vagina. Every time he sits down it's like fucking Pompeii or something."

"These are my mom's cigarettes, dick," Sam said.

And here, here was a moment wielded as a weapon. Even with Toad. Even now, three months later. Like he couldn't help himself.

"Oh," was all Toad said.

And how long, Sam wondered, would this last? How long would he be able to wield her death like a club? How long would he want to? Talking to people—there were minefields everywhere. How fair was it to keep pushing people onto them?

"Anyway, she looked at me like I was . . . not even, you know, a human person," Sam continued. "Like she didn't even know who I was."

Toad raised his eyebrows. "*Does* she know who you are? Didn't you guys work on that horse farm or whatever?"

Sam rolled his eyes. "I've told you this. We hosed out animal cages last summer at her dad's vet office. All summer. We hosed dog shit out of kennels together, Toad. That should count for something, right?" And he was kind of joking and at the same time, kind of not.

Toad nodded sagely, smoke unfurling from his lips. "Jesus, how could she not want to bang you? Her fellow dog-shit-hoser. Her panties should be flying off." Toad, at nineteen, was only a year older but had always been more wizened than Sam. Experienced. By the time he was sixteen, Toad was already going out with hard-faced girls four and five years his senior. Girls with a thing for heavy metal and mascara, who kept Toad in beer and cigarettes and occasionally, if Sam was persistent and lucked into the right air of disinterest and proximity, had younger sisters willing to half-heartedly make out with him.

"Personally, I can't believe you asked her out, dude. What was it for, again?"

"What I've been telling you is that I *didn't* ask her out, Toad."

"Yeah, but if you actually had had testicles, what were you going to ask her out for? Homecoming?"

"No. Homecoming was like two months ago."

"What, then?"

Sam shrugged helplessly. Toad, who on their walks around town would claim—probably truthfully—to have had sex in, around, or on top of any number of various Riptide landmarks, was always dispensing advice in regards to matters of the heart and/or genitals, and rarely was it ever any good. On the walk down to the turnaround, not half an hour before, he'd raised his chin toward the little faux log cabin of the Riptide Pioneer Museum and said, "Me and Carla DeVossy boffed on the roof up there. She got a splinter in her butt that got super infected. Try to boff in bed whenever possible, Sammy, and if you can't, lay one of your shirts down." Sam, who had so far boffed no one and feared he never would, had simply lit a cigarette and grunted. When Toad talked about women, it was like Opposite Day when you were a kid. It seemed like you should do the opposite of whatever Toad, in his motorcycle boots, his half-shaved head showing an armada of acne scars, his Harley Davidson shirt peppered in cigarette burns, told you to do. And yet Toad got laid, and in contrast Sam felt feral and ugly and terribly alone when trying to even ask a girl out.

"It was just a dance that's coming up before winter break."

"Ah," Toad said, lifting a haunch and letting out a pinched, mournful fart. "I remember winter break. The good old days."

"Back in the day. Before you got kicked out."

"Hey, I'm getting my GED," he said. This was Toad's constant refrain, and Sam heard it so often he mouthed the words as Toad said them. They laughed.

After a time, Toad said, "Well, at least you talked to her. That was gutsy."

"Yeah, and she looked at me like she didn't know who I was. Totally blank. Finally I just said, 'Sorry for taking up your time.'"

"You really said that?"

"I really said that."

"Jesus. So you skipped the rest of the day."

Sam nodded. "Yep."

"Well, look on the bright side," Toad said. "You've got the rest of the year to be embarrassed about it, and then we can get the fuck out of here." He pulled a flake of tobacco from his lip.

"I guess."

"Dude, Jordana Benedict sucks. I don't get why you're all freaked out over her anyway. She's lame. She's mean to people. She's not nice. Case in point."

"You don't even know her," Sam said, and what he meant was, *You don't remember her like I remember her.* Those days last summer, those days back before his mother's death, before everything had taken on the full-tilt craziness of a bad dream. The two of them and the dogs. He and Jordana ensconced in elbow-high rubber gloves, booties. They had laughed in the cages as they worked, the dogs yipping and barking in the closed space as if, weirdly, in celebration of them. She had smiled at him in the mornings when he came in.

"I remember her. She's a dick. Besides, when we do leave town? When we go on the Trip? You'll leave, like, a trail of broken hearts up and down our nation's great highways and byways. Believe it, dude. There's a lot more out there than Jordana Benedict."

"She's *hot*, though," Sam said forlornly. "I can't believe she doesn't remember me."

"Of course she remembers you, Sam. Jesus. She *decided* not to talk to you. You know that, right?"

Sam knew he was right, and that he had no chance with her regardless. Their respective social strata were clearly defined. They were in entirely different spheres and maybe, in a different time or a different world, there could be some kind of cross-pollination. But Riptide, Oregon, in 1983? Please. She had been kind to him last summer, yes, and spoken with candidness about her dad; Sam had been surprised at how comfortable she was around the animals, the way the dogs, often frightened in their kennels, had been drawn to her. She'd even seemed a little vulnerable then (and yes, okay, still resolutely hot as shit) which somehow made the blankness with which she'd stared at him today even worse. Like she had amnesia or something. And this was compounded and made all the more baffling because now was a time when *everyone*—in school, in the whole town— knew exactly who he was: the kid with the mother who'd died in a car wreck a week after school started. The kid whose mom may have killed the library lady, *the sheriff's wife*, in a drunken collision.

It was pointless to think about what could be. Toad was right. Even if everything else *was* different—even if his dad hadn't been his dad, and his mom was still around—Sam would still be Sam. Even if Jordana abandoned her clinical distance and no longer ignored him as she strode past in a cloud of bubblegum-scented lip gloss, her bangs in a tsunamied crest at her forehead, wearing those acid-washed Jordache jeans like they'd been spray painted on her ass in a way that literally hurt Sam's heart to look at, he would still be himself. Rail-thin, clusters of acne on his cheeks like paint stipples, jeans blown out at the knees. Wearing his father's old work shirts, punk bands markered on the dirty canvas of his sneakers. He and Toad were like the minor and major versions of the same ruined prototype; but there was a certain girl that *liked* their type and Jordana was not remotely one of them.

The wind shifted and another bouquet of raw sewage wafted over them again. Sam stood up, wiped sand from the seat of his pants.

"Did you hear about the seal down at South Beach?"

Toad shook his head, now burning errant strings from the holes in his jeans with the cherry of his cigarette.

"They found one that was, like, practically ripped in half. Like a whole seal in almost two totally different pieces. Guts everywhere. Everyone's freaking out about it."

"I saw a sea lion once that rolled up onto shore all rotted. It was split in half. Shark got to it, I think. Super gross, it was all puffed up. It smelled so bad."

Sam grinned and said, "It's the monster, dude."

Toad looked at him flatly, pinching his cigarette out and putting the butt in his jacket pocket. Yet another aspect of the Mystery of Toad: he'd straight-up call a cop a pig to the cop's face, and would brazenly inform Sam about the minutiae of a mutual acquaintance's genitals, but he wouldn't litter. "Whatever," he said.

"I'm serious," said Sam. "There's been all kinds of dead stuff on the beach lately."

Toad sighed and put a fatherly hand on his shoulder. "Sam, Sam, Sam. You believe every story you hear? Rumors and lies, my friend. I need you to do something for me. If we're ever going to get out of this shithole? I need this from you."

"What's that?"

"I need you to make a concerted effort to, you know, pull your head out of your ass."

• • •

They crested the hill of the turnaround and then turned onto 101, jackets zipped against the rain, Sam's shoes absorbing water like they were invented for that express purpose. Traffic zipped past them. He and Toad parted with punches to the shoulders and Sam doled out a few of his Newports and then continued on to Trina's school.

The bus shelter flanked the length of the elementary school and he saw her before she saw him. She was thronged by clusters of other little kids running around, screaming and hitting each other with their backpacks, allegiances forming and dismantling in front of his eyes. Parents chatted in oblivious clusters. Trina stuck out both for her silence and her stoicism, how she was unmoving amid the roving knots of children. She was alone. Sam smiled when he caught her eye and Trina grinned when she saw him, her face lighting up.

He threaded his way among the children and their parents, Cabbage Patch Dolls fiercely clutched to chests, Garbage Pail Kids cards passed back and forth among clots of boys with the seriousness of Vegas hustlers, the frazzled phalanx of teachers, a shrill whistle here and there, the pneumatic wheezings of school buses departing, the rain almost always pattering on the roof above their heads. Trina ran to him and took him gently by the arm, started signing right away.

Her third grade teacher, Mrs. Driscoll, gently put her hand on Sam's arm and Trina's face fell. Caught.

"Sam," Mrs. Driscoll said apologetically, "we had another episode today, unfortunately."

Sam looked at Trina, whose eyes had fallen to slits. Trina scowled at her teacher and, to Sam, signed, *I didn't do anything,* and then folded her arms over her chest.

"Trina," Mrs. Driscoll said.

Trina's hands fluttered. *I didn't! Liar!*

"Hey," Sam said out loud, surprised. And then signed to her: *Watch your language.*

"I'm afraid it was another picture," Mrs. Driscoll said.

"In art class?"

"No," Mrs. Driscoll said, adjusting her glasses. She was an older woman with a shell of iron-gray perm and a penchant for shoulder-padded pantsuits that gave her the look of an autumnal linebacker gone to seed. In spite of her formidable appearance, she played the guitar for the children when they were good ("Puff the Magic Dragon," "Ghost Riders in the Sky") and with her husband, an amateur puppeteer, regularly regaled Trina's class with performances. The children adored her, Trina among them. Being deaf, she was not subject to the musical richness of Mrs. Driscoll's charms, but when the woman had found that Trina would be in her class, she had actively made an effort to learn sign language, a first for any of Trina's teachers. For that she had earned Sam's, if not Trina's, respect. His mother had thought the woman walked on water. "It was during her assignment today in English."

"Okay."

"I need to start giving her more difficult assignments, I think. Part of it might be that, she's just not being challenged enough. Her reading and writing comprehension are just wonderful. Well above her age group." Sam was not so stupid that he couldn't see what she was doing: you start out with a compliment and then you show the knife. Still, a part of him was grateful. "But the pictures, Sam, they're getting . . . well, they're getting graphic." She turned slightly away from Trina so she couldn't read her lips (something that used to drive Sam's mother to fury when she saw people doing it) and mouthed the word *violent.*

Quietly, Sam said, "And it was about Russia? The nukes?"

Mrs. Driscoll closed her eyes and nodded.

Sam ran a hand over his buzzed scalp. "I'll talk to my dad about it."

"Okay," Mrs. Driscoll said, patting him on the shoulder. "We want Trina here, and we think it's important for her to integrate with other children. But it's becoming an issue." She looked at Trina and smiled. *I'm glad you're here,* she signed. Trina scowled and turned away from her. Mrs. Driscoll turned back to Sam. "Her speech recognition and lip reading are really improving, too. Every day. I know your parents were considering the School for the Deaf in Vancouver at one point, but I think the socialization she's getting here, even if it's outside of her comfort zone . . . it's important."

"Yeah."

"But the drawings . . ." Mrs. Driscoll shrugged. "She's so immersed in her own head, she doesn't really interact with the other children unless she has to."

She's fucking deaf, Sam wanted to say, but only nodded instead.

"It scares the other kids, is what I'm saying. This is a fragile time for everybody, the way the world is now. You understand?"

"She's been through a lot." Oh, those hidden landmines! Those weapons tucked away everywhere! So ready to use.

Mrs. Driscoll, as expected, softened, suddenly seemed almost near tears. She put her hand on his arm. "Oh, I know, Sam. You both have been through so much. I know that."

Sam looked down at his shoes, suddenly shy. Embarrassed for himself. "I'll talk to my dad."

"Thank you," she said. She turned to Trina and signed, *Have a good day. I'll see you tomorrow.*

Trina, lightning-quick: *No, you won't.*

Sam lightly touched her shoulder.

Trina sighed. *Fine. I'll see you tomorrow. Goodbye.*

NICK HAYSLIP

The new hospital was two stories tall, all glass and right angles. Most modern-looking piece of real estate in town. Fitzhugh, being a cop, had been given his own room, and when Hayslip walked in Fitz had the look of a man shipwrecked and pale lying there in the hospital bed, his torso cinched in gauze. The windows on the ground floor were frosted white and offered little true illumination, and the overhead lights were ungenerous: Fitzhugh's body seemed yellowed compared to the wrappings, and the skin around his eye where the man had dug his finger in was fiercely red and swollen. He looked a little stoned on top of everything, and when someone, a patient, yelled in another room, his eyes didn't track to the doorway for a number of seconds. Still, when Hayslip walked in he gave a slow, spaced-out smile and winced as he tried to sit up in bed. Hayslip held up a hand, his uniform charcoal against the colorless palette of the room. "Don't worry about it, Fitz. It's cool. Relax."

They stayed that way for a moment, a silence between them. Hayslip frowning and looking at the floor, his hands on his hips. Finally he looked up to see Fitzhugh eyeing him: he'd find no kindness there. He wasn't really expecting it—he'd choked, after all, and it could have cost Fitzhugh his life—but hadn't a part of him been hoping?

He motioned toward Fitz's bandages. "How's it looking?"

"Fractured three ribs, the fat fuck. Off active duty for at least a month, month and a half."

"That's from Dobbs?"

Fitzhugh shrugged and then winced afterward. "Ah, Christ. Dobbs and the doctors, yeah."

"How you feel?"

"How do you think I feel, Nick? Hurts like shit. That's a two-, three-foot drop off those steps, man. The guy was not dainty."

"Listen—"

"Don't worry about it. I'll cover for you," Fitzhugh said, and Hayslip turned to the door to make sure they were alone. "But you better just hope the old lady next door doesn't call bullshit on whatever story you decide to run with."

Hayslip sighed. "Has Dobbs actually been in to see you yet?" he asked as he sat in the chair next to the bed. Fitzhugh leaned over, grimacing, and motioned toward the plastic cup on the nightstand. Hayslip poured him some water from the pitcher and handed it to him.

Fitzhugh lay back and looked up at the ceiling, the cup resting on his thigh. "Not yet. There's time."

"Okay."

"But listen," Fitzhugh said, and turned his face toward Hayslip. That one swollen eye pulled nearly shut. "You got to knuckle up, man. You took a dive out there. That was serious."

Hayslip looked away, touched the scars on his neck. "I hear you."

"I mean, you froze up on me."

"I *know*, Fitz."

"Guy runs right fucking by you, practically out the door." Fitzhugh made a pair of scissoring legs with his fingers, ran it down his blanketed leg. "You choked, Nicky."

Hayslip felt a twist of anger uncoil inside him then, a quick, flashing thing that felt like someone stirring through coals with a stick. But he gripped his cap between his hands and nodded at the floor. "Are we gonna talk about this all day? I know I did. You're right."

The look Fitzhugh gave him then: focused, diamond-pure. Had he really thought the man was *stoned* a minute before? Whatever that had been, it was gone now. His eyes beneath that granite-slab of a forehead were cold and assessing. "Nick. You need to get your shit straight. What's going on with you?"

Hayslip shrugged, looked at his shoes, the cold tile.

"You still hung up on that car accident? The married chick? Dobbs doesn't know about you and her, man. You gotta get over it."

Hayslip looked up sharply: to be pegged that easily, to have the workings of his heart pinned so messily to the light. He was torn between asking

Fitzhugh how he knew and not wanting to give that part of himself away. Was it that obvious? A pair of nurses walked down the hall, their voices rising and falling as they passed.

"Maybe," he said. "Yeah. That's part of it."

Fitzhugh nodded, ran a hand along the rasp of his cheek. "I'll turn my paperwork in to Dobbs. They want to keep me overnight. Shit, Dobbs'll probably drop by and bring me the paperwork himself tomorrow, knowing him."

Hayslip's smile felt forced and a little sad: Fitzhugh throwing him all these bones. Saving his ass. "Sounds about right."

"So I'll say you clipped the guy first, not me. But he knocked you down. *Drogas,* baby. High on that PCP and shit. They test him?"

"I doubt it."

Fitzhugh nodded, sipped his water. "Like the town's got the money for it, right?"

"What if the guy says different though?"

Fitzhugh shrugged, frowning. "Who cares what that piece of shit says? You kidding me? There's half your problem right there."

"The EMS guys got a statement from her," Hayslip said. "She says he tooled up on her for missing lunch. Day before yesterday, this was. You believe that? Cuffed her to the table for three days, sitting in her own filth. Burned her. Because the soup was too cold or whatever."

"Like I said," Fitzhugh said. "Who gives a shit about that guy?"

"How many times have we sent people out there? Five? Ten?"

"What, you think *Dobbs* is gonna take his side, Nick? You think the ADA would want a case like this? Please."

"You fractured his skull, Fitz. Might have blinded him in one eye."

"Psshhh," He lifted his cup to his mouth again. "Should have blinded him in both, the prick."

The silence between them more companionable now.

Finally he said, "Thank you."

Fitzhugh eyed him. "You need to eat something at least."

"Sure thing."

"I'm serious. Take a Quaalude, man. Get some rest and eat a goddamned hamburger, Nicky. You look like skin and bones with a really tiny dick attached."

Hayslip laughed and stood up. "Okay."

"And come see me, man. This month is gonna drag. I'll be grateful for the distraction, you know. Sit around, watch some football, bullshit. Drink some beers."

Nick said goodbye, and two hours later he'd gotten through most of the paperwork, pecking two-fingered at the keyboard, cursing under his breath every time he had to pull out the Wite-Out brush. He had decided to get a jumpstart on Dobbs, beat him to it, so everything was in triplicate, and they would still need paperwork from Fitzhugh. Still, he knew Dobbs would grill him the next morning, those searching hound dog eyes staring him down, waiting for a lie or misstep to come tumbling out. Waiting for Hayslip to trip himself up in those expansive pauses of his. At eight p.m. he clocked out, dropped off his reports in Dobbs's inbox. Showered, dressed in his street clothes.

He drove his rust-swathed Datsun hatchback out of the station parking lot and parked at the Sandy Bottom where he watched the puddles in the potholes dance with rain. Supposedly trying to talk himself out of what he was going to do. Supposedly. Mostly just watching the wipers scrape across the glass. He felt small-hearted and angry. Details kept fixing themselves in his mind: the doorbell, the filthy soles of the man's socks. Fitz's hand buried in the bristled fat at his throat. The lady screaming as she looked outside.

Finally he walked in and ordered a burger and fries in the restaurant half of the place. The laughter and jukebox songs behind the saloon style doors that lead to the bar called out to him and still he had convinced himself that no, he'd go home after this. After he ordered his food and the waitress walked away he saw the line cook eye-fucking him through the serving window. Guy's face was familiar, but all faces became familiar after a time, became one face, always a little suspicious and always either a little stupid or guilty-looking. He'd busted the cook for coke possession six months previous, Hayslip decided. That was it. Paltry shit, but something that had probably warranted a few months in county lockup for him.

"Whatever you're thinking," Hayslip called out, "whatever you're thinking, do the opposite. Make a good choice today." The cook grinned fiercely down at whatever ungodly thing he was doing as soon as Hayslip addressed him and when the food came he hardly ate any of it for both mistrust and a profound lack of interest.

He crossed the room and stepped through the double doors at nine-thirty sharp.

One drink, he told himself. He hadn't had a drop in three months, didn't he deserve one drink? Sweet Christ, after a day like today?

The room was lit by the glow of neon beer signs and sagging strings of white Christmas lights tacked to the molding and left up year-round. Everything smelled of cigarette smoke and beer and the stink from the fish plant down the road. The brittle clack and clatter of pool balls in the back. The kick drum from the jukebox like someone else's heartbeat inside his own. He sat down at the bar and Ron the bartender greeted him like a friend home from the war. He ordered a scotch and a can of Hamm's, and they came, and then he drank them, and then he ordered another round and drank those, too, and his heart finally, finally began to settle in his chest.

SAM FINSTER

His mother had called their house the Balsawood Palace. It was a small, single-story, three-bedroom affair that even in summer smelled slightly of mold and would, for as long as it stood upright, creak and moan in bad weather like a haunted house. It sat perched on a hill that overlooked Wolf Point, tacked on in an affluent neighborhood like a strange afterthought, bracketed by two- and three-story homes that robbed it of all but the most direct of sunlight. The sea lay in scalloped green ridges outside the living room window, and moisture frequently beaded the inside of the window-panes. The bathroom, no matter how diligently Melissa Finster or her children (when conscripted) cleaned it, stank of wood rot. Blustery winds rattled the windows like a thief. The floor of the house tilted at various angles here and there, and any marble laid down on the kitchen's peeling linoleum would have taken a winding, drunkard's path from one end to the other. The front door was still painted black three months after Melissa's death.

This was home. Sam had lived here his entire life and when he thought of his family here, the four of them, he thought of them all together lean-ing against the wind, bracing the walls with their weight. The house being held up by them rather than the other way around. Even when his parents fought, when his father was gone on the boat or sleeping on a cot in the gear shed, when his mother left in a rage, her big green Buick throwing gravel out into the street, even when she came back hours later smelling of beer, even when his parents navigated mutual forgiveness by clothing each other (and often their children) in great swaths of silence, they were still *together*. It was still a home.

And what now?

His father, Gary, was down at the docks doing gear work again, the crew prepping the boat for the coming crabbing season that would probably start the day after Christmas. Sam and Trina had hours before he'd be home. The house's new stillness jarred him; he'd thought he'd known quiet before, but no. Not like this. He remembered *wishing* for silence before the accident, just to be left alone, back when his mother was still alive. Trina had always been bothering him about something, and Gary was always wanting him to do something around the house. Melissa had always been trying to rope her children into keeping her company on some errand around town, disguising it as an adventure. And Sam had tried to avoid it all, had always tried to beg off, wishing instead for the communion of his records, his ongoing heartache and lust over Jordana or some other girl. Christ. It seemed so stupid now. He was embarrassed at his naiveté, and cultivated noise, sound, *volume* in the house, as if it could keep something at bay. Noise seemed to beat back some of the fear, the uncertainty about what would happen to them next. It put to rest, however briefly, the notion of his mother's culpability in her own death and the death of Mrs. Dobbs, the driver of the other car. That was the nagging question that he sentenced to the gallows daily with the stereo jacked to the Ramones, Motörhead, the Misfits, the Circle Jerks. Had it been an accident? Was it just one of those terrible things that happened to people? Or had she been responsible?

He and Trina came into the house and Trina dropped her backpack on the floor and sat down on the couch. She grabbed the remote, the television popping to life with a warm hiss. She was nine and had already cultivated the posture of a burnout twice her age: torso level with the seat cushions, shoulders pressed to the back of the plaid couch, feet on the floor. A world-weary air as she distractedly ran her fingers along the numerous cigarette burns on the couch's arm. Melissa would have laughed and then told her to sit up. She would have put her cigarette in an ashtray and signed to her daughter, asking Trina if she was a dirty hippie. Trina would have looked bewildered at such an idea, and Melissa would have laughed again and told her, out loud this time, to sit upright like a human being. And Trina would have.

His mother's ghost: bounding down the hall, alive in every room.

Sam looked at his sister and said nothing.

He put a tape in the stereo and pressed *Play*. Rain ran silver against the kitchen windows. He walked over to the thermostat and turned the heat on.

Half an hour and then homework, he signed. Trina rolled her eyes.

I'm serious.

Fine, she signed without looking away from the television.

Let's do vocals the rest of the night, Sam signed. *Okay? Practice your words.*

Leave me alone, Trina signed. *I want to watch this.*

He tapped the arm of the couch to get her attention.

Do you want me to tell Dad about your picture?

"Fine," Trina said, rolling her eyes.

He washed dishes while she watched the six o'clock news, hoping (he knew this much about her, at least) for improved word of the negotiations between the U.S. and the Soviet Union, the de-escalation of threat. It was a stalemate that had lasted for decades and would, Sam believed, last for decades more, but try telling that to a nine-year-old. Try navigating those waters. He thought she shouldn't watch the news at all, but since their mother's death Trina had directed all of her fear and loss there. That was what she thought about now: nuclear annihilation. The end of the world. Nine years old and that's what she thought about. But she wouldn't talk about the crash, wouldn't say Melissa's name. When Sam or his father tried to talk to her about either her mother or the vast unlikeliness of nuclear war she would look at them with a tired, pitying smile that belied someone much older than she actually was. Like they were the fools.

After dinner, Sam turned the television off and without complaint Trina went and took a seat at her little desk in her bedroom. *Come get me if you need help,* Sam signed, and she nodded, already nibbling on her pencil eraser, frowning down at her math book. This was their cadence and it surprised Sam, its own compacted little heartbreak, how easily they were beginning to fit the remnants of their lives around the absence of their mother. It would be different when Gary went crabbing, of course, when he would be gone for three or four days at a time, but for now the three of them seemed to smooth over each other's loss with silence, with the salve of simple proximity to each other. Maybe it wasn't the best way to do things, but it was something.

At nine o'clock Gary called to say they had about another hour's worth of work at the gear shed.

"Okay, Dad."

Gary sounded tired. "Everything okay over there?"

"Yeah, everything's good."

"You guys eat?"

"Yeah. There's leftovers."

A pause, then, where Gary seemed poised to say something. But after a moment he just said, "Okay, bud. I'll see you in a bit."

It was long past dark when Sam went out to smoke a cigarette on the back stoop. Night had fallen and the rain had stopped and the leaning fence posts around their meager yard took on strange shapes in the gloom. Sam stood in the single cone of the porch light and everything else back there was a pure dripping dark; the cadence of the rain's runoff—from the eaves, from the pines separating their house from the others nearby—was atonal and arrhythmic and comforting to him. The croak somewhere of a frog in the ruinous clot of sticker bushes that grew wild at the end of the yard. Brambles and weeds, the grass ankle high. Through the trees, the gleaming cubes of light from the larger houses above and around their little house seemed clinical in their precision, their straight lines. Nothing was straight or even in their house. Their house was something separate, a shoddy but careworn island among these other, clearer delineations. Melissa had begun sharing her cigarettes with him those last few months before her death, a new and singular intimacy that Gary accepted with a certain muttered unhappiness. Trina would exclaim, every time they came in, how bad they smelled, the exaggerated pantomime of waving her hand in front of her nose. It had been an offering from his mother, it seemed at the time—a hand reaching out—and felt even more so now. Gary had come out onto the back stoop a few weeks after the funeral, testing the give on a plastic cooler before setting his weight on it. It'd been a night much like this one, save for the newness of their ache; to Sam it had felt like he was trying to find his way in the darkened room of a strange house, how he kept navigating the parameters of his loss. Gary had lit a cigarette and clasped his hands together, coughed once and said, not unkindly, "Well, I guess you're old enough to make your own shitty decisions." Tossed him a half-pack of Melissa's unsmoked Newports. And that had been that. Sam still had the box, transferred new cigarettes into it every time he bought a pack, a tangible object that she had touched.

He smoked in the dark and kept finding fresh islands of hurt inside himself. Had she been there right then, he'd have told his mother all about Jordana, the look of incredulity on the girl's face, the rabbit-quick glance at her girlfriends flanking her. The vague understanding that she had more to lose than he did. Three months since the accident and there were still these moments that caught him like a thorn snaring fabric. The totality of it: Never another cigarette on the back porch. She would never say to Trina, with exasperated calmness, "Use your words, please," when a frustrated Trina resorted to signing. The way she would say "Cheese and rice!" when she stubbed her toe, trying not to cuss around them, or once, when she'd been super mad at his father, just the two of them in the other room, Sam had heard her say "Hey Gary, how about you just suck my dick, alright?" and there'd been a moment of heavy silence and then his parents had burst into fierce laughter that lasted sporadically throughout the night. *That* whole person was gone. He kept thinking he had a handle on it and then it surprised him.

He dropped his cigarette in the coffee can next to the screen door and stepped back inside and when he came into the living room he saw Trina sitting on the couch and he could tell simply by the glassed look of terror on her face what she was watching. He understood immediately that something bad had happened.

The six o'clock news, a Portland broadcast. He didn't have Trina's penchant for lip reading—hers was born of necessity and she was much, much better at it than even their mother—but he saw the look of stern resolution on the anchorman's face, and read the ticker tape beneath the footage:

WEST GERMANY ACCEPTS SHIPMENT OF 9 PERSHING II
NUCLEAR MISSILES FROM UNITED STATES, SOVIETS WALK
OUT OF GENEVA PEACE TALKS

And then:

U.S. STRATEGIC AIR COMMAND CONSIDERING ELEVATING
DEFCON EMERGENCY RATING

"Nope," Sam said, hating the way his own heart picked up to a gallop at the news, the shrill, babyish tone of this voice. "Nope. No way, Trina. Not happening." He thumbed the remote, changed the channel. *Cheers* was on, a bunch of laconic old people sitting around a bar, so different than what he pictured when it came to his own parents sitting around drinking beer at the Sandy Bottom. He turned the sound on for himself, for the soothing, idiotic luxury of canned laughter.

Trina became a dervish. Ghoulish in the flickering light of the television, she leapt off the couch and came at him, her little fists hitting his arms. He turned sideways. Her teeth were bared as she struck at him.

She stepped back from him suddenly and stamped her foot. Reached for the remote. *I want it,* she signed. *I need to watch it!*

"No, you don't," he said. "Nothing's going to happen. Everything is fine."
Yes, I do! I need to watch! I need to know what's happening!

"Use your words," he said, and it came out wrong, all wrong, like a mockery, his mother's kindness absent in his voice. He sounded instead like he was taunting her.

Trina paused, her blue eyes wide and glimmering in the light. Her lashes trembling. One tear tracked slowly down her cheek.

With a dignity and patience that surprised him, she said, very slowly and very clearly, "I hate you, Sam."

She slammed her bedroom door and Sam felt it vibrate in the floorboards up through his feet.

• • •

Sam was in the kitchen making Trina's lunch for the next day when Gary came home, a smudge of grease on his cheekbone and the knuckles of one hand scraped raw. He gripped Sam's shoulder as he walked by, the sound of his boots clunking throughout the little house. Leaning in the fridge, Gary came out with a beer and the pot of macaroni and cheese. He looked at Sam as he popped the cap on the beer. "What's up? You look like someone shit in your Wheaties."

"It's Trina."

Gary sighed and scratched his chin. "Sure it is. Bomb stuff?"

Sam nodded. "I guess she drew another picture in class today."

Gary sighed again, ate leaning against the counter holding the pot's handle in one fist and a fork in the other. He smelled of cigarettes and paint and WD40, gear shed smells. "Kids draw weird shit all the time," he said, his mouth full. "Right?" Sam shrugged. They both knew it was beyond that.

Gary sighed again and tossed his bottle cap in the trash beneath the sink. Sam could see his father's pale reflection in the window. He looked older, adrift, tired. He was working insane hours and Sam was suddenly surprised at how angry he was with him. *I shouldn't have to deal with this. Mom should be here. You* should *be tackling this bullshit, not me. This isn't my job, taking care of her.*

"She's not kicked out or anything, right? Teacher isn't booting her?"

"Mrs. Driscoll? No," Sam said. "No way. She's just worried. She's cool, Dad." He paused, and then plunged ahead. "And then we saw the thing on the news tonight."

Gary took his baseball cap off and rubbed at the reddened ring around his forehead. "Christ. What thing?"

"You didn't hear about it?"

"You know how it is down at the shed, bud. No TV. It's all Van Halen and Iron Maiden down there. It's not like those guys want to listen to the news."

"Well, I guess the Russians are pissed about the missiles in Germany."

"What missiles?"

"We put some missiles in Germany that could reach Russia. So Russia walked out of the peace talks."

Gary frowned. "I don't even know anything about this." Sam thought again of the grand luxury of sitcoms, the blessedness of watching the world through a script, everything sweetly wronged and then corrected in twenty-five-minute increments.

"Well, Trina's freaking out about it."

"I'll talk to her," his father said, draining his beer, and the next ungenerous thought came to Sam: *Yeah right, you'll talk to her. I bet.*

TRINA FINSTER

What did other girls dream about? Think about? Whatever it was, it was not what Trina dreamed about. Not when worry cinched her heart tight in the middle of the night. As physical as someone's fist reaching inside her ribcage and squeezing. No. Trina's thoughts were full of a final and terrible heat. A pan-flash of terror and then a great and lasting bleakness. She imagined the sea steaming and roiling like water tossed in a searing pan. She imagined soot-black ash that fell across the world like snow, snow that made you cough blood, made your hair fall out. It would happen—she'd read all about it. She was sure of it.

Most girls thought, probably, of super-fun times. Right? Horses and swimming. Parties. Boys, eventually, though that seemed impossible to her. At least very unlikely. But nice things.

Trina? Trina was nine and she dreamed about the bomb, the bomb, the bomb.

When that fist knocked on her ribs, day or night, in bed or waiting for the bus or seated behind her desk in Mrs. Driscoll's class, she tried to feel good by remembering good things. What else could you do? And when she tried to remember good things she thought of one of the last times she had practiced signing and speaking with her mother. (It was strange how much Trina remembered about it, like some part of her had known how badly she would need it.)

If she could sleep and pick a dream to have it would be this: her mother sitting upright across the table from her, tucking a lock of hair behind her ear. This is the signal, the notice she gives to show that they are no longer at play. That they are student and teacher and now it's time to work.

Okay, you ready?

I guess.

How was school today? her mother signs. Her fingers are long and sure.
It was fine.
Did you do your homework?
We did not have homework today. Today was reading.
Great. That's nice. What did you read today?

. . .

Is it a name? A person's name?
Yes.
Spell it out or say it, please, okay?

. . .

Her mother levels a look at her. "Come on, doofus."
(A sigh. An eye roll.) *J-U-D-Y-B-L-U-M-E.*
She dreams about this. She blankets herself in it: The sight of her mother
smiling at her, her hands clasped between her knees. A fierce, quiet pride
writ on Melissa's face, the set of her mouth. Trina is really good at reading,
can read grownup books if she wants to, but she is a *whiz* at finger-spelling.
She is *so* fast at finger-spelling. (It's strange how these memories can feel
warm, good, and at the same time be like bones lodged in her throat, bones
grown too sharp to swallow.)
Melissa: *Oh, I love her! She's really good. Which book did you read?*
I've read a lot of them.
Which one did you read today?
(She has to spell this one as well.) S-U-P-E-R-F-U-D-G-E.
Okay. Good. Which other ones?
Lots, Mom.
A smile from her mother at Trina's deflection. *Let's practice which ones.
Your signing is great, honey.*
And also, they'd had a video tape that they often watched together when
Trina was little, when she was five or so. Her mother's brow would be knitted
in concentration, a cigarette smoldering in an ashtray on her knee as the
two of them sat in front of the screen watching. There was no remote for the
VCR; they had to sit close so that her mother could hit the pause button every
now and then and they could review. Always the same big-boobed blonde
lady patiently walking them through the same phrases, the same catalog of
words. Trina could picture exactly the woman's expression, her red nails,
the small brooch she wore at her throat, the white background behind her.
The clunky yellow letters that spelled out the words at the bottom of the
screen. She'd had other training—she and her mother both—but this, this

was where the two Finster girls had first knuckled down and got down to it. This was where they really learned to sign. Gary off fishing or asleep, and Sam in his bedroom listening to the stupid Sex Pistols on his headphones. This had been their tutorial, mother and daughter, where they navigated the great and silent depths of the world together. *Girl time,* Melissa called it. The same phrases over and over again, the same letter, even, to the point where their four hands had formed a kind of blazing calligraphy, a fluttering lexicon that would leave both Sam and Gary frowning and begging them to slow down, slow down. *Muscle memory,* her mom called it. They hadn't watched the video in a long time, though—by the time Trina was in second grade they had graduated to the kitchen table, to just signing.

Trina: *Do I have to name them all? All the books?*

Yes, please.

Tales of a Fourth Grade Nothing.

Okay.

I don't know . . . F-R-E-C-K-L-E Juice.

Good! Good, Trina!

I want to read Tiger Eyes *but you said I'm not old enough.*

"Next year," her mother says then, using her voice, and as always, when they make the transition from signing to speaking, Melissa Finster does both at first: takes a drag from her Newport and puts it back, then signs and speaks simultaneously, smoke jumping in pale scribbles around her head. This is Melissa's way of easing her into the world, like the floaties she and Sam had to wear when they were babies learning to swim. This is Melissa's way, by signing and speaking at the same time, of transitioning her into the world of noise and volume. Through the simultaneous cadence of mouth and hand. "What else? Any other books?"

Trina sighs. (Trina sighs *a lot.*) Trina signs and speaks. There is no sound inside her, but there is a vague vibration in her skull with some words, a certain resonance sometimes in her teeth and throat. Trina says, "She's got a new one coming out. *The Wolf in the Basement.*"

Her mother pulls her lips back. "Sssss. An S sound. Like a *snake. Basement.*"

"*The Wolf in the* Basement."

"Good job." Melissa winks, ashes the ever-present cigarette, tucks another lock behind her ear. She rises and gets a beer out of the fridge and this is what Trina wants to dream for sure: before she sits back down, Melissa put her lips to the top of Trina's head and kisses her right there.

Right perfectly on top. When she sits down at the table again Melissa says, "Who else do you like to read?"

"Come on, Mom." Trina thinks, as quickly as she can, which names are easy and which are hard. Letters that trouble her: S. R. Especially R. P and B are easy: they leave her mouth with little detonations.

Her mother smile is generous; she's happy. "Just say it. Don't worry about it. Who else?"

Trina closes her eyes. Somehow this is easier, doing it this way; she sees her hands forming the words behind her eyelids, she feels the silent machinery of her mouth at work.

She names their names, these authors she likes. She names the books she loves.

What do other girls dream about?

What do other girls think about as they fill the world with the grand luxury of their noise?

Trina's deaf, deaf, deaf, and she wishes she could always dream about this. The wavering strands of smoke haloing her mother's head, the beads of condensation on her beer can, the stippling of water at the base of the window outside. And the swaying trees, and Sam in his room, and her father napping on the couch, and most of all, oh, most of all that moment when her mother stands above her and her lips are pressed so sweetly to the gentle curve of Trina's skull.

But her mother is gone now, and sometimes it hurts too bad to think about that moment. It does. Hurts too much to think of her mother at all.

And that's when thinking about the bomb becomes a salve. When thinking about the bomb, about the inevitability of the war—in planning for it, like it says in the book she has hidden under her bed—it seems like she's moving forward, somehow. Or at least away from the ache tucked beneath the fragile cage of her ribs.

Most of the time, thinking about the end of the world hurts less.

NICK HAYSLIP

Oh, a knife-edged morning. Some half-lit dream of Dinkle (sweet Christ, there was a blast from the past!) and Melissa laying on the bed hemming him in, some gore-pressed sandwich with him in the middle, poor legless PFC Stanley Dinkle and poor dead Melissa Finster, and in the real world someone ran a hand up his chest and he bolted upright in bed, gasping.

A woman with a leg on his, just this pom-pom of curly auburn hair on his pillow so unlike Melissa's, and memories from last night, stuttering images that rose from the murk, roiled alongside the ache in his head. Like his skull was packed with old blood and stitched tight with piano wire. Images unspooled: here he was closing out the Sandy Bottom with somebody, presumably the woman in bed with him, and here was a sizable amount of shitty cocaine sectioned out on his coffee table in a paper envelope. And here, look at this, somehow most frightening of all: Rick Springfield on the stereo. Hayslip laughed, and spikes of pain drove themselves into the poor meat of his brain, the wire bands around his skull tightening. He didn't even *own* a Rick Springfield album, did he? Another image: that same frizzed helmet of auburn hair bobbing over his cock as he lay on the couch and ranted about Fitzhugh's *motherfucking temerity.* The *nerve* of the man telling *him* to knuckle up, for Christ's sake. Telling *him* to get straight. That *Fitzhugh* would cover for *him.* He remembered earnest, effortful sounds from down below that might as well have been issued to another man's dick for all he had felt it. And then: that galaxy of cigarette burns on the lady's blue-veined legs inside that house. More: seeing the shrapnel scars on his neck as he bent over the mirrored coffee table. Before the blowjob? After? Scars grown purple with alcohol and narcotics and rage. He felt like someone had shit in his mouth and sealed it closed. He was afraid to open his eyes for fear they might explode. No booze for three months and he had fallen off the wagon hard.

"I think I'm dying," he croaked.

"Mmmm," his bedmate said.

Her hand came to rest in the wire of his pubic hair, gave his cock a tug, that deflated thing, that sad little wretch. The rest came back to him: the Sandy Bottom the night before, the Police purring their stalker anthem over the jukebox speakers, Hayslip loose enough after his scotch and beer back to think a few whiskeys sounded good. The same old bullshit, every stern resolution dismantled in one drink. And then the woman at a table with her friend, her friend overweight and mistrustful of him, unhappy he was there; but the woman had nice tits and an overbite that somehow made her more alluring—Carol? Sheryl?—and here she was now, in his bed, whatever the hell her name was. And he was ruination incarnate, Death's next target, and yes, somebody may have quite literally shit in his mouth at some point during the evening, or he'd eaten a pack of cigarettes, something. Hands down one of the worst hangovers of his life. And the woman in his bed gave his limp little dick another tug, and was it her coke or had they bought it together? Christ, had he worn anything? A rubber? He thought of Joe Lyley leaning forward and hissing "Rubbers," and with that he felt bile rise flush and hot in his throat. He opened his eyes and stood up, groaning, on quavering legs.

"I have to go to work," he rasped, and in the bed, the woman—Sharon? Karen? —uncurled like a cat, pressed her hands against the wall, her wonderful small breasts flattening, and then she retracted into herself, pulling the blanket over her head, just the top of her curly hair visible.

• • •

He vomited in the shower, quickly and efficiently, his guts gleefully flexing and loosening inside him. The woman was still in his bed when he came out and he made a big show of getting dressed, banging drawers, theatrically grunting when he put his pants on. He wondered if Dobbs would be waiting for him when he arrived. He would smell booze on him for sure. Hayslip could feel it easing out of his pores. The woman —he was almost sure her name was Sherry—still just lay there, obstinate and unmoving.

"God," she said beneath the blanket. "I feel like shit." She seemed, to Hayslip, perfectly content.

"Time to get up," he said. "I've got to get to work. I'm late."

"Come on, Nicky. Let me just sleep in a bit. Please? My fucking head, man." This informality seemed so strange in the brazen morning light. Nicky?

"No can do," he said, tucking his shirt in. Trying to keep it light. What was owed here? That was always the question, wasn't it? "Sorry. Let's go."

He went over to the bed and grasped the edge of the blanket and pulled it down. Not a lot. But she pulled the blanket back up to her face and Hayslip felt something move inside him, some skittering animal that felt entirely separate from him. His scars were suddenly hot and flushed. He put a foot up on the mattress and toed her shin with his boot. His head hurt beyond words.

"Get up. It's time to go." Goddamn, what was her *name?*

"Fifteen minutes," she said from beneath the blanket.

He grabbed the bedding in one fist and yanked it off the bed, blanket and all, like a magician pulling a tablecloth. The woman was naked and wire-skinny and unlovely in the morning light. She jackknifed on the mattress like a fish brought onto the deck of a boat.

He said, "Get your skeletal barfly ass out of my motherfucking house."

She came alive then, spitting curses at him as she rose from the bed and gathered her clothes to her breasts, stomping into his bathroom and slamming the door behind her.

"Nope," he said, and she locked the door behind her. "That's not going to work, dear heart. Get the fuck out."

"Fuck you."

"Get. Out."

"A real gentleman," she yelled. "A real fucking asshole." He leaned his head against the door and then recoiled when she threw something against it. Whatever it was clanged against the floor, rolled away.

"Get the fuck out," he said again. He pictured them like this forever, he and Sherry/Carrie/Terry, growing old together, his hair turning white and trundling toward the floor, his hangover effusive and constant through the years, ever present, his skinny limbs thinning even more, his spine curling toward the earth as eons passed. Eventually the pair of them nothing more than a couple of skeletons finally rooted to the ground, the door still between them.

It was when she screamed through the door, "You can go fuck yourself, Nicky!" that Hayslip put his shoulder against it and felt it gave way with sickening ease. It was a kind of particleboard glossed to look like real wood but it gave way in a pair of wide cracking swaths, the doorknob shattering in pieces. Some dim part of him was pleased with it. Some part of him thought, *That was textbook entry right there.*

The room was not large. A rectangle. Sink and counter, toilet and shower.

The woman had one leg in her jeans. She shrieked and fell to the floor and lay tucked up against the sink and sat there curled up like some horror movie starlet, looking up at him with this beseeching look that reminded him of the accident and of the woman in the house with her burned legs and somehow this angered him even more; he grabbed her by an arm and hoisted her to her feet, his teeth bared. She screamed again, slapped and clawed at his face. His head a dark, pulsing planet of pain. She was crying and screaming, gibbous, her mascara smeared, still with her pants half off.

"I need to go to work. This is my house. I'll give you a ride back to your car."

"Fuck you, you—"

He gripped the backs of her arms and shook her. Her head lolled and he heard her teeth clack together. "Get. The fuck. Out."

She reached toward him then with a hand hooked into claws and he gripped her wrist in a lock and pivoted, bringing her to her knees with a gasp. Bent her hand back toward her wrist, the simplest thing, one of the first moves they taught in the academy, and her shriek filled the room, cords in taut relief on her neck. That little overbite she had, her pants like a molting on the floor. He realized he had the stirrings of an erection and let go of her wrist as if it was hot. Revulsion unfolded inside him, and he sank gasping to the floor beside her.

She scooted away from him, crablike, curled into herself in the corner. A pale sobbing apostrophe, holding her wrist to her breasts.

• • •

Ah, Hayslip, repentant.

Hayslip, poisonous.

Hayslip ashamed and shit-scared and sickened with himself.

He drove her to the parking lot of the Sandy Bottom where she'd left her car. His windshield wipers were bad and left beaded arcs on their journey across the glass, the beads like strings of jewels. She sat in the passenger seat with a tissue clasped in her hands, occasionally pressing it to her red-rimmed eyes. He was afraid and recalcitrant. He could see all too well Dobbs welcoming her into his office, a hand on her elbow as he walked her to a chair, or some twenty-two-year-old reporter at the *Riptide Observer* getting a hard-on for a corruption scandal. Allegations of narcotics use and physical abuse within the sheriff's office? That would probably be enough to get him fired, sure. And even with union help, he'd be hard-pressed to keep his badge if he got a piss test on top of it. Would Dobbs push for him to go? If she got an X-ray of her wrist, what would it show? He fiddled with the heater and tried to make small talk, his voice light and airy, insane even in his own ears. She sat with her knees tucked up to her chest, her thumbs tucked into her fists.

Finally he said, "I'm so sorry. I am. I don't really . . . it's been a tough time." He thought of all the things he could make mention of: Melissa, her accident, his three months sober, how he'd frozen on the stoop the day before as Fitzhugh had fought for his life ten feet away—and instead he pulled out that most pathetic of dusty bones and threw it her way: "I did a tour in Vietnam." The tremor in his voice. "I think I told you about that last night." When his dick had been in her mouth and he'd been ranting around Fitzhugh and shrapnel dispersion patterns and any other number of things.

The woman said nothing. The curve of her jaw resolute as she looked out the window.

"It fucked me up. It really did. My buddies blown up and shit, you know? That's how I got this." He motioned toward the scars. Silence from her.

He pulled into the parking lot and she stepped out without a word or a look back, slamming the door hard enough to rock the car on its wheels. He watched her take long, striding, angry steps to her own car and watched her taillights flare to life as she drove away. He was forty-five minutes late for his shift.

"You need to get your shit straight," Fitzhugh had said, and dear Christ, what was this that he was doing? Had done? What was this but the opposite of getting his shit straight? What was this but falling apart? *I did a tour in Vietnam. I got problems.* Sweet Christ. Hayslip *hated* it when guys pulled that nugget out, like it absolved everything, like it should appease people when they were on the receiving end of terrible acts. Like it was some *GET OUT OF JAIL FREE* card. As if nobody was responsible for anything. Nam was something that came back to him intermittently, randomly but without all that much rancor. It was over a decade in the past, after all, and dimmed in his memory; he'd done his tour and come home. He had seen some terrible shit, yes, and had lived with fear like the hum of an amplifier, a constant background noise that would suddenly grow at times to a howl and clatter but would never, the entire time he was in-country, go away. Sure, he thought of it sometimes—briefly—when he looked in the mirror and had one of those strange, polarizing moments where you saw yourself as if for the first time, or possibly how other people, strangers, saw you:

the shiny purple scar on the left side of his neck, nearly to his jaw. The half dozen tightened blotches around his tit and the longer one that ran down his ribs almost to his hip. The neck injury had been the worst, but even that hadn't been enough to get him shipped home for good. He'd gotten stitched up at a field hospital in Nha Trang and was back with his platoon in ten days. He had killed, he was positive, at least three men throughout his tour. Possibly four. The deaths felt weightless upon him. Empty of sorrow or regret. Most of the battles had been little more than a collection of quick, fevered minutes spent firing into the blank green maw of the jungle, into foliage that jittered and shivered with rounds but never fully quieted, no matter what. It had been a long time ago. He wasn't one of those guys that hit the ground when a car backfired. There *were* things to regret, sure, but Nam was not the ghost that ruled his life. Never had been. Nam was a collection of scars that got him a wide berth from most people now, and that a certain type of person saw and latched onto. Nam, if he had to name anything, was personified by Dinkle, legless screaming Dinkle, but it was rare that he thought of it, and rarer still that he dreamed about Dinkle or the jungle at all. He hadn't thought of Dinkle in years, really. To use Vietnam as a crutch was the weakest of things.

Melissa, though? Melissa was the ghost that haunted him, sure as shit. She (and, to a lesser part, her children) was the phantom that trundled down the hallways of his heart. The one he was fiercely inured to, mostly against his own wishes and certainly against hers, the one who had died on that stretch of rarely-used roadway by the boarded up gas station.

His windshield wipers screeched across the glass. As he pulled out of the lot to head to the station he turned on the radio. Now that he'd pissed on three months sober, he wanted a drink, didn't he? He realized he still couldn't remember the woman's name.

DAVE DOBBS

Dobbs leaned back in his chair as Hayslip sipped from his coffee mug and patently avoided the sheriff's gaze. Papers were spread out on Dobbs's desk that Hayslip would cast glances at and then look away. Something about the man had changed in the recent months—a certain hardness had fallen over the deputy since June's death back in summer. A distancing that hadn't always been there before. Like Hayslip was suddenly a fucking Buckingham Palace guard or something, aloof like that. Of course everyone in town had treated Dobbs with kid gloves at first: gingerly, as if he was suddenly some fragile thing capable of breaking if addressed too loudly, if argued with. He was the widower, after all, and June's death had come as a surprise. At first, Dobbs had been touched by the outpouring of support from the townspeople, his staff. It had buoyed him those first dark weeks, lent him a sense of connectedness, a sense of place. He'd *needed* that gentleness at first, had absolutely felt that frailty inside himself. But now? Three months after the fact? He'd quickly grown tired of it, the way his deputies tiptoed around him. There was talk about naming a wing of the library after June, which was fine, it seemed a fitting tribute—she'd worked there since she was a young woman, after all—but he had grown sick of the timidity of his staff. And to their credit, most of them had stepped up, had followed his lead and grown bold again, edged that distance out, stopped soft-shoeing around him. The station's custodian had left him a fifth of whiskey on his chair a few days after the funeral. A scrawled note that said *Sorry for your loss*, and since then the two of them had carried on the same way they always had, bullshitting about the Blazers while the man emptied his wastebasket, mopped the floors. That's what Dobbs wanted now. He and June had been married thirty years, and he understood intrinsically that he would feel chopped off at the knees in some integral way for the rest of his life, would always feel halved. But it was a private thing, one to wade through alone. Yet Hayslip, months later, still continued to act that way. Deferential, stoically nodding at whatever detail Dobbs threw his way. Work a double? Silent nod, eyes on the ground. Heater's out in his cruiser, mechanic won't be able to fix it until Monday? Silent nod, a frown directed somewhere at Dobbs's knees.

And yet.

And yet here was Deputy Nick Hayslip sitting in front of him, an hour late for his shift, stinking of spent booze, and clearly, *clearly* hungover as dog shit.

Dobbs leaned forward at his desk—a lusty groan from his chair— and said, "So I'm smelling booze on you, Nick. You want to tell me about that?"

Hayslip was taking a drink of coffee when Dobbs said it, the rim of his Styrofoam cup a massacre of fingernailed half moons. Dobbs watched the man's Adam's apple bob in his throat like he was working a lure down. "Yeah, Sheriff. I knocked a few back last night. I won't lie to you." He set his coffee down and let out a reproachful chuckle, and then a second later picked the cup again like it was his tether to the world or something. "I just . . . the thing with Fitzhugh messed with me. I should have been on that guy a lot faster than I was. He just tossed me like I was nothing."

Dobbs picked up Hayslip's report on his desk, unfolded his glasses from his pocket and put them on. He made a show of reading the report while waiting for Hayslip to fill in the silence. Gave him room to stumble on his own story. Fitzhugh and Hayslip's reports matched up well, and the injured woman was still being treated at Riptide Memorial. Hayslip was a Vietnam vet and before the silent treatment had not been not a terrible cop. But their stories read very differently from the neighbor's, who had said that Hayslip had stood on the porch watching the whole thing in the yard unfold like it was a rerun of *Three's Company*.

"So you grabbed the guy in the yard after he fell on Fitzhugh but the guy just shrugged you off."

"No, sir. I grabbed him in the hallway. He just threw me off. Then Fitzhugh got a hold of him and they fell off the porch into the yard."

"Like what, he's on PCP? Angel dust?"

"Or just amped up."

"Just amped up, huh?"

Hayslip shrugged. "Did you test him at booking?"

"No, we did not. Should we have?"

Another shrug as he rubbed the palm of his free hand hard against his knee.

Dobbs tucked his chin down, looked at him over the top of his glasses.

"So in lieu of a better idea, you tip the bottle last night and then come to work dragging ass like this? Late?"

"It was a mistake, Dave."

Dobbs frowned. "Excuse me?"

Hayslip cleared his throat and, for the first time, looked Dobbs in the eye. "It was a mistake, Sheriff."

I'm not your friend, Dobbs thought. *Don't make that mistake. I'm not here to help you with this.* "Which part was the mistake?" he asked, taking a sheaf of papers from a manila folder from his desk drawer. "Which part exactly?"

Hayslip gazed into his coffee cup like its contents were going to divine his future.

Dobbs said, "We have a witness that called in late last night—"

Hayslip winced and Dobbs felt a strange and ugly glee at seeing it; it was the first genuine emotion he'd seen on the man's face all morning.

"—a neighbor lady that says you stood there on the porch while the assailant took Fitzy to the ground." He tossed the paperwork onto his desk and folded his hands over his belly. "That true? You just stand there on the porch with your thumb up your ass while Fitzhugh duked it out?"

"I saw that old lady, Sheriff. She was drinking. I'd be surprised if she could see her own hand in front of her face. What is she, eighty?"

"She's sixty-four, Nick. And you didn't say word fucking one about her in your report, did you? She said that you stood there with your weapon at your side—'immobile' is actually the word she used—and that Fitzhugh was pretty much on his fucking lonesome out there. I got no idea why she would lie, do you?"

"That's not what happened," Hayslip said. He dug a thumb and index finger into his temples and the moment stretched out so long that it became obvious to them both that that was exactly what had happened.

Dobbs put his elbows on the desk and steepled his hands beneath his chin. "So you freeze up," he said quietly, "and then you come in to do your shift hungover. That's Nick Hayslip doing police work."

In their marriage, June had tempered him. She would nod at his anger, soothe him with a hand across his shoulders and a kiss on his cheek. She listened, and maybe after her glass of wine would trace a hand over his pants, there and gone. Nothing particularly brazen; neither of them were like that. But she soothed him and laughed at him—usually at the same time. She had always been wiser than him, always. He thought about June as he looked into Hayslip's bloodshot eyes and thought, *No one's going to help you today, deputy.*

"I don't have the numbers to take you off duty," Dobbs said. "If I did, I'd be passing this off to IA and putting you on leave. We can't have guys freezing up, and we sure as shit can't have guys coming in drunk or hungover."

"That's seriously not how it happened, Sheriff—"

Dobbs held up a hand. "Enough with the bullshit, Nick. Please."

Hayslip sat with his hands folded in his lap. Looked out the window at some point over Dobbs's shoulder, out to the parking lot.

"I'm putting this Ms. Clovington's—the neighbor's—witness statement in your permanent file. As an unresolved judiciary complaint. That's in there forever."

Hayslip opened his mouth as if to protest and Dobbs raised his eyebrows, waiting. *Press me and see how it goes over.* Hayslip shut up, and something in his resignation made Dobbs finally soften toward him a little. "I know things move fast at a scene," he said. "I get that. But if you can't keep up, you need to let me know. We can work something out."

"It went down like I said it did, Sheriff. Like me and Fitzhugh *both* said it did. That lady he had tied up? His *wife?* Hospital said he broke the orbital bone around her eye. You know how hard you got to hit somebody? He was using her as an ashtray." Hayslip's voice trembled with indignation.

Dobbs put the folder in his desk drawer. "Get some coffee. You're late for your shift." Hayslip rose and took his jacket from the back of his chair, and Dobbs leaned forward and pointed a stubby finger at him. "Make no mistake: if you choke again or I smell alcohol on you, I *will* put you on four weeks unpaid leave, minimum, while IA rolls all over you. This isn't New York. This isn't fucking Detroit. You don't Wild West it out here. This is Riptide, Nick. DUIs and noise complaints and speeding tickets, that's your job description."

SAM FINSTER

"Hey hey, guys," Mr. Whitlock crowed, and motioned Sam and Trina inside the house with the spatula he held in one fist. Toad's uncle was a big man with a handlebar mustache and any number of blurred and explicit green tattoos lacing his arms. They looked like they'd been drawn there by a child, quite possibly a drunken one, and Toad had long ago informed him it meant his uncle had done various stretches of county time. "Back before I came into the picture," Toad said. Mr. Whitlock had, over the years, insisted that Sam call him by his first name, Stacy, but somehow Sam just couldn't do it. He looked fearsome, even more so than Sam's dad, and like a man who brooked absolutely no shit. But a *Stacy?* No.

It was Saturday; Gary had pulled a sixteen-hour day at the gear shed stripping the boat the day before and was at home sleeping. He had left a ten dollar bill on the kitchen counter beneath the phone—the resting place for missives and communiqués in the Finster house—and Sam had taken Trina out to breakfast at the Riptide Diner. They drowned their pancakes in syrup as Trina signed at great length about the possibility of getting a Cabbage Patch Doll for Christmas. He was happy to listen to her; this was how Trina glossed over her anger, how she forgave him. Their mother had been the same way. She was not one to apologize, like, *ever*, but it was through small deeds, small kindnesses, that what was strained was eventually repaired. Or at least glossed over. Maybe not the best way to do things, but it was what it was. After breakfast, with the sun shining in silvery wands through the scurf of clouds, they had walked to Toad's place before heading over to the park. Sunlight threw daggers off the wet and glittering streets; if it stayed like this, the conditions would be perfect.

Trina walked beside him with a pair of Barbies jutting from her jacket pockets like little naked torpedoes. At one point she reached up and took his hand in hers, wordlessly, another emissary of apology.

Toad's house had been orange once, like a shout sent out against the dreariness of the town, but salt and sea and time had done its work, and beneath the cap of roof the house now was the faded, wind-worn color of sherbet. A leaning dollhouse with a few of its shingles lying glittery and broken in the yard, the steps of the front porch furred in green moss. Mr. Whitlock's Harley sat under a blue tarp in the driveway.

Inside, the house was much like Sam's own: past the scuffed, bone-yellow linoleum of the covered entranceway, it was a warm place heavy with the odor of cigarette smoke and the whisper of mold. Inside the living room, electrical tape lined a crack in a windowpane. Both Toad and his uncle worked at an auto shop on 101, and boxed car parts sat on the kitchen table amid a scattering of tools resting on newspapers. And yet, for all its coarseness, there were signs of domestic life here that were absent in his own. From the kitchen he heard soft flurries of jazz saxophone from a radio. The air smelled of breakfast, bacon and eggs. A whiff of laundry detergent. The Whitlock's orange tabby, a turgid stray that both Toad and his uncle called Shitneck for reasons that Sam could never fully surmise, meowed and spooled itself around Trina's boots, and she smiled as she crouched down to pet the cat.

"You guys want breakfast?" Mr. Whitlock asked. "I got eggs. I got bacon. Does Trina want some juice? Oh wait, shit, we're out. She want a pop?"

"We're good, Mr. Whitlock," Sam said. "We ate down at the diner." Shitneck purred and kneaded the floor in front of Trina's rain boots.

"Todd," Mr. Whitlock called out. "Visitors, bud."

A reluctant mumble came from Toad's room beyond the kitchen.

"I'd say you guys can just go ahead and go in, but he's got a padlock on those doors," Mr. Whitlock said, flipping an omelet in the pan, his bicep jumping like a baseball under his sleeve. He ashed his cigarette in the rusted bowl of a hubcap that sat next to the radio. He turned to look at Sam and winked. "Between you and me, he's got himself a bit of the brown bottle sickness this morning." He turned the burner off and craned his neck. "Todd-o, I'm serious, get your ass up, you got company."

Toad stepped out of his room and into the kitchen, thumbing sleep from his eyes. He wore boxer shorts and a Misfits shirt and a pair of filthy socks sagged around his ankles. He looked, Sam thought, undefended. Like a giant baby, actually. Trina looked up from the cat and laughed quietly when she saw him. Grinning, she signed something to Sam in a flurry, the three of them watching her.

Toad said, "I didn't catch that. She's too fast, dude."

Sam put his hands in his pockets, casting a glance at Toad's uncle, smiling and suddenly a little shy. "She said that when our dad looks as bad as you do, it means he drank way too much the night before."

• • •

Tumquala Park could be considered such only in the most generous of terms. It was a park the way a slab of concrete could be considered a playground, or a hole in the earth could be called a swimming pool.

Near a fire hydrant stood a small mounted placard, its metal face long since grown a lustrous and oxidized green, that gave a brief and, in Sam's opinion, all too blasé account of the Tumquala Massacre of 1858. A remembrance purchased, so the placard said, by the Tumquala Indian Tribe. Judging by the sodden weariness of the park, the tribe had had a budget of about six and a half dollars. Still, in spite of how much it sucked, and how un-parklike it actually was, Sam thought of it as Trina's place, and liked coming here with her. He'd spent a fair amount of time here as a kid himself, and it was one of the few places where Trina seemed to enjoy herself, to unabashedly act her age.

They had stopped by Selwicky's on the way and raided its dumpster for flattened cardboard. Both Sam and Toad carried armloads of the stuff while Trina walked between them, her pink rain jacket singing in the gray light of early afternoon.

The park faced Hastings Street and was bracketed by gravel roads on two other sides. To the west, facing the sea, was a deeply arching clay hill with a series of rickety wooden steps inset into one side. At the top of the hill lay massive thickets of blackberry bushes and, beyond that, the cliffs and thin stands of pine that led to the beach near the Wolf Point turnaround. The park was not large. Besides the hill itself there was a pair of swings, their chains so rust-clotted that Melissa would never let Trina swing on them for fear of her fingers getting pinched and the ensuing tetanus shots. "They give you shots in your *butt*," Melissa had warned her, and that had been enough for Trina to stay away. The park's only other structure was a covered circular bench that was probably supposed to look like a rocket ship but instead looked like a grayed wooden bullet standing on its base.

The darkened insides were a haven for spiders. In many ways, the bullet encapsulated the whole town: worn down, good-intentioned, but obviously well past its prime.

The part of the park that Trina loved, and why Sam considered it her park, was the hill. The weather had remained cooperative—the rain had rendered the hillside slick, layered in a sheath of mud, but hadn't started up again. From the top of the steps to its base near the rocket ship, the hill's height was significant. It even held a slight divot in the center, a shallow trench worn smooth by decades of asses, both children and adult.

Sam and Toad leaned the extra cardboard against the bullet and lit cigarettes as Trina took one of the flats and carefully clambered up the steps.

"Toad!" she cried out, waving, when she got to the top of the hill. "Toad, watch me!" Between the danger of the hill, the spiders hidden in the splintery bullet, the rusty swing set, and of course the requisite filth and mud, Melissa Finster had not been a huge fan of Tumquala Park. But as Trina hopped on the cardboard and rocketed down the hill, a Barbie clutched in each fist as her hood fell back to her shoulders and her hair flowed behind her and she loosed one of her rare, unlovely and joyous screeches, Sam thought his mother was wrong about the park. It was a good place. Trina came to rest in the slurry of mud at the bottom of the hill and Toad laughed smoke from his mouth. "She's already *covered* in mud, dude. After one run. That's hilarious." Trina ran over to them, shoved a Barbie in each pocket. She smiled at Toad and pointed at the hill.

"I know!" he said. "That was some crazy shit, dude."

She leaned her cardboard against her legs and signed something with her muddy hands.

"She wants you to go down with her," Sam said.

Toad squinted and blew smoke from the corner of his mouth. He ran a hand over the stubbled side of his head. "I got to work later, Trina. See, I'm wearing my work clothes."

"Please?" she asked.

Toad laughed. "You keep going. I might work up to it. I'll watch you."

They smoked as Trina slid down the hill again and again. The sky kept teasing them with brief flurries of rain that never lasted more than a minute or two. After a dozen runs, Trina was slathered in mud from head to foot and half of her cardboard sleds were reduced to sodden scraps.

"God, that kid is awesome," Toad said around his cigarette. "Cracks me up."

"Yeah," Sam said, and for a moment was poised to tell Toad that he couldn't go next summer, that the Trip—the cross country trip they had been planning since they were freshmen—would have to wait. That he couldn't leave his sister, his dad. That they needed him here. Travel around the country after graduation? Follow the Ramones on tour, like Toad wanted to do? Shit. There was no way. It was just the three of them now; all they had was each other.

And then Trina fell.

One of her Barbies must have fallen from her pocket. The doll lay toward the top of the hill, resting splay-legged in that shallow rut that had been worn down over time. Trina walked up the steps, and as the rain suddenly let loose a downpour so sudden as to make a sound like an animal hissing, like oil in a pan, she gingerly stretched from one of the steps out onto the hillside itself, leaning over with her hand out, reaching for it. Toad took a step forward and said, almost conversationally, "Oh, she's gonna bust her ass." Immediately Trina's feet went out from under her and she fell forward and knocked her chin loud enough for Sam to hear her teeth clack together. She slid down the hill backward on her stomach, fishtailing, her jacket rucking up around her shoulders.

Sam and Toad bellowed with a mad, terrible laughter—one that Sam would have sworn belonged to fright more than anything—even as they ran out to help her. She lay curled at the base of the hill, rain sizzling around her, a small divot of blood already welling on her chin. Sam picked her up, and she tucked her head into his chest and bawled. Mud had turned her hair into clotted dreadlocks, but the rain was already washing it away.

The three of them ran inside the bullet, Sam carrying Trina, Toad first wildly swinging his arms inside to clear any spider webs.

Sam leaned down on a knee and tilted Trina's chin up. A dot of blood bright among the mud, a watery thread of it that ran down onto her shirt. She was blubbering and red-eyed.

"It's okay, Trina," Toad said. "It's cool."

What did you hit your chin on? Sam signed.

I don't know. I just fell. And I saw you laughing! Her ice-blue eyes were confused and hurt and above the roof of the bullet it roared with rain and his sister had her hands on his shoulders, crying, getting mud all over him, and he hugged her close. She was a slight weight that leaned against him, a weight nearly inconsequential. Christ, like she was mostly *jacket*. He felt blisteringly ashamed at his earlier resentment—he would take care of her. He would protect her. He would pick up Gary's slack. She was *so little*, and she was nine, and afraid, and they had only each other now. He thought, *I'll do anything to make her safe.* He could feel the tiny bones of her shoulder blades beneath his hands as she wept against him.

"I'm so sorry I laughed," he said, and then pulled away from her and signed it.

It's okay, she signed back. She took a shuddering breath and wiped tears from her eyes with the tips of her middle fingers, a surprisingly adult gesture that set his heart to hurting all over again. *I bet it was funny.*

But I shouldn't have laughed. I'm sorry.

It's okay, Sam. She could sign his name, those three letters, as fast as any word.

"Sam," Toad called out. "Check this out."

Toad had stepped from beneath the bullet and was standing, legs braced wide, on the hill where Trina had fallen. He held Trina's Barbie in one fist.

"Come on up the steps. Check this out." His voice was strange and compressed beneath the hissing rain. "Be careful." Toad was getting drenched and seemed entirely unconcerned about it.

Sam hiked Trina's hood over her head, not that it mattered at this point, and they carefully walked up the steps together holding hands to where Toad was crouched in a three-point stance on the hillside. The world was suddenly flash-bright with lightning and then a handful of seconds later a booming crack of thunder that made Trina's eyes go wide. Even with the blood still welling on her chin, she looked around the park with a dazed, gleeful smile on her face: she'd felt the vibration.

"Dude," Toad called out, "I think she whacked her chin on this." Rain fell in a string from his hand where he pointed.

"Don't fall," Sam said.

"I'm not going to fall," Toad said. He pointed to a small, gnarled bump in the clay.

"What is that?" Sam peered over, not wanting to risk stepping off the stairs.

Raindrops jumped silver on Toad's back. He dug his thumb into the earth and pushed a plug of loose mud away. He used the Barbie as a tool, jamming her legs into the crease and flinging more away. Trina watched, frowning.

"I'll get you a new Barbie, Trina," Toad said absently, still digging. "This one's about shit the bed anyways, I'd say. Pneumonia, for sure. Nude. Covered in mud. Boobs hanging out everywhere. Totally unrealistic-looking body type. Super shitty haircut." He wasn't even listening to himself, and Sam had to hope that Trina wasn't trying to lip-read.

"Seriously, what *is* that?"

Toad had sheared a sizable clot of mud away, and leaned over and handed Trina the doll. On the hill where he crouched there was a dull yellow amid the red clay, and even from Sam's vantage point he could see that it was smooth, minutely ridged. Toad crouched over it with his mud-clotted hands resting on his knees.

Sam was covered in mud, soaked through. They were standing in a downpour. Trina was bloodied, still crying a little bit.

"That's not a . . ." Sam said. "Holy shit, man, what am I looking at?"

"You know what you're looking at, Sam."

"Holy shit."

"I know. Exactly."

It was a bone.

The yellowed length of an arm bone, a leg bone. Something.

Toad scooped more earth with his free hand.

Next to the first one, this one unmistakable: the dark, curved hollow of an eye socket. Yellowed as newsprint and filling with rain.

Trina had found a skeleton buried in the hill.

TWO

dobbs in the mud • his face painted blue in the television light • taking the children home • *the looming error,* or how trina learned to fear the bomb • the bonfire • the traffic stop • ronnie radium and the nine fingers of death • a discovery • a brief aside: an excerpt from the *riptide observer,* january 16, 1868

DAVE DOBBS

Noon. A slate-gray sky. Pale beams of sunlight punched here and there through the clouds, and the day had been marked with fierce but intermittent showers. He was in a cruiser, just then driving past the squat cement building of KRPT, the town's sole radio station, when the call came in from dispatch. Some kind of vandalism going on at the old Tumquala Park. "It's the Whitlock boy that called it in, Sheriff," the dispatcher said, and Dobbs laughed.

"You're telling me Todd Whitlock is reporting a vandalism."

"It came in on the non-emergency line but he sounds pretty excited about it. Might be something in progress?"

"Right," Dobbs said. "I'll tell you this, Deb: if Todd Whitlock is actually calling us up and reporting a crime in-progress, I'm buying lunch for the whole goddamned floor tomorrow. You pass that around."

Deb laughed. "That I can do, Sheriff."

"Anyway, I'm en route."

"Copy."

There were days when he muscled through the majority of his day's paperwork, the administrative leanings and expectations of the job, and shunted the rest for a while. Saved it for the next day. Then he would rise from his desk, leave the station, and get in a patrol car and work a shift. Do the part of the job he had been taught as a young man, the part he had grown muscles around. The part still (mostly) couched in muscle-memory and, now that he was in his fifties, edged with the balm of nostalgia. It was something he'd found himself doing more in the months since June's death. There was a certain mindfulness in the responsibilities of sheriff that he relished now: how it required a stepping away from his own loss, how the relentless people-part of the job removed him, if only briefly, from the dumb and constant ache of his own life. His staff, his deputies, the hum of the station, the influx of aggrieved citizens looking for resolution (or just an ear to complain into)—all that ceaseless goddamned *living* going on around him. It was good for him, he knew it. But there were also moments in the cruiser—the familiarity of the wheel around his hands, the wick of the wiper blades against wet glass, the glyphs of static over the radio as the town unfurled outside his windows—in which he felt somehow closer to June. Being in the cruiser made him feel younger, made him almost believe that he was still in some intrinsic way that younger man, the one simply running a traffic shift along 101, some young dipshit watching for speeders, for busted taillights, DUIs. June felt nearer to him then, even if that nearness meant only that he could recall her face, her mannerisms, with a little more ease. Even if it meant it was simply her half-assed ghost, her face in his mind, that seemed to step closer toward him. He would take what he could get.

Tumquala Park had long since fallen by the wayside—as always, the city's budget was comically thin—and was little more now than a sloping hill braced with blackberry bushes and a rusting swing set, and that strange tubular outbuilding that looked like an awkward combination of an out-house and a rocket ship. Besides the beach itself, there were a dozen spots throughout town where kids congregated to partake in the usual shit kids had and would always partake in, and Tumquala Park, with its sad little gazebo, those eroding steps punched into the hillside, and the fact that it was on Hastings Street and just down the road from the Wolf Point turn-around, had been one of them for a long, long time.

The wheels of the cruiser sang out on the gravel road as he approached the park and Dobbs radioed dispatch that he'd arrived. The rain had stopped again. There were three people standing around the gazebo, two young men and a little girl, and he recognized them all and was hardly surprised to feel his heart ratchet itself into his throat.

Oh Junie, he thought. *I do miss you fiercely. Of course Whitlock would be with these two. What did I expect?*

He sat for a moment, staring down at the steering wheel. The gearshift blued to the metal by years of men's hands. The Mossberg pump shotgun at his elbow, the stock locked in place. Of all the people he felt disastrously unprepared to see, the Finster children topped the list. The thin, hard-eyed boy with his shorn scalp and the little deaf girl with the scowl so seemingly permanent that she may as well have come from the womb that way. The strangeness of them, the sadness. He didn't fear them exactly, but through the accident they were bound together in an intimacy that was terrible in its scope, and that intimacy came close to frightening him.

He thought of their mother, Melissa Finster, and the awful ballet of twisted metal on the roadside, how Fitzhugh and the EMTs had found pieces of safety glass thirty yards beyond the wreckage, how June's body was accordioned in against itself, her chest compressed against the steering wheel, the great and terrible velocity of these two women and their two cars meeting on that dark street. Deb had tentatively called him at home and directed him to the location of the scene after they'd identified Junie, her voice fevered with sobs, but when he arrived, there had been no dramatics on his part; they had not had to pull him away from the car, from her poor body crumpled amid the bent steel. Mostly he'd felt too shocked, too wholly cleaved—as if he'd taken root to the ground. The faces of the men speaking to him had wavered as if they were underwater. He kept looking at the architecture of the vehicles as Fitzhugh bumped him chest to chest, gently pushing him away from the scene. Junie's car looked like a building, or a spaceship, or one of the personnel carriers he had kept running in Korea; it did not look like his wife's car. It did not look like a mausoleum that held her body.

He sat across from the park and touched the steering wheel, saw the white hairs on his wrists that crept from his sleeves. The children were looking at him from across the street.

It was not his own voice, or June's, that spoke next. It was simply the voice of the inevitable: You have to step outside now. You have to talk to them. Even if Whitlock turns out to be full of shit, you have to get out of this car. Because there's no one else to do it. Because you're supposed to. And lastly, a thought that almost flooded him with hope, with the expansiveness of such an idea: The errors of the parent aren't owned by the children. He didn't believe it, not really. He was not that gracious of a man. He ached too much for her. But he felt grateful that even a notion like that could occur to him.

Thunder was a raw, roiling mutter in the sky with a sound like God pulling the floorboards up, and the rain came then as if someone had turned on a tap. In seconds the hood shimmered with water an inch high as Dobbs stepped out, his slicker above his head as he ran toward the gazebo.

• • •

The three children—the Whitlock boy, blossoming young criminal that he was, had to be nineteen or twenty, but everyone under thirty looked like a goddamned baby to him these days—stood with their heads peering from the doorway of the gazebo. It was dim and close inside and smelled like salt and damp wood and the smoke from the boys' old cigarettes. Each of their expressions was hooded and solemn, even the little girl's. Whitlock blew into his cupped hands.

"Damn," Dobbs said, pulling the hood of his slicker back. "It's really coming down out there." His voice to his own ears sounded light, jolly, a little crazed. "So, we got a call about some vandalism? Something like that? You guys called in about some destruction of property?"

Whitlock and the Finster boy shared a glance, half-hidden in the dark. "I called you guys," Whitlock said.

"About vandalism?"

Whitlock frowned. "Oh, I get it. I called it in, so automatically it's about *property* or some shit like that. Vandalism."

The Finster boy (Sam, Dobbs remembered the kid's name was Sam) said, "It's not about vandalism." His jacket hung off him like a drapery. He ran a hand over his scalp.

"No? Okay. So? What do we got, fellas?" Still with that cheerful, half-mad brightness to his own voice.

"We found something out there." Finster gestured vaguely toward the open mouth of the gazebo.

"What, in the park?" Dobbs had a fleeting remembrance of Joe Lyley screaming about beasts of the field. He paused, wondered very briefly about notions of leading a witness, then plunged ahead. "You didn't find a bird out there, did you?"

"It's a body," Whitlock said.

Dobbs looked at him. Whitlock's face was cowled in shadow and for a moment Dobbs thought of how strange it was, the four of them huddled against the elements like this, here in this dark shell, the day's failing and meager light hardly reaching them. He pulled out his notebook, a leather affair June had gotten him years ago, the cover long since bowed from the curve of his ass. He clicked a pen open, smiled at the children, felt an anger uncoiling. The boys were having a run at him, bullshitting him. Whitlock he could understand; the boy would be housed within the Oregon State Penitentiary, and sooner rather than later, most likely. But Sam Finster? Their lives were entwined, messily. And still he'd do something this stupid? A prank this callous?

There was a knife-edge to Dobbs's voice. "Okay, Todd. You found a body here at the park?"

"It's not really a body," Finster said, and thunder boomed so hard and close that everyone recoiled from it save for the little girl, who suddenly grinned, her eyes springing open as if she'd just been told some delicious secret. Their feet all made gritty scraping sounds on the cement floor. "But it's definitely bones we found," he said. "A skeleton."

Dobbs clicked his pen, stared hard at him. "When did you find it?"

"Just a bit ago," Finster said.

"I ran over to one of the Coke-bottling warehouses and called," Whitlock said.

"You called non-emergency for a dead body in Tumquala Park?"

Whitlock shrugged, pulled a pack of cigarettes out. "It's a skeleton, man. That shit ain't going nowhere."

Dobbs started writing. Absently he said, "Don't smoke that in here, there are kids around." He wrote down their names, their numbers, the time of day. Finally, it was the little girl who patted him on the arm. When she looked up at him, Dobbs saw a weal of fresh scab on her chin.

"It's over there," she said, her little hand at the end of her muddy pink jacket, her words slow and exaggerated. There were flecks of mud dotting her cheeks. She was pointing toward the sloping hill and its stairs carved into the side.

"Okay," he said, still looking at the girl. Trina, her name was; the memory of it came like a quick little hammer-jab to the sternum. Trina Finster. She was deaf, he remembered. "Listen, why don't you guys tell me what happened and we'll start from there."

The boys shared a glance, some mantle being passed between them. The Finster boy ran a hand over his scalp again and began haltingly telling their story. The girl's cardboard slides down the hillside. The rain, how she fell down. Trina Finster, who had been watching her brother speak, turned to Dobbs then and lifted her chin again to show him the little pearl of dried blood. Whitlock on the hill, digging enough of its red clay away for them all to recognize what lay buried there. Whitlock's run to the bottling plant.

"Okay," Dobbs said, folding his notebook back into his shirt and buttoning up his yellow slicker. "Let's go over there and take a look." They emerged from the doorway, his slicker a noxious and horrific yellow in the strange gray light. The rain by then was falling steadily again so he bid the three of them back in the gazebo to wait. It was unlikely there would be any evidence remaining in a downpour like this, footprints or otherwise, but he was going into this blind. Three extra set of footprints trampling around? Not wise.

Oh, the soothing nature of precedence. How procedures and muscle-memory bit back so lovely against the fangs of grief.

The steps up the hill were treacherous things, little more than chunks of splintered, ancient wood tiered into the hillside. Each rotten step pooled in its own slurry of mud. *Slick as shit through a goose,* his father would have said. Yeah, the idea of footprints was a joke. Promptly, the heel of one of Dobbs's shoes slid from one of the steps and he went down to one knee, the warm mud painting him nearly to the thigh. Both hands slapped the step in front of him for purchase and then he was drenched to the forearms in mud as well. Rain fell in strings from the brim of his hat. "Sweet jumped-up Christ," he muttered, feeling the weight of his years, his paunch, the stiffness in his bones. Luckier than hell he hadn't just pulled his back out. Crouched on one knee there in the mud, he spied a glance back at the gazebo at the bottom of the hill and—to his surprise—even the Whitlock boy was frowning and serious.

"You okay?" he called out.

"Yuh," Dobbs said, rising carefully, flicking his hands free of mud as best he could.

A few more steps and there it was, a dull yellow crease of bone against the slick red clay of the hill. Around the remains were the craggy blemishes that Whitlock's hands had rent in the hill; divots already being worn smooth and rounded by the falling rain. He stood on the steps and peered down, his hands on his hips.

He turned back and called out, "I don't quite think it's a good idea to step out there," he said.

"I hear you," Whitlock said, and just like that, something changed between them. He would never be bosom buddies with Todd Whitlock; they'd never stop and shoot the shit if they ran into each other in the butcher's aisle at Selwicky's, but for right now, lines had been drawn and they were all on the same side.

A pale bowl of skull, the eye socket filled to overflowing with rainwater. A little teacup. Over another foot or so in the hillside, another knob of bone lay revealed. Dobbs suppressed a shiver as he felt a rill of water run down his back. He realized the skull was small, childlike.

He walked gingerly back down the steps as Trina Finster watched him from the doorway of the gazebo. Her brother held one hand, and with the other one she lightly explored the wound at her chin.

"I'll be right back, guys," he called out, and jogged across the street.

He sat carefully in the cruiser's seat, not wanting to get it muddy, then deciding that in regards to cleanliness he was already well past fucked. He shut the door and started the engine, turned on the heater. Soon the inside of the car smelled earthen and raw. Things fell in clear delineations within him. The things they would need to do. Protocol. There was no crime here, at least not a recent one—probably—but even then there were things to be done. And besides, habit was habit, and he felt the relief of habit's locomotion. Across the street, Todd Whitlock spit and then stubbed out his cigarette on the wall of the gazebo and put the butt in his pocket. Dobbs thumbed the radio handset, and when Deb responded he said, "Looks like we're gonna need someone from State Forensics in Salem out here at Tumquala Park, hon. ASAP."

"Calling the Staties?"

"Yuh. Got a body here. Some remains, anyway. How old I don't know, but they'll want to check it out. Meantime, get Fitzhugh and Ridges down here to cordon things off and set up tape and all that."

"Mark Fitzhugh's off duty with those busted ribs, Sheriff."

Dobbs closed his eyes. "Goddamn it, that's right."

"Nick Hayslip's got the day off. You want me to call him in?"

"No, no." He had an image of Hayslip blundering around the scene. Drunk, most likely, police tape wrapped around his stork legs. At the very least moping around, kowtowing and deferential. "Just send Lonnie Ridges down here and get the State people on the horn."

"Roger, Sheriff."

He had an evidence kit in the trunk. He should lay tape around the site and start a cordon. Secure the scene, have clear directives for his arriving deputy. There were things to be done. But for a moment he simply sat there. He could put the Finsters and the Whitlock boy in the car, get them warm. He knew in his heart that it was not the children's fault, what had happened to his June, that they should be exempt from judgment. A better man would have maybe moved beyond it by now. Maybe someday he would be that man.

He sat and waited just a moment longer, that rich smell of baking earth filling the car as he waited for the park to come alive with movement.

NICK HAYSLIP

He lay in bed as the day slowly broke open outside the window. A sky of flat burnished steel. Awakened after three hours of fitful sleep, capped off with a nightmare. Finally Hayslip sat up, put his clothes on and went out for a run. What was it that Melissa had said once? He had so few bullets in the chamber. She'd said it kindly, jokingly, but it was true. So few things worked. Yet running—running was one of them. It had always been one of his keys. A solution.

He ran. The slow unfolding promise of footfalls on wet pavement, the engine of his breath loud in his ears. Trees devoid of their leaves, their reaching limbs like skeins of ink scribbled on the pale paper of the sky. The quiet, drizzly early morning traffic. He turned and ran along 101 for a time, the same route he frequently drove on patrol, and headed toward the Wolf Point turnaround, the beach. The few people he saw were just limned shapes inside the buildings he passed, shapes he caught brief glimpses of before moving on.

He crossed the highway and ran down Hastings Street, the charcoal expanse of the sea visible between pale ridges of crabgrass and thin stands of slash pines. Past industrial warehouses and clapboard apartment buildings. Empty lots and those very few towering homes built on stilts, anchored into the cliffs. He ran down the paved loop of the turnaround and then down the concrete ramp to the beach itself. Running, with the fierce piston of his heart pumping like that, the images from his dream carried less weight. The dream wasn't as deadly out here with his legs burning from exhaustion, the tide roving in and out beside him. The panic had faded, the blued throb of vein at Melissa's throat, the way her hands flexed into fists in his hair as she came; this stirred him but did not hurt his heart as much as it would have in a dream, in the dark. The spill of sand on Dobbs's desk. The woman screaming as she looked out the window, like she'd been reading from a script, the laugh track on the TV. The man putting his finger in Fitzhugh's eye. Fitzhugh in his fucking martyr bed. *You got to knuckle up. You need to get your shit straight.*

And Dinkle.

That'd been the dream, hadn't it? Private First Class Stanley Dinkle, twenty years old and just high as fuck, and still plenty of dope left in his pack from his last R&R to Saigon, and look: his bandoliers of M60 rounds lay unfurled around him as he writhed in the dust, screaming, his legs reduced to a spray of red paste a yard or so away, and really, *what* was with all the war bullshit now? The blurred dreams of Dinkle—what was it about? You lived through something and then you made it home and you moved the fuck on. He hit a dune of soft sand, a sullen little rise, and staggered, touching down with one hand. He spit and rose up, sprinting even harder. His breath was a constellation of hot knives in his side. Clots of dark sand flung in his wake, his pale legs pumping, calves flexing like fists. The few other beachgoers saw him, this scarecrow man with his manic pace like he was being chased, and gave him a wide berth. And he *was* chased, here and there: a dog or two briefly loped after him, tongues lolling, until their owners called them back. (The feral ones knew better, presumably. Nobody that skinny would be offering them shit.) He ran until the knives of pain disappeared, until the molten core of him turned into something else, a looseness. Like he could run forever, like the world was sloughing off of him. He ran, the sea a great expansive blanket to his left, the dullest quilt on earth, the mournful bellow of ships clashing against the seaside cliffs and tumbling back. Gulls rode the thermals and hung nearly motionless in the sky above him.

He was a man destined, it seemed, to be fearful. Afraid of what both the past and future held for him.

He fell to the sand gasping, his hands gripping clots of wet sand.

The woman from the Sandy Bottom, he was sure of it, her name was Sherry. Of that, at least, he was almost positive.

• • •

He jogged his way home, cooling down, feeling something close to calmness wash over him. Those few good post-run minutes. His mind finally wrung out, punch-drunk into submission with the fatigue of the body. He made it to the door of his little house just as the sky unleashed a torrent. It had been raining off and on but fell now so hard the lawn turned silver and out on the street it hissed like some great and unhappy animal.

And it was only that evening—well after the day had dimmed and darkness had fallen, after he had paced the floors and done the laundry and the dishes, and in his head had visited the Sandy Bottom a dozen times, and been harangued by mental specters of Sherry and Melissa Finster's husband and Stanley Dinkle and all the others, specters rife with their vengeful recriminations against him—it was only then that he changed the channel on the blaring television and saw Dave Dobbs on the screen, jowled and red-faced and looking terribly old and irritated.

There was Tumquala Park, garish and bright in the newscaster's lights, the little wooden gazebo like a grayed shipwreck in the background. The footage cut to a trio of kids, obviously shot earlier in the day when it was still mostly light out. Melissa's children and Todd Whitlock, the blossoming criminal, pointing at a spot up the hill. The whole park was ringed in yellow police tape and the footage showed the little girl turning toward the camera and scowling and turning away again and for a moment she looked so much like her mother—that same fierce determination, the same eyes— that Hayslip felt that everything was possible: that goodness abounded, that lost and unnavigable things could be regained somehow. The little girl was holding her brother's hand. He looked pale and drawn, his acne glaring in the merciless light. Whitlock stood smirking with a cigarette in his hand.

The children, the reporter said, had discovered what appeared to be the remains of a body in Tumquala Park. They had called in specialists to discover the nature of the crime, and more details would be released as soon as possible.

Hayslip stood there, mute, his face blue and slack-jawed with wonderment in the television light.

DAVE DOBBS

It was an early starless evening by the time he finally drove the Finster children home from the park. Strange how, in a few scant hours, that ugly little swath of mud had gone from empty to thronged with people. He and Lonnie Ridges laying a perimeter around the lot with yellow police tape, the children clustered around his cruiser across the street, then the forensics team finally arriving from Salem as the sky started to darken. The hours following that had marked, to Dobbs's surprise, the arrival of news crews and passersby both. First, a pair of disheveled reporters from the *Riptide Observer* who'd clearly been monitoring the police channel. From there, the word had clearly gotten out; reporters began arriving from Salem and Albany. The most surreal moment came when a news van— all the way from *Portland*, for God's sake— had pulled to a stop beside Lonnie's cruiser, with an honest to-Christ satellite dish mounted on its roof. The cameraman and boom operator stepped out, gathering their gear. The rain was still coming down and Dobbs, beneath the hood of his slicker, saw a female newscaster in a maroon pantsuit step gingerly from the sliding door of the van. She'd held a clipboard over her head to protect her from the rain. Her perm was a formidable thing, and Dobbs recognized her immediately from the ten o'clock news. He felt both irritated and a little flustered at her arrival.

When the forensics team arrived, they consisted of a pair of mute, stone-faced men in rubber booties and latex gloves that they snapped on with the solemnity of morticians. They might as well have been brothers, considering how almost featureless they appeared. Pale and fearsome as saucers of milk. They introduced themselves and one of them asked, "Mind if we take it from here, Sheriff?" He and Lonnie had watched from beneath the gazebo as the two men quickly assembled a trio of squat, mercilessly bright klieg lights from their van and set them up outside the tape. They double-checked the park perimeter and photographed the grounds and measured footprints, and then, after that, examined the meager allotments of bones showing on the hillside. Their cameras flashed like lightning in the fading daylight. (Dobbs, before any of the news teams had shown up, had felt a small, ugly tear of happiness run through him when one of the forensics guys had fallen to a knee on what was probably the exact same step he had slipped on earlier that day.) He quietly warned Lonnie not to speak to the press until the investigation was entirely under way and they had a better idea of jurisdiction. Dobbs himself had some macabre vision of someone dumping some poor child's body in lye, stripping it down to the bones, trying to make some recent travesty seem old. Something from a Hollywood cop show. Finally, forensics had kicked both Dobbs and Lonnie out of the wooden bullet so they could photograph its interior. So, he'd sent Lonnie out for pizza. The kids ate in his cruiser.

After they'd taken their photos, and as the news crews began setting up their cameras, Dobbs had cornered the forensics men by their van and asked them if they could just go ahead and interview the children now. "I'd like to get that part over with and send them on home. They've been here for most of the day."

"We don't need to interview the kids," one of them said as they slammed shut the sliding door of the van and clambered in the front seat.

"You don't?" Dobbs said, peering in through the passenger window.

The other one peered over at Dobbs's cruiser still across the road and turned back to him, smirking. "Not unless they've aged remarkably well."

"Not unless they qualify for the senior discount at Sizzler."

They fell into a cadence. "The senior *senior* discount."

"Social Security, even."

"Adult diapers!"

"Depends!"

Dobbs sighed. "Guys, I'm not following you."

The reverie was broken, and they turned back to face him, grinning. "Pretty certain these are pioneer-era remains, Sheriff. Doesn't really matter how these kids found the bones. I mean, I know there's no statute on murder and all, but even if this was a death due to foul means, it happened a long, long time ago. As a crime scene, there's nothing here for us."

It was decided that Dobbs would leave a message with the Anthropology Department at the university in Corvallis some ninety minutes away. Offer them an opportunity at excavation. It rained and stopped and rained again, and the information traveled among the news teams, who seemed disappointed to hear the age of the body, the lack of a fresh atrocity. It sat strange inside him. He felt relief that it was not a new murder, and yet some part of him was already disliking the inevitable messiness of it. The news teams hung around, first trying to film and interview the children, who as dusk fell proved less than photogenic; they wanted nothing to do with Trina Finster once they realized she was deaf and couldn't provide a soundbite, and Sam himself seemed more interested in protecting her. He gave only monosyllabic answers to their questions. They gave up interviewing Whitlock after he proved incapable of answering a question without saying "fuck" every fourth or fifth word, contenting themselves with short interviews with Dobbs and Lonnie and the forensics team, and long pans of the park under the kliegs. Finally, during a break in the rain, and in that last twenty minutes of twilight, the Whitlock kid asked to leave and Dobbs gave him his business card and bid him well. Lonnie asked if he needed a ride and Whitlock said he worked on 101, a straight shot.

The news crews left. Dobbs asked Sam Finster if his father would worry about them and the boy had simply shrugged. The inside of the cruiser stank of pizza. The windows were fogged. Dobbs rubbed at the windshield with his sleeve. "You guys ready to go home? Been a long day, huh?"

"Sure," Sam Finster said.

"Where we headed, folks?" His voice was again falsely bright. Inside his head he heard June tell him not to blame the children and knew it was just some hopeful part of himself trying to rise up.

• • •

They wove their way through the early evening streets. The little girl seemed fascinated by the grill separating the front and back seats, and every time Dobbs would look in the rearview he would see her, mouth slightly open, her hood still hooked over her head as she held a half-eaten slice of pizza in one hand and, with the other, traced the diamond-shaped meshwork. They were strange children, though he couldn't say if it had been their mother's death and the nature of it that had made them that way. Who could know? Maybe they'd been that way before. He thought momentarily about making a joke about Todd Whitlock being no stranger to the backseat of a police car, then thought better of it. He felt suddenly old and fat and useless, his bones loose in his body, poorly gathered things. It had been a long day.

He was soaked. The cruiser whirred through miniature lagoons that lay curbside, and he slowed when he saw pedestrians on the sidewalk for fear of splashing them. The children sat silently in the back.

"Sounds like you guys are going to be on the news," Dobbs said, looking in the rearview mirror again. Cursing himself for his own inanity.

A grunt from the boy, as his sister traced designs in the fogged window glass.

"Those forensics guys, in the white van? They said those bones were at least a hundred years old. You believe that?"

A pause, and then Sam said, "She can't hear you. She's deaf."

Dobbs cleared his throat. "Well, I was talking to both of you, I guess."

The boy looked at him for a moment, their gaze held in the rearview mirror, and then Dobbs looked away. He smoothed his mustache and turned the windshield wipers on high until they strode once across the glass with a screeching sound.

• • •

He pulled the car into the driveway of the Finster house, other larger homes looming over it. It was like something from a fairy tale, that little house among the big ones. The driveway was empty of any cars.

"Your dad home?"

"He's doing gear work down at the docks," Sam said, and Dobbs got out and opened the back door. The night smelled of pine, wet earth, the sea. Sam walked to the front door without another word, his head down. The doorknob gleamed silver among the front door's black paint. Dobbs felt a tiny warm hand brush his wrist and he looked down to see the girl gazing up at him.

"I told Sam to save you some," she said carefully, her words just a little rounded. She leaned into the back seat and took the grease-spotted pizza box and handed it to him. She walked to the open door but before she stepped inside she turned and gave a small wave. The hood of her pink raincoat was still up and one eye was obscured but he saw her smile before she went inside and shut the door. The pizza box was cold but he looked at the door as it closed and something caught in his throat and wouldn't let go of him.

TRINA FINSTER

Trina learned to fear the bomb two weeks after her mother died, and she fell into that fear like someone slipping into bed after a hard day's work. Fell into it with a relief that bordered on gratitude. When she thought of the bomb, she felt like someone who was gravely ill witnessing a terrible and violent event: a merciless distraction, but at least one outside of her own body.

When thoughts of her mother came now, thoughts that made her ache and curl up in bed like a plant without sunlight, she read *The Looming Error*. She read about *Mutual Assured Destruction—M.A.D.*—and at night those three letters ran the plainsong of their zippered teeth along her heart as she stared at the ceiling wishing for sleep. It was a lullaby that made her heart fearful and clumsy, those three letters, that *idea*, but—and this was the important part—it took up too much room to worry about anything else. To feel sad for herself. To miss her mom. The world, Trina knew, was doomed, and it was terrible, but there was some part of her that felt glad that at least this part of it would be over. The world wouldn't survive, and there was something freeing about that, like finally throwing up after you've felt sick for a long, long time.

Those three letters, M-A-D, and how they spelled the end of everything.

The book lay under her bed and sometimes it felt like she slept above a bomb for all the power it had.

The thing she hated most about the Soviets and the United States both was their babyishness. How much they seemed like grumpy, spoiled kids playing with toys they didn't want to give up. There was a lot about the negotiations in the book, and she could picture it all too well, the two countries discussing things in a big room somewhere, everyone with their own glass of water by their hands, old white men in suits trying to work out trades in practically the same way that she and Sam had bartered the gross parts of their school lunches when she was a baby back in first grade:

United States: We want you to reduce the number of your SS-20 missile launchers in Europe, okay? You have 243 of them and we want you to only have 75.

Russia: Hmm. Okay. If you also only have 75 launchers for your Tomahawk cruise missiles there as well.

United States: Fine by us.

Russia: Ha! Except we both know that your Tomahawks carry four warheads compared to the one warhead of the SS-20, so you would have like 300 warheads to our 75! Cheater!

Trina knew they did not actually talk like this, but still. Practically.

It went on and on. And this, she knew, was just *one* type of nuclear missile, when both sides had so many different kinds, *thousands of missiles of all different kinds,* and all of them capable of doing their little part for M.A.D. *One* Tomahawk, *The Looming Error* said, carried a nuclear yield up to *ten times* the one at Hiroshima! And still they argued about it like little babies over their toys. Their tens of thousands of toys.

ICBMs. NCBMs. SLBMs. IRBMs.

B-1s. MXs. Poseidons.

These characters at night became like glyphs to her, these names a hidden language that battled the shadows skirting her wall, battled the shapes of the trees outside her window, the yawning realization that her mother was never, ever coming back, that Trina would never see her again, that she was *dead in the ground right now even—*

Trident IIs. Pershing IIs. Tomahawks.

Soviet SS-4s. SS-5s. SS-18s. SS-19s. SS-20s.

She read them in the book and repeated them; it was a cadence that had become familiar, intimate. *The Looming Error* was overdue but she couldn't imagine turning it back in to the library. She carried it in her backpack to school; she could practically feel it under the bed at night, whispering like a bad friend.

Trina and Sam had gone back to school two weeks after their mother had been found wrapped around the steering wheel of her Buick, Mrs. Dobbs dead in the other car. The school year had practically just started when it happened; she hadn't missed much. Trina had walked to her classroom amid throngs of staring children whispering behind their hands. Mrs. Driscoll had greeted her with a hug so fierce it threatened to loosen something vital inside of Trina's chest. Her mother's absence still made her look around corners, as if she was somewhere down the hall, in another room, if only Trina could find her. All else in her life—Sam, her dad, Judy Blume, Anastasia, her toys, Face from *The A-Team* (whose unpredictability and strangeness Trina found privately thrilling)—had been shunted to the sidelines. She felt ghostly, half-formed.

Coming back to school was about as she had expected it. She was not only the deaf girl now, she was the deaf girl whose mother had died in a car accident. Whose mother, she found out from a gleefully malicious group of fifth graders on the playground that day—girls with lacquered bangs and zebra-striped tights, girls who over-enunciated each word to make sure she understood—had actually killed Mrs. Dobbs in a head on collision *because she was drunk*. Her mother was a drunk driver that had killed the nice librarian who had held a book drive for their school the year before where *every kid in the entire school* had gotten a book, including Trina, and how did she feel about that? How did that little factoid, those fifth graders wanted to know, sit with her?

She was the deaf girl, and her mother was dead, and a killer on top of that.

The silence, Trina's silence, had always been there, but now it became a feeling like drowning. The word *murderer* in her head felt distended and ugly, like a snake with the shape of an animal inside of it. *Killer* felt cold, like a knife made of carved ice. This was her mother?

A book report had been assigned their first week of class. Mrs. Driscoll had, of course, given her an extension, and had also offered that she could turn in a two-page report instead of the five pages due the rest of the class. But this had felt like cheating to Trina, like another avenue in which she would be placed separate from everyone else.

No, I can do it, she'd signed upon her return. *It's almost done anyway.* A lie, but a necessary one.

Mrs. Driscoll smiled. "Can you turn it in by next Monday then?"

Trina had nodded, looked away.

"—about, dear?"

(This happened frequently, and was possibly the most frustrating, infuriating part of being deaf: how she would lose entire threads of conversation if she looked away from people's mouths.)

Sorry, what?

"What's your report about, dear? I gave everyone a list of topics about Oregon history, remember? Which one did you choose?"

Over Mrs. Driscoll's shoulder some of the children in the front row were behind their hands silently mocking the exaggerated cadence of the woman's speech, their shoulders rising and falling. She looked back down at Mrs. Driscoll's desk. Everyone—her brother, her father, certainly her mother—felt so distant, like people she had only read about.

The Indians, she signed. *I picked the Indians.*

"Excellent," Mrs. Driscoll had beamed. "I look forward to reading it."

When she walked back to her seat there was a folded piece of paper on her desk. She knew she shouldn't open it, knew it desperately, but she did anyway.

In looping, patient cursive: *I heard your mom was so drunk when she killed Mrs. Dobbs that beer cans flew out of your car and went all over the road.*

• • •

After school that day, Sam had picked her up and taken her to the library to get books for her report. She had folded the note into tiny squares and placed it in a pocket in her backpack, where it sat like a little poison pellet waiting to be discovered again. What if it was true? She wanted to remember her mom's scratchy laugh, and the way she would run a cool washcloth behind Trina's ears after Trina had been crying, and the time she'd gotten a perm from a lady at a salon in Depoe Bay and came home embarrassed and Trina's dad laughed so hard that he cried and said she looked like the meanest poodle he'd ever seen and Mom smacked him on the arm and then started laughing too and said there was nothing to do but wait for it to grow out. And all four of them had laughed so hard about it. And the bad stuff too, even that was important to remember: how her mom would get all grabby after a few beers, would grasp Trina close, would ruffle Sam's hair, tell them how much she loved them, her eyes red-rimmed and close to tears. It was nice but it had always felt strange, like another person was trying to wrestle loose from inside of her. The sour smell of her after a night of drinking and how she said she was all "achy," when really everyone knew you got a hangover if you drank too much. How Trina would find her leaning over the washing machine in the back room sometimes, the light weak and everything smelling of detergent and mold, or in the bathroom, and how she always smiled but Trina would see her quickly wipe tears away. When Trina asked her if she was okay the answer was always the same: *I'm fine. No problem, baby.* But people didn't cry against washing machines for nothing. Like Sam said, *I call bullshit,* but she never told Sam about it, because doing that would be like telling on Mom.

The Riptide Public Library was a small four room affair with wide windows that, in the front, reached all the way up to the ceiling, windows that—on those rare sunny days—showed galaxies of dust motes drifting through the air. It was a place that she knew was always quiet if you were deaf or not, and because of that alone—not even counting the rest of it— made it a place she loved fiercely. The floor was checkered black and white and held the rich smell of books and the warm smell of the mimeograph machine, two of the best smells in the world, things right up there with angel food cake and the muddy hill of Tumquala Park after a good rain. Old men sat at tables in the grown-up section, licking their thumbs and turning newspaper pages. The librarians always smiled at her when she came up with her stack of books. She always made a point of checking out her books with her own library card and the librarians always handled her card and books with a respect and seriousness that she found nowhere else, and this also was something that Trina loved about the place. And there were aisles and aisles of books, entire new worlds waiting to be stumbled upon, and you could either find something specific or let your eyes wander along the spines and wait to be surprised by something interesting.

She would sometimes play a game where she would step into the adult section and grab a book at random and peruse the cover. Looking at the text was cheating; you had to guess how good the book was just by the cover. If it looked good—say if there was a lady in a dress leaning against a shirtless man who was kissing her neck—she would take it up to her mother for approval. Her mom would frown at it, open the cover and read the description, chewing the inside of her cheek, and then flip to a random page. Almost invariably she would grimace and pass it back to Trina and nod her approval, shrugging. "That's a cleavage-heaver," she'd warn, a saying that still mystified Trina. (The fact that she was allowed to read an adult book from the library but not read *Tiger Eyes* yet was just one of those things that made no sense. That was how grownups were.) She would try reading them, and while the stories would be decipherable—her spelling was terrible, but Trina could read pretty much anything—they were also almost always insufferably boring. Anastasia made sense to her. Judy Blume's stories made sense to her. Stuff *happened* in them.

That day in the library, everything was different. In the foyer they were stopped by a large photograph of Mrs. Dobbs, a black and white photo that had been mounted on a stand. Beneath it was a bouquet of white flowers in a vase as tall as Trina's chest. The smell made her think of her mother's funeral and a placard beneath the photo read *June Dobbs, Beloved Community Leader, Library Advocate and Loving Wife.* There was more writing but Trina's vision had been suddenly prismed with tears and she'd looked back up at Sam, her heart thumping like a curled fist in her shirt.

Sam scowled at the photo. "Come on," he said, and he took her hand and began to lead her in.

I don't want to go inside.

"We've got just as much right to be here as anybody," he said, which was not the point at all.

He walked her to the kids' room, Trina's eyes to the floor, and then he left to check out the issues of *Rolling Stone* they kept in the magazine section. She didn't tell him that she needed grown-up books for her report; her mouth felt like it was full of dust. Sam left and she traced her fingers along the ridged topography of the books on their shelves, tried to quiet her galloping heart, tried to make her lips stop quivering. She looked at the spines of the books. She crossed her eyes and saw only fuzzy swaths of color and felt a little better.

She had actually smiled a minute later when there, on the *New Arrivals!* shelf, she saw both the new Judy Blume *and* Lois Lowry books that she hadn't read yet. Lowry's Anastasia Krupnik would be a friend to her, Trina thought, if she lived in real life; a girl who was just as intractably awkward and weird as her, but who seemed somehow impervious to harm, who lived in a world of frazzled parents and annoying brothers, yes, but not a world in which they died. Not a world in which girls left notes like the one in her backpack. Trina gathered the pair of books (Judy Blume's *The Wolf in the Basement* and Lowry's *Anastasia at Your Service*) to her chest. Kids were allowed to take out five books at a time until they were thirteen, and then they were considered adults—at least as far as the library was concerned—and could check out as many as they wanted. *A hundred of them even?*—Trina had asked once. She tried picturing herself at thirteen and couldn't do it.

Was it true what the girls had said? That they'd found beer cans all over the road? That her mother had been drunk? Maybe they were Mrs. Dobbs's beer cans, she thought. But she couldn't picture the gray-haired lady in the photo, smiling, with her nice earrings, drinking anything. Maybe a glass of wine. Trina pictured her mother's old Buick so full of empty Hamm's cans that it was like a bright silvery explosion when the cars struck each other. She considered asking Sam if it was true or not but was worried that he would say yes or, worse yet, that he would turn away like he was afraid to answer her.

She went to the history section in the grown-up wing of the library. Outside the big windows, leaves lay in colorless strings in the gutters and the trees wobbled in the wind, their few remaining leaves trembling as bright as flames. The history section was big, practically as big as the entire kids' section, and she hadn't known where to start. She kept thinking of the picture of Mrs. Dobbs in the foyer. Her hands were slick with sweat. She was mad at herself for being afraid and tears made her vision leap and tremble again and panic started to edge up into her throat like water in a sinking boat. So she'd done what she always did in the grownup section and picked a book at random, pulling it off the shelf and simply liking the heft of it, how heavy it was compared to her other books. She hadn't even looked at the cover this time.

She'd walked up to the checkout counter then, thought briefly of putting the hood of her raincoat up on her head to hide her identity, but decided that would just be too weird and probably make her more obvious. *What would Anastasia do?* she thought. *What would Face from the A-Team do?* Face would probably jump out the window and run away.

At the checkout desk, her cheeks burned while she filled out her cards with a stub of pencil. She'd slid the cards and her books over to the librarian and removed her library card from her velcro Star Wars wallet (the other contents being her Riptide Elementary ID card, an old blue paper card that said she was deaf, and four worn single dollars that had been in there forever) and handed it to the librarian. She waited for the librarian's eyes to bulge wide in rage, in fury, in contempt once she recognized Trina's name. *The daughter of the killer here to check out books! Can you imagine the nerve?*

But the librarian, another old lady who had a wart on her cheek the size and color of a chocolate chip, had simply smiled at her, and Trina had felt a terrible flush of gratitude toward her, that library lady with her wart and her black and white-striped blouse that made Trina's eyes go funny if she stared at it too long. The lady stamped the back pocket of her books, stamped her cards, and then slid the books over to Trina.

"Due in two weeks, dear," the woman said, and smiled.

"Thank you," Trina said.

She'd found Sam sitting at a desk tucked in the back of the library. Sam, she saw, had been crying as well. He had been looking at the same *Rolling Stone's History of Rock* book, with its chipped leather cover and half dozen pages dedicated to punk rock, that he looked at every time they came here. "You ready?" he said, coughing and rubbing at his eyes like he had allergies. "Let's get the fuck out of this place."

It was only when they got home and Trina had taken off her shoes and socks, after Sam had turned on the heater and made them each a snack of grilled cheeses and Ritz crackers, that she had sat on the couch and looked at the history book she had checked out. It really was gigantic. The Lowry and Blume books looked babyish in comparison. The title was in shiny gold lettering, like tinfoil, on an ominous black background. A gray mushroom cloud rose from the bottom of the cover. It was not, she realized with dismay, a book about Indians. Not even close.

And yet.

And yet she'd taken a bite of her grilled cheese and opened the cover.

And there on the title page again, but now in immutable black on white:

THE LOOMING ERROR
Russia, the United States,
and the Inevitable Nuclear Catastrophe
by Gen. Paul D. Forrester, USAF

Trina, her heart suddenly full of a delicious, distracting kind of worry, had taken another bite of her sandwich and turned the page.

SAM FINSTER

Beyond a curve in the cliff side, the bonfire was a good half-mile from the turnaround ramp. Tucked in a cove, the firelight was obscured and some enterprising redneck had, earlier in the evening, driven their truck down onto the sand and unloaded a stack of pallets, which people had been doggedly going through as the evening progressed. The fire was huge, undoubtedly throwing a glow to the cliff tops and streets above the beach. The cops would show up, but this was Riptide, and a Friday, so of course the cops would show up.

The fire threw up great columns of whirling sparks and Sam stepped a little closer, weaving just a bit, liking the way he could feel the skin of his face tighten in the heat. The closeness, that comforting wood smoke stink of it when the wind changed and it washed across him. The clusters of kids around the fire were limned shapes beyond the wavering flames. The flow of chatter and laughter, bravado and flirting and shit-talking. Smokes in his pocket. His father has taken a rare night off from gear work—he'd be going out on nearly week-long trips soon enough, and things would get complicated in ways that Sam was still trying not to think about—but tonight he had mentioned the bonfire and Gary had waved him out of the house, pressing a twenty into his hands. "Go crazy," Gary said. "Not arrested-crazy, but you know."

"What about Trina?"

"What about her?" Gary said, his arms thrown over the back of the couch. "Trina will be fine, Sam. What the hell. We're not crippled. We're not infants."

"She's been having more dreams."

Gary frowned, serious. He looked at the wall and scratched his nose with a black-rimmed fingernail—Lava or no, his father's hands were never entirely clean—and turned back to Sam. "More bomb shit?"

Sam shrugged, pocketing the twenty, already figuring out who he could tap for a beer run at Selwicky's. "Bomb shit, yeah, plus the bones we found."

Gary sighed and leaned over, testing the weight of his beer on the coffee table. He stood up with a groan. "That goddamned park. Your mother would have had a conniption."

Sam just shrugged again. Not feeling that generous, honestly. Gary was beginning to say things like this, beginning to place her in the ground, cement her in the past. It hurt. "I'll take care of it," he said. "Go ahead and take off. Have fun. I'll talk to her." When Sam's hand was on the doorknob, Gary called out, "Don't get in a car with any drunk people." This last thing had been spoken almost absently, or like his father couldn't help himself, and the two of them had looked at each other for a moment and then Sam had stepped out, his footfalls on the gravel loud in his ears.

He and Toad had met up beneath the glaring white lights of the Selwicky's parking lot and hung out with the scattering of other underage kids there, shoulder-tapping haggard fishermen until one of them agreed to buy a case of beer in exchange for a six-pack of his own. "Man, two more years of this shoulder-tapping shit and then I'm getting drunk every night," Toad had said wistfully as they walked toward the beach with their paper sack. "Swear to God. Shitfaced for a decade, at least. Just go in and buy it."

"Aim high, Toad," Sam said.

The interiors of the businesses they passed, the dry cleaners and the hair salon and the auto shop where Toad and his uncle worked, were all filled with the ghostly electric half-light reserved for the off hours. Headlights painted their backs and moved on while those approaching flared briefly in their eyes in passing and then moved beyond them. Puddles reflected streetlights, their surfaces scudding with the wind. At the cove, the bonfire was raging, a loose array of kids already ringed around it, and the pair of them sidled up and set their bag in the sand with the meditative, contented air of men hunkering down for a while. The bottles (the fisherman had bought them Budweiser, which Gary called Shitweiser every single time he drank it, it was practically a nervous tic) were beaded and cool in his hand. The taste of beer was still thrilling to him.

They shot the shit, the ring of people around the fire shrinking and swelling as kids left and others took their place. Someone had brought a boombox and they listened to cassettes of Mötley Crüe and Bon Jovi until the batteries ran low and the music slowly took on fearsome, uneasy overtones as the tapes started to drag. Then they tuned in to KRPT, hoping the

DJ would play just one song appropriate for someone under ninety. Finally, the batteries died for good, the lights of the boombox fading to darkness, and they were left with the sound of the surf, the roar of the fire, their own voices suddenly fragile and small against the dark around them. At one point, a small brown dog, well-fed and clearly not one of the half-feral ones that roved the beach in summer, walked up to the fire and made the rounds, grinning happily and sniffing at all the outstretched hands. Sam could hear the jingle of his tags and saw that he was trailing a yellow leash behind. Some local's dog gone loose.

"See, what you do is you piss on the dog's back when you're at a party," someone genius informed them all. "And then everyone pets him. It's awesome."

"Yeah," someone else said, "except we just heard you explain it. Kind of defeating the purpose, isn't it?"

A girl's voice: "And nobody wants to see your dick anyways."

"I'm just saying," said the first guy, a little sullenly. "It's funny. Like at a party. Not on the beach. Like in a house or something."

"Yeah, we got it."

"Whatever, dude."

Sam kept his eyes open for Jordana Benedict—hopeless, hopeless—and after a few beers the stringency of his heart seemed to loosen just a bit, and he felt better; he found himself full of any number of magical, moving things to say to her should she arrive. He was drunk.

A few minutes after the dog trotted away trailing its leash, a cluster of rednecks showed up, five or six tough boys in their baseball jackets, boys already balding at the temples from a lifetime of wearing baseball caps, their cans of Skoal and Red Man wearing rings in the back pockets of their jeans. A cluster? Sam thought. A passel? What was plural for redneck fuckhead? They just appeared like smoke, like a sunny day where you're walking down the street and you look down and realize you've stepped in dogshit.

They stopped a few feet away from the fire and spread out as if it were an orchestrated thing, shouldering their way to the fire's edge as if in some kind of attack formation. They were boys just used to elbowing their way through the world, boys with an innate understanding, through experience, of the many versus the few.

"Looks like a fudge packing convention out here," one of them crowed, which got a few laughs—Toad's loudest of all, harsh and metronomic and dense with mockery: "Ha. Ha. Ha." Sam saw him tilt his bottle up to the sky, the glimmering edge of it jumping with reflected firelight as he drank. A piece of wood shifted in the bonfire and threw up another funnel of sparks. Again Toad laughed that stilted, mocking laugh: "Ha. Ha. Ha."

Another one of the rednecks said, "Seriously, though. What are you fags up to tonight? Who's playing the skinflute?" He pointed at two boys with his beer bottle. "Are you blowing him or is he blowing you?"

"Shut up, Kenny," said a girl across the fire.

The boys finished their slow strutting circuit around the fire, settled into their spots. Sam, all one hundred and sixty pounds of him, his blood singing with Shitweiser, was feeling loose-limbed and dangerous. He stood with his head tucked down, his arms folded, imagining himself whipping his arms like pistons among the crowd of boys, a pair of fluid counterweights dealing wreckage and ruin with impunity, with a terrible accuracy. He pictured hats flying into the bonfire; gibbering, bloody boys begging apology; wet sand darkening the knees of their jeans, eyes glittering with fear. Something to crack their veneer, that sense that they were little more than strutting roosters in some dooryard looking to claw at someone.

A few people began to make their leave then, edging away down the beach like phantoms. Finally one of the boys spit a jet of tobacco juice onto the sand and sneered at Toad, "The fuck do you keep looking at me for, faggot?"

Everyone took a step back, some animal awareness running through them. Sam lifted his beer bottle up and tasted dregs, foam. He tapped a rhythm against his thigh with the bottle, imagined the hollow *thwock* it would make against a skull. Pictured all these boys in the dugout of some baseball field glum and salted in bruises, rife with bandages, slings. Something from a TV show. Sam smiled at the bank of glowing embers.

Toad frowned as if in concentration. "I keep looking at you because you're a dumb motherfucker. Like, *shocking* dumb. You know? What do you think about that?" The boy, surprised, took a step backward and Toad shouldered his way past someone and closed the distance between them. Someone pressed a hand against the boy's shoulder blades and pushed him forward and Toad's big pale hands came up as fists near his jawline. Adrenaline tumbled through Sam's veins like someone had turned on a tap, poured it into his skull. The back of his knees quivered with tension.

One of the rednecks said, "Don't touch him, Kenny. That's that Whitlock kid. He's got AIDS, man. Don't touch him."

Big and nineteen, that half-shaved head, Toad's form was almost shapeless in his dark jacket with its patches for Valvoline and 76 at the shoulders.

The boy—Sam recognized him now as Kenny Pritchard, a leanly-muscled baseball player who, as a junior in high school, still found some measure of hilarity in snapping girls' bras in the hall—spat loose another string of tobacco. He held his gaze with Toad for another five seconds, his fists balled near his hips. It lasted long enough for Sam to wonder if Toad was just going to hit him anyway, just piston one big arm out and knock the fucking kid out, send his baseball hat flying into the pink-coaled center of the fire, drive his chaw into the back of his throat. Finally Kenny shook his head and said weakly, "You're not even worth it, is the thing." Within seconds the group of boys had walked off back toward the turnaround, some of their bravado gone. Within moments they were invisible beyond the fire's corona.

Later, when all that was left of the firewood was a few splintered pallet slats and a silence had fallen over everyone, that part of night where people were left staring into the flames with equal measures of introspection and drunkenness, Sam and Toad stuffed their last few beers into their jacket pockets and walked further down the beach. North, away from Wolf Point and the turnaround. Before they left, Sam threw their beer box and paper bag into the fire. They flared brightly, savagely, and then faded to glowing pink ashes.

"Don't let the Beast get you," someone yelled out in mock horror as they walked away. Sam cinched his coat tight around his throat.

"He'll find ye and cut ye from asshole to Adam's apple, he will!" called another boy. "He'll rip your titties right off ye, boys!" he crowed, cackling like a witch. Toad raised a middle finger as they trudged on. The moon was a bone-colored coin beyond a scrim of clouds and away from the fire the wind made them hunch in their jackets.

"You should have dropped that guy," Sam slurred. His throat ached from so many cigarettes.

"What, five against one? No thanks."

"People would've gotten into it. *I* would've dropped somebody."

Toad laughed. "Sam, I appreciate it, but come on, man."

"I'm just saying, fuck those guys. Fucking redneck douchebags."

"Well, yeah." Toad smacked him on the shoulder hard enough to sting. "But here's the thing. Think big picture, Sam. By June we'll be out of here and on the road. The Trip awaits. So who cares? The last thing I need is jail and probation for stomping some dipshit seventeen-year-old."

There it was: another opportunity to tell Toad that he couldn't go. That the Trip had to be put on hold, at least. He felt brave enough to say it, as drunk as he was, but the words seemed paltry, clumsy in his mouth. Instead he said, "I can't believe that guy said you had AIDS. Kenny Pritchard. That guy's a piece of shit."

Toad shrugged. "That's just what people say. That's, like, the go-to insult now. Half those dudes are probably gay."

They sat on a stretch of driftwood and looked at the sea, the rising clay cliff and roil of dunes at their backs, the bonfire a trembling spark down the beach. They always wound up at the same places. The clouds had moved on and the sand was nearly white in the moonlight now. Sam laced his arms around his knees. Toad pulled his little one-hitter out and packed it, bending down to capture the wavering flame. He held it out to Sam, who shook his head. They sat there like that. Toad finished the hit and clacked the pipe against the log and tucked it back in his pocket. Sam opened another beer. Out in the dark were the glyphs of some tanker's working lights. A foghorn rolled above the surf, low and mournful.

"How's Trina?"

"She's freaked out still." Sam dug a pair of divots in the sand with his heels.

"The nuclear stuff?"

"Yeah," Sam said. "I should have thrown that fucking book in the trash the second I saw it."

"The library book?"

"Yeah. She says she returned it but we keep getting overdue notices. I think she's hidden it somewhere."

Toad blew a bass note into the open mouth of his beer. "Kid's a weirdo," he said, not unkindly.

"True."

"Hell, she may be right. All it takes is one warhead and we'll glow for years. You hear about all this shit with Germany?"

"Never gonna happen," Sam said, rolling his eyes.

Toad shrugged. "I'm just saying—"

"*Never gonna happen.* And even if it does, she shouldn't be worried about it. I mean, it's not like anyone can do a thing about it. Right? She's *nine*."

"I guess, yeah."

"And now there's the whole thing with the skeleton."

"I still feel bad about laughing," Toad said.

"Me, too."

"No disrespect, but what's your dad doing during all of this?"

"My dad?" Sam's voice took on a deep, serious tone. "'Oh, I better make sure these fucking crab pots are in tip-top shape, Sam, that's really important. Better pull sixteen-hour days stripping the boat and let my kids raise themselves.'"

Even as he said it he felt ashamed. He could see the weight of things bearing down upon his father in a hundred different ways: he was navigating his own mourning, after all, and suddenly had two kids to take care of, entirely on his own. Sam got it. *And yet*. And yet the resentment was there, pulsing and buried beneath the skin like a toothache. "I don't know. I mean, he's got to feed us, right?"

Toad nodded, conceded the point. He tilted the bottle up to the moon.

"It just feels," Sam said, "like everything's happening at once. Like things are coming up too fast."

"Like what?"

Like the Trip, Toad, for starters. "I don't know. Take your pick. Skeletons in the park. Everyone ready to blow the world up. My mom."

"Yeah," Toad said quietly, and the silence between them after that was companionable enough.

Finally, Sam murmured, "We just miss her. We just miss her a lot, Toad." He looked out at the black expanse of sea and lifted his beer to his lips as if to stop himself from saying anything more.

They rose and walked away from Wolf Point and the bonfire; there were trails all up and down the cliffs, trails worn into the clay like the frayed end of a rope. You just had to know where to look. They lead to the woods above and then, eventually, Hastings Street. Sam was tired, the threads of a hangover beginning to knit itself together behind his eyes. He looked out at the beach, heard that constant wavering call of the surf, thought of how ageless this place was, touched by time's ferocity so much more than by man's. Such lofty thoughts inspired by a few bottles of shit beer.

They had hardly walked around a gnarled little outcropping of rock—he looked back and could see the whitened clutch of driftwood that Toad had sat on—when all of the heat in his body seemed to vanish. His hands and feet plummeted with cold. It was just fear, fear galloping through him. He thought it was a tendril of seaweed at first, the thing that lay at his feet, something some kid had pulled up from the tideline. He'd done the same thing when he was younger, usually to try and whip it at Trina until his mother yelled at him to knock it off. But the sand was white and dry here. No way the seaweed, this single strand, could have washed up this far.

"Holy Jesus," he said. "Oh my God." The wind ran through him and he felt that he and Toad were suddenly surrounded by a great swath of unmapped land, a number of unknown things surrounding them. The fear stood up inside him, found it had room to move around, stretched out. The dunes next to them seemed suddenly alive with movement, with a hundred different things.

"What is it?"

Don't let the Beast get you!

Toad peered at him, frowning. His face looked strange and masklike in the dark.

"Dude, what is *with* you?"

Sam pointed at his feet.

It was the dog's leash. The happy dog at the fire, the dumb mutt that some local was probably worried sick about, maybe someone with a little one-bedroom shack that sat perched along the scrub woods along Hastings Street, or in one of the houses near the bottling plant. Maybe, Sam thought wildly, even as far as Slokum Beach. It was possible, wasn't it?

The leash, Sam remembered, had been yellow. And it was still yellow, save for a foot or so at the end that under the moonlight now was an ebony black, dark with blood. Frayed at the end, it lay in a curled S shape in the sand at his feet, nothing else around it, like it was just dropped there, and he and Toad had sat thirty yards away and hadn't seen a thing. Whatever had happened had taken place right around that outcropping, there in the dark right around the corner from them.

NICK HAYSLIP

The town had put its holiday decorations up over the weekend, and as he drove along the spine of Highway 101, he saw small plastic lanterns wreathed in holly and anchored to light poles, and the Michelin Tires place had once again provided its roof as a platform for Riptide's Christmas tree. It stood there like a sentinel now, strange and totemic in the daylight, limbs all jagged diagonal slashes against the sky. Salvation Army peddlers rang their bells in front of the doors of Selwicky's and the pair of life-sized plaster of Paris candy canes once again menaced the doorway of the Community Center like a couple of thugs. Meager decorations, maybe, but they should have buoyed him. As a boy he'd always loved the trappings of the seasons, the physical manifestations of each: barbecues at his parents' friends' homes during the summer, the concussive, thundering bluster of the fireworks lit from the jetties at South Beach and flowering in the night sky, the candy and jack-o'-lanterns of fall, the turning trees, and spring's bejeweled green grass, its return to sunlight. And in winter: Christmas, with its lights and decorations and fake snow, its forced good cheer.

It should have lifted him, but it didn't. He came home and showered and the newscasters on television were dour with their continued litanies of doom. Reagan and Chernenko were still in a freeze-out. Tensions were escalating, they said, as Germany had given permission to the U.S. to install the mounts for the Pershing IIs. They were going ahead with it. "The strain between the two nations," Bryant Gumbel said, "continues to mount." But then—*the salve of America!, our saving grace!*—he'd moved on to a segment about a group of schoolchildren in Detroit who had written and performed a school musical based on Michael Jackson's *Thriller*. Footage after the break.

He ate a piece of toast, found that he could stomach it, and so he risked an omelet. The ritual of cooking felt strange to him, and when he cracked an egg into a bowl the sight of it was enough to leave him dry heaving against the counter. The children danced on the TV. They were good.

Gingerly, carefully, he poured the bowl's contents into the sink, rinsed it. Drank a glass of water. *What world*, Hayslip thought, *could really perish that housed such grave luxuries as these?* The comfort of the television, that resolute *sameness,* the lapels sharp as knife blades on Gumbel's ridiculous suit, his put-on earnestness. Michael Jackson in his leather pantsuit, dancing among a cavalcade of zombies in a questionably well-lit alleyway? No world could end that managed to simultaneously house such lunacies and such intimacies.

A few hours into his shift he drove down to Tumquala Park and sat watching from across the road. The anthropologists from the university in Corvallis had arrived and he sat and watched as they methodically dismantled the hillside. There were three of them, two men and a woman, and they had erected a massive blue tarp over much of the park. The blue tarp against the red clay made his eyes jitter in a way that was almost pleasant. They had already shaved a significant amount of the hill away like someone curling slivers of ice cream with a scoop. With their chisels and trowels, their rolls of chamois and spray bottles, their folding tables littered with sample boxes, he witnessed their obedience and supplication toward the ground's contents; it seemed nearly religious to him. The base of the hill's excavations were demarked by spikes and twine, and they gently pried their findings with tweezers and sprayed them clean with solution and laid them in their sample boxes and placed them on the tables. All of them muddied in their smocks, the red clay lending them the air of battlefield surgeons. He wondered again how a world that managed such reverence and care for one lost, forgotten body could ever be destroyed. The woman walked over to the wing of tables beneath the tarp and began organizing some of the boxes, occasionally looking up to peer at Hayslip in his cruiser across the road.

Eventually he got out of the car and walked over, lifting his leg over the safety tape and raising a hand in greeting. The sea was loud, right over the hill and beyond the scrim of blackberry bushes.

"Morning, everybody," he said, standing with the tables between him and the woman. A few errant drops of rain pattered on the tarp above his head, loud on the plastic. "How's everyone doing?"

They were all probably mid- to late-twenties. The men seemed *tweedy,* Hayslip thought—reed-thin and pale in a way that bespoke a coming lifetime behind a podium, of leather patches on the elbows of patterned jackets. Was this Hayslip's ignorance? A contemptuous little bird fluttering around his head? His father had been a foreman at the bottling plant for forty years. His mother was the first person in her family to graduate from high school. Hayslip himself had come home from Vietnam and worked a variety of jobs before enrolling in the academy. Riptide was a small place in the world, a pebble on the earth, but it was home to him. The field hospital at Nha Trang had been as far from the town as he ever wanted to go again in his life; college was just another unnecessary destination, one just as foreign. So, was he contemptuous? Probably. Probably a little. The most marked difference between these two men was that one wore glasses and a mustache and one had neither. Other than that their faces seemed as bland as unbroken slate, so bland they didn't even look guilty of anything. The woman was different: lanky, sure, but with a great dark mane of curls she kept tied back as she stood there glowering at him behind the table. Where the men seemed placid she thrummed with a vibrancy that sang with contempt. The men turned from the hill and stepped under the tarp; the trio stood there in their muddied smocks with tool belts and rubber gloves, assessing him. He'd been greeted with silence the first time, so Hayslip went ahead and again asked how everyone was doing.

"We're fine," the woman finally said, rubbing her forehead with the back of her gloved hand. "Can we help you with something?"

"Oh, there's no trouble or anything," Hayslip said, looking around, thumbs in his belt. "I was just hoping to speak to your boss. Whoever's in charge."

"We're all in charge," said the one without the mustache.

"And none of us are," said the other, and a smile traveled among the three of them, some joke passing through them like a current. Hayslip resisted the urge to roll his eyes.

"Okay," he said. "That makes it easy, I guess. I'll just ask all of you. How's the dig going?"

The woman snapped her gloves off with a squelch of rubber and dropped them on the table. "Is this about our permits?" A gust of wind sloughed through all the trees and brambles around them and the hems of their smocks fluttered and pressed against their legs. She opened up a satchel lying on the table and started rooting around in it, the pale cords of muscle in her forearms leaping out. No ring. "We've got all our permits, our licenses."

"We're all squared up," one of the men called out over his shoulder. He and the other man had gone back to work on the hillside. "Your own forensics people signed off on this one. They handed it over to us." The woman found the papers she was looking for and thrust them out at him. Hayslip held up his hands in surrender. "I'm seriously just here because I'm interested," he said. "You know, I just think this is cool."

It was a moment before her face softened and then she tilted her head back toward the hill and Hayslip stepped beneath the tarp and followed her to where the men stood, a spot marked with dowels boxed off into those precisely stringed quadrants. Each quadrant was roughly two feet by two feet and demarked on the dowel with a number and letter. The mud here was thick as gruel.

The anthropologists had wrought serious changes to the park. Beyond the twined sections, there had been a curvature of hill here; where the skeleton had been found, midway to the top of the hill, they were now carving a wedge into the earth. Like a retaining wall, almost, or a big sliver of pie. The wedge ran with dripping mud like an Impressionist painting and the twined sections at the bottom of the hill made more sense: fragments of bone and other things would slide down the hill over time, collect at the bottom. Smart. As always, the scar at his neck itched in this weather. He nodded appreciatively at the work they had done and the woman stepped under the tarp and lit a cigarette and the men followed suit. It surprised him. He followed them, stood next to one of the tables, frowning down at the fragile treasures resting in their tabletop boxes.

"Can you tell me anything about the body?"

"Well, it was a girl," the man with the glasses said. They showed him the slivers of yellowed bone that lay in some of the boxes. Most of the bones were no larger than the joints of a finger, though here was one he recognized as a tibia, and of course they had excavated the skull; Hayslip stared for a moment at its hollowed sockets, the sinuous bowl of the brainpan. A series of perforations, some as thin as a nail head and some the width of his finger, spanned the crown of the skull, gave it the appearance of a delicately fractured eggshell. Her specific age, they told him, was still indeterminate, but she was doubtfully even a teenager. A young girl. The body had been dead a long time.

The wind shifted and a cold rill of rainwater ran down his collar. "How long's a long time? When do you think it happened?" If pressed for an answer he could not say why the bones had suddenly stirred such an interest inside him. A part of Hayslip wished it was just the woman standing across the table from him, something as simple as that, but it wasn't. The bones moved him, the idea of them cast here in this lonely swatch of ground, tossed and forgotten.

"We won't really know until we can take the stuff back to the lab. We're finding new stuff every day. But we want to make sure we have everything before we leave."

"But are we talking, like, Cro-Magnon or something?" At this the trio shared another look, more wry smiles traveling among them at the expense of Hayslip's ignorance.

The woman said, "If I had to hazard a guess—"

"And we all know you're *loathe* to do that, Dana."

"Oh, shut up. If I had to guess, I'd say she's between a hundred and a hundred and fifty years old. Just judging from the cohesiveness of the bones and the depth they were buried."

"Buried?"

"Oh yeah," the man with the glasses said. Hayslip watched as he ashed his cigarette in the pocket of his slicker. "This little lady was definitely buried." Hayslip realized they were all either ashing their cigarettes into their pockets or their hands.

The woman, Dana, saw him watching. "Don't want to contaminate the excavation."

"Got it. But listen, the nearest cemetery's way the hell over on the other side of 101. How'd she get over here?"

"Who said anything about a cemetery?"

"Was she in a coffin?"

"Don't think so," the one with the glasses said. "Haven't found any lumber, and we'd probably find at least something. But we found swatches of the cloth she was wrapped up in. And we found this." He gingerly handed Hayslip one of the samples boxes. Resting on a bed of cotton batting was a small wooden cross of roughly hewn wood, its crossbar bound in twine. Slivers of bark still visible while the flesh of the wood had long since been dyed the red of the clay. It was the size of his palm and looked ready to crumble into fragments at the slightest touch. "It's hard to tell *where* the exact burial site was, since this claybed is constantly shifting and eroding. Two hundred years ago, this hillside was probably a lot more flat. But nine times out of ten, in cases like this, someone harvests all the rooted materials—there used to be a whole copse of pine and fir trees up on that ridge there, it was way more forested, and now it's mostly just blackberry bushes—so there's all this runoff. The bones just started coming down the hill along with everything else. That's why they've been displaced over such a relatively big area."

"That's crazy," he said. "Are you sure it's just one person?"

Dana shrugged. "At this point we're not sure of anything. But that's what it looks like so far."

"And it was a kid. Not even a teenager."

"We're still piecing together all of the major bone groups, but from what we have now, the length of the skeleton says that she was probably between the ages of eight and twelve."

"Christ. You can tell all that already?" He thought of seeing Melissa's daughter on the news, a deaf girl frowning and pale in the glare of the news reporters' lights. "Okay, listen. One, no, two more questions and I'll get out of your hair." The scar on his neck itched madly. Dana bent to the ground and snubbed her cigarette out, dropped the butt in her pocket. "How did she die? Who was she?"

"Look at the skull," she said.

He went to it, a small and yellowed thing resting on its cotton bed. "Those marks on the top of the head?"

"Exactly."

"It looks like bird shot. From a shotgun or something."

Dana bit a thumbnail, raised her eyebrows. "Interesting. See, we were thinking teeth."

• • •

He met Melissa Finster on a traffic stop.

It was a summer afternoon roughly fifteen months before she would die. (How else to consider it? Hayslip's life now was bifurcated by two ages: Before the Accident and After the Accident. That was it.) His radar gun had clocked her at thirty-eight miles per hour in a twenty zone, and on Hastings Street no less, a winding, mostly-residential road that snaked along the cliffs all the way from Slokum Beach to the bridge at the southern edge of town. There was a speed trap between two copses of blackberry bushes, and it was just the right size to back the cruiser into and set the radar. He clocked her and drove out, gravel popping under his wheels, and pulled the vehicle over a few blocks away. He was a little surprised to see that the car's plates were marked from an auto dealership in Lincoln City; it meant the driver was most likely local. The car was a Buick, seven or eight years old, one of Reagan's gas-guzzling wet dreams. A Detroit monster that probably got about eight yards to the gallon. As he approached he saw the side panels were salted with rust, which told him, again, the car was local to the coast. Normally, on that road at that time of year, Hayslip encountered oblivious tourists, people in a hurry to get to the beach or one of the motels that dotted 101. People thirsty to start their vacations. It had been a fine, sunny day. He remembered sunlight trembling on the bumper of the Buick as he walked up to the driver's side door, a gentle breeze hinting at salt and warmed blacktop.

The driver smiled up at him. She was pretty, beautiful even. Wearing a blue t-shirt with *Slokum Beach Sluggers* in cracked script, faded jeans, her dark hair tied back in a ponytail. A dusting of freckles across her collarbones, the bridge of her nose. Blue eyes already bright with a look of apology. A young girl sat in the passenger seat with a book splayed in her lap.

"Afternoon," Hayslip said.

"Hi," the woman said, her hands still hooked on the wheel. "I bet I was speeding, right?" Catalog it: wedding ring, kid. The backseat held a few jackets, some newspapers. Part of it was habit— always scan the interior of the vehicle for threats or violations—and part of it was simply that she was pretty enough to make him nervous, Hayslip with his scotch-scars. It was hard to look her in the eye.

"I'm afraid so," he said. The little girl turned and frowned, scanning him intently, her own small hands clasped around the leaves of her book. "Thirty-eight in a twenty."

"Yikes. Jesus."

Hayslip nodded. "And this is a residential street, too. Lots of kids around here. Can I see your license and registration please?"

"Sure," the woman said, sighing and deflated as she fumbled through her purse. Here again was habit at work: Hayslip with his hand on his belt, near but not on his holster, paying great attention to what she pulled out of her purse. Habit. And yet! As she leaned over to peer in her bag, Hayslip caught the barest glimpse of cleavage and looked away, and what was that about? At the very least it was dangerous, sloppy traffic work. (He would wonder this for a long time after: why it had been her, someone else's wife and mother, who had done so much to stir the embers inside him, to make him careless in so many ways. What great shortcoming lived inside him that Melissa Finster turned out to be such a catalyst?) She took out her wallet, thumbed through it and removed her license. Then she motioned at the girl—Hayslip recognized immediately that the little girl was deaf, that they were using sign language—and the girl opened the glove box and handed the woman a sheaf of papers. The woman began shuffling through the random effluvia that gathers in glove compartments: receipts, bills, maps, pamphlets to notable places that had been kept either as a remembrance of going or a reminder to someday make the trek. She handed him the registration.

"I'll be right back with these." He walked back to his cruiser and sat with the window down, one boot hooked on the pavement. Melissa Finster. Thirty-four years old, five-foot-seven, a hundred and thirty pounds. He radioed it in and sat a few minutes more until dispatch came back with a clean run on both the plates and her ID. He went back to the Buick and handed Melissa Finster her paperwork.

He leaned down toward the window and smiled. "It's twenty miles an hour through here, okay?" He rested one hand on the roof of the car.

"Yes," she said, nodding. She turned and looked out the windshield, a measured look, as if reviewing the drive ahead of her. "Okay."

"I'm going to let you go with a warning this time," he said, and the little girl smiled at him. Hayslip realized she had been reading his lips. He surprised himself and smiled back. The woman had been sitting with a rigid posture, preparing for the worst. She sighed in relief.

"Thank you so much," she said, and if he knew why he'd done it, he didn't know himself well enough to put it into words. She was beautiful, yes, and Hayslip felt some minor part of himself responding to that. That was part of it. But there was also something about the way she'd signed to her daughter, this hidden language they shared, and the way the daughter had scanned him up and down, as if she'd been silently gauging his worth. The way the woman had sat rigidly, staring out of the windshield, waiting for judgment. That stoicism. It was all of it, and none of it, really. Sometimes his insides were a great hollow. Sometimes it seemed a mystery, how people moved through the world, how they seemed to know themselves so well.

She gave him a little wave as the Buick came to life, mouthed *Thank you*, again. He stood with his hands on his belt and watched her drive away.

• • •

Four or five nights later, he was drinking at the Sandy Bottom and waiting for Fitzhugh to show up when she came in with her girlfriends. The air conditioner had died, and in its place a series of standing fans had been set up in the corners of the room, which did little more than push the fug of cigarette smoke around the place. Hayslip was parked at the bar, the sad and foamy dregs of a Budweiser in front of him, the taste as bitter as rust in his mouth. When they came in, a trio of women in tight jeans and perfume and the music of their laughter, every man in the place turned and looked. Men bent subtle as magnets, leaning toward them. That eternal salve of women laughing in a bar. Hayslip looked over his shoulder and recognized her right away. He was out of his uniform, wearing a baseball hat, jeans. She turned his way and saw him. Looked him up and down, brazen about it, her arms hooked around the waist of her friend. Hayslip looked away.

He ordered another beer from Ron and someone sank quarters into the jukebox in celebration of the women's arrival and Eddie Money's saccharine, straining moans of "I Think I'm In Love" filled the air. Hayslip laughed and shook his head. Ron gave him his new beer and Hayslip sat for a time with his eyes on the mirror before him. Something was wrong with the mirror, some error in its manufacture, and his face in it was warped and strange. Distorted and terrible with every one of his movements. The warmth of the bass vibrated in his ribcage, and there was the laughter of the women behind him, the sudden uptick in chatter and bravado from the other men, the clatter of a game of eight ball at the back of the room. Neon painted the tabletops red and blue. The glossy wood of the bar. The night slowly unwound before him and he finished another beer after that and tried not to sneak glances at the woman. Fitzhugh, it seemed, wasn't coming.

He stood up to go and there she was leaning on the bar next to him.

"You're not leaving, are you?"

Hayslip, bashful, felt his scar tissue flush, knew what it looked like rising from his collar, grateful that she was standing on the other side of him. "Well, I was thinking about it," he said.

"Let me get you a drink, at least. What are you having?"

It was a bad idea. He knew it. The ring on her hand plain as day. He thought of the flush of cleavage there in her battered Buick, the chipped blue ice of her eyes, and said, "Just a Bud. Thanks."

"Two, please," she said to Ron, raising her fingers in a peace sign.

Ron dropped them off and she said, "Cheers," and raised her glass.

"Cheers."

They drank and she put an elbow on the bar, squinted at him. Hayslip again felt a heat pulse through his scars. He traced a burn mark on the wood of the bar with his thumb, frowned at it.

"I just want to thank you for the other day," she said.

"It's really no problem."

She nodded, looked back at her friends behind him. There was some signal given; she smiled and almost imperceptibly shook her head and turned back to him. "So when you're not pulling people over for speeding, this is what you do? Drink at the Bottom?"

Hayslip laughed. "This is pretty much it, yeah. I run sometimes."

Again, he was aware of both her closeness and the ring on her finger. It would have made more sense had she been there awhile, been intoxicated; it would have lent at least some credence to what was happening. But she seemed clearheaded, sober. He couldn't understand it.

"So your daughter's deaf?" he blurted, and then winced. She raised an eyebrow at him.

"God, I'm sorry," he said. "That was tasteless. Just ... Jesus, wasn't *quite* how I meant to say it."

"No problem," she said, frowning and smiling at the same time. "Little weird, but no problem." She fished a cigarette out of her pack and Hayslip lit it as she cupped her hand around his, steadying the flame. He should be running in the other direction. He should be going home. And still he found himself anchored there in the smoke and light, reenacting the ageless story of a man and a woman in a bar.

"Not the most graceful guy," he said.

"I guess not." She blew smoke at the ceiling. "But yes, she's deaf. She was born that way."

"That must be hard," he said, but for who, he couldn't exactly say. Everybody, probably.

"She gets by okay," she said. "Most of the time."

"So you learned to sign?" he blustered ahead. "I mean, where'd you learn it?"

"The hospital offered a class. Up in Portland."

"Portland, huh? You go there a lot then?" The inanity of it: his mouth opened on a hinge and they both watched the idiocy tumble out.

"Something like that. Listen, can I ask what your name is?" she said. "You mind if I ask you that?"

"It's Nick," he said.

She held out her hand. It was dry and cool. "Hi, Nick. Melissa."

"Sorry," he said, wincing. They shook and then he held his hands up to his chest in surrender.

"What are you sorry for?"

"I just don't talk to a lot of people outside of work."

"That's a fucking lie," Ron the bartender said, startling them both. Melissa laughed. Hayslip shot him a look and Ron winked. "Nick, Fitzy just called. He's running late with paperwork but he says he'll get here when he can."

They drank their drinks and she seemed content enough just to be there near him. And why shouldn't she? She was married, had children to go home to. A life. She knew her own trajectory. This night, he told himself, meant nothing. This was two people talking. He made his way to the bathroom and was surprised to realize on the way that at some point he had gotten drunk. When he returned to the bar she was still there and their talk was suddenly easier now that he had accepted their circumstances. She was married, yes. Two children, yes. Her son was born when she was very young. Husband a fisherman. She worked part time at the cannery on the bayfront, but it was seasonal work, like much of Riptide's offerings. She had learned to sign by necessity, she said, had driven to Portland once a week for two months once her daughter's deafness was discovered. After that they had taught themselves, she and her family, through videos and books. Her daughter's teacher knew how to sign. She and her husband talked sometimes of sending her to the deaf school up in Vancouver. Melissa worried that they were robbing the girl of a childhood, that her isolation here was a kind of cruelty. "But I might as well wait for a unicorn to trot on by and hand me a lottery ticket," she said.

"Why's that?"

She looked at him over the rim of her glass. Even in the meager smoky light her eyes were the deep, cold blue found inside a glacier. "Because her dad's terrified of doing anything outside of his little bubble."

Hayslip, muddled with drink. Hayslip, scarred, scared, heavy with want. Some internal mechanism switched inside him: Hayslip, drunk enough to hold her gaze now.

He ordered them a pair of whiskeys.

Later, Melissa-with-the-Wedding-Ring stood so close he could smell her perfume, a hint of sweat, the whiskey on her breath. Her leg pressed firmly against his beneath the bar. "What happened here?" she asked. She was sitting on his scarred side now, and with her fingertips gently touched the old wound seeping from his collar. The hint of a slur to her voice. He felt nothing but a faint pressure where her fingers lay.

"Shrapnel," he said, closing his eyes. He held his breath. His heart thundered at the simple closeness of her. His cock was hard. He looked into the dregs of his drink and she took her fingers away.

"Does it hurt?"

"Not anymore. I mean, it did. At the time. It hurt like a motherfucker."

One of Melissa's friends lurched up to the bar, a woman in a terribly unfortunate sweater that reached her thighs, threatening to double as a dress, and patterned in an abstract smattering of circles and triangles. Her hair was bottle-red and she eyed Hayslip suspiciously. "What are you doing, Melly? Who's this?"

"Belinda, this is Nick," Melissa said.

Belinda squinted one eye at him and then the other. "She's a fucking married woman, you know," and both Hayslip and Melissa laughed. Hayslip somehow felt relieved that someone had finally said it out loud. And yet, it made what was happening seemingly all the more apparent for it.

They got on the dance floor, and Hayslip felt ridiculous, especially when Belinda danced over and took Melissa away and he was left alone to lurch and flail in his little pocket of space. The music was terrible, and his dance was a passable impersonation, he was sure, of someone being electrocuted. It felt good, though—his nerves hot with booze and movement, edged with an exhaustion different than running. Then she came back to him, her arms raised above her head, her hips sinuous. The jukebox played a slow song and they moved closer together, coiled against each other. Melissa was a palpable heat, perfume, smoke, sweat. The press of her breasts against him. Her blouse was damp at her spine where his hands lay. He was bent a bit at the waist so as to hide his erection as much as possible, but she pressed herself against him regardless.

They returned to the bar, and around midnight, Melissa looked at the clock and motioned to her friends across the room. She stood and gathered her cigarettes, her purse and jacket. Her bangs lay in sweaty curls on her forehead. Hayslip was crestfallen. "You're leaving?"

"I've got to get home to my kids," she said, slinging her purse over her shoulder.

Hayslip, drunk, felt bludgeoned with his own ugliness, his want. "Well, it was nice meeting you," he said lamely.

"It was very nice meeting you," she said, and leaned over and kissed him. In the grand scheme of things, it was nothing epic. There would be no string section, no film scores written as counterweight. Moonlight did not burst through the windows. And yet Hayslip, fearful and drunk, had nearly swooned with it.

"Come home with me," he blurted.

Melissa laughed. "Can't do it, Nick. Everyone's at home. Everyone's waiting for me there."

"Can I see you again?"

She walked away. "I'm sure I'll see you around," she called over her shoulder. "Keep your eyes open."

Hayslip stared after her. She and her friends were twice as loud and brash leaving as when they'd entered. Hayslip squinted and saw that Fitzhugh had arrived, was actually holding the door open for them. Red-faced and grinning, he leaned out the doorway of the bar, tracking their asses as they walked away down the sidewalk. "I don't want to see any of you ladies driving drunk," he called out. Whatever their response was, it made him smile.

"The fuck happened to you? What took you so long" Hayslip said as Fitzhugh sat down next to him. He sounded bitter.

Fitzhugh lit a cigarette. Sat there in Melissa's seat with his giant freckled biceps and green polo shirt that looked like it'd been vacuum-sealed on him. "Somebody lost a fucking week's worth of my arrest reports and I had to redo 'em all." He cocked his head toward the doorway. "What was that? You're not actually getting some pussy, are you, Nicky?"

"She's married," Ron said, pushing a pint of beer Fitzhugh's way. Fitzhugh turned and looked at Hayslip with something approaching respect. He raised his glass in a toast. "Well, you know what I say, Nick: A ring never plugged a hole."

Hayslip winced. "Jesus Christ."

Fitzhugh drank from his beer, wiped the mustache of foam away. He socked Hayslip on the shoulder with a casual indifference to his own strength; Hayslip would have a bruise the next day. "Seriously, though," he said. "It's about time you dipped your wick, hitched or not. I was starting to feel bad for you."

DAVE DOBBS

You could not manage a branch of law enforcement in a county of this size without being shrewd and careful and a politician of some deftness. Dobbs was a man who had done any number of small favors to a great many people and kept a constant tally of what was owed him. He cared greatly about his elections, and he cared about city taxes and levies, budgets that shrank or expanded or infringed upon his staff's capabilities or law enforcement in the state in general. He was a Republican in the sense that people in his county viewed Democratic *anything* as soft on crime and criminals, especially Democratic-leaning sheriffs, so when asked, he was a Republican and that was that. Mostly, though, it hardly mattered to him. The day-to-day mattered: paperwork and performance reviews and the tread of his deputies' boot heels on the hallway floors, the sharp clip of cruiser doors slamming shut in the parking lot outside his window. *That* was politics to him.

Junie, though. Junie had lived and died a Democrat. Staunch and fierce. A believer in social responsibility, in society's innate indebtedness to one another. June loathed Reagan not only for what she claimed was his murderous bravado, his foolishness, but because even without the assassination attempt on his life in August of '80, that deadly club that the man would wield for years and years, he would have won the election anyway. By 1980, the American people felt like Carter was just too god-damned soft on the nuclear question (among most other things) and the Russians just kept gnashing their teeth and puffing up their chests and toeing the line. First Brezhnev and, by the time June died, Andropov. It was a dangerous time, and the American people were afraid, and they were *tired* of being afraid, and tired of weakness, and Reagan in 1980 had strode in like a cowboy-savior come to life from one of his films, a stoic, grizzled man covered in trail dust and spattered in blood. The relief that people felt—*most* people—was palpable. Save us, they said, from this doughy-hearted peanut farmer.

That was what had irked Junie: that he'd already been winning in the polls. Then, on Saturday, August 23, 1980, roughly two months after becoming the Republican nominee for President of the United States of America, Reagan was shot twice on the heat-softened tarmac of the Peachtree-Dekalb Airport in Atlanta, Georgia. It was 98 degrees in the shade and John Hinckley, Jr. (who had by then already given up on stalking Carter, knowing even then which way the political winds would blow), got within twelve feet of Reagan and fired six rounds from his little Röhm .22 revolver. Six rounds in less than two seconds. Saying it out loud—*boom boom boom boom boom boom*—took more time than doing it.

All but one bullet found a target.

Junie always said the Republicans might as well have put the man on salary.

Six shots and then that old familiar chaos: madness and bellows and a chorus of bodies hurling themselves to scorching blacktop. The familiar names: Reagan's campaign manager, Carl Dwyer, took a round in the skull, and his foreign policy rep Tom Teer was grazed on the neck. Secret Service agent Bernard McCleary took one in the guts as Special Agent in Charge John Wanatabe tackled Hinckley. The fourth shot was the one that went wild. It was a shit-show. But it was the last two rounds (Wanatabe had even cinched his hands around Hinckley's wrist by then) that were imbued with the freaky, unnatural luck that would forevermore leave the conspiracy nuts whispering.

The fifth round took off Reagan's left thumb as neatly as if someone had lopped it off with a pair of fabric scissors, leaving a simple ragged hole centered with a knob of bone. That same round then hit his ribcage and traveled up the pectoral muscle to shatter his collarbone before exiting.

And the last round? Lucky number six?

The last bullet entered beneath Reagan's armpit, tumbling through bone and tissue, finally coming to rest woefully near the heart.

He lived ("Of course he did!" June would say. "There are social services to dismantle! Missiles to build!"), and poor, bumbling Carter should have just conceded the race right there. Reagan, wounded and gasping, soon became the people's knight, bloodied but unbowed. The bullet, so said his running mate, George H.W. Bush, in a hushed press conference that afternoon, was lodged too close to the soft tissue of the heart to be removed. To do so, Bush said gravely, might kill him. His speech was lush with pauses, the click of cameras in those silences so dense and frenzied they sounded like the hissing of some great reptile.

Reagan was still bandaged up in November when it was announced that he had won the election in one of the most marked landslides in Presidential history, seventy-five percent of the popular vote, and carrying 46 states. His first speech to the public after taking the oath of office included those oft-repeated lines: "The American people, and the world, have suffered too long under the soft and, at times, misguided conceit of diplomacy. There are times in history in which diplomacy *fails* a nation, *fails* a people. When it places a country and its citizens in grave danger. With me as your President, *that changes today.* We live in the greatest and most powerful, benevolent nation on earth, and with that power, and that generosity, there lies a willingness to act and a staunch refusal to kowtow to tyranny and evil." Then he held aloft his ruined hand and you could hear the roar of the crowd like something ageless, the same sound heard down millennia of bloodied, brutal politicking. ("They yelled like that in the Coliseum, David, when the senators of Rome threw people to the lions," June would say dourly from the couch. Dobbs would just smile.)

She had loathed the man from the start. The night of his inauguration speech she had set her knitting down and pointed at the television with one of her needles. "That man," she spat, venomous, "wants to start a war so badly he tastes radium when he takes a shit." Which hardly made sense, of course. But June hardly ever swore, and she was furious, and with Dobbs's tumbler halfway to his lips and his eyebrows raised, he turned to his wife. June's mouth was trembling, and a moment later the two of them had laughed so explosively and suddenly that the dog woke with a yelp at Dobbs's feet. June had *cried* laughter, wiping tears away with her thumb. Dobbs had been bent over in his armchair, literally slapping his knee, breathless, almost with a kind of panic. The two of them slowly gathered their breath again and the rest of the night there would be brief bouts of mad laughter, no provocation, but frequent enough so that the dog finally had risen and gone to sleep elsewhere.

After that, she called him Ronnie Radium when she saw him on television, and usually left the room.

• • •

Dobbs's house was four miles north of town. Flanked by big pines on all sides, one arrived by a long and curving driveway that branched off from

101. It was practically their own road. The property consisted mostly of thick plots of Douglas fir and rolling patches of sand-clotted crabgrass, though he and the dog, back when her eyesight was good enough, would sometimes find surprisingly large swaths of stinking, knee-high standing water that he supposed qualified as bogs. They'd bought the place a year after he and June married in '53. Dobbs was freshly home from Korea and nearly everything between Riptide and Lincoln City had been standing timber and brackish, rock-hewn scrub that ran straight to the cliffs bracing the beaches below. Beautiful country in its own right, but windswept and forlorn, too. Back then, Riptide had been a town of four thousand souls, or so.

The house had been too big for them. Two stories tall, four bedrooms, two baths, as well as an attic and basement. A detached garage held the history of Dobbs's half-hearted attempts at hobbies, at finding something besides police work to fill his days: model building, golf, fishing and camping equipment, his-and-hers skis leaning like robbers in one corner. It was too big for them but June had had the mumps as a child and, as a result, could not have children. They had talked in their thirties of adopting, but it was distant and vague talk; they had always found solace in each other, in their work. He had the station and she had the library. For thirty years, June had sanded off the harshness in his heart, had smoothed the jagged edges inside him. Made him laugh. Excited him. In bed, after they made love, they would lie together and talk, him pressed against her ass, the scooped curve of her back, his hand cupping her breast. He had taken great solace in it throughout the years; children or not, he had always been grateful of their intimacy, a little awed by her. He heard other men complain of their wives, of their boredom or frigidity, towards June he felt none of that. The opposite of that.

They bought the house and got a puppy, an Irish setter, and when that one died they had gotten another one. It was their third dog that now greeted him as he opened the front door, and she was old and mostly deaf and nearly blind. An arthritic female Golden Retriever named Lea that, since June's death, would occasionally rise and walk around the house, navigate the many empty rooms, her poor eyes marbled and almost beautiful with cataracts. Nosing the corners of each room she passed through. Looking and looking for June.

The land was different now, too. Clusters of houses, whole neighborhoods, had risen through the decades. Businesses and warehouses and gas stations seeping out from the heart of the town like blood from a wound.

Running alongside 101 like an infection. The inside of the house was the same as it had ever been, changes so incremental as to be practically unnoticeable. It had been too big for them but together they had managed to fill it, hadn't they? Dobbs's recliner fuzzy and pilled at the headrest, the blond wood floors, June's seashells clustered on the mantle above the fireplace, the kitchen's pale green Formica countertops glittering like they held trapped chips of gold. They had made such an expansive space smaller with their closeness, the singularity of their living.

Now his footsteps took on the echo of a mausoleum as he stepped inside and dropped his keys on the kitchen counter and slung his jacket over the back of a high-back chair. He put his holstered revolver next to that morning's unwashed coffee cup and Lea came toward him, grinning and silent, not even barking anymore at his arrival. She grazed his palm with her wet nose, then licked the back of his hand and pressed her flank against him heavily, as if grateful for the support.

He fed her and then turned the television on in the den, the sudden brash noise and light an envoy against another night's worth of silence and darkness. Beneath the television's laugh track he could hear the wind among the eaves, the sharpened corners of the house. Dinner was served in a sectioned Styrofoam tray, warm from the microwave: gray turkey in its thin gruel of gravy, tiny cubes of carrots, and applesauce. He ate in his recliner; June would have shuddered. He sectioned an apple with his pocketknife as he watched the news and when he was done he threw the Styrofoam tray in the trash and poured himself another drink, padding back to the living room in his socks. There were those moments—a hundred of them a day at first and now maybe only slightly less—when he kept waiting for the sound of her car in the driveway, the headlights to wash across the wall of the living room. Or he would be watching television and look over, expecting to see her in her spot on the couch, cross-legged on the cushions as she sipped a glass of wine, her knitting in her lap, reading glasses perched on her head. Books in a stack near the lamp. He found himself doing it again tonight, and finally stood up and turned on both of the room's lamps and the overhead fixture, as well. In the dining room, he turned on the hanging chandelier so that it shone through the doorway into the living room. The place was surfeited with light now and Lea raised her shaggy head from her paws and looked at him.

"Don't worry about it," he said.

M*A*S*H* was on, a show that had played itself out any number of years back but one Dobbs still found comfort in, and that was what it was all about, right? The laughs were forced and spare; it was the familiarity that he wanted. The known. He went into the kitchen and poured another Rum and Coke.

As he walked into the living room again he looked over at the empty couch and then veered away from his recliner so suddenly he surprised himself. He sat down in June's spot, the same room from a different view, a collection of strange angles. The way June had seen their home for so long, so often. To one side was the television, to the other his recliner and, beyond that, the fireplace, the bookshelf full of her novels and his history books on the war. A stack of old crossword puzzle booklets lay in a wicker basket next to the end table. Rain pattered against the window behind his head.

Dobbs sipped his drink. "Come here," he said, and patted the cushion next to him. Lea raised her head again, her rheumy eyes searching him out. June had never let the dog on the couch, or the bed.

"Come here," he said again, and the dog rose gingerly on quavering legs. A labored process. Old dog, old man. He had to help her up onto the couch, but then they passed a number of hours that way. Sitcoms, a crime drama, and then the ten o'clock news—Ronnie Radium and the Soviets in their ceaseless ballet. The dog's head in his lap, the warmth of it, the resolute curve of her skull beneath his hand.

• • •

It was past midnight when he entered the bedroom. He'd made no effort yet to remove her things. How could he? Her nightgown still hung on a hook on the bathroom door, frail as smoke. Her slippers, one tiered slightly on top of the other, still at the end of the bed. But June's scent was fading after three months and there was some part of him that was afraid to remove any object lest his overall memory of her somehow become diminished because of it.

Lea, emboldened by her time on the couch, stood in the doorway with her head lowered, seeking him out in the room, casting her head this way and that. As if she was both seeking permission to enter and aware of the intimacy of his next act, what he was about to do. Dobbs had taken a pair of the pillows from the couch—the long ones, which June had always insisted on calling "body pillows"—and laid them end to end on her side of the bed. (And it *was* her side—they had slept this way for three decades and Dobbs still slept on the left. He would do so until he died, he was sure.)

He took all the blankets and sheets off the bed now, piled them on the bureau. He took one of June's nightgowns from her dresser—one that still smelled at least of the detergent they used, the fabric softener—and laid it on the bed, placing the pillows inside the nightgown. Lea was a sentinel in the doorway, unmoving, her long shadow falling across the carpet. He laid that creation, those pillows in their cocoon of nightgown (misshapen and strange and so unlike his wife's body), and placed it on June's side of the bed and remade the bed then, tucking the edges in tightly. He turned off the light and Lea chuffed softly and Dobbs stood in the dark looking at the bed. The rising clefts and valleys, the shape under the blanket.

It looked nothing like her body. It looked like nothing alive.

He disrobed and masturbated quickly in the shower while his head was a dark void full of heat and a great yawning expanse. His blood sang quietly with rum. After he was done he stayed for some minutes under the shower looking at his wrinkled, calloused hands. The yellowed cracked talons of his toenails. An old man. He cleaned himself, toweled off and padded into the bedroom and found Lea asleep at the foot of the bed, her head resting on June's slippers. He was struck for a moment with the surety that he could not go on. Could not continue any more. And yet. He put on his pajama bottoms, checked that the telephone at his bedside had a dial tone, went to the kitchen counter in the dark and got his revolver and put it in his bedside bureau.

He drifted to sleep with the dead weight of the pillows against his chest. The worn fabric of June's nightgown soft against his arm. The cheap and hollow comfort of it all.

NICK HAYSLIP

The bones sang out to him, snared him, called him, fucking *worried* at him ceaselessly. The bones demanded their resurrection. Demanded the discovery of their passing. Demanded justice—and he had brought such pain to those he knew, hadn't he? Couldn't he do this one thing? Christ, this hurricane in his waking hours. This hurricane behind the eyes. And you just want to sleep and you can't.

He began including Tumquala Park in his patrols. Sometimes he'd radio in that he was hitting the bathroom—"10-100, dispatch, might be a while"—and Deb, ever the professional, would dispassionately radio back confirmation. He'd sit in his cruiser, turn the radio's squelch down and would, for a while, simply watch the crew at work. If anyone at the station was surprised in the uptick of shits he was supposedly taking throughout the day, nobody said a word. (Though he could easily picture Dobbs checking Deb's dispatch log and taking him to task for it, advising him, with his old man's hands cinched around a doughnut and a cup of coffee scorched to dark sludge, to alter his diet. Proselytizing about fiber intake, awkwardly pushing sheaves of paper from one side of his desk to the other before he pinned Hayslip to the wall with those heartbroken, bloodshot eyes.) The anthropologists had by now sheared out a great and precise section of the hillside alongside the wooden staircase, a section probably ten feet high and maybe fifteen feet wide. The ground itself was sectioned out in a grid, larger now, marked in those dowels and twine. Exact and precise, and yet twenty feet away great mounds of culled clay sat in piles that turned to mud in the rain. The yellow tape lining the perimeter of the park sagged now and bowed toward the ground between its leaning posts. Tumquala Park had always been a sad place, and good Christ if it wasn't sadder now. Shit, the town itself seemed sadder to him, squalid. He was still getting his few random hours of sleep at night. Harangued by

Stanley Dinkle in his dreams and with the girl's bones nattering at him in his waking hours, incessant as a skipping record. And Melissa was in there too, wasn't she? The dead owned him.

Finally, he brought four cups of coffee in a Styrofoam tray and got out of his cruiser and stepped over the perimeter tape. The rain fell in fat drops and sang on the ground as he walked. The archeologists were examining a section of hillside and had their backs to him, the tarp above them sizzling with rain like static on a radio. He set the tray on one of the folding tables laden with their boxed artifacts: chipped slivers of bone, a blunted arrowhead, what may have been a loose chorus of beads or pellets. Rough-hewn things all, made reverential and totemic as they rested on their cotton batting. The woman, Dana, finally turned and saw him. She blew a lock of her hair from her forehead and put her hands on her hips; the smeared clay gave her the appearance of a butcher.

"What do you *want?*" she called out. "Seriously. Why do you keep coming by here?"

Hayslip responded with his familiar gesture of conciliation: his hands up, a smile on his face. "I'm just interested. I'm not trying to trip you guys up."

She pulled the hood of her yellow slicker back, rolled her head on her shoulders. Waited him out. The men shared a look and went back to work. "Seriously, though. You keep saying that, you keep saying what you *aren't* doing. What *are* you here for?"

"Okay," Hayslip shrugged. He tapped the lid of his coffee cup with his thumb. "I feel bad for her."

"You feel bad for her."

"It seems like a bad way to die, you know? Lonely." His own voice sounded strange in his ears. "It makes me want to know what happened."

Dana seemed to study the boxes laid out on the table and when she looked up at him her eyes were hard. "Can I tell you something?"

"Yeah," he said.

"I find your sentimentality a little weird. No offense."

Hayslip shrugged and laughed a little, gesturing at the other coffees in their trays. "Fuck, so do I. Believe me."

She sighed and walked over and took a cup from the tray.

"Can I ask you something now?"

"I guess."

"Do you know how she died yet?"

Dana sucked at her teeth as she cracked the lid off her cup and stared at its contents, gently swirled it around. Hayslip was reminded—who knew where you picked shit like this up—of one of those Roman diviners, what were they called? *Haruspices*—that was it. People who claimed to divine the future through the blood and entrails of animals. A hell of a racket, but that's what Dana looked like in her rain gear slicked with red mud, gazing into her coffee. Some haruspex. He wanted to appease her somehow, figure out a way to—

"She was attacked," she said.

A stone on his chest. "Murdered?"

She shook her head. "That's not what I said. She was attacked. By an animal. There are gouge marks all over the bones. Remember those punctures on the skull?"

"I do, yeah."

The men walked up and took a cup of coffee each. Finally, Hayslip got their names: Aiden was the one with the mustache and glasses, Brett the one without. They still looked nearly interchangeable to him. "We ran a bunch of tests in the lab. Stress fractures galore in all those puncture marks," Dana said.

"Mean fucking jaws," Aiden said.

"So they were teeth, then. Like you figured."

Aiden nodded above his coffee cup, the lenses of his glasses starting to fog over. "It was like putting the kid's head in a vice, man."

"Her whole skull," Brett said, "the whole setup's like a house of cards. If one little bit ever gets knocked out of place, the whole skull's just gonna fall apart. It just crushed her, pretty much."

"Jesus," Hayslip said.

"Do you want to hear the weird thing? Hey, do you have any sugar, by the way? No? Okay, the weird thing—"

"Brett," Dana said.

"Dana, chill. He's a cop. So the weird thing is, you know about the cross we found, right?"

"Yeah."

"Okay, so here's the weird thing: you see the cross and you just think Christian, right? Back in the 1830s, 1850s, whatever decade this kid's from, Christianity's big time out here in all the settlements. Within this thirty miles of coastline there's already a half dozen little community churches. So she's probably just some Christian kid, out foraging with the family, gets attacked by a wolf pack or something, right?"

"Sure," Hayslip said.

"No wolf pack did that," Aiden muttered.

"Shush," Brett said. "Here's the weird thing: we found some beads too. Probably sewn into her clothes, and beads, especially these kind that we've found, almost always signify some kind of tribal affiliation." He held out one hand, palm up, and then the other. "So was she Christian? Was she native? And if she was, what tribe was she? Tumquala? Alsea? Tillamook? The Tumquala Reservation's closer than Siletz, but neither one's *particularly* close to here, you know. Not by foot."

"The Tumquala Reservation's right off of Highway 20," Hayslip said. "It's almost a straight shot from here."

"That stretch of Highway 20 was built in 1940, man."

"Oh."

"Besides, that was *town*."

"What do you mean?"

"No Indians allowed," Brett offered. "Not unless you were just passing through, not unless you had papers from your Indian agent or from a white man you were doing business with."

"What if she was an Indian kid that got a Christian burial?" Hayslip said. "Weren't they into that? Helping the poor savages find the Lord and all that shit?"

Brett nodded, lifted his cup Hayslip's way. "That's an idea we were kicking around too. Not bad, man." Dana rolled her eyes.

"Here's the point I was making," Aiden said. "Indian, white, whatever. Whatever happened to her was bad, okay? Like what my dad would call 'guts for garters' bad. I don't know what kind of animal could have done it."

Brett tilted his head back and sighed. "We've gone over this. You're not, you know, a veterinarian, Aiden."

"I know I'm not a fucking veterinarian, *Brett*," Aiden said scornfully. "But this is some straight-up *Cujo*, werewolf shit. Those fractures around the punctures? Those little cracks you saw? That's from her getting her skull, like, *pressed* down," and here Aiden slowly lowered his tented hand toward the top of the table. "Do you have any idea how much psi something like that requires? No wolf did that."

"Jane Goodall over here," Brett said quietly.

"That's chimps, you fucking idiot," Aiden said. "I'm just saying, if it was a big-ass black bear or *whatever* took her down, whoever buried her probably had to pour her in her grave like a margarita."

That was when Dana slapped Aiden on the shoulder, a little *pap* sound bright under the tarp. "That's *enough*. It's time for us to get back to work.

You want to know what happened? *Get back to work.*" She turned to Hayslip. "And thanks for the coffee and all, but it's time for you to go."

"I didn't mean to upset you. I really do want to help."

"I hear you. The best way you can help—"

"Okay, okay. Got it."

"—is to get the hell out of here."

Dinkle and Melissa and the girl in the hill. The dead owned him, steered him like a ship along some great dark river.

· · ·

The small, wood-paneled room the doddering librarian had placed him in was heavy with the smell of ink from the mimeograph machine out in the hallway. The microfiche machine itself exuded a warm electric hum and he could hear the rattle of men and their newspapers out on the main floor. Murmured conversations and one codger with a ceaseless wet cough, the old man seemingly ready to expel his very lungs right there next to the scuffed, oaken card catalog.

He had to go out to the front desk and ask the librarian to teach him how to change the spools of microfiche. "What do you think about getting that fella some cough drops?" Hayslip asked.

"Oh goodness, he's terrible, isn't he?" she whispered back.

"Goddamn, we should take him out back and put him out of our misery, know what I mean?" he said, and grinned, and there was something in it—he knew it as soon as it came out of his mouth—that set her on edge. She took a step back and began twisting the button at her collar with her gnarled, arthritic fingers. "Anyway," she said, "notch left for forward, notch right for back."

"Got it, thank you," Hayslip said, shamed. His father, Fitzhugh, Dobbs. The woman in the bathroom. Was there a person alive he had not disappointed or frightened? Was it any wonder he sought solace elsewhere? Christ.

He started the search in 1861—easy enough because it was the beginning of the library's spools of microfiche for the *Riptide Observer*—and moved his way up from there. It had never been a large newspaper, especially then, and the yellowed pages beneath the lens sped by quickly, though the ink had sometimes bled so badly as to be nearly indecipherable.

All in all, it didn't take long.

Still, it was with a moment of savage recognition—a sense of triumph as sure as an arrow notching in a bowstring—that he found an *Observer* article from an issue dated January 16, 1868. The headline had all the titillation and glee of a tabloid: WOODLAND CREATURE SAVAGES YOUNG INDIAN GIRL ON BEACHFRONT.

"There you are," Hayslip cried, slapping the tabletop loud enough that the rooms beyond his were temporarily quieted. Even the goddamn coughing man stopped for a moment.

"Oh, there you are," he said. "Goddamn, kid, I see you. I see you right there."

A BRIEF ASIDE

-Excerpt from the *Riptide Observer*, January 16, 1868 (p. 3 & concluded on p. 8)

WOODLAND CREATURE SAVAGES YOUNG INDIAN GIRL
ON BEACHFRONT

On the morning of January 11 of this year, Mr. Robert Meachum, a well-respected and honorable member of this township, did come across a corpse that had been horribly and savagely disemboweled and killed by some sort of animal. The body belonged, so says our Sheriff Watts, to that of a young Indian girl. Individual recognition was impossible, so brutal was the attack. Said Indian girl was found midway between South and Slokum Beaches, on a stretch of mostly desolate and undeveloped beach-land. Mr. Meachum did hurriedly go about and bring the proper authorities to the spot of the girl's passing first things first.

Sheriff Watts has now requested that all children and those of the fairer sex avoid the beach-land in the coming days. He would like it noted that he's offering a bounty of five dollars, in the form of hard currency, to any man who brings the deceased body of the offending animal or animals to the Sheriff's office.

There has been much talk in recent days of the increased number of birds and woodland creatures found also to be disemboweled and killed upon our good town's beach-lands, and as this marks the first human attack, all citizens are well-advised to take care. A Christian burial will be performed upon the Indian girl forthright and those who have information leading to her identity are urged to contact Sheriff Watts or this newspaper at their earliest opportunity.

THREE

SAM FINSTER

The flagpole held no flag and its chain rattled in the wind. It was a lonely, forlorn sound, the way it rattled and clanged against the pole, and it fit perfectly with the iron-gray sky above and the roughened cries of the children circled the two of them with their fists raised. Sam Finster and Kenny Pritchard, their knuckles up as they each bounced on the balls of their feet among the tennis court's broken black slabs of pavement. There was laughter and sneers and a wheeling carnival of faces. Taken without sound, the faces would look insane, blood-maddened. With the jeers and cries and the loose clanging chain on the flagpole, it was simply a darkness around him, a spinning blur. At the circle's edge, there was Toad smoking a cigarette, calm as Buddha, the side of his head freshly shaved. Looking bored and elbowing people who jostled too close, he had met Sam at the school doors only minutes before; Sam had unslung his backpack and handed it to him. All business. It could have been choreographed. "I have to go fight Kenny Pritchard at the tennis courts," he said, and Toad had shrugged, and said, "Sounds good," and that had been that.

The tennis courts were at the far end of the high school, beyond the athletic field a minute's walk away. The two courts were flanked on all sides by a chain-link fence and hidden from both the high school and the street by lines of shrubbery that had, for whatever reason, long been allowed to grow riotous. One small gate to get in and out. Almost an empty cage, save for a few rusty tetherball poles, the flagpole, and the courts shorn of their nets. No one came here anymore except kids from the high school who wanted to fight.

Kenny arrived a minute after Sam, complete with his own entourage. The courts were already thronged with kids. Boys in puffy camo and baseball jackets gathered around Kenny, their caps on backward, plugs of chew bulging from behind their bottom lips. Not a pair of jeans among them had both knees. Kenny handed his jacket to someone and adjusted his baseball cap with the delicacy and concentration of a man trying to find a transmission from Europe on a ham radio dial, his eyes never leaving Sam's. He spit a clot of tobacco juice on the pavement and raised his fists, rolling his shoulders a few times. He said, "Let's go, fucknut," and then raised his chin toward Toad. "And once I beat the living shit out of this quimby, you gotta promise me you're not gonna step in."

"I'm not promising you a thing," Toad said flatly.

"I'll take him if he does anything, Kenny," someone said, and someone else agreed, and Toad shrugged again.

Sam was thinking too much. He couldn't help it. He was thinking of how he was going to be late to pick up Trina from school, and he was thinking of his mom, and the Trip, and also the fierce bloom of love he felt for Toad when he said he wasn't promising Kenny anything. And then he ran forward on legs that felt like poorly-joined sticks and started throwing straight, fast, ugly punches. His arms stiff with fear. Graceless. Kenny's eyes were small dark marbles, hidden and mean and deep-set in his skull. But the muscles in his arms rolled with a terrible fluidity as he blocked Sam's volley of punches, slapping almost all of them away and ducking the rest.

"Ah, fuck," Sam heard Toad mutter very distinctly, and then a star exploded in his eye. His skull filled with a deep, hollow purr, like the way the world might sound far down in the sea, and he felt his asshole tighten up in pure animal panic as adrenaline sang out in his blood. He swung again, blindly, and Kenny grabbed at his wrist and pulled him forward, hooked a leg out. Sam fell to the wet pavement on his elbows—God, that hurt—and felt water seeping through the belly of his shirt. The crowd's volume rose. He was in trouble.

But Kenny let him go.

Sam hopped up, a part of him knowing that if Kenny had really been invested in the fight, he'd have kept Sam on the ground at any cost. Would have beaten his ass there on the concrete. But it was only Sam Finster, so who cared? Jesus, maybe Kenny even felt a little *sorry* for him. It was this last thought that pissed Sam off even more and he stomped toward Kenny with his fists down at his hips. His eye pulsed in time with his heartbeat. Toad moaned, "God, get your hands up, Sam. Jesus."

Sam swung, Kenny dodged again and jabbed back and mashed Sam's lips against his teeth. And again. *Pop. Pop.* Kenny was so fast it almost looked casual, and even apart from the pain, Sam's head was suddenly throbbing

with confusion, regret, and embarrassment. His mouth felt numb and positively huge; he thought he could feel warm blood running down his chin.

Discernible through the roar: "Fuck him up—"

"Dude, you see that—"

"Getting his friggin' ass kicked—"

"You see that blood, it's all over him—"

"Fight's over man, jeez—"

Kenny stepped close again and Sam reached out and hooked his shirt-
front with three fingers. Lucky. He pulled Kenny forward, and Kenny's shirt
gave with a lush tearing sound like a fart. People laughed. Sam saw drops
of blood on his wrist, drops that wandered crazily up his arm, realized it
was his own. He grappled with Kenny and punched him in the ear, glanced
one off his jaw. He was close enough to see the angry cluster of pimples at
Kenny's temple, and he punched him there. Again. Rabbit punches, but the
crowd let out an almost orgasmic *oooooh* as Kenny's eyes fluttered. Sam
hooked a foot around his ankles and pushed hard on his chest and now
Kenny was the one on the ground, his legs splayed wide, his back pressed
on the pavement.

"No, Sam," Toad called out. "Don't do it."

Right before he reared back to boot Kenny Pritchard in the testicles
as hard as he possibly could, he saw Jordana Benedict among the jeering,
screaming circle of students. Her crest of bangs, her wide gray eyes ringed
in mascara. What was that look on her face? It was different than the rest
of them, he was sure of it, but what was it?

Kenny started to rise and Sam reared back. Kenny rolled, and the steel
toe of Sam's boot instead hit him in the ass with such a meaty thwack Sam
could feel it roll up his leg. Kenny, poor shit-for-brains Kenny, bellowed
like a sea lion.

• • •

By the time it got to Sam via some kid in his history class, it was apparently
old news. Tracing it back to its source—which took a while—brought him
to this: that Kenny Pritchard was apparently responsible for telling people
that Sam Finster had for months been stalking Jordana Benedict, had in fact
been caught "yanking his pud" outside of her house the previous night. Her
father, the story went, declined to call the cops only because Sam's mother
had died so recently.

Had his mother been alive, she would have almost undoubtedly told him that this was exactly how rumors got started.

"What?" Sam had said, as a cold, thrumming kind of feeling—a strange cocktail of anger and fear—settled in his legs. "*Yanking my pud?* What?"

"That's what I heard, man," the kid next to him said, dutifully filling in a penciled Iron Maiden logo in his history book with pen. Almost laconic in his pleasure at spreading bad news. "That's just what somebody told me."

"*Who* told you?"

The kid looked at Sam with something like pity. Not quite, but close. He said quietly, "Dude, it's all over school. I mean, everybody knows."

"Well, it's bullshit."

The kid shrugged, like *Don't shoot the messenger.*

Sam asked around and Kenny's name came up a few times. And that was that. With that strange comingling of dread and anger that made his hands feel icy cold, he had found Kenny Pritchard at his locker during third period. Kenny was not a particularly big guy, but he still had a few inches on Sam and the easy, loping confidence of an athlete. Sam put his hand on the cool metal of the locker next to Kenny's. "I heard you were talking shit about me." It was a terrible line in the best of circumstances, but he was past caring.

Kenny smirked and kept putting stuff away in his locker. "Please. Like I don't have anything else to do? I just sit around and talk about you?"

"I heard you said I was, like, stalking Jordana Benedict. That her dad caught me outside her house."

"Wasn't me."

"Good. I don't want to hear you talking about me," Sam said. What would Toad do in this situation? God, what would Lemmy Kilmister of Motörhead do? "Just make sure you keep your fucking mouth shut when it comes to me."

But he'd gone too far, and he knew it, and Kenny slowly closed his locker and looked him up and down, like Sam was a piece of questionable machinery. A sneer curled his lips. "You know what? Fuck you, Finster. You little queer."

"No, fuck *you*," Sam said, and pushed him, both palms to his chest, and then Kenny pushed him back, and then they were grappling, and it was as stupid as that, and thusly all requirements for a fight at the tennis courts had been met. After a clumsy pirouette that knocked to the ground various students' textbooks and someone's can of Coke that exploded on the floor like a bomb, they were separated by a teacher. Neither one of them was sent to the principal's office—mostly, Sam presumed, because of his dwindling currency of mourning with the school staff—and it was tacitly agreed with only a look that they would meet after school. There was no need to say where.

"I'm gonna fuck you up," Kenny called out.

"Depart, gentlemen," the teacher said.

"Your ass is grass, and I'm gonna mow the shit out of it," Kenny said with such sudden and fevered menace that, as Sam walked away and the hallway erupted in laughter, he felt his scalp pull tight in anticipation and worry. It should have been funny, what Kenny said, but it wasn't.

• • •

And yet, here they were. Kenny had gone easy on him and was now writhing on the ground, his hands cinched over his ass, his face closed tight as a fist. *Did* Kenny even start the rumor? Sam had heard other names mentioned too, after all. *Stomp him*, Sam thought. *It doesn't matter*. Some lizard part insisted on it, some hugely hurt part of himself. Some part that missed Melissa the way someone would miss an arm; integral, vital.

Just stomp him.

Kenny lay on his side, still bucking like a fish on a gunwale. Sam stepped forward and raised a foot, some other part of him closed off and distantly watching, knowing he was doing the wrong thing, knowing he would regret it, but *wanting* to regret something. To regret something that he could control. A regret that he was fucking *responsible* for, for once. Kenny raised himself on one elbow and put his other hand up in the air as if to ward him off, and there were bits of gravel stuck to the palm. A constellation of dark pebbles on the pale map of his hand. And if Sam looked up at Jordana now, what would he see?

"Dude," Toad said behind him.

And then Sam was airborne, his own shirt collar tightening at his throat as someone pulled him back. He scrabbled on his feet to remain upright. He lashed out, his fists connecting with stone, saw in his peripheral vision the quick, nervous procession of kids leaving through the gate.

"Let him go," Toad called out.

Sam caught a glimpse of a black leather belt, a baton and revolver.

The cop said, "Shut the fuck up, Todd," and yanked on Sam's collar again.

"Let him go," Toad repeated. The cop whirled Sam around as easily as he would a doll, and pushed him. Sam bounced off Toad like a pinball, a loose collusion of jarred bones and clacking teeth.

Kenny Pritchard slowly rose to his feet with the help of a few loyal teammates. The cop standing before him was probably in his mid-thirties. Skinny as hell, yet he'd tossed Sam like a toy. The man had the red-eyed, punchy look of a man long running on little sleep, and a latticework of purple scars crept out of the collar of his uniform. He pointed a finger at Toad. "I know for a fact you're over eighteen, Todd."

"Come on, Hayslip. Jesus Christ."

"You want to go to jail for obstruction, say one more motherfucking word to me. Seriously. Try it out."

Kenny finally stood up, limping between two other baseball players. There was half a red leaf stuck to his face that he brushed angrily away. One of the boys bent down and handed him his baseball cap.

"I think you broke my tailbone, you little faggot." His face was red and pinched.

"That's enough," the cop said.

"This guy started it," Kenny said. "This guy hit me first."

"Look at him. I'd say you gave pretty good there, too. Right?"

"He hit me first though."

"Go home," the cop said, shrugging. "See you later."

Kenny was incredulous. One of the boys holding him up started to say something, and with a sigh, the cop took a notebook from his hip. His fingers started searching for a pen in his breast pocket. Kenny muttered and hobbled away, held aloft by his two friends.

The cop sighed, looked around the court, up at the rattling flagpole. "I'll give you guys a ride home," he said.

Toad looked uneasily at Sam. "I got to get to work, dude."

Sam nodded, touched his bottom lip. "I have to pick my sister up at school."

"Is it okay with his Highness if I go to my place of employment?" Toad asked. "I can walk there."

The cop tucked his notepad back in his belt. "Goodbye, Todd."

Toad clapped Sam on the shoulder. "You cannot fight for shit, dude."

"I know."

Toad left and Sam followed the cop to his cruiser across the street. The air stung his split lip and his hands shook with adrenaline, his saliva sour with it. Scraps of trash lay flattened and colorless against the fence. A curled rubber lay like a milky snakeskin in the gutter. A gust of wind scoured the park, and back behind them, the flagpole chain clanged and clanged.

Sam stood at the passenger door of the cruiser and the cop shook his head.

"Get in the back," he said.

"For real? I'm bleeding."

The cop stared at him over the roof of the car. His eyes were cold and appraising. "Tell me what I just saw back there. Tell me what that's about and you can sit in the front. You were going to stomp that kid's face, right? Before I came along? That's what it looked like."

Sam didn't say anything.

"Yes or no?"

Silence. The clanging chains.

"That's what I thought. Get in the back."

Sam got in the back.

NICK HAYSLIP

He'd asked her once what her husband was like. They had been lying together in his bed, and he'd surprised himself with it; they had not been sleeping together long. He was still navigating the newness of it and still a little stunned by it all, but as soon as he said it he knew enough to realize that it was a topic laden with landmines.

It seemed to surprise Melissa as well. She had been tapping a rhythm on his chest, and after he said it, she stopped. Her breath caught and then she gave a little laugh and hooked a warm leg over his thighs and said, "Did you ever have any pets when you were a kid?" The last of the day's sunlight shone pink and red through the thin curtains and a band of it lay in a distinct swath along the bed and the wall behind them. It was summer and she would have to go home soon. His whole house seemed a different place with her in it. Expansive, heavy with possibility.

"Sure," he said. "We had cats. And a black lab named Devin. God, that dog. He'd run through fire if he knew there was a pile of cat shit at the end of it."

Melissa laughed. The room was close, smelled of sex and spent alcohol. She said, "I had a little Yorkshire Terrier that my dad got from a neighbor. Mandy, her name was. God, she was *so* sweet and *so* adorable and just, you know, dumb as a post. Just *dumb*. Every time she walked by the mirror in my bedroom, every single time, she'd see herself and freak out. Just bark her head off at her own reflection."

"Okay."

She leaned over him and took the pack of cigarettes from his nightstand. He felt her breast pressed against his arm and smiled, the ridiculous ease with which his want stirred to life. Like a kid. She put a cigarette in his mouth and one in her own. She lit them and put the ashtray on his chest and then considered him as she leaned on one elbow.

"Well, that's Gary," she said.

"He barks at the mirror?"

She blew up a plume of smoke at the ceiling. The blankets lay in tangles at their feet and she reached down and pulled the sheet up to their waists. Absently ran her fingernails up the outline of his cock and then lay back, hooked her leg over his again. He was still bashful around her in the light, his scars shining and purple against his skin. He felt freer as dusk fell.

"I mean," she said, "Gary gets these random moments where he's reminded of his life. Okay?"

"Sure."

"Suddenly. Out of the blue. And he's, like, pleasantly surprised almost every time. He is. He's good in that way, and he tries. But then life goes on. He forgets again and then eventually everything goes back to being all about him."

"Got it," Hayslip said.

"Like Mandy. She was *amazed* every single time she saw herself in the mirror. She never learned. Gary will get these reminders, like, I don't know, my daughter gets pissed off because she doesn't know how to sign a word, or my son comes home and we know for a fact he's been drinking down at the turnaround. And you go to see where your partner is, where this guy is to help you out, to get your back, and he's just not there most of the time. Gary gets these reminders that there are other people in his life, his family, and for a while he's on top of it. Makes an effort. Shows up. But then . . ." She shrugged.

"But then."

She stared at the ceiling and a wry smile formed around the cigarette. It was a fine armor, the way that she could be with him while not really being there at all. Hayslip couldn't do it. He was all desire and stunted angles and exposed nerves around her. Lust and a bumbling gratitude.

"But then he just forgets all over again," she said. "He just checks out."

• • •

The boy, Sam, seemed like his father. What little Hayslip knew of the man, anyway. Sullen, distant, and an anger inside the boy ready to simmer over. Hayslip was reminded of certain guys in his platoon, as well—quiet, scared guys who would finally crack in a firefight and wind up screaming their throats raw as they emptied rounds into the dripping darkness. No thought to it, just anger and fear, all that tension finally unspooling. Maybe that tension was just youth itself, its yawning ceaselessness. Had he been that furious as a kid? Before Nam and that field hospital in Nha Trang? Before Dinkle? Before the M67 had tumbled from Mendez's hand and left him scarred forever?

Following Melissa's children around town was not a thing he'd planned. Christ, no.

It had started by accident, almost. It helped him remember her, and it distracted him from the dreams. Because the dreams of Dinkle had become a nightly thing. And, as of last week, Mendez had begun making appearances as well. The nightly show flickering behind his eyes as soon as the anvil of sleep fell upon him: they are in the village, and like always, they've received reports of VC using the village as a staging area, but also like always, when they arrive the place is quiet, *mama-sans* and little kids and nobody's saying shit. Everyone's eyes are downcast, and through the whine of flies above the paddies skirting the village, Hayslip can hear their interpreter grilling the old folks and getting nothing back but one-word grunts. And then the little kid comes out of nowhere, out of some hootch Hayslip's sure they've already been in, and he just hugs poor old Stanley Dinkle around the legs like Dinkle's the kid's long-lost pop, like something out of a made-for-TV movie; then the hollow cough of the explosion and the kid's just gone, the kid's just paste and a few pieces—a few *actual pieces*—and Dinkle's legs have just turned to slaughterhouse remnants from the thighs down, and that's when Mendez and Hayslip see the VC rise up from the paddies at the north side of the village. In the dream, Dinkle is just getting that first big lungful of air that he'll use to scream with, and Chuck's rising up, three or four of them hunkered at the field's edge but visible enough in their dark button-up cammies, four, no, *five* of them, and it's chaos, shots cracking off in the haze, steam rising from the paddies in threads that grow hazy a few feet up. Hayslip's heart is a hot ball of iron tucked smartly into his throat. It's broad daylight and he will marvel later at the boy's willingness to sacrifice himself, but at that moment—both in real life and all those years later in that ceaseless fucking dream—there's no time to marvel or ponder or anything like that at all because Mendez pulls out his M67, olive green and round as a piece of fruit, and he pulls the pin, and he's gonna what? Throw it fifty yards to the paddy? Drop those Charlies with a Joe Namath pass? Mendez, who'd even re-upped, got as scared as any of them.

And then—in real life and in the dream—Mendez catches that AK round in the throat that ends his life with the punctuality of someone flipping a light switch. Had to be a stray round. Just pure bad luck. Had to be. But Mendez's hand loosens and the grenade bounces off his leg and rolls like an obedient pet right toward Hayslip's feet, like Hayslip whistled for the thing. People screaming and firing all around, Dinkle still howling, the first lackadaisical green puffs of a smoke grenade starts wafting next to Dinkle's writhing body, tendons in his neck rising as thick as coaxial cables as he screams and screams, and it's nothing so conscious as a thought: Hayslip scoops the M67 up, and *here's* where the dream pays off, where he really gets his money's worth because it's some kind of *Tom and Jerry* cartoon shit: instead of the grenade rising in an arc like it did in real life, detonating far enough away to only get his left side fragged to ribbons but leaving him alive, nah, in *this* version the M67 sticks to his hand like someone's lathered super gluc on it. And Dinkle starts screaming laughter in the mud and Mendez, flat on his back like a KO'ed boxer, looses a big throaty chuckle from that black hole in his throat. Hayslip's shaking and shaking his hand, the M67 stuck fast to it, the seconds ticking off and those guys just laugh it up.

Dinkle, in the dreams, Hayslip could manage. Even the kid, the hug around Dinkle's legs. But the first time Mendez had appeared—the comedy with the grenade—he'd awakened to his own gasp echoing in the little bedroom. Leafless trees outside skulked and shimmied like dancing skeletons on his walls.

. . .

After Mendez made his first appearance in his dreams, Hayslip took to driving past the children's schools during the day and to sitting outside of Melissa's home before he slept. Some half-assed salve. Ghostly. Hayslip hollowed out with sleeplessness, a bone-deep fatigue, thinking half-heartedly about yanking the wheel and driving off the cliff, the white expanse of sand and rock beneath his wheels looming bigger and bigger. He'd drive past his father's house, just to check on him, and then park down the sloping hill from the Finster's with a beer or two, KRPT on low, the window cracked and full of the quiet static of the sea behind him, the moon hanging bright as cheap jewelry in his rearview mirror.

On those nights he'd drink a bottle of Budweiser he'd brought with him, and finally, finally, his heart would slow as he watched the dark windows, the family's door still painted black. The sparse lawn. If he got close he knew he would see the patch of dead grass where she had parked her car, where the grass had given up for want of sunlight. That spot empty; Melissa's car a twisted sculpture of metal in some junkyard. He'd think of that one-sided leer she got when she was drunk, the wiry thatch of her pubic hair, the slickness of her. The warmth of her leg across his own. His heart would settle back in its own house, and he'd drop the bottle on his floorboard and open another one.

He would wonder again why it was her, what it was about her that clamored for such ownership of him. He could talk to someone about it. He should probably talk to someone.

His work at the library, his visitations to the girl's burial site, all the bullshitting with the anthropologists: these were the other ways he divided his days into definable increments now, and they all seemed like things that should have helped him sleep, but didn't. If he truly missed Melissa, why didn't he dream of her? Why not, for that matter, the little girl buried in the hill? Why Mendez and the grenade? Dinkle? It was fucked. It had all happened such a long time ago. But he felt closer to Melissa on those nights he sat in his Datsun and watched her house, tiny as a fairytale cottage among those other larger homes. Watched the children and their father walk from their black door to Finster's truck. It felt like a way of being near her, it did. And then he would drive home and eventually reach toward a few hours of stilted sleep before his alarm woke him.

Yes, he should probably talk to someone.

• • •

Hayslip didn't believe in God, a divining force, an underlying schema that propped up the splintered workings of the world. Which meant it was pure chance, then, statistics in action, that he'd been patrolling past the high school that afternoon and seen the phalanx of school kids stepping from the doors with Sam Finster and Todd Whitlock in the lead. Even if he hadn't been familiar with the Finster boy's lope by then, hadn't been watching him and his sister, he'd have recognized the group as a whole, where they were going. Their intent to fight. He'd been to the tennis courts himself enough times as a teenager.

He'd circled the school a few times, his heart doing a clumsy ballet in his ribs, wondering, wondering. What to do? It seemed like a sign but he couldn't portend what it meant. Finally, he'd parked the cruiser and walked through the gate of the tennis courts and could see nothing beyond the circle of jeering teenagers.

Clearing a path through them, he'd found Sam Finster standing above a boy that lay on the ground. Sam's boot was raised, poised to stomp on the boy's head. This look on his face, like he'd tasted something sour, was already regretting what he was about to do. Hayslip had grabbed the boy by the collar as people began spilling from the gate.

• • •

People stared at them as they snaked their way along neighborhood streets instead of the highway. He wanted to give the boy time to calm down. He caught Sam's eye in the rearview mirror and Sam looked away.

"What was it about?"

Hayslip didn't think he would say anything, but finally, touching his split lip as he looked out the window, he said, "He just said some things about me."

"Yeah? What kind of things?"

"About my family."

Hayslip's heart quickened. "Yeah? What about? About your mom?"

Sam gave him a hard look in the rearview mirror. Moments before, he had looked a lot like his father, those few times Hayslip had seen him in the Sandy Bottom. But now, with the mask he wore, heavy with distance and guardedness, he looked just like Melissa when she was angry, when she was avoiding giving too much of herself away. It twisted some knife inside him. "What the fuck do you know about my mom?" Sam said quietly.

"Everybody knows about it," Hayslip nearly stammered. This time he was the first to look away. "I'm sorry, kid. But everybody knows."

They parked across the street from the elementary school, the cruiser getting glances from parents picking up their children. For a moment, Hayslip felt bad about it: Melissa's kid stacked behind the mesh like he was being arrested, paraded around. He was quiet in the backseat as the little people in their little raincoats and boots, their puffy jackets and bright backpacks, fled from the school in twos and threes or trundled alongside their parents like ducks. The sun broke through for a moment and sunlight threw jittering knives off the hood of the cruiser. Dimly, through the glass, came the high clamor of the children's voices, the occasional shrill whistle from a teacher.

"Actually," Sam said, "it was about me and this girl."

"Not about your mom?"

Sam shook his head and laughed a little. Looked down at his hands. "Goddamn, could you make this a little more embarrassing for me?" he said. "Making me pick my sister up in a cop car?"

"Shit, you're lucky I didn't arrest you."

"Well, there's Trina. Right there."

Hayslip stepped out and opened the back door and Sam walked across the street to the breezeway that flanked the school entrance where the children gathered. Two yellow school buses stood idling. Melissa's daughter wore the same pink raincoat she'd had on when Dobbs was interviewed on television.

• • •

"You're seriously gonna make us *both* sit in the back?"

Behind the mesh, they seemed to be swallowed. Sam Finster looked smaller, somehow, next to his sister. Like his custody of her shrank his bones. In the rearview mirror, he saw the two of them were holding hands; moments before, a conversation in sign language had taken place and now Trina Finster seemed content and unworried to be sitting in the back of a police car. Trusting of her big brother. Something in Hayslip softened. Something in Hayslip, too, told him to beg off. Some internal mechanism that ran a cup along the bars of his ribs and demanded that he stop. That he leave the family alone, that he forget about Melissa, stop revisiting the pale remnants where her life had intertwined with his. To forget any notion of sharing words or deeds with her children, of intersecting with their lives. *Leave them*, a little voice said, *leave them the fuck alone. Move beyond them, out of their orbit. Nothing good will come of it.*

Whatever it was between you, the voice said, *it wasn't love.*

"Listen, I can drop you guys off wherever you need to go."

Sam was silent, eyeing him through the mesh. Suspicious of his change in fortune.

"I'm not in trouble?"

Hayslip started the car. "Hey, people fight, right? If you'd stomped that kid's face, yeah, you'd be in deep shit. But now, no, you're okay with me. I know . . . I knew your mom a little. She was a good lady." He cleared his throat once, twice. "So, where am I taking you?"

Sam looked out the window. They sat there in the idling car until he said, "Home." It sounded like a question. And then, more assured: "Home."

DAVE DOBBS

June's funeral had been held on a Saturday. It had been scheduled for Sunday until the funeral director, flustered and apologetic, had called him to ask in hushed tones if he would consider doing it a day early; while the Finster woman's funeral would be held at another church, it was scheduled for Sunday, as well. "So that everyone who wishes to, may be allowed to pay their respects to both families," he'd said. "I'm very sorry, Mr. Dobbs. I know this is difficult." The notion that there were people who knew both of them, who would mourn both his Junie and the Finster woman, seemed baffling to him. Profane. But he'd succumbed to it, he'd agreed, and June's sisters had hissed in contempt of him when they'd heard. He didn't want trouble; he was too punch-drunk for it. So, Saturday it had been, and his grief was slowly unfolded and unpacked and jammed into the vast empty rooms of his heart a day earlier than his liking.

It had been a beautiful day, the sun throwing shadows in stark relief. It was early September and the wind, normally malevolent and constant, was barely noticeable. Clouds gently scudded along, curling and wavering into strange new shapes above the town. The accident had taken place on the previous Tuesday night, and the time between had taken on a strange half-light in which Dobbs recognized the rest of the world going on about its motions—cars passed by, commercials still aired on television, people still fought in bars and broke into houses and drove with expired tags—while his interior workings seemed to have ground to a standstill. He had hardly slept. He seemed hardly to have *moved*, really, and yet his joints ached terribly, like he was continually on the verge of coming down with a cold. He discovered you could feel both frail and unmoored from your body at the same time.

The church was regal by Riptide standards. Right on the highway and surrounded by a large parking lot, a great expanse of gleaming dark blacktop. Dobbs drove there alone. He had no family to speak of; his only brother had died of a heart attack five years prior, his parents were long dead. June's two sisters refused to stay at the house, instead holding camp at the Silver Sands, the bed and breakfast on Hastings Street. June had been a surprise to her parents and her sisters were significantly older. They were stoic in their grief, the two of them, their silence taking on the unmistakable air of blame toward Dobbs—for bringing her here, perhaps, to such a small town or, at the very least, to such a ruinous and undignified death. They certainly blamed him for kowtowing to the funeral director. After that, he had handed them the reins, let them handle the details.

He had sat for a moment in the parking lot of the church, the ceaseless traffic of 101 at his back. People in their mourning clothes exited from their cars and made their way toward the church doors and he knew all of them, or almost all. The pants of his suit pinched his gut unmercifully; he hadn't worn it since his brother's funeral. (June would've taken them out for him. She'd have laughed at him for it, too, at least a little.) Gulls perched, squawking on the church's bell tower, exuberant splashes of guano running down its sides.

Between Korea and his years as sheriff, he'd become acclimated enough to death's workings, its resolute finalities. The single card it played over and over again. His wife's was not, after all, the first traffic accident he'd come upon. He'd seen nothing in his years that indicated anything at work beyond the visible and tactile: June was gone, and that was that, and he felt such a yawning hopelessness at the idea; it was a notion that bordered on the insane simply for its breadth of seeming impossibility. Dobbs, alone, without June? Yeah, right. He pressed his forehead against a steering wheel hard as bone and felt the constant, stupid engine of heart and lung at work beneath his shirt.

• • •

Riptide came to the funeral.

The church was full, beyond full, and for a moment Dobbs was buoyed, lifted from his grief. Junie had been loved—adored, even. While Dobbs had spent his life eliciting contempt and hatred from many of the people he came in contact with, spending his time among petty criminals and thieves, people who at their most base level loathed and feared him and what he represented, June had always been the gentle one. The library was her second home. The people there, especially the children, had been fiercely loyal toward her. She was not perfect—she grew short with people when she was tired, could be acidly sarcastic then, and Dobbs in his doubt had worried at times that their own lack of children had perhaps driven her to the town's children as a kind of surrogate. That she was more bitterly disappointed then she'd ever let on. But she had balanced him, had gathered those elements of love and sweetness around her; she had carried an innate goodness that balanced the petulant greed of the people he sometimes had to surround himself with.

Dimly, Dobbs heard the newscaster on the radio remind listeners about the Korean commercial airliner the Russians had shot down a few days earlier. U.S. officials were claiming that the Soviets were obstructing search and rescue efforts, and that they had something to hide. It was all noise to him. We will all die in flames, he thought, these two groups of spoiled children will draw their lines in the sand for the rest of us. Ignite the world with their lethal sense of righteousness.

He looked at the church doors, blackened for the occasion, and told himself he would go inside when the news was over.

In the foyer of the church, he stood grimly next to Stacia and Mary, June's sisters, the three of them forming a kind of way station of grieving and condolences, a gauntlet each funeral goer had to pass through. He shook hands, had his cheek kissed, felt the hands of men constantly at his elbow, his shoulder. He was the recipient of their sorrows and their pity. Red-faced men like him grown bashful and shy beneath the church's hushed vaulting, the fug of incense. The women, June's coworkers and friends and even those who still remembered her from their childhood visits to the library decades before, all hugged him and told him that they had loved her, just loved her.

And Dobbs offered his cheek and patted their arms or shoulders and said quietly, "Oh, thank you, honey. She thought the world of all of you." A vast, spiraling emptiness inside him.

He took a seat in the front pew next to Stacia and Mary, both of whom sat silently dabbing at their reddened noses beneath their veils. Old ladies sheathed in black. Two crows, he thought ungenerously as he sat down, wincing again at the pinch at his waist. The air on the back of his neck was supercharged with the sure knowledge of hundreds of people behind him. The church smelled cloyingly of incense and the flowers mounded before June's white casket. Dobbs and the sisters had spared no expense there, the coffin flanked by the tiered bouquets of pale carnations and pastel tea roses. He thought, again: *That is my wife in that box.* And again it felt like he was a man talking in his sleep, or listening to a voice down the hall. He felt it wasn't true. He felt that the intrinsic things that had constituted *June* were as dissipated as vapor now. Now she was a woman defined by her absence.

After the memorial, they would go to the cemetery and lower the casket into a rectangle sawed from the earth. The body in the casket. June, with her elbows that she put cream on every night, June with her lovely dimpled ass and the wisps of hair at the base of her neck and how the sight of her trying to pin her hair up in the mirror had always stirred him to hardness for reasons he could never quite explain. How she almost always killed their infrequent arguments before they began by simply pointing a finger at him and, with a wry smile, saying, "That tone? That tone just isn't going to work with me, friend." Even going from the living room to the kitchen she would reach down and squeeze his hand as she passed. All that, gone.

It had been a head-on collision on a rarely used street. In front of an abandoned gas station with broken windows covered in squares of cardboard. Its marquee dented and punctured by children's rocks, long devoid of any lettering. June had been coming from a late-night budgetary meeting at the library. She had taken the back roads, even though 101 would have been mostly deserted at that hour. One of those decisions, probably only half-considered (and Dobbs knew himself well enough to know that this was a hole he could fall into, a dark hole with no bottom, wondering why she had taken that route and not the other). That summer, a Riptide widow had left the library a posthumous ten thousand dollar donation and the library staff had had a delightful dinner and planning meeting to discuss where the funds should be allocated. Nothing like free money, June had told him before he'd left for work that morning. Her coworkers had said she'd had a glass of wine at dinner. One glass. Pete Doyle did the autopsy and said her alcohol levels were negligible. (Dobbs was more grateful for this fact alone than he would ever tell anyone.) Melissa Finster had been, in Pete's words, "shithouse drunk." He had delivered the news with no shortage of venom. "If you could prosecute a corpse, Dave, I'd say you should. I'm so damn sorry." Dobbs had seen it for himself: the backseat of her Buick had been a riot of beer bottles. The windshield had been entirely shattered, a galaxy of safety glass on the pavement. She hadn't been wearing her seatbelt.

There, in the church, he thought only momentarily of the crash. How the EMTs had parted before his badge but Fitzhugh, the little redheaded bastard, had gone so far as to get in Dobbs's face as Dobbs surged toward Junie's car, had blocked him with one massive forearm to the chest. The red light of the emergency vehicles had strobed on Fitzhugh's teeth, the whites of his eyes, as he said, "Sheriff, there's nothing over there. We've moved the bodies. There's nothing there, Dave." Which had been a lie, of course. Pebbled glass flared on the pavement in the revolution of a police cruiser's trouble lights, and then he'd seen her: June's forehead resting on the steering wheel, her lower half wed to the metal in a way that spoke of little more than death's efficiency, its calculated pairing with inertia. In the church, he cleared his throat, crossed his arms, and frowned at the marbled floor.

The priest began walking toward the pulpit and Dobbs suddenly leaned over and touched Stacia's hand. She startled as if shocked, her eyes wide and surprised behind her veil.

"She would have hated this," he said, nearly whispering. "All this fuss."

Stacia stared at him as if he'd blasphemed. "I don't think so, David. I don't think so at all."

He nodded, still smiling. "She would have. I'm glad we did it, Stacia. But she would have shit a brick."

Stacia turned away from him and the priest shuffled some pages and the room quieted. Programs fluttered behind him with a sound like settling birds. And Dobbs had put his hands in his lap and fallen into the vacuous rhythm of the man's words while hardly hearing them at all.

NICK HAYSLIP

He was spooked by the visit to the house. Melissa's husband had come to the door when he saw the cruiser pull into the driveway and Hayslip had lifted a hand in greeting as the children got out. Finster had stepped out into the yard and Hayslip had rolled his window down and said, "There's no problem. Just giving them a ride home." He'd stood frowning before their black door and gently corralled the kids into the house. The man hadn't looked like a little dog surprised at his reflection, and not at all like a man who had forgotten his family, his obligations. He had nodded once and stepped inside and there was nothing particularly thankful or gracious about it. Hayslip's hands were slicked with sweat when he backed out of the driveway.

He dreamt that night of the same strung-out section of time: the boy hugging Dinkle with the grenades between them, the explosion, and then Mendez pulling his own M67 free, catching the AK round in his throat, dropping the grenade, and Nick watching it trundle toward himself like he'd called its name. There was one difference this time, a new wrinkle: there was something else out in the fields with the Cong. It was out there and making a positive mess of them. It was something low to the ground and four-legged as a motherfucker, and he could hear the men screaming like children as it moved among them. Still, he tried to shake the grenade from his hand as Dinkle and Mendez bubbled their black laughter. The same hot-nerved panic as he woke, the sheets like grappling hands.

• • •

The blue tarp over the excavation site snapped loud as rifle shots while the rain tapped him on the shoulder like a bully. "My folks live in Cleveland,"

Aiden told him over his cup of coffee. "Shittiest place on earth, but I'll tell you what. I'd almost take Ohio over this rain, man. Seriously." He looked around; he'd grown a beard in his time here and looked older for it. "This place is finished anyway." The anthropologists were done with the dig, and Hayslip loitered as they busied themselves that morning with stacking their sample boxes into plastic tubs and loading them into their van. All three of them had colds and the hill was carved back now to the point where the clusters of blackberry brambles at the top hung over the edge like forelocks of hair. The hill had become a cliff now. Walk to the base and look up and all you could see was sky. A tremendous amount of work for three people. Dana grudgingly allowed him to help pack a few samples into the tubs. He picked up one box the size of his palm and saw slivers of yellowed bone resting inside, a few shards no longer than sewing needles.

He had saved his findings from the library, carried a mimeographed printout of the *Observer* article in his back pocket. Some talisman against his dream of the rice paddies, against the shape moving through it. Against his nightly stakeouts of the Finster house. Robert Meachum and the poor dead girl he'd found on the beach in 1868. The tarp and tables were the only things left but the archeologists seemed reluctant to dismantle them, so he handed the printout to Aiden.

Hayslip sipped his coffee and waited, looked at the park's red mounds of slurry that bled into the gravel road. "Yeah, this is cool," Aiden finally said. "This could totally be her. I mean, like, it almost definitely *is* her. Dana, Brett, you guys should check this out. This totally could be our lady."

They came over. The paper rattled in Dana's hands and she turned against the wind. Finally she turned to face him. "Can we keep this?" she said.

"Sure. Do you think it's her?"

She folded it up and tucked it in the front pocket of her jeans. She nodded. "Yeah, it's probably her. Where was this place they mention in the article? Where they found her body? 'Between South and Slokum Beaches?"

Hayslip smiled. "Are you fucking with me?"

Dana looked bewildered. "No."

He pointed over the ridge of blackberry bushes and scrub pines. "Right over that cliff, pretty much. Around there, at least."

"Are you serious? Right on the other side of the park?"

"Well, I mean, roughly, yeah. But Wolf Point's midway between South Beach and Slokum Beach."

"So if she was killed there, they could have just bundled her up and buried her here," Dana murmured. She looked at Aiden and Brett. "That makes sense."

Brett nodded. "Wrapped her up, maybe found a trail from the beach, or even just pulled her body up the cliff with a rope winch. Couple guys pulling her up."

A truck came alongside Hastings then; mud splashed up its wheel wells. It pulled to a rattling stop and parked behind Hayslip's cruiser. A man stepped out and trotted across the road with his hands in his pockets. His smile didn't falter in the rain. Dana looked over Hayslip's shoulder. "Ten to one says this is nothing good," she said. Hayslip, not knowing what else to do, sipped from his coffee. Dana, Aiden and Brett, consciously or not, flanked themselves behind him.

"Hey there, everybody," the man said, smiling. Skin the color of weak coffee. The white at his temples sang out vividly, two quick smudges of chalk, and the rest was a glossy, coal-black that he had tied back in a ponytail. Delicate, whitened scars marked his eyebrows, the bridge of his nose—the man had taken a beating more than once—and he wore a canvas jacket and jeans faded to stringy thread at the knees. He shook Hayslip's hand with a calloused and work-roughened grip, low-grit sandpaper. He ducked behind Hayslip and shook the anthropologists' hands.

"Leon Davies," he said.

Aiden nodded and said, "What can we do for you, Mr. Davies? We're just packing up here."

"Hopefully you can do quite a bit, friend," Davies said. His teeth were big and slightly yellowed and his grin was unabashed and ceaseless. The five of them had formed a loose constellation beneath the tarp and it reminded Hayslip of penguins huddling up to each other for warmth. The wind snapped the tarp above their heads and an occasional gust flung rain down Hayslip's collar. "I'm a representative for the Tumquala Indian Tribe," Davies said, and Brett sipped his coffee wrong and turned from the group, coughing into his fist. Davies stood there with that implacable grin, his arms folded against his chest.

Finally Dana said, "What can we do for you specifically, Mr. Davies?" She was standing in profile, a hip toward him, radiating fight-posture now, a stance that screamed confrontation.

Davies unzipped his jacket and from his pocket took out a manila envelope. He held it out toward Dana. "Well, hate to say it, but I'm the bearer of bad news. For you folks, anyway." To Hayslip, he didn't look like he hated it in the slightest.

Dana kept her hands on her hips, and finally, Aiden reached out and gingerly took the envelope from him. "That," Davies pointed, "is a document from the tribe, calling for the return of the bones of the Tumquala girl you've been exhuming."

"Exhuming?" Aiden said.

Davies shrugged. "Digging up a hill for a little girl's bones? What would you call it?"

"We're excavating a *historical site*," Aiden said. Hayslip assumed he was shooting for a tone of moral outrage but instead sounded like a prig who had been punched in the throat. "We're not *exhuming* anything."

"Well, you say tomato," Davies shrugged. He looked at Hayslip and actually winked. He said, "Deputy, that's a cease and desist order from tribal lawyers, and a formal request that the remains be remanded back to us for proper burial. The fine print says that no more exhumation—or digging, or whatever you care to call it—can be done until the matter's brought before a judge for a preliminary hearing."

Hayslip looked at Dana and shrugged. A small shake of her head—pure contempt. Disgust. With him or the situation? There was a stutter-flash of lightning and they all waited for the thunder. Moments later it unfolded slowly, rippling, reverberating among the carved hillside.

"We've sent copies of everything to your dean already, as well as to Governor Atiyeh's office, but I thought it'd be respectful to deliver them to you personally."

"Respectful," Dana said. "We're packing up anyway. We hardly even have any samples here."

"They'll need to be delivered to our offices then."

"Sounds like some PR bullshit to me."

Davies shrugged, nodded as if he'd expected them to say such a thing. "Well, I'm sorry to hear that."

"Listen," Aiden said. He put the envelope on the table and then put his coffee cup over it to anchor it. "I just really feel like we're on the same page here. We want the same things, you know?"

"And what's that?" Davies said. He was still smiling, and Hayslip realized that the man's façade hid a great and significant anger. "Why don't you tell me what it is we both want?"

Aiden shrugged helplessly. "I don't know. Preservation of culture? Respect and acknowledgement toward the past? The, the misdeeds of the past—"

Davies nodded, suddenly solemn. When he spoke his voice was low and hushed. "Those *are* important things. You bet. This isn't an attack on you or your work. But putting those bones on display in a museum? Or laying them on trays in some anthropology archive? So you and your friends can write your papers and make careers out of her? That's not respect. That's vampirism, boss."

"How do you even know the body was a Tumquala?" Dana asked.

"Or a her?" Brett said.

"You're saying it wasn't?"

Dana shrugged helplessly. "Why don't you let us find out?"

"Come on. You've taken measurements of the bones. Where they were found. Taken thousands of photographs, marked everything to hell and back. You people aren't stupid. Why not take those materials—the photos, the reports, you can *keep* all the paperwork—and give us the little girl's remains? That's fair, right?" He nodded at Aiden as if they agreed, as if this was all something Aiden had come up with himself. "That's more than fair. And *that's* acknowledgment, don't you think?"

"That all sounds very noble of you," Dana said, her mouth curled in a semaphore of bitterness.

Hayslip said to Davies, "You know about the *Observer* article, don't you?" He was struck with the surety of it. A hunch. "The Meachum article, right?" Hayslip said. "The Indian girl 'disemboweled and killed.'"

"I do indeed."

Dana said, "That's what you're basing all of this off of? It's just guesswork on your part, then."

"Okay, sure. Guesswork. Here's something I'd put money on: She was running from a bounty hunter," Davies said. "I'll bet you. They had Indian hunters running all up and down this coast here, the valleys. All up and down. Guys who made their living at it, you know? Some of these guys even got out of the gold business to go into the Indian hunting business. You believe that? Shooting some redskin in the back while they ran through the brush turned out to be a fuck of a lot easier than being bent over panning for dust twelve hours a day."

"Okay, okay," Hayslip said, his hands up. He was familiar with the trammel of rhetoric, and of a man sliding from composure toward a sloppy, ill-edged anger. (Christ, he had done it himself enough times!) "I think everybody just needs to calm down now and take a minute."

"She was mauled by an animal," Dana said. She had taken the envelope from the table and was running her thumb under the seam as she spoke.

"Okay, maybe," Davies said. "Maybe she was." He ran his tongue over his front teeth as he nodded and then he said quietly, "But one thing doesn't change the other." He pointed at the envelope. "And it doesn't change what's in there, either." He took a step back from the rest of them. "I just wanted to let you know that we've started formal proceedings to gain custody of the remains. I thought it was the considerate thing to do."

"Oh, super considerate," said Dana.

"Also—and again, we're just trying to be professional here—the Tribal Council's arranged a press conference on Thursday."

"On the reservation?" Brett asked, and Dana's eyes grew wide with understanding.

"*Here?*" she said. "You're doing a press conference *here?*"

A little more of that anger spilled loose from Davies, quick and hot as kindling. "Well, I was told that you folks were gonna be out of here by tomorrow. We applied for a permit with the city, and now that you've taken every last goddamned splinter of that girl's body out of the ground, this is just another muddy hole as far as you're concerned, right?"

"They'll be battling over this for years."

"You think so? You think your school wants that kind of attention?" Davies asked.

Dana looked down at the envelope in her hands. "This is ridiculous." She turned and held out a hand toward the desiccated hillside, the black clots of dead blackberry bushes spilling over its edge. Her mouth was a knitted red line. "Look at that hill. *We* did that. We took her out of there. She was *lost* in there." Her voice trembled; she sounded on the edge of tears.

"I know," Davies said, putting his hands in the pockets of his jacket and taking a step backward. He squinted up at the clouds and when he looked at Dana again it seemed that all his anger had dissipated. A sadness, a sudden fragility to his features, was all that was left.

"I know you did, dear. But if you really think she was lost, let us take her home."

TRINA FINSTER

Her dad was not good at signing.

And that was being nice about it. He missed words, got words wrong. His sentences left her confused half the time, a collection of words colliding and strung together in ways that made no sense. Worst was when he didn't know a word and she would have to wait the million years it took to watch him finger-spell something.

They were at the turnaround. This was Trina's favorite part of town, even more than the park: Wolf Point, down the wide cement ramp and onto the beach. Thick hazy tendrils of mist hung low to the ground and there were some mornings, before the sun burned it off, when someone might as well have hung a white sheet ten feet in front of you. It was that thick. The mist made everything like a dreamworld, softened the edges of things, blunted any sharpness. If there were ever a time when something strange and unexpected could happen, it would be on a morning like this one. Not scary things, though. Something nice. She knew it was dumb, knew it was impossible, but if there were a place where she could imagine seeing her mother again, it would be here. Could almost picture her coming out of the mist like she had traveled through a cloud. Even at noon some days the sun was a glimmering silver coin up in the sky, like something spied through gauze.

As they walked on, a part of her wondered if this was what nuclear winter would look like. But no. She imagined it would be both colder and hotter than this. *The landscape, what is left of it, will be charred and heavy with irradiated ash.* That was a line straight from *The Looming Error.* She'd memorized large swaths of it. Carried it in her bag. Kept it under her bed at night. Still read it when the memory of her mom threatened to overwhelm her. The library kept sending overdue notices, but so far, she had been quick enough to grab them from the mailbox before her dad got them. She wondered when the library would stop sending them. Of course, there were also those nights when she couldn't sleep *because* of what was she had read in the book. It was all a big mess. Everything in her whole life seemed ready to tumble; like dominoes, one thing would fall and everything else would fall down after it.

Her dad signed, *I need to wash out my shirt.*

She signed slowly and exaggeratedly in response.

Gary frowned. "Do it again, I didn't get that one. You think what?"

It took him two more tries to get it: *I think you're getting your words mixed up, Dad.*

"I am?"

Trina nodded. *A little bit,* she signed, and then said out loud: "You said you needed to wash your shirt."

"Gah!" Gary cried out in mock exasperation, and signed, *I have no money!* with his own big, exaggerated gestures, his feet kicking up little fantails of sand as he waved his arms around in big circles. A gull picking at a wash of seaweed hopped away in alarm. It was an old joke of theirs: *I have no money!* was an easy sign and her dad always went to that one when he got frustrated. It still made her laugh every time.

Down the beach they went, the mist so heavy it was like the surface of another world. The sea was a washed-out gray, as flat and colorless as a dirty sheet. Her father lit a cigarette and scratched his eyebrow with his thumb. His beard was brown and gray and she watched his face because she knew that he was frustrated with signing and would probably just start talking instead. It was easier for him.

He turned his face toward her. "Your mom was a lot better at this than me."

Trina nodded.

"She worked hard at learning it. I should have tried harder."

"She got mixed up sometimes too," Trina said.

"Really?" Gary smiled a little at this. You could hardly ever tell when he did now, because of his beard, and because he did it so rarely; it happened mostly in his eyes. Today she saw it and felt a flush of happiness run from her head down to her boots, to the very tips of her toes.

"Sometimes," she said.

"You're a good liar, honey bear."

She laughed and signed, *It's true! I promise!*

Down the crooked spine of the beach. Trina was always amazed at the things that the tide brought to shore and left behind. There were two ways of looking at it, she figured: the things that washed up could be considered gifts from the sea, like presents. Or they could be things expelled, a sickness, things the ocean got rid of because they weren't healthy. She had seen a report on television once where a bunch of needles from a hospital had washed up in Japan, and Trina knew for sure that something like that was the second kind, an illness of the world. As she and her father walked along the beach, her hand in his rough hand, she saw a gigantic piece of driftwood worn smooth as glass on one side with the other side wet and densely carved from seaworms. The intricate lines and dottings looked like patterns, like its own language. Something like that, she thought, was the first kind.

They would sometimes come down here when Trina was really little, six or seven, before her dad started working all the time and her mom began disappearing. She and Sam would build driftwood forts while their parents sat on blankets and drank beer. Her mom would bring a book and wear sunglasses that made her look like a movie star. Sometimes they would help build the fort and then they'd all take their blankets, as well as Trina's blue plastic bucket with the white dolphin for the handle, and they would sit inside the fort, the four of them. On sunny days, the strange patterns of light would fall on the sand from the delicate architecture of sticks leaning and stacked above their heads and Trina would look at these shapes against the sand and think that this was the best place in the world to be. Her mother's arm warm against hers, the smell of suntan lotion, her father saying something in her mother's ear that made her laugh. Then Sam would grow restless and decide the fort needed a moat and they would crawl out of the fort and begin digging. Sometimes, when she went back in to enlist one parent or the other to help she would find them kissing, her mother with a finger holding her spot in whatever paperback she was reading. Sam would always cry out in disgust as if it was the grossest thing he had ever seen, but it made her happy to see it and both happy and sad to think about it now. But it was better than imagining her mother dead in a car with beer cans scattered around her.

Her father stopped and sat down in the sand in front of her. "I've been thinking about school."

Trina reluctantly sat down, too. The wind was at her back and she pulled a hank of hair away from her mouth. She didn't want to think about school. Her hands played over the gritty surface of the sand.

He said, "I hear you're having a tough time right now." He took a drag of his cigarette and turned his face away and blew out the smoke, still looking at her with his eyes. The smoke tore from his mouth.

She shrugged, looking away. The end of one of her shoelaces was coming unthreaded and she picked at it. Her dad tapped her on the knee.

His face was red and wind-scoured above his beard. "How are things going at school, baby?"

Okay.

"Is Mrs. Driscoll helping you?"

Yeah.

"What about the kids? How are they?"

For a moment she stood still, and then, violently, surprising herself, she gave the pantomime of a pair of chattering voices with her hands, her face feeling like an ugly mask as she sneered. "They're talking about it all over the whole school. Everyone is talking about it."

Gary nodded. "That's how kids are," he said. "A lot of people are assholes, Trina. A lot of people only feel better if they make you feel bad. You gotta be tough."

I know, she signed glumly.

He said, "I hear you might be worried. About the Russians, I mean. About us being safe."

No. I'm not.

"You're not worried?"

No. She looked back down at her shoelace again and her father put a hand on her elbow.

She sighed and rolled her eyes and looked up at him.

He spoke slowly. Behind him a pale man in a blue shirt jogged down the tide line without looking at them. Ghostly in the gloom and then gone just as quickly. "You are *safe,*" Gary said. "There is not going to be a war. Countries have problems, sometimes, but they talk it out. That's what's happening."

It might happen. There are wars all the time. Kevin Merlin's uncle got killed in Vietnam.

"It won't. Sometimes countries get mad, just like people, and they have problems. But they talk it out. Nothing is going to happen to us."

But something already did *happen to us.*

It took him a minute to decipher that—she had to do it twice—and when he did such a look of pain walked across his face Trina wanted to take it back immediately.

He looked out at the ocean and she saw his pale neck wrinkled beneath his beard. He turned back to her. "She didn't want to leave you, Trina. You know that, right? It was an accident. She loved you so much."

I know, Dad. I know that. The threat of tears began to tighten her throat, to make her vision prism and tremble, and she swiped at her eyes almost angrily.

"Okay. Good. Because that's the one thing you should never, ever forget."

He stood up then, and pulled her up by the hand. They started walking again. The mist was getting heavier. Another man passed through the gloom with a bright yellow windbreaker and a little black-eyed wiener dog whose belly almost scraped the sand when it walked. It made her smile.

Gary signed, *I love you, Trina.* He knew that one by heart.

I love you, too.

"Can I ask you a question?"

Okay.

He adjusted the bill of his cap and put his hands in his pockets. "You know you're smart, right? Really smart."

Trina shrugged. *I guess so.*

"Come on."

Okay. Yes. I know.

"Do you want to go to the deaf school in Vancouver?"

She looked at him and then looked back the way they had come because it seemed like she might cry again. She used to want to go to the School for the Deaf. Before. A million years ago. Back when her mother was alive and lines were clearly divided—back when these people had been her family and around them had stood everyone else. Even last year, in second grade, when she realized the offhanded cruelty of her classmates hadn't been a first grade fluke, that this was how she was going to be treated, she would have given anything to go to the School for the Deaf back then. To be among people like her. Just for once. Just for a little while.

But now?

Her father and Sam were all that she had left. Riptide's places—the park, the library, the beach, even school—these were the things she knew, the history her heart clung to fiercely. She'd already lost a lot, it would hurt too much to leave everything else. To leave what remained of her family. And what of the world? How could she leave Sam and her father and go somewhere new with this old world tumbling all around them? They needed to stay together.

No, she signed. *I want to stay with you.*

Her father's look of relief was so obvious that she started crying for real.

He picked her up, even though she was way too old for it, and hugged her hard. She cinched her arms tight around his neck, felt the scratchiness of his beard against her neck, the smell of cigarettes, the cold circle of a button on his jacket. He set her down and they both wiped their eyes, Gary laughing a little bit, embarrassed. They turned around and began walking back home.

"Things will be okay," he said. "We'll be okay."

And she wanted to believe him, she did.

But Trina had learned one thing a long time ago: just saying something didn't make it true.

A BRIEF ASIDE

-Excerpts from *The Looming Error: Russia, the United States, and the Inevitable Nuclear Catastrophe,* by Gen. Paul D. Forrester, USAF, Retired (Goldmine Publishing, 1981, pgs. ix, 66-67, 112)

. . . implore all readers to recognize this as a falsehood. The likelihood of a world-scare nuclear event became inevitable after the tactical use of nuclear weapons against the Japanese people of Hiroshima and Kokura in 1945. We, as a race, are wholly incapable of stepping back from such an error, from *unlearning* our mistakes. There is no turning back. The world has ever since lived in the shadow of those events, and the inexorability of a worldwide nuclear event escalates every year. Unless drastic measures are taken, it *will* happen. Our only solution now as Americans—and much of what the material in *The Looming Error* is concerned with—hinges on the willingness to do what is necessary to ensure that the vital structural, civil and democratic anchor points of our great nation survive the oncoming catastrophe. That we as a people are eventually able to rise up from the ashes . . .

• • •

. . . is true that atomic weaponry has altered the very notion of human warfare. It is the culmination of man's aggression toward one another, the pinnacle of man's resourcefulness, brilliance, brutality, and thirst for his own destruction. Such weapons in the arms of madmen and despots have shown us: never before have we been poised this close to the precipice of annihilation. And never before have we felt our national divide—our sense of *us* versus *them*—so clearly. And justifiably! As a bomber pilot in World War II, a decorated officer in both the Korean War and Vietnam, and finally as a General intimate with both the battlefield and the theater of wartime policy, I have long been familiar with the notion of "The Other." "The Other" is the great salve of warfare, the concept that allows us to do these things to other men, *necessarily*, in the name of an assured liberty and freedom and safety.

But again, reader, when it comes to the nuclear question, such an idea is a falsehood—and a luxurious one we can ill afford. There will be no "Other" once that first warhead is fired, here or in Soviet Russia. There will be no "us" verses "them" when the missiles burst from their silos. There will be no Russians or Americans, no Chinese, no Europeans. At last estimate there were an assumed *55,000 active nuclear weapons* tallied between the two powers. Enough to annihilate the planet thousands of times over.

Mutually Assured Destruction—the theory of deterrence in which both parties are armed and willing to respond with equally deadly force if attacked (supposedly resultant in a tense but stable peace)—has long held sway over the majority of the policy-makers within both the United States government and the American military. The concept of M.A.D. (and its concurrent concept of "fail-deadly", i.e., an immediate, automatic and overwhelming response to a nuclear attack, and coined so because of its directional opposite to "fail-safe") is, as of the time of this writing, a strategy that has become frighteningly outdated and the notion which, if continued to be used as a diplomatic tool, will be the one act of supposed diplomacy that will *resolutely* sentence us all to death . . .

• • •

. . . should our respective stockpiles continue to grow, and our archaic and blundering solution of Mutually Assured Destruction continue to be used as a diplomatic bludgeon, then peace—in the best of times a fragile thing—will finally become impossible to sustain. History has taught us that generations cannot keep their finger from the red button. History has taught us that someone will *eventually* press it—in a fit of pique, a transgressed border, a perceived slight, a misunderstood radar signal, an act of diplomatic thoughtlessness, a coup. It is in our nature.

DAVE DOBBS

He woke the same way every morning now. There was no quaint, touching moment before wakefulness, a moment when he thought of her as still alive. No half-lit world where that was possible. He knew even in the pale coloring of dawn against the shade that she was dead and lost to him forever. And that he was pressing himself against the scarecrowed corpse of her memory; the couch pillows inside her clothes, the last vestige of her scent on the nightgown. Each morning he woke with his arm over this thing, her effigy. Always the same flare of shame in the morning, disgust, but like a drug addict, the contempt would fade by nighttime and he would be lost to it again. Even this falsehood was better than nothing, better than her being gone forever. It was better to awaken with shame at his own weakness than to only the pure and unbridled loss of her. Good god. Heartache every fucking morning like a burr catching on your clothes.

He put June's nightgown back in the dresser, put the cushions back where they belonged, firmly resolved that it was the last time he would do such a thing and, even as he thought it, knew it was not. He dressed and, in the kitchen, listened to the coffeepot gurgle as he cooked a half a dozen strips of bacon, then ate them sandwiched between two pieces of toast, the kitchen stinking of scorched meat. He fed Lea and looked out the kitchen window at the copses of birch and Douglas firs beyond the back lawn as he sipped his coffee. The morning out there mist-shrouded, sky the gray of new weaponry.

He gathered his keys, his shirt covered in the scent of bacon. Smelling it on himself, he was suddenly nauseated. So this was what was happening to him, the man who had assisted EMTs with brutal multi-car collisions dozens of times, who at the motor pool near the infirmary became familiar with the raw velocity of shrapnel against skin and muscle, who had seen death in any number of guises, and now the smell of bacon made him sick. This was the man he had become? He walked into his bedroom, laughing a little as he unhooked his badge and threw it on the dresser. He threw his workshirt into the hamper and put on a fresh one, grabbed his badge, gathered his keys again and stepped out his front door. The misted air felt like a baptism on his skin.

The birds lay in a number of pieces on the welcome mat.

More gulls—it was hard to tell how many, at least two—wrenched smartly in half and dusted in sand the way a cutlet gets dusted in flour. Some pieces lay next to June's godawful ceramic troll planter, a thing she had picked up on one of their trips to Lincoln City, this terrible juxtaposition, a dark mirth. Intestines lay in blue-gray spools amid jellied clottings that could only be the remnants of organs. Viscera coated the sharp green bristles of the mat and lay in great splashes on the cement walkway. *Welcome,* the mat proclaimed. One bird's open beak laid next to it, a brash carnival yellow in the morning light. Feathers lay pasted to the bottom of the front door, some grown nearly translucent on the lawn. He stood for a moment, one hand hooked around the doorknob, leaning out of the doorway on the balls of his feet. His heartbeat thrummed in his neck and the back of his hands felt cold. He went to the hallway closet and grabbed the Polaroid. Lea stepped from the living room and he sharply bid her away. She looked at him a moment, confused. He never spoke this way. He snapped at her again and she shuffled away, her head down. There was film in the camera and he took a large step over the welcome mat and shot a half dozen photos from a number of different angles. He set the photos on the kitchen counter, and put the camera back, then grabbed a handful of garbage bags from beneath the sink and put on a pair of Junie's gardening gloves. As the photos developed, he gathered up the pieces of birds as best he could, the stiffened pieces and bony, unforgiving legs, marbled clots of effluvia and gore. He cinched the whole mess in a wad of plastic and threw it in the garbage can at the side of the house. He threw Junie's gloves in there afterward, took the welcome mat and hosed it off in the driveway, spraying the walkway much longer than he needed to.

Driving to work, a red coal of anger seemed to grow larger in his chest the closer he got to town. The photos lay stacked on the dashboard. He pulled into the parking lot of the station and sat there for a few minutes, gauging his anger. He slammed the heel of his palm into the steering wheel three times and smoothed his hair back and stepped out of the truck. Walking toward the station he saw his harried reflection in the station window.

He strode through the station floor, fists at his sides—he didn't see Hayslip anywhere. He checked the tiny changing rooms and showers, scanned the roster to see if he was still on patrol, even looked in his own office. He finally found Hayslip in the bathroom, a green-tiled place of two urinals and a single dented stall, a window of wired glass set high into the wall. An echo chamber with a drain in the floor. Hayslip was pissing at a urinal; Dobbs sidled up to the other one and very slowly set a photo on the white porcelain of Hayslip's urinal. The image was garish, the splayed remains shadowed in high-relief. Hayslip's face in profile was sleep-stunted and bristled. Nightmare thin. Dobbs couldn't tell if he was just waking up or nearing sleep. He watched as Hayslip frowned at the photo like a man trying to divine the glyphs of another language.

Dobbs's voice was tight. "You know anything about that?"

Hayslip cast a worried glance his way then turned back to the blank green tile. "Christ, not me, Sheriff. Why would I?"

"That was on my doorstep this morning."

"You kidding? Jesus."

"Meet me in my office."

"Dave—"

"Ninety seconds, goddammit."

Hayslip came into his office moments later, sat down in the chair. Dobbs sat at his desk, the Polaroids fanned out before him like a hand of poker. Hayslip cocked a boot up on one knee and then dropped it back down. His eyes pin-balled around the room. His clothes tented on him like a man crafted of sticks.

Dobbs tapped the photos on his desk. "You don't know anything about this?"

"Sheriff, I'm being straight with you. Swear to God. I mean, why the hell would I even do a thing like that?"

"Why would anybody?" Dobbs said.

Hayslip shrugged helplessly. "I'm not . . . That would not be in my best interest, you know what I mean? I mean, that's some crazy shit right there. Why would I even do that?"

Dobbs leaned over and planted an elbow on his desk, pointing a thick finger Hayslip's way. "The worst idea you can have right now is the one where you consider fucking with me, Nick."

"Dave—"

"I read activity logs. You think we're all idiots here? Heads up our asses?

Everybody knows you've been hanging out down at Tumquala Park. Calling in 10-100 at the same time every day. Spending hours down there. People see you, son. You think you're invisible but you're anything but. You sticking it to that girl digging up the bones? That college kid? Is that what's happening?"

"*What?* No. No."

"This some kind of payback for that dressing down I gave you?"

"*No, I—*"

"Shut the fuck up. You come to my home in the middle of the night, do something like this? Who do you think you are? I mean, really. Tell me, Nick, I'm fascinated." He was yelling; the floor outside his office was tomb-quiet.

Hayslip, his head down, lifted his hands up wordlessly and slapped them on his legs. Didn't say a word.

Quieter, Dobbs said, "Fitzhugh's back on active tomorrow. You two will work that park detail in the morning and then you're done with that place. Do you understand? Maybe now that your little girlfriend's gone you'll start acting like a cop again, because your police work is shit these days. You look strung out, Nick. If I had the numbers for it I'd put you on forced leave."

Hayslip tilted his chin up, wearing a thousand yard stare now that went right past Dobbs and through the window and along the horizon where the world started to bend. He'd just reached that saturation point. Sitting upright now, hands on his knees. "Yes, sir," he said.

Dobbs held up a Polaroid. "And if I find out this is you? Suspension's gonna be the last thing on earth you need to worry about, I swear to jumped-up Christ."

"I'm being straight with you, Sheriff."

A beat of time and then a phone rang and the moment changed to something else. "Tread carefully," Dobbs said, and stood up and walked out of his own office with Hayslip still sitting there.

• • •

The Silver Sands was a bed and breakfast on Hastings, the street that wove itself north to south all the through town. The Silver Sands was an immaculate three-story Victorian braced by a white fence and postcard-quality lawn. A line of tulips, purple and yellow and nearly glowing for the lack of color around them, grew beneath a pair of hanging benches that ran along the length of the porch. There was a small parking lot attached and Dobbs stepped out of his cruiser, his knees barking in protest. What was it Lyley had said when he'd dumped that first bird out on Dobbs's desk back in November? Not even two months ago? What fine little gem of quasi-religious wisdom had he provided?

The Great Redeemer puts His mark on all of us.

His footfalls were hollow and loud on the steps. He opened the heavy oak door. The front room was paneled in dark wood that seemed to swallow all the light that bled from the lace curtains. Framed doilies hung on the walls and deep molding ran along the perimeter of the room and was lined in seashells, pieces of twisted driftwood, agates. In one corner of the room stood a taxidermied seagull on an end table, its eyes glass-bright, standing amid travel brochures gone warped with the damp. Dobbs was reminded of the gull legs he had gathered up less than an hour before, that same pale yellow, the feeling brittle as tree branches beneath his hands. The floor of the place was polished to a gleam and creaked when he stepped inside.

The counter ran the far length of the room. There were nooks and shelves built into the back wall and Dobbs saw more curled driftwood, commemorative plates, a number of crucifixes nailed above tiers of decorative bells and thimbles. The woman behind the counter was in her mid-forties and had no makeup on. She wore a green cable-knit sweater rolled to the elbows, and a silver cross hung between the nubs of her breasts. At his arrival, her mouth became a scar, thin enough to be nearly invisible.

Dobbs clapped his badge on the counter. "Sheriff Dobbs with the Lincoln County Sheriff's Department."

"I know who you are," she said quietly, her eyes sparking like chipped flint.

Dobbs smiled and nodded, taking a savage satisfaction in the contempt in her voice. "That's good, then. I'd like to speak to Mr. Lyley, if he's around."

She seemed poised to say something and instead nodded once and walked through the doorway behind the desk, letting it slowly shut behind her.

Moments later Lyley walked out. He looked much the same as their first meeting but now, rather than righteous, his eyes were wide and worried behind his glasses. Dobbs lifted the panel in the counter and stepped quickly over to him and grabbed him by his shirt collar. He yanked Lyley forward so hard he heard a button tumble to the floor. Lyley gasped—the sharp stink of coffee washed across his face—and Dobbs pivoted behind him and wrought the man's arm up, bringing Lyley's fist toward his shoulder blade as he pressed the man's face against the counter. Hadn't Hayslip done the same thing to him in Dobbs's office? Lyley's feet kicked out and thunked madly against the wall behind them, searching for purchase. A plate fell and shattered. Dobbs's heartbeat boomed in his throat. He felt a ripple of disgust at the man's malleability. Part of him wanted Lyley to fight back.

The woman came through the door, her eyes wide, and Dobbs with his free hand held up his badge.

"Back up," he said. "*Back up.*"

The woman backed through the door and disappeared and Dobbs put his badge in his pocket and dropped three of the photos on the counter in front of Lyley's face. Dobbs hiked his wrist up further between his shoulder blades and Lyley gasped and let out a pathetic little fart, the only sound in the room besides the grit of broken porcelain beneath their feet.

"Harassment of a police officer's a felony, Joe. Didn't you know that? Haven't we talked about that?"

Lyley gasped, his lips pulled back from those stunted yellow teeth. "I don't know—I don't know what you're talking about."

Dobbs palmed the side of Lyley's head and slammed it against the counter. One of the photos stuck to his face and then fell facedown. His glasses hung from one ear.

"Proof of our sins?" Dobbs said, holding a photo in front of the man's eyes. "The Mark of the Redeemer, or some such horseshit? Isn't that right? Isn't that what you were trying to show me, Joe? When you dumped a bunch of dead fucking birds on my front steps?" He hiked Lyley's arm up again and Lyley loosed a watery scream, the cords in his neck rigid. The woman came out of the doorway again, her fists wrapped around the fabric of her sweater. She was crying. "Please," she said. "*Please.*"

"I did nothing," Lyley gasped. "I don't even know where in the world you live. It's a Day of Reckoning, is what it is. It's End Times. Terrible things are afoot. It's not *me!*"

"Enough."

Lyley said, "The Great Redeemer *has* marked us all, Sheriff," and even with his wrist hiked up nearly to his neck he seemed unable to keep a thread of sanctimony from creeping in.

"My wife and I, we pray, Sheriff. We give thanks to God and we wait for a great and terrible justice to be wrought upon the land. We expect it. For the sinners to be bathed in flame. We're ready. That's what we do, my wife and I." Dobbs realized he could break this arm and the other one and then do any number of other things to the man, could keep transgressing against him and finally, *maybe,* Lyley would admit to putting the birds there—but would it be true? Christ no.

Dobbs let go and stepped away from him, swiping his hand down his own mouth as he put the photos in his pocket and moved around the counter. In a voice that surprised him with its new timidity, with his hand resting on his own throat, Dobbs said, "If not you, then who, Joe? Tell me that. Who would do it? If you're so goddamned smart." His voice was plaintive, searching.

Lyley stood, put his glasses back on and cradled his arm to his chest. The woman in the doorway was still crying. He said, "You've been marked, Sheriff." Dobbs was only mildly surprised to see that his smile was a pitying one. He took great care in putting his glasses back on. "You are of particular consequence. Whatever's happening, whatever nature of the great unraveling, you're a part of it."

"You've made that clear, Joe. But *who* is doing this?"

Dobbs backed up toward the door, his fingers brushing the warm metal of the doorknob. He wondered if, in a way, wasn't he envious of Lyley? Was he actually envious of the man's conviction?

"Why, a beast of deliverance, Sheriff. It's God's arrow, and it's searching for you."

"Right."

"And you'll suffer for it, Sheriff," Lyley said. "You will. Through suffering we are shown God's path, and it's a hard path, but one that leads to righteousness and redemption."

And Dobbs, as he stepped outside and walked quickly toward the cruiser, as he looked up and down the street like some criminal, his heartbeat loud in his ears, was arrogant enough to think: *But why me?*

Haven't I suffered enough?

NICK HAYSLIP

The park was thronged with people, Hastings Street lined with vehicles on both sides. A crew of Tumquala men had arrived promptly at dawn and quickly built an impromptu stage and erected a tarp over it, moving with the focus and efficiency of a hit squad. Christ, it had still been dark out when a tribal lawyer had presented their permits to Hayslip. He'd waved his hand away and taken a sip of his coffee, feeling like his hangover was a cloud shifting and wavering over his head. "Hey, it's your show," he said. He and Fitzhugh had cordoned off both ends of the street with orange and white sawhorses. In spite of a sky that continually threatened rain, the morning had the taken on the joviality of a party. All save for the group of Tumquala tribal reps who stood grim-faced on the stage, as dour as funeral goers in their suits and dresses. Fitzhugh was at the north end of the blockade, motioning cars to move on and park the next street over. Hayslip made his way through the crowd, his hands on his gun belt, nodding at those always half-familiar faces. Tribal members circulated among the crowd, passing out leaflets about the rally and peopling a few booths near the stage to further dispense information; some enterprising souls were even selling fry bread and sweet corn from behind their own makeshift stands. Some people had brought boomboxes, and the sounds of both funk and solemn flutes comingled through the air.

"Those permits didn't say anything about food," Hayslip said as he finished his circuit and made his way over to the cordon where Fitzhugh stood. The air was rich with frying onions, grilled fish. It was ten in the morning! Nausea rippled its fingers along his guts. "And especially hot food. That fry bread? Some little kid gets hot oil dumped on him, who's that fall on? Us or them?"

"Forget about it," Fitzhugh said. "You want to be the guy that shuts that down?"

"I'm just saying."

"How's that gonna look for us, Nick? Use your head."

Hayslip toed the mud and looked around, his hands on his hips. He was so tired his eyes felt like chipped marbles housed in the poorly-formed sockets of his skull. "I think we should get more guys down here," he said. "Get Lonnie down here at least." Fitzhugh squinted at him. He was wearing a rain jacket with *Sheriff's Department* stenciled on the back, and one hand rested on the sawhorse at his waist. His face was pockmarked and jowled in the unpleasant morning light and he seemed to move a little more trep-idatiously than usual. But the look he gave Hayslip was clear as day, and Hayslip just couldn't understand what was with the *attitude* Fitzhugh was giving him. When, he wondered, did everyone start looking at me with such contempt? Jesus Christ. Fitzhugh with his pissy glances and Dobbs apparently convinced that Hayslip was leaving *massacred birds on his front porch.* That was the level of devotion he inspired these days. Christ, who was left to alienate? Food still held no appeal, and he could now trace the clear topography of his ribs through is shirt. His sleep was still infrequent and nightmarish. The trajectory of his life had long been strange, but now it seemed to lurch down jagged, lonely avenues he couldn't even come close to being able to foretell. He was running blind. When had that happened?

A group of children got up on stage and the crowd quieted, their music winking out. On the side of the stage a phalanx of Tumquala men and women sat down and began a low stuttering drumbeat with a selection of drums held between their legs or on their laps. The children wore long tunics, dyed turquoise and white, with tassels that hung past their knees. Some wore necklaces studded with feathers and painted reeds. The children began dancing as the susurration of the drums rose in both tempo and volume and one of the men's voices cut through the air, a voice heavy with—to Hayslip's ears—lamentation and loss. One child circled another and then pivoted and turned and circled still another, and the man's voice rose and began a call and response with the singing voices of the other drummers. Parents in the crowd held their children aloft on their shoulders. The dancing rose in momentum, and the singing in volume, and soon the dancing children were whirlwinds of blue and white, the drums loud enough to reverberate in Hayslip's chest, and all the men and women were singing as one, this wending ululation that left Hayslip awestruck and a little afraid, as if it were giving voice to some lost part of himself. The sound rose, the children whirled, and with a final thunderous close—every drummer with their hand flat against the skin of their drum—the children froze in place and the silence stretched out for a moment until the crowd roared its approval. The children's façade broke and they smiled as they trotted offstage to their parents, and up on stage, Leon Davies stepped to the podium while the rest of the Tribal Council reps sat in the seats the drummers had vacated. Still the applause went on. Davies wore jeans, a dress shirt and a tie beneath his corduroy sport coat, his hair tied back in a ponytail. Occasionally, one of the council members would lean over and whisper in another's ear, but other than that they were grim and silent.

Finally the applause died and Davies leaned into the mike and said, "Let's give those kids a hand, what do you say?" and the applause started up again.

The anthropologists had left the day before, and when Hayslip had asked if they were staying to watch the rally, Aiden had rolled down the window of the van and shrugged. "The school president can get into a pissing match with these guys if they want. Our professor and the head of the department have already given up." He scratched at his beard. "We did the best we could, you know?" And then Hayslip had tapped the sill of the van door and bid them all well and they had driven away. He couldn't imagine what would need to take place before he ever saw any of them again, and somehow that seemed to make the girl's bones—and the responsibility of them, their fate and caretaking—entirely his now, rather than the opposite. When it came to the Tribal Council, he was conflicted. On one hand, they were right—there were centuries of appropriation and genocide and all of that to contend with. On the other hand, he couldn't help but feel that Davies viewed the girl's bones as an idea. A matter of principle. Hayslip himself felt them walking up and down the hallways of his life, as if the girl was someone who could still be rescued.

Fitzhugh eyed him dourly over the sawhorse. His jaw was working a piece of gum hard enough to make the cords in his neck leap. "More guys? We don't need no more guys, Nick. This isn't the Democratic Convention. Shit'll be over in half an hour. Just relax."

"You have an issue with me that we need to talk about, Fitz?"

"Actually I do, Nick. You bet your ass. But now's not the time."

"Listen. If you have something you need to say to me—"

"Ladies and gentlemen," Davies said over the mike, drowning him out, "thank you all for coming. This is a great turnout, isn't it?" He had that same smooth cadence Hayslip remembered from when he'd served the anthropologists their cease and desist papers: the rich tone of a radio DJ or a politician, one intimately familiar with talking circles around any naysayers. It wasn't a matter of pure charisma, but goddamned if that wasn't a part of it. The crowd quieted again and their faces rose in unison toward the stage beneath the tent.

Fitzhugh spit his gum onto the gravel. "Looks like things are getting started, Nick. Better go work your section." He lifted his chin, nodded down the road. Somewhere in the crowd a kid started crying.

"What," Hayslip said, "you're freezing me out here? I hurt your feelings?"

"We'll talk about it later. Go do your job."

Hayslip looked at him for a measured beat of time. Fitzhugh eyed the crowd, turned his face away. "Fuck you, Fitz," Hayslip said, and walked away.

"I'd like to thank the citizens of Riptide," Davies said from the stage. He took the microphone in one fist and stepped away from the podium, stood there before the crowd with his fingers laced in front of his chest. "As well as the dedicated team of cultural anthropologists from the state university who, with care and precision, recently extracted the remains of one of our ancestors. From this exact spot, people. Right here"—and he held out an arm toward the carved, shunted hillside—"in Tumquala Park. Kind of funny, and kind of fitting isn't it? Their care and respect for our culture was immediately apparent, and I can tell you that the Tumquala people and the Tribal Council are grateful for it." Ripples of applause ran through the crowd. Hayslip walked the perimeter of the park, gently urging a few stragglers out of the street. Furious, he could feel sweat lining his brow, making his back itch.

When he saw the Finsters in the crowd he did a double take. It probably looked like something from a movie. It was the three of them midway through the crowd—the girl, the boy, and the father. Hayslip remembered seeing Gary Finster from the doorway of their house when he'd dropped the children off after the fight at the tennis courts. The man seemed to have lost weight in the interim, become more frail, even, in that short time. Every man who loved Melissa Finster seemed to wind up the worse for it. He still looked formidable, sure, but there were new creases around his eyes, the skin on his neck was loose. Even as Finster smiled down at something the girl signed, Hayslip felt something darkly joyous leap inside him like quicksilver at the man's humanity, how he was at the mercy of the same things that Hayslip was.

Sam Finster stood scowling next to his father, a red smatter of acne near his mouth. He caught Hayslip's eye and they locked gazes for a moment. Hayslip nodded and Sam looked away.

"We have issued a formal request," Davies said from the stage, "for the bones of what the local press is calling the 'Tumquala Girl.'" He walked around the stage holding the microphone as he spoke, and Hayslip was again reminded of a politician or a game show host. "It is our great hope, the tribe's hope, that the girl's bones be returned to us for a ceremonial burial. The experts have noted, have told us personally, that she died a tragic and unfortunate death and was buried right over there in an unmarked grave." He paused, looked down at the stage, his voice lowering. "We would like to do the right thing for her. The experts have also mentioned that this young girl was a possible victim of the Tumquala Massacre of 1858. I'm sure I don't need to remind anyone about that; it's a scar on our collective memory, isn't it? When nearly half of the Tumquala Indians residing on the reservation were slaughtered by state militiamen after protests regarding their living conditions." Murmurs ran through the crowd and Davies held up his free hand. "Now, I'm not blaming anyone. Those were different times. A hundred and twenty-five years ago, those were very different people than you and me. A whole different world. But just take a second and think of it. Just imagine it for a bit. What if it had been you and yours? If you'd found an ancestor's remains, one of your people. A *relative*, when you get down to it. Wouldn't you desire the same? Wouldn't you want someone from your family, *the blood of your blood*, to be given a proper burial? I'll tell you, we're interested in moving forward. We just want what's right, what anyone would want."

Hayslip edged his way through the crowd toward the family. Trina Finster stood next to her father, her mittened hand in his. She looked a little bored, her gaze traveling among the sea of legs around her. Why shouldn't she be bored? What was there down there to interest her? Melissa would have lifted her up, Hayslip thought. So that she could at least see the man speak, read his lips. He felt himself walk toward the Finsters on legs that weren't entirely his own. Through clutches of people, brief blips of cologne and cigarette smoke and fry bread, that toddler still crying. He thought wildly of just telling Gary Finster, walking right up to him and saying it: *I loved her. That or something close enough to it.* Through it all, Davies talked on and on, the PA system thumping in response when he pronounced *p*s and *b*s, the words booming against Hayslip's ribs. *Problematic. Bitterness. Prevent. Beliefs.* He elbowed his way through the crowd and people looked over their shoulders at him, frowning and angry, and then parted, their faces softening in apology once they saw his uniform.

Don't do this. Just leave them alone. Why can't you just leave her family alone?

He touched Gary Finster lightly on the arm. "Would you like to take her up front so she can lip read?"

Gary Finster turned and looked at Hayslip, each hand falling automatically on the shoulders of his children. His eyes were dark and unreadable beneath the brim of his cap.

"Your daughter. She's deaf, isn't she?"

"It's fine," Sam Finster said.

"She's deaf," Gary said. "Yeah." He looked from Sam back to Hayslip. From the podium, Davies kept on.

"I can lead you up front so she can lip read, if you'd like. Seems a shame she just has to stand here."

Gary's eyes skated from Hayslip's face down to the scars on his neck and back up. Even as worn and weary as he was, Melissa's husband still exuded that glowering restlessness that Hayslip had recognized in him straight away, that seemed so fierce inside his son as well. Just something within the both of them, compact and coiled, ready to spring.

"We're fine," Gary said. "There's no need."

Hayslip cleared his throat. The image came unbidden of this man fucking Melissa, this man's cock in her mouth. And beyond that, the schoolyard hurt of it—all their years together, a lifetime's worth of hidden intimacies between them. A family's worth.

"It's no trouble," Hayslip said. "No trouble at all." His voice couched somewhere between panic and a bright, unhinged joy.

Trina's eyes roved between them.

"We're fine," Sam said, stepping closer to his father.

"Do we know each other?" Gary Finster asked, and you'd have to be a fool to miss the challenge in it.

Hayslip's grin felt wolfish and crazed. "I dropped these guys off from school a while back."

"That's right," Gary said. "Well, we're fine, deputy."

"Great injustices took place," Davies said from the stage, his voice rising. "I don't think anyone will argue with that. But this—*this*—is an opportunity for us all to set things right. To correct, finally, one small, broken piece of the past."

A BRIEF ASIDE

-Excerpt from *Myths and Legends of the Coastal Indians,* transcribed from an oral tale and compiled by Meredith Briggs-Jenson (Western University Press, 1911, p. 77-79)

HOW THE *TAH-KEE-NA-TEH* CAME TO WALK THE LAND
(Tumquala legend)

Shortly before the whites came to this area, and many of the people took sick with disease and hunger, and there was a young brave who was mourning his wife. She had died in the wintertime and the brave's heart was heavy with sadness. He had cut his hair in mourning and the people had taken her body to the burial cairns, but the chief of the tribe had seen the brave's sadness and saw how it was like a lake with no bottom. He told the brave to go to the spawning grounds at the river where the tribe made their camps in summertime. "Go and see that things are as they should be," the chief said. The chief was wise and knew that the heart hurt less with the body's movement upon the skin of the world.

The brave agreed and left the camp. The people gathered and said to him, "tah-ne, tah-ne" ("We will see you" -Ed.). As he traveled, his heart lifted at seeing the country before him. Here was mountain and forest and river and ocean, all the places he had lived, the familiar ground. He saw beaver and elk and cougar and raven, along with the trees, which were turning their colors and shining. But still his heart was heavy like a rock sinking down in the water.

The first night on his travels, the young brave was asleep in his teepee. He heard a noise and peered outside of a hole in his blanket.

In the darkness, by the coals of his fire, he saw the face of his wife. He became afraid because she was a ghost come to visit.

"Do not be frightened," she said. "Come see me. I see that you are sad."

"No," the brave said. He was afraid!

"I am your wife," she said.

"You are a ghost!" the brave said.

The thing with the face of his wife grew angry then and called him many bad names as he hid inside his teepee with his knife. In the morning the brave discovered a dead bird by the fire, a raven. The bird lay in many pieces. The coals of his fire were scattered; winds and rain had come and he could find no tracks.

He traveled that day with much concern. He kept his fire brighter that night but woke to see his wife's face peering at him at the hole in his teepee. "Do not be afraid," she said. "Come see me."

"I will not," the brave said, looking for his knife in his blanket.

"Come outside," she said. "I see that you are sad. I want to talk to you!"

"You are a ghost," the brave said and kicked at the hole in the blanket and the thing with the face of his wife grew angry again and called him bad names again.

That morning, he saw that the coals of his fire had been kicked around once more and that there were many more birds in pieces nearby, including owl and gull, and the creature's tracks had been erased with the boughs of trees scraped across the ground.

The third night the brave was very tired. He built a large fire and slept hardly at all. But he did sleep. That night, he woke to feel a hand on his leg and he opened his eyes and there inside his teepee was the creature. It had the face of his wife and the body of a cougar and then, in a moment, the body of a fox.

"Come see me outside," the creature said. "I see that you are sad."

The brave tumbled out of his teepee with his club and his knife. The two of them circled the fire. "You are not my wife," the man said. "Who are you?"

The thing sat and licked its paw across the fire from him. "I am *tah-kee-na-teh*," it said, "the low walker, the Sorrow Eater."

"Why do you have the face of my wife?"

The *tah-kee-na-teh* smiled, which hurt the brave's heart even more, to see the face of his wife like that. "Because you are in mourning, and I am hungry."

"Go away," the brave said, and raised his club. "Don't see me again."

The *tah-kee-na-teh* hissed and started to call him bad names again but the brave found courage and chased it with his club where it ran into the forest.

That morning the brave saw still more dead birds around his teepee, and also saw that the ground around his fire was covered in the tracks of the cougar and fox and the handprints of a woman. He knew it had not been a dream.

And that is how the *tah-kee-na-teh* came to be, part of this world and part not, the thing that feeds on our sadness.

NICK HAYSLIP

He drove by his father's house after his shift and, in the scant moonlight, saw the old man standing bowlegged on the roof, knots of unlit Christmas lights in his hands like clusters of barbed wire. The tail of his robe flapped in the wind and showed off the skinny fenceposts of his legs, flattened against his pajamas. It was raining and his father's back was turned to him, and as Hayslip slowed to a stop, Ernie nearly lost his footing, his arms pinwheeling for balance. A hammer slid down the shingles, clanged off the aluminum ladder angled against the gutter, and fell to the lawn.

Hayslip got out of his car, afraid to call out, afraid the distraction would startle him. But then his father turned to stare down at the lip of the roof, the missing hammer. His mouth was drawn in a sour frown, hanks of hair blowing in his eyes. He saw Hayslip standing there on the street, frozen with his car keys in his hand.

His father held up the Christmas lights looped around his hands. "Probably should have untangled them first, I guess," he called out. His voice was a fragile thing shunted by the wind. It was almost bashful, the way he peered down at the tangled wires.

"Dad, come on down. Please."

His father dismissively waved a hand Hayslip's way—shooing a fly away. "These lights aren't going to hang themselves, Nick. I should've had them up a while ago."

"It's *raining.* I don't want you to fall."

"I'm not going to fall," Ernie said, even as he began cautiously scooting toward the edge of the roof.

Hayslip went to the ladder and held it flush against the eaves of the house, the sound of the rain loud as it fell on the hedges. He had to close his eyes for a moment when his father's leg appeared over the edge, gingerly searching for purchase. He was wearing *slippers*! Jesus Christ!

Inside, the house was the same as when he'd been there last, the same, essentially, since his childhood. Ordered and tidy, the kitchen sink devoid of dishes, the counters gleaming. His father's bed would undoubtedly be made. But lights burned in various rooms, even, he saw, the laundry room and the attic, as if his father needed these buoys to navigate the darkened spaces of the house. For comfort or guidance, Hayslip couldn't say.

Ernie looked like a drowned fucking rat, shivering in his soaked robe and pajamas. Hayslip started the shower, and when his father protested—even as he shivered, and drops of water rained down, trailing his passageway through the house—Hayslip shook his head and said, "I don't want to hear it." Gently enough, he pushed him into the bathroom with a towel and a change of clothes and, while steam began creeping from beneath the bathroom door, he went to the small bar in his father's den and poured himself a drink. The uncoiling heat in his guts calmed him and he stood watching beads of rain run down the front windows.

He heard the shower stop running and, eventually, heard his father rummaging around in his bedroom. The house was very quiet and Hayslip could hear the wind lean into the house and occasionally the rattle of the ladder against the eaves. His father stepped into the den in a sweatshirt and chinos, his hair standing up in puffed white thatches. So childlike in his frailty that Hayslip felt something like despair at how inadequately he was prepared for this, how rapidly their positions seemed to be changing.

"I was fine up there," his father said, shrewdly eyeing Hayslip's glass. "Just so you know."

"Kidding me? You'd have busted your ass up there."

"Oh, bull pucky."

"You'd have busted your ass, fallen off the roof, and laid out in the yard for who knows how long with a pair of busted legs or worse. Gone into shock, gotten pneumonia."

"Psssh."

"And then you'd have croaked, Dad. For Christmas lights. How's that sound?"

Ernie turned away, went and adjusted—minutely, so little that Hayslip couldn't even tell the difference—a frame on the wall. "The whole street's got their lights up, Nick. I'm gonna be the guy without lights up? 'He's just too old,' they'll say. 'Just doesn't have the same zing, old Ernie. He's lost it.'"

"Fuck the neighbors," Hayslip said.

His father's mouth knit itself shut, became a thin red line.

"You *are* too old, Dad. Call me, I'll put 'em up for you."

Ernie turned and there was something restorative in his anger, something that took years off his face and seemed to ratchet his spine up, remove some of that terrible hunched quality he had of late, as if his very confusion had been weighing heavy upon him. His voice was hard and direct, even as the finger he pointed in Hayslip's direction wavered and trembled. "And you, Nicholas, you're the man to be telling me how to live? That's what I'm hearing?"

"I'm worried about you."

"I'm worried about *you*. You look like a damned skeleton. Are you eating anything?"

"You're changing the subject," Hayslip said.

"I'm fine," Ernie said, shoving his hands in his pockets. "A man can put his Christmas lights up whenever he damned well wants. This is still America, last time I looked around."

"Jesus."

"Are you done lecturing me? Drinking my booze and lecturing me?"

"I'll put them up tomorrow," Hayslip said. "When it's not pissing rain. When it's light out."

"Don't bother," his father said stiffly. "I don't want to disrupt your busy schedule starving yourself to death. Or whatever in God's name it is you're doing."

"I'm just trying to help. I'm worried. The thing with the fridge, and now this. I'm worried."

His father's mouth quavered with anger. "A man my age has earned the right to be a little confused at times. I was tired. And as far as the G.D.'ed Christmas lights go, Sunny Jim, I'll be putting them up at my leisure, thank you much."

They hadn't always spoken like this. As a boy, his parents had been the totality of his world. Honest and benevolent gods, the two of them; his father's hands rough on his back as he guided Hayslip's bicycle down its wobbling sidewalk travels. His mother handing him the keys to their pickup as a birthday gift when he turned eighteen. What had changed between them? Vietnam? The job? Melissa? Or was it simply time doing what time did, drawing wider the chasms between people?

He sipped his drink and in the reflection cast back from the front window he saw his father standing next to him, ghostly but present, his hands still thrust in his pockets, his hair fluffy and uncombed. Both of them swallowed in their clothes, the shape of Hayslip's skull clearly visible beneath the skin. Looking at the two of them in the reflection, their resemblance was obvious. And he didn't know what to do. He didn't know how to help either of them. The world was narrowing.

SAM FINSTER

School let out for the break as the days inched toward Christmas. The weather turned even more sour, and the decorative lanterns tied to the power lines along 101 swayed in the wind, some of them coming loose and skittering down the highway, as if gleeful to escape. The Christmas tree atop the Hamm's warehouse shivered like some bowing gentry and occasionally people would see a worker up on the roof making sure it was lashed down tight. There were power outages that sometimes lasted through the night, people staring at the blank black faces of their clocks, the eyes of televisions suddenly gray as cataracts.

Gary would start fishing in a few days, but in a break between gear work, he and a couple of the other guys piled into a truck and headed out to the valley and cut down some trees, the group of them returning to town loud and triumphant as if they'd felled some army, the trees laying stacked in the truck bed like trophy animals. His father came back to their little house smelling of pitch, clapping the tree stump to the floor, both proud and possibly a little sad looking at the thing. Melissa's memory, of course, sat bright and heavy among them. Their first Christmas without her. Sam looked at the tree and back to his father, saw the look on his face. Like he was asking Sam if they were ready for it. "That's cool, Dad," he said. "It's a good one."

The next day, Gary screwed the big metal bolts into their Christmas tree stand and locked the tree in place. Sam was splayed out on the couch, eating a bag of Doritos and gazing, glassy-eyed, at *Fat Albert*. The break stretched out before him, the idea of school starting back up not even remotely on his radar. All this time.

Gary stood up and looked at him, crossed his arms. "Put your shoes on, bud."

Sam looked up at his father, his fingers covered in orange dust. He saw the look on Gary's face and did as he was told.

Gary met him outside with the paint scraper. Mist rose from the ground and dew gathered heavily enough on the limbs of trees to occasionally patter to ground. The sound of everything was close; a neighbor started their car and it sounded like it was right there in the yard with them. Gary laid a paint-spattered tarp at the front door. He handed Sam the scraper handle first and Sam's look must have been questioning and lost because Gary, gentler than Sam would have thought possible, put his hand on the back of his neck and said, "It's time."

He spent the morning scraping the black paint from the door, erasing the sigil of their family's mourning, those flakes falling dark and psoriatic onto the tarp. He felt tears gathering in his eyes and swiped his hand down his face as if he was sweating. It didn't take long before the black door was gone, and then Gary gave him some painter's tape and a gallon of white from the laundry room and Sam painted the door. Somehow, this was supposed to mean that their mourning was over or that they were moving beyond it. Sam felt that neither was true. He was finding ways of making the expanse of it navigable—it was no longer a hole his heart tripped into every minute, but that didn't mean he was fine. The three of them—he and his father and Trina—seemed these days like buoys with their lines cut. He felt, in her absence, that they were drifting further apart from each other.

Perhaps because of this, Gary seemed to have chosen the day as some kind of marker. By that afternoon he had enlisted Sam and Trina in making sugar cookies as their next project. They'd been Melissa's specialty and a family tradition. This big, rawboned man who had to scrub his hands free of machine oil with Lava and a wire brush each night. He started by putting on Melissa's apron and, for Trina's benefit, cracking an egg one-handed into his mouth to her delighted screams. But they forgot to add something—baking soda?—and the cookies came out of the oven pale and flat, with the brittle consistency of chalk. Trina stormed to her room, bawling, but with the timidity of a kitten had crept back out and sat on the couch, watching them as they adjusted the tree in its stand and trimmed the excess branches.

After Gary had pulled the boxes of decorations from the hall closet, Trina at first refused to help decorate. She sat, instead, on the couch, getting up every minute or two to change the channel and occasionally sneak a look to check on their progress. The two of them kept at it, laying on lights and tinsel that shimmered when the heater came on. By the time they began sifting through the boxes of decorations, Tina was sitting with her fists shoved in her armpits, frowning, not even pretending to watch television anymore. It was Saturday afternoon, one of those dark days that quickly blued to evening before it seemed hardly to start. Trina was still wearing her pajamas; she hadn't brushed her hair that day and it lay mounded in matted whorls on top of her head.

"It looks like you're getting dreadlocks," Sam said, putting a devil ornament on the tree. It was one of his favorites, one he'd made in first grade: resting in half a walnut shell and looped with a hank of yarn for hanging, a little devil baby tucked into a cradle.

No, I'm not, Trina signed. You're *getting dreadlocks.*

"Good comeback," Sam said. "You might want to think about brushing your hair today, Trina."

And you might want to think about not smelling like pee, she signed, and Sam laughed.

Indignation parked itself on Trina's face, and for a moment, it looked as if she might cry again. And then something loosened at her mouth, then her eyes, and moments later both of them were laughing and Gary came into the room with a cup of coffee, a small smile on his lips. He'd been, Sam knew, strengthening his coffee with brandy much of the day and had the look of a man committed to muscling through the day however he could. "What'd I miss?"

"Nothing," Sam said. "Trina said I smell like pee."

"Ouch." Gary sipped from his cup and nodded. "Well, if the shoe fits."

Trina rose from her spot on the couch and walked over to the boxes of ornaments. She picked one up, a small reindeer made from clothespins, a single googly eye on its face. The Cyclops Reindeer, Melissa had called it. Trina held it up for Gary's inspection and he smiled and said, "You made that one for your mom in, what was it, first grade?"

Kindergarten, she signed.

"Didn't catch that one, hon."

"Kindergarten," Sam offered.

Trina frowned in concentration as she selected a branch of the tree. She held up another ornament, a small glass star on a hook, and they went on like that. Gary calling out as best he could where each ornament had come from. This litany, this history of theirs. If Gary did not know it, Sam usually did. There were a large number of ornaments made for Melissa, or purchased for her by the children, and Gary had to make numerous trips to the bathroom where Sam knew he was blowing his nose and trying not to weep in front of them. Sam thought that maybe this was how it happened, how new memories were formed, how new traditions became bound in the bones of the old ones. That they could remember her this way and still move on. It was after one such trip that Gary went to the kitchen, came back and wordlessly handed Sam a beer. Sam looked at the bottle of Hamm's in his hand and then back at his father, who shrugged. "Put some hair on your tits, I don't know," Gary said gruffly, and then put a gold bulb on a limb without looking at his son again.

Later that night, Trina was taking a bath and Sam was smoking out on the stoop. There were still almost two weeks of vacation left and he wondered what he would do with it all. He felt the stirrings of all of this useless goddamned time yawning ahead of him, wondering how the adults did it, how they filled all the hours with work and worry and children and sound and light—all the trappings of living a life. He felt ageless and ancient and, yet, also like the years would never catch up to him. How did people stand it?

Gary's cheeks were drawn and sharp under the porch light. He took his hat off, rubbed at his forehead, and then pulled a pack of cigarettes out of his breast pocket and lit up, the cigarette smoke wreathing him in blue under the light. The night was impenetrable beyond the scrim of light on the porch. Somewhere out in the dark, rain pinged incessantly on a garbage can lid, frenzied and then metronomic. *Pingpingping. Ping. Ping. Ping.*

"Well, we fucked up those cookies pretty good," his father said, biting at a thumbnail, his cigarette next to his eye. It was that time of night when, if he'd been drinking, he got sentimental, the closest Sam ever came to seeing his father cry. The visits to the kitchen for brandy hadn't diminished throughout the night.

"It's no big deal, Dad."

"I know this is hard, Sam."

"We made it," Sam said. "It's just another day. The tree was good."

Gary smiled. "The tree was pretty good, wasn't it?"

"Yeah."

"Thanks for doing the door."

"Sure."

"I just . . ." Gary cleared his throat. "I just want things to be good for you guys."

Sam kept his cigarette curled in his palm—he was still unused to smoking in front of his father—and blew his smoke away from the light, out into the darkness. "Maybe we should try new stuff. New traditions. Maybe we should go somewhere else next year, you know?"

His father was silent, and Sam turned, worried that he had angered him, had hurt him somehow, but Gary was looking out at the backyard and nodding slowly. They smoked some more, and finally he said, "Maybe you're right about that," and dropped his cigarette where it hissed in the coffee can. He stepped inside with the rusty croak of the screen door banging behind him. Out in the dark night the rain went *Ping. Ping. Ping.*

• • •

Christmas Day began with Trina sneaking into his room while he slept and nearly squashing his balls into oblivion when she leapt on him in bed. "Jesus, Trina!" Sam curled into an apostrophe, hoping to avoid the slow ache that threatened to blossom into fire in his guts.

Trina rolled off the bed and looked around, her nose working like a rabbit's. She tapped Sam on the leg to make sure he was looking at her and then signed, *It stinks like a butt in here. You need to do some laundry.*

Sam took his hands away from his stomach and signed, *You need to fuck off.*

Trina's eyes grew wide and her mouth dropped in a merry O. *I'm telling Dad!* She practically skipped out of his room and Sam heard his father say, "It's too early in the morning, baby. I can't think right now. Can you just say it?"

Her voice husky and gleefully scandalized, she said: "Sam told me to fuck off."

Gary sighed. "Hold this," he said, and then came the tread of his father's boots through the kitchen and down the hall. A moment later he peered in Sam's doorway; Sam by this time having graduated to a sitting position, hunched over and breathing slowly. (The fug of his laundry was admittedly pretty intense.) Outside, a limb scraped against the window like a squawking bird.

"Riddle me this: did you just tell your nine-year-old sister to fuck off? On Christmas Day?" Gary's hair was sleep-flattened, the blood vessels in his eyes visible from across the room. The recipient of one of his stronger hangovers, Sam assumed.

"She comes in here and jumps on me, smashes my balls, I'm sleeping—"

"You're grounded. One week."

"Dad, come *on*. Are you *kidding* me?"

"I'm not kidding you. And you're not going out on New Year's Eve. You're not doing dick until 1984."

Sam leaned forward, intimate, man-to-man. Quietly, he said, "Listen, she jumped on my nuts, Dad. It seriously hurt." *Be reasonable.*

Gary yawned and pushed himself from the doorway with both arms.

"I don't care if she played hockey with 'em, Sam. Makes no difference. You don't talk to your sister that way."

"I'm eighteen years old, Dad."

Gary turned back to him and smiled. "Meaning what, Sam?"

"Meaning I'm a little old to be getting grounded, don't you think?"

"You're still in school and you still live under this roof. And I know for a fact you're too old to be talking to your sister like that. That's what I know."

Gary managed breakfast—Lucky Charms, bacon and toast, even orange juice, which Sam had to admit was akin to a seven-course meal, given his father's usual culinary inclinations. As they ate at their leaning kitchen table, Trina kept sneaking longing glances at their Christmas tree. Beneath the limbs lay a surprising amount of gifts. Above the television set hung four stockings, sagging and angular, each of their names written in glitter. They had reached an unspoken consensus when hanging ornaments on the tree the night before: their mother's stocking would be hung along with everyone else's. Trina had stuffed it full of extra ornaments to give it shape.

Can we open presents now?

"Finish your breakfast," Gary said, his jaw working. He held his spoon like a toddler, gripped in his fist, elbow cocked. KRPT played low in the living room, Christmas schmaltz. The colored lights on the tree reflected themselves in tiny, warped galaxies on their glasses of juice. Sam had to admit it was nice.

I'm done.

Gary pointed with his spoon. "I see a piece of toast and some bacon there. Don't let that monkey die in vain."

What?

Sam nodded and tapped the table to get Trina's attention. He was still a little pissed at both of them—where had the beer-giving father gone? Why the hell had this stern one suddenly decided to make an appearance?—but this was too hard to resist. "Yeah, you didn't know?" he said. "Dad bought some orangutan bacon off some guys on the boat."

Trina's eyes cast suspiciously among them. She signed one-handed, wiggling the fingers of one hand in front of her breastbone, her eyebrows skyward. *Ha ha. You're so funny.*

"Oh yeah," Gary said. "You didn't notice it tasted a little different? This is *extra special Christmas orangutan bacon*. Twenty-two bucks a pound, Trina, so eat up."

Trina sighed. Nine years old and she sounded seventeen, exasperated with the world. *Orangutan*—she had to finger-spell it—*is an ape, not a monkey. We studied them in World Geography.*

• • •

The floor soon after became a riot of wrapping paper and contoured Styrofoam shells, plastic and bows, bright ribbons unfurled and gleaming with light. Melissa had been the fussy one among them, the paper-folder and bow-keeper; the Finsters now unwrapped their gifts like dervishes.

Before the presents were opened, Sam had pulled out their careworn VHS copy of *A Charlie Brown Christmas* (the captioned version) that they had recorded off of the television, with its stuttering five or ten seconds of commercials and then the stuttering returns five or ten seconds into the program, someone always a bit too late on pressing the *Record* button. Trina would cast reverential glances at the screen in between their rounds of opening presents and here, at least, they still clung fiercely to tradition. Melissa may as well have been out on the back porch smoking a cigarette for the nearness Sam felt toward her, and he realized this was one of the ways that time could hurt you and help you simultaneously.

Gary had done surprisingly well in the gift department, and it occurred to Sam to wonder where he'd found the time. Sam got a battery charger and some AA batteries for his Walkman. He also got a pair of black Converse (Trina looked fussily over his shoulder at these, a pair of new and naked Barbies in each fist) and, most surprisingly of all, a pair of cassettes. Sam looked at Gary like he'd pulled a rabbit from his mouth or informed Sam they'd be moving to Moscow. His father had actually laughed out loud. The tapes were brand new and still in their shrinkwrap: *Rocket to Russia*, by the Ramones, and Motörhead's *Ace of Spades*.

"Where'd you even *get* these?"

His father balled up a piece of green wrapping paper and tossed it toward Trina, who batted at it with a Barbie. "Your mom kept a list, actually. One of the guys had to go get a motor part up in Portland, so I had him stop in a record store up there."

"That's so awesome, Dad. Thank you," Sam said. "Thanks a lot." Suddenly not entirely trusting his own voice.

"Those Ramones guys look like a bunch of space aliens," Gary said. "You should listen to regular-guy music, Sam. Aerosmith. Van Halen. Now those are real bands. Those dudes can play."

Flipping the cassettes over, reading the track listings and hardly listening, Sam said, "Sure thing, Dad. I'll get right on that."

Trina had gotten her new Barbies and a few outfits for them. Another box revealed more Judy Blume and Lois Lowry books, their sale tags mostly rubbed off of the covers. *The Wolf in the Basement. Tiger Eyes. Superfudge.*

Thank you so much, Dad. Trina rose onto her knees from her spot on the floor and hugged Gary, her side-ponytail poking him in the face.

"Are those good ones?"

Yes. Real good.

Gary drank his coffee and they watched the Charlie Brown tape again from the beginning. Trina was enrapt. She put one of her Barbies inside her shirt, the arms jutting out at right angles from her collar. *It's like she's my kangaroo baby,* Trina signed to each Sam and Gary separately.

They cleaned up the mess, Gary throwing everything in the trash. Sam cringed, knowing his mother would have insisted on saving at least half of the paper, meticulously peeling the tape from the ribbons and bows. They made grilled cheese sandwiches for lunch, and when Trina dipped one of her Barbie's faces into her tomato soup as if she was a horse drinking from a trough, Gary made her put her dolls in her room. When she came back, Gary went into the kitchen and opened a beer and when he came back to the table, he frowned and made a big show of looking around the room as if something had gone missing. "Actually, I think I might have seen something in the washer for you guys."

What is it? In the washing machine?

"I think so," Gary said. "I can't quite remember. You should go look."

Trina ran toward the back of the house. Gary nodded at him. "You too, bud."

Sam followed his sister to the back of the house, feeling the spongy give of the floor beneath his new shoes. The laundry room was narrow and drafty. Shelving hung from the walls, full of brackets and planks of particleboard, storage for Gary's tools. Leaning stacks of plastic-netted lawn chairs, their legs mottled with rust. A Styrofoam cooler missing its lid. A trio of lethal metal-tipped lawn darts. The laundry room was the black hole where half-broken things went to be forgotten, the last stronghold before they were thrown away or taken outside and leaned against the house, the Finster equivalent of exile. Opposite the shelving, the washer and dryer sat behind a pair of warped wooden accordion doors. Trina went over to the folding doors and opened them.

Resting on top of the machines and leaning saucily on its kickstand was a red and white bike, a Huffy. Trina squealed and from down the hall Sam heard his father laugh. Sam helped Trina muscle the bike down to the floor. Which was when Sam finally spied, hanging from the inside doorknob, a leather jacket. Gleaming black, shot through with zippers, brand new.

"Holy shit," Sam said.

"You been wanting a jacket for a while," Gary said from the doorway, his fists tucked in his armpits.

Sam hefted the jacket while Trina ran her hands over the frame of the bike with the same reverence she would a pony. The jacket was heavy.

"Thank you, Dad. I can't . . . This is so awesome. Thank you."

Gary did this thing where he grimaced and smiled at the same time. His version of joking. "I guess I'd rather you look like one of those Ramones guys than a hippie any day. Lesser of two evils and all that shit, right?"

• • •

Their mother's friend Belinda came over later that night. Trina had already crashed on her bike in the driveway multiple times, studding her knees with bits of gravel and crying until Gary finally told her it was too dark to continue and they came inside. Sam tried to remember that fearlessness, that willingness to struggle against inertia and velocity no matter how badly your wheels wobbled, how badly you swerved. Gary greeted Belinda warmly but awkwardly—they had known each other for years, but Melissa had always been the anchor point between them. Yet Trina was thrilled to see her and the two of them sat together on the couch as she regaled Belinda with the many adventures of her day, proudly showing off her bandaged knees. Belinda was one of the few people that Trina made a conscious effort to speak out loud to. Unable to help herself, Belinda would occasionally grab Trina in a one-armed hug or lean over and kiss her on the crown of her head—Belinda, Sam knew, missed Melissa as much as any of them did. Gary busied himself in the kitchen and Sam sat at the kitchen table listening to his Walkman, nodding his head to the staccato rhythms of *Rocket to Russia,* songs like gunfire wrapped in bubblegum. The new and comforting weight of his leather jacket, the smell of it, the sense of being ensconced in it already felt like a part of him. He felt like a badass, truthfully, or a little closer to being one, and couldn't wait to show Toad.

Belinda said something to him from her spot on the couch. He took his headphones off. "What's that?"

She said, "You look like you should be in the movies, Sam." Trina lay against her shoulder, her eyes drooping with sleep. Belinda smiled. "But like a bad guy, don't worry."

"Like Jeffrey Ramone," Gary called out from the kitchen.

"Joey," Sam called back. "Joey Ramone, Dad."

"Hmm," Belinda said, squinting. "I don't know. Maybe. I was thinking more like Eddie Van Halen or something. You know, like a *rocker*."

From the kitchen came Gary's laughter. "See, what did I tell you, Sam? Get with the program, man."

DAVE DOBBS

Had she been alive, he'd have confessed to her. What he'd done to Joe Lyley. He'd have been unable to keep it from his face. It had gone against everything he'd propped himself up against his entire life, and yet he'd done it, felt the tensile give in the man's arm, driven his skull against the counter. Threatened and abused the man. Wielded his power like a club. And why?

Because he was afraid.

It was New Year's Eve and he had taken advantage of one of the rare luxuries his position afforded him: a night off on a holiday. He shouldn't have; Riptide's statistics for *everything* shot up like mercury in a heat wave on nights like these—domestic violence, assaults, drunk driving. But since finding the birds, since doing what he'd done to Joe Lyley, Dobbs felt a ragged stitch coming loose inside himself. Felt a great bolt of shame too, yeah, and while he was not a superstitious man, he felt that this year marked an ending, and when he moved past it, it would signify something. He would place himself out of harm's way tonight and the next day would mark a new year. A new start. Dobbs sat on the couch with Lea's head in his lap, his living room positively incandescent with light, and watched an ageless Dick Clark grin like a dentured lunatic beneath the shimmering apple in Times Square.

The look you would give me now, June. You would give me that look of yours and I would deserve it. That and more.

"It wasn't unfounded," he said to the television set. "Goddamn it, it wasn't." The dog's ears twitched and settled at the sound of his voice. "Man brings a dead bird into my office, dumps it on my desk. *In pieces.* Muttering about the End Times, for Christ's sake. What was I supposed to think?"

He had started doing this recently, defending himself. Speaking out loud, petitioning the walls. When had it started? The June that lived in his head tut-tutted, a little disappointed in him, and said *The better question might be: had he begun doing things that needed defending?* At the very least, he had done away with June's sad night-time effigy of pillows and nightgowns; he lifted the old dog into bed with him now, and they both seemed more contented for it, snoring and farting their collective way through the night. But the photos, still in his jacket pocket, were irrevocable proof of *something*. Someone was cultivating this, was responsible for what was happening to the town.

"I was pissed," he said, the rum igniting in his guts like pooled gasoline. "You can't . . . you can't do that to a person. Dead birds on a porch? It's sick."

Ghost-June, *mind*-June, yes, the June of his lovesickness and loss who followed him, who listened, who judged without damning (mostly), who was patient with him—even she would have gazed at him over the tops of her glasses with her no-bullshit look. This was pandering.

"I was afraid," he admitted, and held up his drink and peered at the television through the prisms of glass. A commercial came on, and spied through the tumbler, it was simply a loose collection of colors that shifted and bent. Dobbs thumbed the remote, the television winking out to a pale white star that faded away to nothing.

As soon as he did it the phone rang with a shrill, piercing cry that reverberated through the house, and both he and the dog started, Lea turning her marbled eyes toward the kitchen and chuffing softly. Dobbs's heart was a fierce and fluttering starburst in his chest.

He rose on unsteady feet and walked into the kitchen as the phone rang again and again in that terrible jarring sound. "This is Dobbs," he said when he picked up. He cleared his throat and fished in his shirt pocket for his glasses. "This is Sheriff Dobbs." The clock above the stove said it was 11:39.

"Sheriff," Deb said. Her voice was a curious mixture of shakiness and solemnity, and of course, he should have known right away: no good news ever came from a midnight call. Unease coiled with the rum in his blood.

"What's up, hon?"

Deb said, "We got a real issue here, Sheriff."

"Okay," Dobbs said. He looked down and was surprised to find that he had brought his empty glass with him to the kitchen. He put it in the sink with a clatter.

"It's out at the turnaround, down on the beach. You know that little cove tucked away there?"

Dobbs knew it—a little inlet where bonfires weren't visible from the turnaround or from the ramp. For decades, Riptide's teenagers had partied down there, and his deputies, the good ones, made it a regular spot on their patrols. He hadn't been lying to Lyley about that.

"Yeah, I know it, Deb," Dobbs said, a little irritably. "Of course." Trying to quell his growing unease with crossness. But he closed his eyes and took a breath and said more softly, "That first one about a half mile down from the ramp? With all the boulders?"

"That's the one."

"So what do we got? A fight down there?"

A pause, and then Deb exhaled and said, "Some kids just found a body, Sheriff. It looks like it just happened too. Lonnie Ridges just radioed in from the scene."

Dobbs pressed the heel of his hand against his eye socket, battling the way his head wanted to run loose with the rum. At the same time, he felt a curious sense of things locking into place. That was just pure habit, a lifetime of doing the job, and something to be thankful for. The inevitable check-lists began to unscroll before him. Secure the scene. Gather evidence. Get statements from witnesses. Things fell into place inside him. But goddamn, he shouldn't have drank tonight. He should've known better. "I assume we aren't talking about natural causes here, Deborah?"

"No, sir. Doesn't appear that way. Lonnie says it's real bad."

"Okay. Get everyone down there. Every unit we've got. Part-timers too. Get someone to block the turnaround entrance, and get folks stationed from Slokum Beach down to the South Beach jetty. Call folks from the volunteer list if you need to and get cars stationed along Hastings Street, see if anyone comes out of the woods. If you still need people call Waldport and Lincoln City for extra bodies."

"Everyone's gonna be drunk, Dave."

"Christ, don't I know it. I'll call the Staties right now and ask them to send a K-9 unit. I'm serious, Deb, I want this shit locked down. Do we know who it is? The body?"

She was a professional, Deb was. There was a tremor in her voice, but hardly any trepidation at all. "We don't, Sheriff. Apparently it's real hard to . . . Lonnie said you can hardly even tell it's a person."

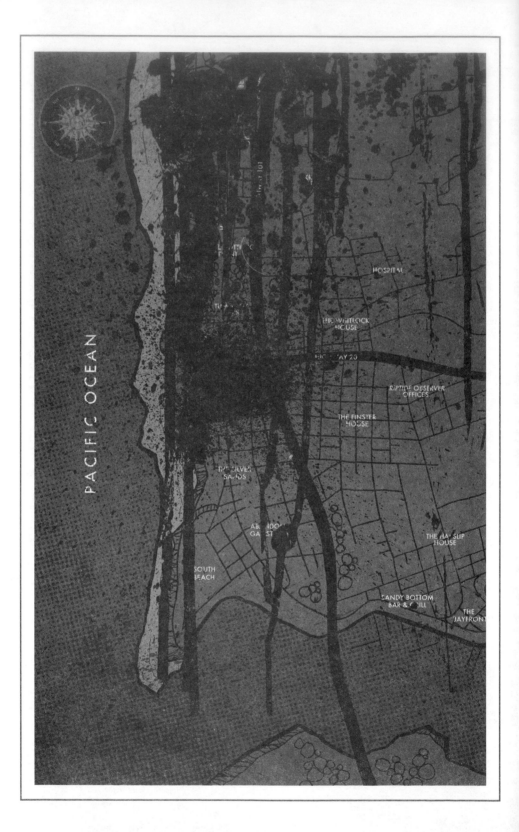

RIPTIDE, OREGON

January 1984

FOUR

a brief aside: the bad death of ada two trees • how many funerals is too many funerals? • walking papers • hayslip visits the res • to paint your door in mourning • fisticuffs at the sandy bottom

A BRIEF ASIDE

The morning of January 11, 1868, was cold, damp and mist-heavy, like a cloud had settled on the skin of the earth. One of those Oregon mornings.

Ada Two Trees, nine years old and the only child of Otto Bordst and Louise Two Trees, was running for her life. She ran through the woods with branches whipping across her cheeks and the air in her lungs ripping in and out beneath her shirt like hot stitches. Greenery like a blur as she ran. She ran for miles, she ran for hours. She ran through the woods and the morning gave way to afternoon and then to dusk and finally into the night. She ran and rested and ran and rested. She ran toward the scent of the sea and away from the man with the rifle, away from their little home with its two real leaded windows and the tiny shoots of a cucumber plant she had been growing in a little tin on the windowsill. She ran through scrub brush and among the lashing tree limbs that left welts on her arms and rills of chilled water running down her collar. She leapt over streams, past clots of poison oak and tangles of sticker bushes, over falls of dead jack pines stacked like bleached bones, across carpets of jagged stones and beds of browned pine needles gone soft as clouds. She ran until her feet were punctured and bleeding. She ran until finally the pain in her side became too great and exhaustion trembled the edges of her vision and then she hid in the spongy earth between two fallen trees, the ground fragrant with rot, buoyant with give, the gray flesh of the trees covered in moss and clusters of tiny white and orange mushrooms. She pulled clutches of ferns over herself and lay there listening to the sound of the forest around her.

The man had been astride his piebald horse, his form warped through the cabin window, when she watched him shoot her father in the face. He'd laughed as Otto Bordst had tumbled to the ground, inert, a suddenly broken doll. Her mother had grabbed her, shoved her through the other window in their little house, her voice hushed and bright with panic.

Ada wiped tears away beneath her bed of ferns, heard the chorus of dripping rain above her as the world slowly darkened to night. Nine years old, Ada Two Trees, and close enough to the ocean to smell its brine and tang in the air.

• • •

The man who had killed her parents in the dooryard of their home was a woefully hungover Indian hunter named Timothy Long. Initially a prospector, Long had only recently discovered that a lifestyle of unhindered travel, government bounties, and sudden black flurries of violence greatly agreed with him. He had heard it on good authority (a fellow drunkard in a Riptide tavern the previous night) that a woman named Louise Two Trees was actually a full-blood squaw who had, years earlier, escaped the reservation and was now apparently living in the woods without proper papers. Sitting next to him in the bar, the flickering oil lamps thankfully obscuring the majority of grime covering the man's countenance, he claimed that Louise Two Trees had spent the past fifteen years gallivanting around with her kraut husband and kicking out any number of half-breed babies, the whole lot of them living in filth out in some squalid cabin in the woods, the children so depraved and brain-scarred they ate their own waste and the bark off trees. "If it was me and I had the go ahead from the governor," the man leered through a cloud of body odor so severe it actually made Timothy's eyes water, "I'd be putting a plug in that bitch promptly and dropping her skullcap off at the Sheriff's office. If it was me and I was a man interested in a paycheck."

This information was, like most things, mired in half-truths. For one, Ada Two Trees was an only child. More importantly, Louise Two Trees had her papers. They had been issued to her by the state of Oregon and signed by David E. Muyner, acting Indian Agent of the Tumquala Reservation. Otto had been a frequent visitor to the Tumquala trading post and Muyner, impressed with the man's humility and work ethic, had willingly passed Louise on beyond the walls of the reservation. If only more could be like those two, the Agent had mused more than once. Willing to eschew the dark animism of the Indians' ancient ways, in exchange for hard work and belief in family and home. So, yes, she most certainly had her papers. And as far as it concerned Ada Two Trees, most of the men in Riptide knew of her only vaguely, and not by name but rather simply as one of those young *sitkum siwash* (a not-so-nice term in the Chinook jargon that meant half-breed) gals who populated a small number of homesteads in the dark nooks and crannies along the coast. All things considered, Long should have grown suspicious after his barmate had archly suggested, "Them kids ain't worth nothing, but that Louise, you'd get you some guv'ment money for her scalp sure as shit. I'd say that information's worth a drink, don't you? At least one, maybe two." But Long had also been morbidly intoxicated, and had simply nodded his agreement and raised his hand for the bartender's attentions. Sometimes, we only hear what we want to hear.

In roughly eighteen months Timothy Long had gathered the scalps of eleven unchristian and paperless Indians. The states of Oregon and California had paid him between ten and fifty dollars for each of these, and Oregon, at that time, was offering fifteen dollars for the scalp of a proved-rogue Indian. That morning, it had gone like this: Timothy had gotten directions to the cabin, and at first light, a hangover's terrible fangs still stuck in his head, he had stood in the dooryard and called Otto out of his home. Timothy managed to sound jovial as hell, in spite of his headache, greeting the man like an old friend. Dawn had shown blue through the fragmented sky between tree limbs as he shot Otto through the forehead with his revolver from fifteen paces away, astride his horse. Otto still had the straps of his coveralls around his hips when he died. Louise began screaming inside the cabin, a hot and bright sound that reverberated in the tiny rooms, and Long dismounted smartly and fired another round into Otto's head as he stomped his way happily into the doorway of the cabin, where little Ada's legs could be seen wriggling out the far window. Louise came at Long like a dervish, howling and mad, a cooking knife gleaming in one fist. Another shot rang out in the tiny room, a curl of flame licking from the barrel, and Timothy Long walked over to the corpse with a spring in his step. Fifteen dollars was a fine payout for a minute's worth of work.

It was only after scalping Louise and ransacking the little house that he found her papers in a wooden chest beneath the bed. A flurry of cursing ensued. He rode back to town, fury at a slow boil— never even coming close to following little Ada. All this happening while she ran and ran, certain that he was after her.

That evening she rose from her bed of ferns and ran again toward the sea. It had been long dark by the time she made it through the scrim of pine and fir trees to the cliff side, the beach glimmering below her. The moon hung low and bright and lit the ocean swells like sculpted white fire. The sand glowed. She made her way carefully down the cliff, holding onto exposed roots and stones for purchase, and it was only when she had made it down to the beach, where the sand was hard-packed and cool, where she could see around her in all directions, that she sat down and wept—loud, wracking sobs—for all that she had lost.

• • •

Perhaps it could be argued that the *tah-kee-na-teh* is no more to blame than a bullet fired from a gun is to blame. That we should question, perhaps, the rifleman instead. That it is fulfilling a simple purpose, less than an animal, even, and no more capable of awareness or rationality than a lung or a blinking eye or a trigger. That it was simply doing what it had been created to do.

And yet how much did *intent* matter to Ada Two Trees right then, with moonlight gleaming off the ocean surf like sparks from a fire and her heart feeling like it had been rent in pieces? Did *blame* really matter when she looked up and saw what suddenly shared the beach with her, that sinuous form slinking toward her, skulking and low to the ground? Did it?

• • •

Timothy Long traveled back to Riptide and, that evening, found the man who had told him about Louise the night before. The man was sitting in the same bayfront tavern, on the same stool, drinking, perhaps, from the same glass. He certainly smelled the same.

Timothy threw Louise's scalp down on the bar in front of the man, and next to it the signed papers illustrating her freedom.

"Get that shit out of here," the bartender said. "Good lord."

Timothy said to the man at the bar, "You owe me fifteen dollars, I'd say."

The man took a drink. He looked at the papers as he wiped a ghost of foam from his mustache. "I never learnt to read, myself."

"Well," Timothy said, "you can pretty fucking well imagine what it says."

The man nodded. "I guess I can. I guess I'd say that's about right. I was just telling you what I'd heard. Making conversation, you know."

"Means not a good goddamned whit to me," Timothy said. "You owe me fifteen dollars and the price of a drink or we'll have an issue momentarily."

"Okay, then," the man sighed, reaching into the bag on his hip.

At the same moment, on a stretch of beach very near what would later become known as Wolf Point, Ada Two Trees looked up from the cave of her hands and saw a thing in front of her that, put simply, made the eye unsure of itself. This animal coming toward her, that slunk with its four legs low to the ground, this thing that slalomed among the low rises of dunes, the fur on its back scalloped in whorls of matted gore.

And as it fell upon Ada Two Trees, it made a joyous and gleeful sound, so akin to a human voice as to be practically indistinguishable from one.

A man named Robert Meachum, the owner of a feed and grain store on Riptide's growing main street, was out for his morning walk when he found Ada. (What was left of her.) Meachum went running for the sheriff with bile hot in his throat as Timothy Long woke up hungover in a rooming house near South Beach around the same time. How the world hands us ruination by the handful, and in a million small ways. Long would never read the article published in the *Riptide Observer* a few days later, having moved on further down the coast. Sheriff Watts and his deputies would wind up burying the little girl in the woods above the cliffs; the Tumquala Massacre would take place less than a week later, and alongside the state militia, they would have their hands full quelling a goddamned Indian uprising; there was no inquiry into the girl's identity.

For the rest of his life, Robert Meachum, who had discovered Ada's body, would, on infrequent but oft-sleepless nights, with the darkness beyond the window glass spun out seemingly forever, consider this: how, at its best, the world seemed indifferent to sorrow and pain and, at its worst, seemed an engine that ran on it like fuel.

SAM FINSTER

Rain on the church roof made a sound that was distant but ferocious, like a giant radio dial spun to static above them. The same cloying stink of perfume and flowers, scents almost common to him now. And the same odd collusion of hard-scrabble people dressed in their finest clothes. The priest was an old, wizened gnome of a man with a hawk-like nose and the weight of years bending his spine, a little man in black curled like a question mark at the pulpit, a man Sam had never seen before. A man expected to know what he was talking about, to speak regarding someone he'd never met before.

It was the same church that Sam's mother's funeral had been held in. Many things were the same then as now: Sam wore the same suit, the coat too small and riding up past the knobs of his wrists. Trina wore the same dark blue dress and dark stockings. His father wore the same charcoal, broad-shouldered suit he'd gotten married in, his hair slicked back, his tired, red eyes blinking owlishly.

"Ours is not to wonder," the priest said, his hands visibly trembling around the edges of the lectern. There was an occasional cough behind them, once a child crying out and being shushed. "Pain comes with loss, friends. The terrible loss of one so young." The priest looked down at his notes, cleared his throat. "Some would say he was troubled. Others—his friends and family—would attest to his generosity, his fierce loyalty. If you were his friend, there was little Todd wouldn't do for you." A lady behind Sam let out one honking gasp that would have been funny anywhere else. The old man paused again, and Sam wondered if something like this had become rote for him over the years, the mouthing of these same platitudes that might as well have been drawn from a hat for their minute interchangeability.

Sam himself felt gutted, an automaton consisting of heart and lungs and little else. A wind-up toy that went from place to place with no point to any of it.

They had found Toad's body in the little tucked-in cove past the turn-around. He'd been making the rounds among the New Year's Eve bonfires up and down the beach and was found only because of his bright white tennis shoes. They had been his Christmas gift from his uncle, the only thing really visible among the clotted shadows, the boulders and driftwood. Sam had heard the stories: every other part of Toad had been gored and drenched in blood, black and unrecognizable. Entire limbs missing. Trunk eviscerated. Only the shoes visible. He didn't know what was true and what was just a story, but the police hadn't even been sure it was Toad until his uncle was able to identify a homemade tattoo on this shoulder.

"We have much to be sorry for," the priest said, licking his lips. Sam thought—no, he knew—that Toad would have laughed at the man. "It is impossible for us to see the great and overarching will of God, his plan for us. Not in such an act as this. Not in the taking of such a young man, in such a painful manner. But rest assured, friends: *his soul is at home now.*" The priest waited, met gazes throughout the crowd. "The body is but a vessel. We are a part of the material world, with all its trappings and joys, but for an instant."

More coughing. Trina frowned at the priest as if she was furious at him or trying to divine some truer meaning from his words. Sam recognized a lot of kids from school in the pews, even some teachers. Buck-toothed boys with dustings of mustaches who surreptitiously pulled at starched shirt collars, and girls who didn't normally wear dresses allowing them-selves the luxury of tears at the funeral of a boy they hardly knew, a boy they had since childhood made fun of or ignored. Toad's uncle sat next to Trina. He sat with his big chapped hands in his lap and jailhouse-green ink creeping from his sleeves, the corners of his handlebar mustache ghosted with nicotine stains. He stank of dope and thrummed with heartache, his reddened eyes looking at the floor as he occasionally ran his fingers down his mustache. *Vacant.* The same difficulty came to Sam, now, as it did when his mother had died—just the sheer impossibility of reconciling the living person with the remains. He tried to picture Toad's remnants situated in the box. Resting on the felt—the velvet, whatever it was—there was a reason it was a closed casket. His body piecemealed and put back together, a pale and stiff man-doll full of more stitchwork than stuffing now. He marveled again at the idea that they were soon going to put his friend in the ground and leave him there forever.

After the ceremony, people filed out and paid their respects to Mr.

Whitlock on the way to their vehicles. Sam stood smoking a cigarette next to his father's truck. Wind pulled the smoke from his mouth and rain pattered smartly against his leather jacket (Gary hadn't let him wear it inside the church.) He traded nods with passing kids and the occasional teacher who frowned at the cigarette in his hand but said nothing. Sheriff Dobbs walked up to him, looking strange in his suit and tie. Just an old man in a terrible suit.

"I'm sorry to hear about your friend," Dobbs said. He seemed almost bashful, frowned down at his feet. "We're doing everything we can."

"Okay. I know."

Dobbs seemed poised to say something more but, instead, nodded once, grimacing as he rattled his keys in his hand and walked away. Kenny Pritchard walked by with a group of younger boys following him, a few of them scooping pinches of dip from their chew cans as soon as they exited the church doors. Kenny had tucked his shirt in and even worn a tie. Most surprisingly of all, he raised his chin at Sam as he passed.

"Hey," he said quietly.

"Hey," Sam said, the confusion likely apparent in his voice. Toad, Sam thought, you're letting me skate here. Even Kenny Pritchard's giving me a pass. If this keeps up, Jordana's gonna come by and offer me a mercy hand job or something.

He'd heard the talk. It spread like a virus throughout the school, quick and efficient; a game of Telephone that mutated and grew more outlandish with each telling. First, Toad had, according to the gossip, been murdered by a hitchhiker, some 101 vagrant who'd carved him up with a knife. Then, it'd changed to a man and a dog, because how could a man do what had been done to Toad, and the man had probably sicced the dog on Toad after he'd been knifed. Finally, the version that Sam was told directly from a pimple-faced freshman who had no idea who Sam was, was that Toad had been dined upon by both the man *and* the dog, a New Year's snack right there on the beach with the stutter and flash of nearby fireworks serving as candlelight.

Sam had felt a little sick when he heard that one. "That's bullshit," he said. "You know that's bullshit, right?"

The freshman, whose locker was near Sam's, shrugged as he probed a zit on his chin with monk-like concentration. "Whatever, dude. That's what I heard from a guy that, like, knew the Whitlock kid personally."

"Oh yeah?"

"That's what I heard." It was said with the great luxury of not needing to know the truth. What, really, did this kid have to lose by saying this? By talking out of his ass? There was a buried *deliciousness* to it, even. Just people throwing words out into the void. Making shit up. The more fucked-up the better. His mother's death had been taboo to some degree. But *Toad Whitlock*? Gossip and shit-talking about Toad Whitlock's death bloomed around the school like a newspaper blaze, fast and hot.

Sam pitched his cigarette when he saw Trina and his father finally step out of the church doors with Mr. Whitlock. Gary held Trina's hand and Sam felt a starburst of heartache flare inside himself seeing the two of them walking across the parking lot, his father in his outdated suit, his hair combed back like that. Trina so small next to him, carefully avoiding puddles with her good shoes.

The difference between an accident and malevolence was something that Sam's father, in the way he looked at him, seemed to be trying to bridge. To talk about. The way he searched his son's face. Hadn't Toad been out on that beach on New Year's Eve alone because Sam had been grounded? That he'd grounded his eighteen-year-old son, and wasn't that the long and short of it? Would things have turned out differently if they'd been together? That was what Sam saw when Gary looked at him, that war between sorrow and gratitude on his father's face. The great selfishness of the heart: *I'm so sorry it happened to yours; I'm so glad it didn't happen to mine. And I hate myself a little for it.* His father's face had never seemed this naked and plain. Sam knew that if Gary ever spoke of it, it would need to be in darkness, smoking out on the porch, and his father would probably need to be drunk. So much rested on the things unsaid between them these days.

The three of them walked up to their truck and Sam opened the passenger door and hoisted Trina inside, out of the rain. Mr. Whitlock stood with the same posture he'd held in the church: head dropped toward the ground, frowning, absently running his thumb and forefinger down each side of his mustache.

"Anything you need," his father said. "Anything at all."

"It's different," Mr. Whitlock said in a small voice, as if Gary had asked him a question. As if he was testing out the idea of speaking. "It's a different thing, for sure."

"I know it is," Gary said quietly.

"I'm not real sure how I feel about it," and he looked at them as if he had just discovered this about himself. The hearse sat idling in the lot, waiting for Mr. Whitlock to get in his truck and follow, to lead the rest of the procession through town.

"He was just a fucking kid," he said. He kept swiping his hand down his mouth and chin as he spoke, as if some part of him still wanted the words kept inside, like he could shove them back in. "His dad was an asshole. Did you know that, Sam?"

"No," Sam said quietly.

"Ratty little speed freak, always talking about his connects with the Hell's Angels and shit. Popped cross tops like they were Tic Tacs, swear to God. Got sent down to Chico for armed robbery when Todd's what? Three months old? Gets a dime for it because of priors and, right away, within a week, gets his head caved in over some yard beef. Always the swinging dick, that guy. My sister knew how to pick 'em." Cars sat scattered throughout the lot, their headlights on, their wipers working across windshields. Waiting for Stacy Whitlock to lead them to the cemetery. "My sister hears about her old man croaking and loses it. Runs off. Leaves me with this baby. And what? I'm the guy taking care of him now? Kidding me? I'm like twenty years old. So I take him to the shop, I don't know what else to do. And here's this baby in a cardboard box with some blankets." He laughed and it sounded like he was being strangled. "Kid's trying to gum a socket wrench to death while I'm trying to get cars out the door. I'm just *lost,* you know? Just *lost.* Who the fuck knows where Amanda is. But we stick together, him and me. Grow up together. To the point where he wasn't like my nephew or even my own kid but just this other person I was with. That knew me the best. You know?" He looked at Sam with those terrible, blood-veined eyes. "He wasn't no rocket scientist, but he was fearless. You know that. He'd give you the shirt off his back. Right, Sam?"

"Right."

"He was doing good at the shop, too, they were thinking of moving him up, teaching him bodywork next. He was good at it. Guys at the shop liked him. Hell, they'd grown up with him, too, right? He was just some dumb kid." He voice broke on the last word and he gave Gary a wide smile, heartbreaking for how out of place it was. They were all soaked through now and Mr. Whitlock's hair fell in a dark comma on his forehead. "Bummed cigarettes off me all the goddamned time. Just a pain in the ass, ha. I just don't know what I'm going to do, Gary. I don't think I can do this."

Sam's father nodded, tucked his chin to his chest, absorbing these things the way men in Sam's life absorbed such things. Finally he raised his head and said, "But you can. Because you got to. Because there's nothing else to do. There's no other way to go about it."

Mr. Whitlock turned and looked out at the parking lot. Rain fell in a string from his chin. "I hear you."

Softly, Gary said, "We were thinking of coming by and painting the door for you. Sam could help you with Todd's stuff. If you needed."

"Would you do that?" Mr. Whitlock said with the gratitude of a child. His voice so naked with hurt Sam had to look away. "Would you do that, Gary? Thank you. Thank you, man. I don't think I could stand it." A bluster of wind sent leaves skittering across the black pavement. He pulled a pack of Newports from his jacket and lit one, then ran a knuckle under one eye and let out a shaky breath. "God, it's pissing. Guess we should get going."

"You need a lift over there?"

Mr. Whitlock shook his head. "My truck's just right there."

"You okay to drive?"

"Course."

"Okay. We'll see you in a few minutes then."

Mr. Whitlock began shambling across the parking lot toward his truck and a few weak swaths of blue even became visible through the clouds as they drove to the cemetery. On the radio, the DJ mentioned a massing of Soviet troops at the borders of Latvia and Lithuania. "Jesus Christ," Gary sighed and snapped the radio off, as if Trina might suddenly be capable of hearing. She sat between them reading one of her new books and Sam watched the town unspool out the window. It was another thing that he was unable to manage: helping his sister navigate her own loss. Toad had been her friend, as well; Toad had fucking adored her, and Sam was smart enough to understand that, to Trina, he and Toad occupied a different place in the world than his mother had. He and Toad were teenagers, after all—impervious to harm, bulletproof, demigods, and perhaps, because of their proximity to childhood, even more powerful than the grownups were. And now that Toad was gone—and in this terrible and strange and bloody way—what did that mean for her? What did that say about the fragility of the world and her place in it? How could he help her? She'd said little to him about it all, had taken the fact of Toad's death silently, like a punch to the gut. They had learned everything they knew about loss from Gary, from their mother. All the wrong things. Trina had always cultivated these great tides of silence within herself and now he feared the silence was hardening into a shell around her. Not for the first time, he wondered if maybe the school in Vancouver would be the right place for her. They had shut down the beach entrances for the time being; everyone from Animal Control to Fish and Wildlife was looking for whatever animal had savaged Toad. He looked at the same rain-drenched streets outside the window, the same hunched little buildings and houses. They looked flimsy and frail.

The sun came out, and in the cemetery parking lot, the roofs of the cars glittered like fire. The trees rose skeletal, gray and leafless along the cemetery fence line, bracketing the worn headstones and the expanse of emerald lawn. It was beautiful, really. Threads of black-clad men and women made their way toward Toad's gravesite; not as many kids from school as had come to the funeral, but some. He saw a red-faced Sheriff Dobbs in his suit and something like gratitude walked through him.

Sam's leather jacket felt like a suit of armor, dense and impenetrable. His Motörhead and Ramones tapes sat in each pocket like talismans; you never knew when someone would have a tape deck, and in a way, the tapes felt like a bridge to everything that had once been. The last time he'd seen Toad—only two days before he'd died!—they'd listened to the tapes in his room, where Toad, ashing his cigarette into a beer can, had declared Lemmy Kilmeister of Motörhead the baddest motherfucker around, even more than Bon Scott and, easily, *easily* more than Glenn Danzig. High praise. And the tapes were also the last bridge to his mother, the way she had left the list for his father, had written these titles down on paper, expressly with him in mind. When it came to his mother, he was the worst sentimentalist. This, he recognized as he followed his father across the dewy grass, was exactly the sort of shit he'd have told Toad. *Should* have told him.

The little priest stood beside the precisely sectioned piece of ground in which Toad's coffin would be laid. He droned on and on. Mr. Whitlock stood frowning with his hands crossed before him. Trina stood blinking in the sun next to Sam, her little hand as cold as ice in his. Occasionally an eddy of wind passed among the crowd and a flurry of raindrops fell from overhanging branches and pattered on Sam's jacket, the grass at their feet, dotting the dark brown wood of the coffin and sliding off, leaving small beads in their wake. Yet again, he thought of the body of his friend being lowered into the ground. All that dark weight, all that dirt thrown on him. It seemed more than macabre, a burial like that; it seemed fucking obscene. Something from the middle ages. A practice perhaps born out of necessity at the time, but something now transformed into a mockery of its old intent. To bury his friend in the lightless ground like that seemed almost worse than the death itself.

The priest finished his prayers and a pair of cemetery workers lowered the coffin into the slot of earth with a winch. With a trembling hand, Mr. Whitlock threw a handful of dirt on the coffin where it fell with a loud, almost metallic sound.

Afterward, everyone—in twos and threes—made their slow trek back to the parking lot. Sam walked beside his father and Mr. Whitlock again, his hands in his pockets, each wrapped around a tape like they might warm him. Trina walked ahead of them all, lightly running her fingers along the moss furring some of the older gravestones.

"Like I said, if you need anything."

Mr. Whitlock smiled down at the ground, a brief blip, there and gone. He nodded, "I hear you. Thank you."

They got to the Finster's truck first and Mr. Whitlock, on the way to his own rig, suddenly leaned down in his suit gone shiny at the elbows, and hugged Trina. Those scarred, red-knuckled hands gently patting the girl between her shoulder blades; Trina, surprised, held her arms out at her sides. Mr. Whitlock rose and shook Sam's hand, his other one gripping Sam's shoulder with an easy strength.

And this was when someone stepped from around the hood of their truck and called Stacy Whitlock's name.

Sam immediately recognized the cop from the press conference, the one that had stopped his fight with Kenny Pritchard. Today, he wore wrinkled chinos and a blue windbreaker and his face was dusted with days of stubble. He looked to be the survivor of some cataclysm where food and rest were scarce. His hair was flat on one side, as if he'd recently slept on it, and yet he looked worn, beyond fatigued. Those fingers of scars climbed, purple and shiny, out of his collar up to the bottom of his jaw. His eyes were so swollen and dark with sleeplessness it looked like he'd been recently knocked out.

"Mr. Whitlock," the cop said, walking toward them, "I'm very sorry for your loss. I'm with the Sheriff's Department." He held out his hand and, Mr. Whitlock—it seemed to Sam, at least—numbed by the day's repetition of the act, shook the man's hand. "I was just hoping to ask you a couple of questions, sir."

Sam's legs had gone watery and loose. The man did not look well at all and, in his street clothes, was so emaciated that Sam half expected him to tumble to the ground from sheer exhaustion. And yet, he thrummed with a kind of manic intensity, seemed seized by it.

"What kind of questions?" Mr. Whitlock asked. "What about?" A few mourners had paused in passing to speak to Mr. Whitlock and then, seeing the cop's face, the patchy beard and wrinkled, ill-fitting clothes, quickly moved on.

"Well, if I could just have a minute of your time," the man said, nodding his chin toward the Finsters standing nearby. "If we could speak alone."

"You can go ahead and ask here," Whitlock said. "It's okay with me."

"I think that would be unwise," the man said.

Gary took a step forward, touched Stacy Whitlock on the arm while he eyed the cop. "Listen, you're not in uniform right now, guy. I don't think now's a good time for this." As a group they began walking forward and the cop stepped around the front of the Finsters' truck and stood directly in front of Mr. Whitlock. The way he clasped his hands in front of his heart reminded Sam of those few times he had gone to church with a neighbor kid, before Trina was born. The fervency of it. *My man's got the spirit!* some strange, disconnected voice inside of Sam cried out, and he had to suppress the urge to let loose a laugh. The man's knuckles were white with the tension of it, knuckles pressed against the bottom of his jaw as if in prayer. He spoke with his eyes closed. "Was your son involved in any occult practices? Dark magic? Séances? Ouija boards, anything like that?"

It was a helpless look that Mr. Whitlock gave them all, a look gravely wounded and confused as he searched the cop's face for some punchline, some placement of context. When none came, when the cop still stood there with his hands clasped, the wind ballooning his pants against the sticks of his legs, Mr. Whitlock smiled a terrible smile, a smile vacant and punched-in and lost. But when he spoke, some vestige of his old self seemed to have returned. "Who the fuck are you, again? This guy's a cop?"

"I don't know why you keep showing up," Gary said, putting an arm over Trina and, again, gently corralling Mr. Whitlock toward the parking lot. "But we're done here."

"Please," the man said, walking backward with them, his hands still clasped beneath his chin, "anything will help our investigation. Was he acting strangely before he died? Did he talk about people following him? About the beach? Did he talk about the Tumquala? An old Tumquala legend?"

"What? What are you asking me?"

"There's a *reason* this happened to him," the cop said. Sam saw the man's red-threaded eyes when he opened them wide and realized that, whatever the nervous thing was that had rested inside the man when he'd driven Sam home from the fight the month before, that had seemed poised and ready at the press conference, that part of him had kicked free now. It was one of the most frightening things Sam had ever seen. "Mr. Whitlock, there's a *reason he died—*"

Gary took two steps forward, his shoes rasping on the pavement, and punched the cop in the mouth. Trina let out a little squawk and squeezed Sam's hand and the cop's head bounced against the driver's side window of their truck. Someone behind them screamed.

Sheriff Dobbs pushed his way through the crowd that was forming. The man sank to one knee, the fingers of one hand splayed wide on the ground, the other at his mouth. The scars from his collar were a vibrant, garish purple. Gary leaned over the man, shaking the pain from his hand. Dobbs touched him on the back and Gary turned and took a step back.

"I don't know who this guy is," his father said, "but I want his name and his badge number. I want this guy shitcanned. You can't do this to people."

"We'll take care of it," Dobbs murmured, gripping Gary's arm and maneuvering him away. "Step back, please."

"*He wasn't involved in none of that stuff,*" Mr. Whitlock suddenly cried out. He wheeled around at the faces in the parking lot. Trina began weeping and took Sam's hand in hers. The man slowly pulled himself upright from the ground. "He was a good kid," Mr. Whitlock cried again, his voice hoarse and cracking. "*Nobody deserves that, what happened to him. You hear me? Nobody deserves that to happen.*"

DAVE DOBBS

"I just want you to look at something," Hayslip said. "Please, Dave."

Dobbs watched the line of traffic exiting the cemetery, cars inching slowly along, a line of ants trundling grief and obligation. He shook his head. "I must have done something pretty horrendous in a past life to get saddled with you. Sweet Jesus."

They sat in Dobbs's pickup; he'd found a handful of napkins in the glove box and Hayslip, in the passenger seat, kept pressing these to his split lip. He was fussy about it, too—he'd blot and examine the tissue, blot and examine. He did not seem particularly concerned to have interrupted a young man's funeral, or to have sent the man's guardian into hysterics. He just sat there folded up in Dobbs's seat like a goddamned skeleton, dabbing at his lips like a teenager blotting her lipstick.

Dobbs thought back to those mornings of burnt coffee and bullshitting with his staff, the luxury of an infrequent patrol. Had that only been two months ago? Before everything in his life went south? And now what? June was still gone forever. A young man mauled to ribbons on his beach. Multiple branches of law enforcement were swinging their dicks at him trying to commandeer his investigation, and now he had a cop on his staff—a staff already strung thin as rice paper—who was clearly succumbing to some sort of prolonged and unpleasant mental fuckery. (And wasn't Dobbs partly to blame? Hadn't this particular deputy been on his radar for some time?) The beaches had been shut down, Fish and Wildlife was convinced there was a rabid animal on the beach itself or roaming the woods above the cliffs. Staties still weren't sure it wasn't the work of a sociopath and were threatening to intervene. People were terrified; just last night Fitzhugh and Ridges had to talk a group of men in the parking lot of the Sandy Bottom out of a night hunt along Slokum Beach. A half dozen drunken dipshits with shotguns driving along the dunes with a jacklight on their Jeep? Shooting at every twitching frond of crabgrass? Some drunk high schoolers gone to neck in the dark would've gotten their asses blown off, for Christ's sake. It had taken Fitzhugh and Ridges threatening to make arrests to diffuse it all. Yet Dobbs doubted they'd *actually* wound up diffusing anything at all; it would happen sooner or later. Vigilantism soared when people were afraid. He knew that. Especially if they felt the law wasn't acting on their behalf. And wasn't that what this was? A distinct lack of movement on his part? He was in here chastising Nick Hayslip when he should've been out working.

"I'm giving you a paid leave of absence," he said, running his thumbnail along the groove of the steering wheel. "Thirty days. That's a good deal, and you're lucky to have it. So if you're thinking about siccing the union on me, don't. I'll weather you out, and I'll wear you down, and after what I just saw out there in the parking lot, it won't be tough to fuck you ten times to Sunday, Nick. I'll downgrade you so fast any pension you'd get in retirement wouldn't keep you in breath mints. It's a promise."

Hayslip nodded and sucked at his teeth. His laugh was bitter and contemptuous, the kind that came out as just brief exhalations. "That's some real team loyalty you got going on there, Dave. You're not even going to listen to what I have to say."

"Nope. I feel like, personally, I've held your hand for months, Nick. Given you every chance."

"Yeah, well." Hayslip looked out the window and Dobbs saw in profile his Adam's apple jutting out like the man had swallowed a fishing lure.

"Once you're brought back on duty, you'll be on a ninety-day probationary period, in which you'll file daily reports to both me and Deputy Fitzhugh. You'll be in two-man patrols with Ridges and Fitzhugh, depending on the shift." Dobbs turned the heater on and it ratcheted to life. "I'll monitor your progress, check the reports, and we'll talk about letting you go back on single patrol at the end of the three months."

Hayslip gazed down at the bloody tissue in his hands. "More people are going to die if we just sit on our asses. This isn't a thing that's going to fix itself."

"Do you hear yourself? You hear the things you're saying? I would *strongly* suggest you get your ass up to the VA in Portland and talk to somebody. I wish we had those kinds of resources here, but we don't."

Hayslip reached into his pocket and Dobbs lashed out and grabbed his wrist; the man had grown so thin his fingers nearly circled the bone.

"I'm just getting a piece of *paper,* Dave. Jesus."

"Slowly."

"Christ. You think *I* should talk to a professional?"

"You're acting like that wasn't crazy out there. That was *shithouse crazy,* Nick. Harassing Stacy Whitlock like that." The lot was emptying out, but traffic on 101 was as steady as it ever was. Softer, he said, "I know how sometimes being in the shit can creep up on you. Years later. I've seen it happen. There's no shame in it."

A wry smile from Hayslip. "In the shit?"

"Yeah," Dobbs said. "If that's what this is about."

"What, you mean Nam? That's what you're talking about?"

Dobbs nodded.

Hayslip smirked. "You were in the, uh, the *motor pool* in Korea, right, Dave? Worked on engines and shit?"

Dobbs leaned back in his seat, his arms crossed. He nodded again. Knew what was coming.

"So no combat experience."

"No," Dobbs said flatly.

"Well, I'm sorry then, but you don't get to use terms like 'in the shit.' Not if you were in some barracks with your Miller High Life, listening to Bing Crosby on the jukebox in the officers club."

"Goddamn. You're just dedicated to burning every bridge you have, is that right?"

"You have no idea what's going on, Dave. You don't have a clue." He held out the piece of paper; the leather seat squeaked beneath them. "Just read this."

"You're coming unhinged. You're strung out. You harass the Whitlock kid's uncle at his *funeral?* Talking about devil worshipping? You look like you haven't slept in weeks."

"I'm the only one in this town that has any idea what's going on."

Dobbs laughed and ran a hand down his face. "I'm trying to talk to you. You know who you sound like, right? You sound like Joe Lyley."

"Maybe Joe Lyley's on to something," Hayslip said and Dobbs raised his hands up in defeat. He turned and put one arm over the steering wheel and the other over the back of his seat, faced his deputy.

"You positive you didn't put those birds on my porch, Nick?"

Hayslip held the paper between his first two fingers. "Read it."

Dobbs pulled his glasses from his shirt pocket and unfolded the paper.

Mimeographed pages from a book. The header at the top of the page read *Myths and Legends of the Coastal Indians.*

"It's all there," Hayslip said. "The birds, everything. The Tumqualas dealt with this thing long before we ever came here."

Dobbs closed his eyes, shook his head again.

"Dave, *read it.* This thing's *malevolent.* Do you understand what I'm saying?"

There had been certain times, when he'd done patrols as a young man and later on, after the job had gotten softer and had become more couched in diplomacy, where Dobbs just hit the wall. The feeling itself never changed, even if the situation did. It was when he had reached his saturation point, when he had simply had enough of the bullshit, whether it was someone he had pulled over or someone he was interviewing or a loudmouth at a town council meeting or, now, with one of his cops who had apparently, over a short period of time, become broken and mad and believing in a monster under the bed. When Dobbs hit the wall, he would just shut down, become suffused with a certain blankness. He was just *done,* sure only of the fact that he had trucked with enough idiocy for one day. If the county had had a shrink, he'd have assigned Hayslip to mandatory sessions, but as it was, he dropped the pages on the seat between them and said, "Deb'll have your paperwork at the station tomorrow. Make sure you're there first thing, and make sure she signs off on your service piece and your badge. And talk to somebody, Nick, my God."

Hayslip seemed poised to say something else but, instead, took his pages and opened the passenger door and stepped out. The sky was like a gray sheet dappled with shreds of blue behind it. Dobbs started his truck and drove away and didn't look back at Hayslip once.

• • •

That afternoon the Staties dropped in on him again. Tolker and Watson, a pair of State Police detectives who looked like they could be father and son. Like Salem was spitting out a singular bloodline of the same stiff-necked, uptight, bureaucratic shithead. The two men wore the same cut-rate charcoal gray suits, the same buzzcuts, the same rings of fat pushing up around the collars of their shirts. They'd been in and out of Dobbs's office for three days now and had yet to call him anything but sir, treating him with a respect that absolutely sang out with condescension. Like whatever had happened to Todd Whitlock down at the Wolf Point turnaround was indicative not of nature or chance or a sick animal, but rather of Dobbs's inept staff and, specifically, his own shoddy policing.

Deb knocked on his door and mouthed, "They're back." She grimaced and pointed a finger toward her open mouth, pretending to gag, and Dobbs smiled sadly.

Of the two of them, he could never remember who was who. Tolker, he thought, was older, with the burst-capillary nose that hinted the man was no stranger to a barstool. Watson was the younger one, the even more soft and pliable one. An untested Gumby-version of a cop.

Tolker came in, smoothing his tie down, offered a nod by way of greeting, and dropped a piece of paper on his desk. Watson didn't even bother hiding his grin. They stood in front of his desk, arms crossed, crowding him in. Over thirty years in law enforcement, and it came down to this bullshit, this dwindling down. Muscled out by these two.

Tolker nodded at the folder. "We just got the fax. It's confirmed: State's taking this one over."

Dobbs looked down at it, didn't even reach toward it. Not for the first time, he thought, *Good. Maybe this is for the best. Maybe I'm in over my head.* But it felt like poison, didn't it?

Watson said, "We'll need all the files regarding the Whitlock case. Everything. All the auxiliary files too. There's a writ in there, so don't bother trying to hide anything that's missing because it will come back, sir, and undoubtedly bite you on the ass."

"We're all on the same team here," Dobbs managed.

Tolker and Watson shared a look.

Watson and his shark grin: "Are we, Sheriff? You sure?"

Dobbs stared at him, counted to ten. Felt a muscle leaping in his neck. "What the fuck is that supposed to mean?"

"You know, they've put us up in a real nice place while we're working on this case. State budget's on this case is pretty fat."

Dobbs's heart was likely a body tumbling down a staircase.

"The Silky Sands?" Watson said. "What is it? That bed and breakfast over by the beach?"

Tolker raised his head and frowned at the ceiling, as if trying to remember. "That's not *quite* it, nope."

"The Silver Sands," Dobbs said, his own voice seeming to come from the other room, from someone else entirely.

"That's right," Watson said. "The Silver Sands. You've heard of it, haven't you, Sheriff Dobbs? You're pretty familiar with that place, from what I hear."

Tolker smoothed down his tie again. "Would you care to you describe your last interaction with Joseph Lyley, Sheriff? Because we just came from speaking with him and he's got quite the story to tell. And we've convinced him to file charges."

"DA's gonna want to have a talk with you, Sheriff. You're welcome to have representation present," said Watson.

Now even Tolker was smiling. "It's probably a good idea, actually."

NICK HAYSLIP

The Datsun's windshield wipers soldiered on through the rain. Highway 20, out to the Tumquala Reservation, was surfeited in flats of stilled water that sent fantails up to the doors as his little hatchback slogged through them. It was only mid-afternoon, and already the headlights of passing vehicles were dim and ghostly things that slowly cut past him in the gloom. The scenery on each side of the highway—thickets of trees, fields green and bogged with skeins of water, crumbling outbuildings leaning and wreathed in vines and various hues of rust and weathered wood, the poor odd field animal with its head down, hunched against the downpour—seemed blurred for all the rain, all of it taking on the shimmering, blurry air of a poorly-shot photograph. The only sounds were the clatter of the wipers and the radio turned low, rock songs from his boyhood. The driver's side window was cracked open to let the cigarette smoke out.

Dinkle was only a bit part in his dreams now. Mendez, the grenade, the Cong, it was all second-tier shit these days—the movie had changed reels. The locale had switched too: no longer the village, everything took place instead on the carved-out hillside of Tumquala Park or, across the cliffs, on the beach itself. Only one thing was constant: the *tah-kee-na-teh* was the main attraction, growling and muttering and *almost* visible through the phosphorescent dunes, an almost-shape spied at a glance through the trembling light, the wavering grasses.

He passed the sign demarking the reservation and turned off the highway down a winding road with sodden, empty fields on each side the color of burnt hide. In the distance lay a thumbing of dead trees, and beyond that, a horizon of dark and sloping hills. Ruts in the road filled to the brim with rainwater.

He arrived through the reservation gates to a dilapidated and scattered village of trailers and outbuildings and, here and there, the hulking skeletal frames of vehicles seemingly left to sink into the ground. The ditches on each side of the main road were choked with trash and weeds. He passed a pair of men in bright yellow slickers spearing the trash with hooked sticks, who stopped and stared at him as he drove on. Further out, like spokes from a wheel, he caught glimpses of sheds and tin-roofed houses, mobile homes, some of them manicured and cared for and some gone to rot, as if an apocalypse had already taken place or was well underway. Hayslip realized that he had never been to the reservation in all of his years as a cop—had never needed to, since the Tumqualas had their own tribal police. Funny though, now that he'd turned in his badge and gun, been stripped of them, here he was.

The tale of the *tah-kee-na-tch* had been found in the library, in a book that collected myths of Northwestern Indians; he had been studying the legend since the day that Leon Davies had shown up with the cease and desist order at the dig site. He had discovered a fervor for it, and an inclination that surprised him. When Hayslip read the story, it had felt like a series of locked tumblers aligning in his skull. Like a flashbulb of recognition. Nothing else that he'd found resonated the way this story did. The brave, and his poor dead wife, and the collection of birds; the nightly, constant visitations; every element was there. The venomous, *playful* quality of it all. Had Dobbs read it, taken the time, he'd have seen it as well, he was sure of it. Hayslip had reached a place where sleep hardly mattered, food was a thing endured. It was fine; since the discovery of the story, it finally felt like the end was in sight. All of this—all of the loss and confusion and searching—had fallen into place once he was willing to make the leap of faith to believe that there was something long-lived and of ill will prowling the town. Once you made that concession, everything else was a cinch. There were still questions, sure, riddled with unknowns. But the *how* of it all was answered, and any cop would tell you that all the rest was secondary to that. All else fell into place.

The Tribal Council office was a squat, mustard-colored building with a rickety ramp entrance, ringed by a gravel parking lot. Hayslip turned off the engine and, by habit, went to adjust the gun belt that no longer sat on his hips. He sat there listening to rain fall on the roof. He had little in the way of a plan, and was almost positive that any answers he'd get would be because Davies wanted to tell him. There would be no cajoling or trickery. Davies was smarter than him, and Hayslip had long since surpassed the point where he could physically overpower someone Davies' size. Anything given here would be given as a gift. But Hayslip had seen the crime scene photos of Todd Whitlock's body, and how the tenets of a body's archi-tecture had been entirely, gleefully, disbanded (there lay an arm where a leg should be, and that was probably a leg over there, and look: strings of intestines unspooled like tape from a cassette and strung everywhere in the blood-darkened sand) and he was positive now that Dobbs would do nothing. That the man was willfully blind. Hayslip was the only one that could help the town, and he sat for a moment beneath the thrumming roof and tried to prepare himself. As always, when he sat still for more than a moment, he felt his eyes drooping closed, felt his head begin dipping toward the steering wheel, and he slapped at his cheeks and stepped out into the rain and up the splintered ramp.

He was surprised to find Leon Davies alone in the office, seated behind an oak desk at the far end of the room. He wore a red-checkered flannel shirt, his hair loose on his shoulders. He peered at Hayslip over the rims of his bifocals and, surprisingly, seemed to brighten at his entrance, rising from his desk. Above their heads, the fluorescent lights buzzed. Wooden paneling lined the walls, and a pair of elk horns lay mounted on felt near the clock. A pair of glass cases was set into one wall; they held a collection of woven baskets and reed pipes, and a headless mannequin wore a beaded shirt. There was a pair of metal folding chairs in front of Davies's desk, and he shook Hayslip's hand and motioned him toward one. They both sat and Davies said, "Haysworth? Was that it?"

"Hayslip. Nick."

"That's right. How's things, Deputy Hayslip? Looks like you've gotten into it recently."

"What's that?"

Davies pointed. "Your mouth."

"Oh, right. Yeah." Hayslip smiled. "Now that you mention it, we'd better stick with Nick, actually."

Davies frowned. "Oh?"

"I'm here informally. A personal day."

"Really."

"Really. I'm doing a little investigative research into the case of the Tumquala girl, was just hoping you had a second."

Davies nodded and took off his bifocals, tucked them into his shirt pocket. His hair shone glossy under the lights and Hayslip wondered again about the whitened scars on his eyebrows, his nose. He could hardly imagine the man throwing a punch, but that kind of underestimation was advantageous, wasn't it? "So this is independent research?" Davies asked. "For yourself, or is there a third party involved?"

"A third party?"

Davies smiled at him, indulgent. "Come on, Deputy Hayslip. Nick. Give me a break. I'm happy to share information, but I want to know who I'm speaking to. You were there at the gravesite when I handed the papers to those kids, so you'll understand if I'm a bit trepidatious, right? I just want to know who I'm talking to. Where your loyalties lie, and all that."

"Well, my loyalty's with the truth," Hayslip said, and Davies actually laughed out loud.

"I'm serious."

Davies leaned forward, bracing his forearms on that big desk. The clock thunked out a new minute, and in the silence, Hayslip could hear the gentle purr of the rain on the roof. "You're not here in the capacity of a police officer at all? This is off the record, that's what you're telling me."

Hayslip shrugged. What did he have to lose? "I'll be straight with you, Mr. Davies. I'm on administrative leave."

A slow and measured nod from Davies. "So we're definitely off the record then."

"Absolutely."

Davies leaned back in his chair, ran his tongue over his teeth. He shuffled some papers, straightened them and put them in a drawer. Running a hand over the surface of the desk, he said, "Okay. Shoot."

Hayslip, surprised, was unsure what to say. He realized he'd hardly expected to get this far, hadn't expected anything to get green-lighted that quickly. "I guess I was wondering, in part, about the actual forensics involved."

"Well, that's not really . . . that doesn't have a whole lot to do with our aspect of the girl's death."

"I understand that. But surely you know some of the specifics."

"Well, we got copies of the reports from the anthropologists' field studies, copies of their photographs, things like that. The university's actually being very forthcoming, so we know about as much as they do. But like I said, that's not really in our scope. We just want the bones so we can perform the proper death rites on them. To bury the girl where she belongs."

"Which isn't in a museum," Hayslip offered.

Davies pointed at him from his clasped hands. "Exactly. The Tribal Council is really just hoping that once we get the actual bones—which, according to the university's Anthropology Department, is supposed to be any day now—the whole thing just quiets down. Like I told those kids, we don't want years of litigation and cross-suits. It's messy and expensive and self-indulgent. And it doesn't really help anyone in the long run."

"Like I said, I'm not here to stir any political pots."

"Well, the university is being very helpful, and we appreciate that."

"I'm curious as to what you think happened to her."

Even as exhausted as he was, he caught it: how Davies's eyes skated away from his, rabbit-fast, to the door and back. "Again, that's not really in the scope of what matters to the Council."

"I understand. But what do you *think* happened? You mentioned something before that stuck with me. About Indian hunters up and down the coast. Ex-prospectors."

Davies nodded grimly. "I shouldn't say *just* prospectors. Some of them were farmers who tried to make a go of it but the land didn't hold up. Or ex-soldiers. Drunks. Psychopaths. Whoever could stomach hunting and killing people for a living."

"The anthropologists' evidence suggested defense wounds on her hands, bite marks."

"It sounds like," Davies said with a dismissive smile, "you've read more of the report than I have."

"They said it's likely the girl was killed by an animal of some kind."

"Like I said, cause of death isn't really in the Council's scope. Or interest, frankly."

Hayslip folded his hands in his lap and leaned forward. "So it's a coincidence that the Tumquala girl died in 1868 the same way that a man did just last week, not half a mile from where her remains were found?"

It was unmistakable now, the way Davies's eyes skirted the room. When he looked back at Hayslip a hardness had been cast on his face, an anger. *Fuck,* Hayslip thought. *Looks like the politician's taking a backseat. Who's this I'm talking to?*

"It sounds like you've got an agenda, Nick."

Hayslip reached into his jacket and tossed the sheaf of mimeographed pages onto Davies's desk. Davies just stared at him, his mouth a knitted line.

"That's the story of the *tah-kee-na-teh,*" Hayslip said, "an old Tumquala—"

"I know what the *tah-kee-na-teh* is," Davies said. "It's probably time you hit the road, Nick."

The chair was rigid and unforgiving against his back; the clock, again, notched loudly in its housing. His hands gripped his knees, and he could feel his heartbeat thud in his chest like a pool ball, wrapped in felt, colliding clumsily against his ribs.

"Two months ago," he said, "a citizen brings a dead bird into the sheriff's office. Thing's ripped in half. Someone—something—leaves more of them in front of the sheriff's house a short time later. All the while, we're getting reports of dead birds and dead dogs on the beach in record numbers. Dead seals. You name it. Crazy shit. And now this kid, Todd Whitlock, gets literally pulled apart near Wolf Point. Just *dismantled*, right? And everyone—"

"I can't help you."

"And everyone's standing around with their heads up their asses, Mr. Davies. We're all way off the mark, I think. We're not even looking in the right *neighborhood*, know what I mean?"

He paused a moment before he decided to go for it. Lay it out. What could be lost at this point? "What *is* it, Mr. Davies? The *tah-kee-na-teh*? What's happening to the town? I don't—I don't know what to do anymore, man. I've lost my badge over this, I can't sleep. Can't eat. I'm having *dreams* about this thing, these fucking nightmares."

"You know you sound crazy, right? Batshit."

Hayslip nodded, shoved his fists into his armpits and leaned back in his chair. "I know. But I also know the Tumquala girl was discovered, according to the article in the *Observer*, right where Todd Whitlock was found. Just a hundred and twenty-five years apart." Whatever surety he'd had was a distant thing now; he sounded simply desperate, ragged.

But some new and galvanizing thing had made Davies raise his chin sharply, made his eyes bore into Hayslip's, the creases on his forehead suddenly standing out in vivid relief as he frowned.

"Stand up."

"What?"

"Stand up. I'm going to frisk you."

Hayslip rose and held his arms out at his sides. Davies stepped around his desk; his work was efficient and quick as he laddered his hands up and down Hayslip's ribs, his legs. "I'm going to tell you something. If you repeat it, if it ever gets back to me that the information's left this room, I'll deny it, and you'll come to regret speaking out. I won't say how, but I'm sincere about that. Are we clear?"

"We are."

"I need to know you understand me."

"I understand."

"Wait here." Davies walked to the doorway below the antlers and took a key ring from his pocket. He fished through the keys and then opened the door and stepped inside; when the light came on Hayslip saw nothing save for another wedge of cheaply paneled wall and part of a steel bookshelf heavy with plastic binders and books. Some of the books were new and some were old enough to have cracked leather spines, the color flaked and worn to illegibility. Davies came out with one of these tucked under his arm and shut the door carefully behind him. He stood next to Hayslip's chair and opened the book on his desk. It was large, leather-bound, and with pages of yellowed vellum that were ragged and uneven. Beyond the smell of the leather itself, Hayslip caught other ghosts: tobacco, dampness. Davies thumbed through the book quickly and the pages fell with a particular severity, a heaviness. He found the page he wanted and pointed.

"Here," he said. "What does this look like to you?"

Half of the page was an illustration, a woodcut of some kind. The columns of text beneath were written in English, but the script itself was so heavy and serifed that it was nearly indecipherable. The inks were faded as well, almost the same off-yellow as the pages. A few words leapt out from the dense text—*and, a,* that right there looked like it might be the word *night*—but it was the drawing that Davies had rested his finger on.

The illustration was detailed, rich in contrast, heavy with blacks. It showed the floor of some valley and at the outskirts were buildings, more small huts fringing the sides of the panel, but central to the panel were bodies. Hundreds of bodies littering the floor of the valley—men, women clutching babies, small children with their arms curled around their knees. Dead and dying.

And, in the distance between hilltops, was a silhouetted shape. Its back bristled with spines as it stood hunched over like a man, but with the great darkened head of a wolf, a coyote. And it raised its skinny arms toward the sky, toward the blackened outline of a fleeing bird.

"I don't understand," Hayslip said.

"I know," Davies said, not unkindly.

"What's happening to them?"

"Here? In this picture? That's the pox, deputy. Everyone is sick and dying. The end of the world. The white man came and the world changed." There was no humor in Davies's grin.

"I still don't get it."

Davies pointed at the shape in the dunes. "It's an early warning sign. A harbinger." He stepped back inside the room where he'd retrieved the book and came out with another one. Smaller, well-kept. Cracked it open, and Hayslip recognized it immediately: Briggs-Jenson's *Myths and Legends of the Coastal Indians*. The origin story of the *tah-kee-na-teh*. Hayslip's mimeographed version lay right next to it.

"It arrives and it begins cutting through the people right fucking smart. Just mowing them down. Taking children in the night, harrying the camps. There's a mention here that some of the elders dreamt of it before it arrived."

"So it's real," Hayslip said.

Davies gave a sad little laugh. "Wake up! You asked, and I'm telling you. Read this first sentence." He pointed to *Myths and Legends of the Coastal Indians*.

Hayslip read, "'Shortly before the whites came to this area, and many of the people took sick with disease and hunger, there was a young brave who was mourning his wife.'"

"The key's in the first sentence. *Shortly before the whites came* this thing shows up. Shortly before the people were stricken with disease and starvation. Shortly before the world ended. When did the article appear in the *Observer* about the Tumquala girl?"

"1868?"

Davies nodded. "January 16, 1868. She was discovered by what's his name, Meachum, on January 11."

"Okay."

"The Tumquala Massacre happened on January 22. There's a less than two-week gap between the girl's death and the massacre. *That's* what the Tumquala girl is. She's a preemptive sign. That's *all* she is, in the big scheme. She's a warning: tragedy's coming down the pipeline. The *tah-kee-na-teh*'s like some shitty by-product, that's all it is. There's no meaning to it, there's no great plan. It's just this piece of darkness that runs scattershot through the world, a precursor to larger, more awful events that'll be perpetrated by man upon man."

"So, what, it's showing up now because something terrible's going to happen? When?"

Davies shrugged. "I don't know."

"Well, what is it? What's going to happen?"

"Nick, you're asking questions that just don't have answers."

Hayslip laid his fingers on the book; it felt clammy, the leather ridged, the vellum almost tacky. "Well, this, at least—this needs to be stopped. If it's an animal, it can be killed."

The smile Davies gave him was a pitying one. He put a heavy hand on Hayslip's shoulder. "There's no stopping it." He smiled at the look Hayslip gave him, shrugged again. "There's not. It's a vanguard. It's—it's a muscle flexing. It's idiotic. There's no purpose to it."

"Why even tell me this then?"

There was a moment of silence between them. "Because," Davies finally said, "you look like you're dying. No joke. Like this is killing you an inch at a time. Whatever's going to happen will happen no matter what you or I will do. I want you to understand that. *That's* why I told you. Some members of the council think that once we get the bones back and perform rites, the *tah-kee-na-teh* will change its mind. That the tragedy will be avoided."

"What do you think?" Hayslip asked.

"I think it doesn't have a mind. I think it's pure function. It's performing a duty, something it was built for. There's no petitioning that. You might as well try to bite the wind."

"That's some real spiritual shit."

"You know what I mean." Davies gingerly took the book from beneath Hayslip's tented fingers. "There's something bad coming down the avenue, and there's nothing you, me, or anyone can do about it. What is, is. We're at the mercy of the workings of the world."

Hayslip looked at his face, at the worn carpet, the cheap paneled walls. "Why even bother with the bones then? Why worry about what happens to them?"

Davies had turned away by then, and the keys rattled in his hands as he opened the door with the books tucked under his arm. He said, "Because it's the right thing to do."

• • •

Bottles grew on his coffee table like stalagmites. His television stayed on, the ceaseless struttings and shouts and laugh tracks and gunfire soothing him better than the silence, which seemed to yawn ahead of him, which seemed suddenly laden with threats. He murdered the night's hours at the Sandy Bottom, where he sat in a corner booth away from everyone and tilted beer bottles up to the neon lights until he drove home drunk and angry at questions that sang out in his skull in a dark litany. *If Sherry came in right now, right through that door, what would you say to her? If Melissa did? What is your greatest sorrow, Nicky? Why the rift between him and Fitz?*

Was Dinkle grateful that he lived, legless and all? Dizziness threatened, at times, to overtake him and he stood stock-still until it slowly crept away, until the swimming, pulsing darkness at the edge of his vision went away. The dreams continued, and one night after waking, he punched a buckled crater in the wall above his bed and then wept with exhaustion as he cradled his knuckles. Drinking was beginning to become difficult; he couldn't keep it down, at least not very much of it. A shot sent him reeling into drunkenness. He was becoming a vessel for something, and in doing so, he was emptying himself out. A week into his suspension, he woke up and drove along Hastings Street and parked in front of the Silver Sands. Even with its shock-bright tulips and white paint, it seemed as foreboding as a haunted house. There were no cars at the curb, but an OPEN sign hung in the curtained window of the front door.

The office was shadowed, dark paneled and couched in gloom. Crosses and driftwood and taxidermied birds. Little decorative plates everywhere. Lace on all the windows that gave the daylight a misty, damp quality.

Recognition didn't take long, but Hayslip was surprised when Lyley's eyes bulged behind his little John Lennon eyeglasses, and he shrank theatrically against the wall, the back of his head thocking against the wall. "I don't know anything about it!" he cried, his voice high and reedy.

"Take it easy," Hayslip said, putting his hands up.

"I told the Sheriff, it's nothing to do with me! With anybody! I don't know anything!"

A woman stepped from the doorway. "Joseph?"

"Wait, what are you talking about? Sheriff Dobbs?"

"Yes. Dobbs." Without looking away from Hayslip he said, "Go on, Dolores. Go back to the living room."

"He assaulted Joseph," the woman said reproachfully, stepping out of the office and closing the door behind her.

Lyley adjusted his glasses and said, "Someone left an animal on his doorstep. Some birds. He thought it was me. He came here and threatened me."

Hayslip squinted, thinking of Dobbs laying the Polaroids next to him at the urinals. But Dobbs coming to Lyley's place and strong-arming? It seemed so unlike him, but who was acting the way they were supposed to these days? There were angles upon angles at work here. "What's the *tah-kee-na-teh*, Mr. Lyley? The low walker? If you had to describe it to me, I mean."

Lyley frowned, searched his face. "I don't . . . I don't know what you mean. I don't know anything about that."

"No? The sorrow eater? The Tumqualas? The girl in the hill?"

He should be used to it by now, that look of careful consideration everyone gave him these days, like they were trying to hold a conversation with a man juggling grenades. That look that was reserved, clearly, for those coming undone. And the fact that *Joe Lyley* was giving it to him probably should have worried him more than it did. Carefully, Lyley said, "This has nothing to do with the bones. The park, none of that. This has been foretold. It's the End of Days."

The same flat proclamations. Lyley knew nothing; he was doing nothing more than reading from a script, a man shouting from a street corner. Hayslip took a brochure from the rack near the door—*Visit Riptide's Waxworks Museum of Oddities!*—and wrote his phone number down. He handed it to Lyley, who leaned over the countertop and gingerly took the brochure as if there was a lava pit between them.

"If the Sheriff comes back, Mr. Lyley, please call me."

Lyley, obviously, was dubious. Hayslip almost smiled.

"Believe me, sir," he said, opening the front door. "If Sheriff Dobbs comes back here again, no good'll come of it for you. You'll need every friend you can get."

• • •

Sometimes, he woke on the floor, at other times curled between the right angles of two walls. Two weeks into his suspension, he woke from the dream and saw it was hardly even eleven yet. The night yawned huge and mean against him, promising no sleep. He put on his pants, washed his face, grabbed his keys. There was no one at the Sandy Bottom. His Colt .45—the same kind of sidearm he'd used in-country, and one that that still felt strange against his hand now that he'd turned his 66 in to Dobbs—sat like a brick in the waistband of his pants, warmed metal at the small of his back. Tumquala Park was falling back into disrepair; the sharply defined edges of the hill were beginning to slope down again, to curve; Hastings Street was a wash of red mud where the slurries had bled out onto the gravel. He drove down to the turnaround. There was supposed to be someone stationed there, but instead, there was only a sagging swath of police tape between two sawhorses. He ducked beneath the tape, a six-pack of beer in one hand. He traveled to the small inlet where the Whitlock boy had been found and discovered a small scattering of wilted flowers, blackened candles, a few miraculously untouched cans of beer. All of it leaning against a large boulder, the word TOAD scrawled on its face in hazard-orange spray paint. He left a beer, frightened more by his sentimentality than anything else, and moved on down the beach. He stood in the wind and tried to drink one of the beers; a few mouthfuls in and his head swam. He poured the rest of the bottle out onto the sand. As he walked, the foghorns of distant ships occasionally hung their music, low and lonely, over the ocean. Finally, he stopped and made his way back to the turnaround. He left the beers on one of the large fence posts that braced the turnaround and drove home beneath a nickel moon.

It was only when he pulled into his own driveway again did he realize that a plan had formed.

The next night, he drove north and parked near the entrance to Slokum Beach. A light rain was falling and traffic was sparse, and next to the walkway that led down to the beach, he saw a Fish and Wildlife truck parked next to another pair of sawhorses. It was laughable; he jogged a hundred yards down the street and walked through a thin copse of trees and then slid down the embankment to the dunes below. He sat down between two dunes and changed his clothes, stuffing his civvies into his backpack. He removed a pair of binoculars, a Maglite with the lens covered in black paper save for a small aperture in the center. Handcuffs. His .45 heavy in his waistband again. A flask, though he doubted he'd be able to partake. The lampblack felt cool on his face and he began walking north on the beach, away from the Fish and Wildlife truck, keeping to that narrow valley between the escarpments on his right and the dunes to his left. Some notion of stealth had come back to him with strange ease, the same rigid silence that had cocooned him in Vietnam, but it felt like a luxury now, like a gift. Like putting balm on a burn.

He did this each night, crept amid the dunes, staying in one spot for a few hours and then hiking further down the shore, or back up to his car to another spot. Waited and listened and readied himself. Looked for tracks as best as he could but found little to recommend anything out of the ordinary. The wind buffeted his ears, the howl of it a constant companion. Occasionally, he would sip from his flask, feel the warmth of it course through him; but no matter how much he drank, he didn't feel drunk. He finally just put it away. Alone, out in the dark, hunting for the low walker. It was the calmest he had felt since Melissa's death. Probably before that, even.

One Friday night, a group of high schoolers ducked the tape at the turnaround. Hayslip was a quarter-mile north of Whitlock's death site and he saw their bonfire like a winking jewel in the distance. It was raining, and yet, there they were. There was something ancient about it: a group of people gathered around a fire, something timeless. He lay on his belly between two bushes of crabgrass. The pistol lay on his backpack, out of the sand, as he glassed the party with his binoculars. Would he hear anything if the *tah-kee-na-teh* came up behind him, the wind in his ears like this? No. And yet, he trusted fate—fate itself had put him here, placed him in this position. Within an hour, he saw the glowing beacons of a pair of cops, bright in their yellow rain ponchos, walking down the paved ramp of the turnaround and heading toward the fire. He felt a stitch of excitement when he recognized Fitzhugh. They still had not spoken since the day at the rally but he recognized the man's walk, a certain unhurried swagger. He traced the scar tissue on his neck with his free hand, hardly aware he was doing it.

He realized that he had been waiting for this his entire life. This stringed-together section of nights. Everything prior to this had been a kind of preparation, he knew that now. Vietnam had steeped him in it, had familiarized him with the shocking speed of sudden violence. It had taught him that there were many, many things larger and stronger than one's will to live. Police work had sharpened him, kept that part of him from atrophying after the war. The dreams had dismantled him enough to be awakened to what needed to be done, had culled from him all the unnecessary accoutrements. Had brought to him the understanding that the *tah-kee-na-teh* was real, more than a myth. And the loss of Melissa Finster—to have had love, however paltry or hidden, and then have it so brusquely taken away in a broken-music-box stutter of collapsing metal and glass—had brought him here, to this.

He had become an envoy of sorrow himself, and he was courting the thing's arrival.

Fitzhugh and the other cop stood by as the kids poured out their beers and kicked their fire out, the group of them leaving in one ragged cluster. Who was it with Fitz? Lonnie Ridges? A Fish and Wildlife guy? He couldn't tell. Hayslip picked up his binoculars and glassed the beach both ways. He saw nothing for another hour, two. He was just about to put his gear in his pack when, through the glasses, he saw a dim shape loping down the shoreline. He thumbed the safety off his .45 with his free hand. His body felt suddenly cold and empty, like the wind was blowing right through it. He whistled and the head of the animal turned his way and trotted toward him. In a break in the wind, he heard the jingle of a chain.

It was just a white and brown dog, a mutt of some kind, that crested the dune and trotted toward him, happy and dumb and lost in the dark, pink tongue lolling. Someone's pet dragging its leash, just the kind of thing that didn't last long out here.

SAM FINSTER

"Call me if you need anything," Gary said. The truck sat idling in the cracked driveway of the Whitlock home. A Saturday morning, the day gray and droll. Trina, still in her pajamas, sat between Gary and Sam, reading an Anastasia book.

"I will," Sam said.

"Don't rush the job."

"I won't."

Gary sucked at his teeth and nodded. "I know you won't, Sam. That's just me talking out my ass. Did he have any dope or anything in there? Anything that'll fuck with Stacy if he finds it?"

"Maybe." Yes.

Gary drummed his thumbs on the steering wheel. "Well, be sure and take it. This is hard enough for him. Don't leave him with any surprises."

"Okay."

"I'll pick you up at noon."

Sam removed the tarp and gallon of black paint from the bed of the truck, his backpack slung over his shoulders. He stacked them next to the front door. Mr. Whitlock let him in, ducking his head like a butler, deferential and quiet. Sam was quiet, too; he'd never painted a door before. The solemnity of it lay heavy between them.

The living room felt different. No radio played, no scents of breakfast. The sense of a place being lived in was gone, had been shunted into something else. The house could be a relic, a mausoleum. Even the light seemed to shy away from the windows, leaving the place murkier than he remembered. Though maybe that was just his own heart working against him, wanting to paint the world differently since Toad's death.

"Where's the cat?" Sam asked. They stood at opposite ends of the small kitchen, both of them seemingly a little afraid to look at each other.

"Shitneck?" A small, distracted smile from Mr. Whitlock. "I don't know where that cat is. Just took off."

"Oh."

"I got you some boxes." Mr. Whitlock shoved his hands in his pockets and looked down at the scuffed kitchen floor. He was wearing oil-stained jeans and a black Harley Davidson t-shirt that showed his freckled arms and jailhouse tattoos. He had shaved his mustache since the funeral and his face looked strange and full of new contours. "I haven't gone in his room yet, Sam. If he left food in there it's gonna be a nightmare."

"Maybe I should do the door first."

Mr. Whitlock's eyes cinched tight for a moment as if some internal pain was passing through him. He nodded. "Sounds good. You got everything you need?"

"Yeah, thanks."

"Okay. I'll be . . . I'll just be inside here. Holler if you need anything."

He had a roller and a brush in his backpack and it didn't take long. It was cold and windy outside but he was afraid of getting paint on his leather jacket so he left it inside. He laid the tarp down and taped off the doorknob and poured paint in his father's dented tray. Of course he thought of Toad as he worked, and he remembered when Jeff Greenwood's father had died when they were all in junior high; Mr. Greenwood had been a crabber and was pitched overboard. They hadn't been able to get to him in time. The body had never been recovered. Jeff's uncle had painted the door for the family and Mrs. Greenwood had kept the door that way for *three years* before Jeff, in high school, had convinced her to scrape it clean. Sometimes it took people that long. The crazy part was that Jeff's mom had been seeing another guy for over a year by that point, some other fisherman. It had baffled Sam then, and still did, how you could go into a family's house for over a year and sleep in someone's bed when you had to walk through a black door to get there. It wasn't right.

He cleaned his tray and roller with the hose at the side of the house and wrapped everything up in newspaper. He found Mr. Whitlock sitting at the kitchen table, smoking and looking out the window, the one with a crooked blue line of electrical tape sealing a crack in the glass.

"I'm all done."

"Thanks, bud." Mr. Whitlock didn't look away from the window, just tapped his cigarette into a scarred hubcap he was using as an ashtray. The house groaned against a gust of wind and Sam felt a draft like a cavalcade of ghosts brushing against him. Yes, the house had changed. It was empty now. "I don't quite think I'm up for looking at it now."

"Sure," Sam said. "That's cool."

"Why don't you go check out his room. Boxes are over there."

Toad's room was at the back of the house and had been hastily added on from some earlier incarnation of the place. Instead of a single door it featured a pair of wing doors that opened in the middle. The doors stopped at Sam's knees and nose, and to balance this toward some small measure of privacy, Toad had cinched a chain and padlock around the inside door-knobs and hung a curtain on the inside of the door. The effect, to Sam, was a little like entering an unkempt saloon. Maybe a head shop. Toad had long made it a habit of locking his doors with the chain and padlock and then scooting out beneath them.

Sam picked up a cardboard box that had once held a case of Valvoline antifreeze and tried the doors. He felt them give but they didn't open. He turned and gave a little smile to Mr. Whitlock, who looked at him from the table in the living room. He seemed almost happy. "About what I figured," he said.

Sam pushed the box beneath the door and then got on his knees and followed it, both of them laughing a little.

The room was musty and smelled like mold was getting a foothold. The carpet was a lime green shag that didn't match the rest of the house and a pair of northern-facing windows gave the room a weak, diffused light. The walls were covered in a kid's pastiche—a few flyers for shows Toad had certainly never been to: Motörhead in Leeds, the Circle Jerks and Bad Religion in L.A., the Ramones at CBGB's. A large poster hung above his unmade bed: a Lamborghini, its sinuous curves stippled with airbrushed water droplets, shouting sex as clearly as a curved leg. His bass and amp in the corner. A boombox and a scattering of tapes next to a mattress on the floor. A small desk with a reading lamp on top. There wasn't room for much else, save for a splintered dresser covered in auto-motive decals. Car magazines and tattered, coverless copies of *Rolling Stone* lay in scattered heaps along the floor. Beneath the mold, it smelled like pot, cigarettes, and old socks. The fug of a young kid, or, Sam thought, of Riptide itself. Above the desk was Toad's map, his outlined route of the Trip, a scattering of colored pushpins all over the country. Way more pushpins in his than in Sam's.

He sat on the bed for a moment and turned away from the map, too overwhelmed to look at it. He took Toad's tapes, put them in the box. Even the shitty ones. Blue Oyster Cult, Boz fucking Scaggs. He opened the drawer in Toad's desk and found about an eighth of ditch weed double-sealed in a plastic bag. He put it in his jacket pocket. The closet was small, had a dozen shirts and a stack of cardboard boxes knee high. Toad had been good at that—where Sam had gathered physical artifacts around himself, the tangible as proof of his living, an ardent need for all of this *stuff*—Toad just lived. While Sam lived in his head, Toad walked around town, stirred shit up, got in fights, hung out with Sam, worked at the garage, saved up money for the Trip. Just howled his way through life.

The money, Sam thought. *Fuck.*

The floor of Toad's closet was made of the same scuffed, near-colorless linoleum as that covering the entrance to the house. He peered into the four corners of the closet, pushing the stacks of boxes around and wondering if he wasn't even close—maybe the desk?—and then saw the one corner of the closet floor with a rectangle neatly cleaved out of it. A ghost of an outline. Sam bent over and picked at the crease with a fingernail until he was able to pop that section of linoleum up, and inside was a dark hole, a space smaller than a shoebox.

Sam put his hand down, pulled out a paper bag rolled tight at the top. Before he opened it, he explored the rest of the hiding spot, found nothing else. He slid the linoleum swatch back where he'd found it.

The bag had been handled so many times it was worn smooth as skin. He opened it and peered in at tubes of bills rubber-banded together. He dumped them on the mattress and pulled the rubber band from one. A roll of fifties. Another revealed a band made up entirely of hundreds. Sam ran a hand over his scalp, felt his cheeks flush with heat. How long had he been saving up for this? They'd been talking about it since they were in eighth grade. Had Toad been saving up the entire time? Saving his garage money, his dope money? Sam had maybe six hundred bucks, and that was after working a summer with Jordana and her dad. He kept his stash in a milk bottle under his bed and would pull money out of it for stupid shit, cigarettes, beer runs. Tapes. Toad had saved thousands of dollars. Toad had a rainbow of pins in his map.

He stacked some fanzines in the box, a couple of shirts, and tried not to cry. It all felt mercenary. But he also knew that all of this would be harder on Mr. Whitlock than it was on him, and that Toad would want him to have these things. He found a notebook of Toad's, couldn't bring himself to read the scrawled, childish handwriting, but put it in the box anyway. He pulled the thumbtacks from the map and held the map up to the window and saw the galaxy of pinpoints shining through the paper. He folded it and put it in the box like something reverential.

He went into the living room and set the box down. Mr. Whitlock was watching *The Price Is Right* with the sound off now, a beer on his knee. "Got everything?" He cast a glance at the box and quickly looked away.

"Did you want me to take the bass?"

"Yeah," Mr. Whitlock said after a moment. "Yeah, go ahead, Sam."

Sam went back into the room and came back out to the living room holding the bass and the practice amp and leaned them against the arm of the couch. He reached into the box and pulled out Toad's paper bag and held it out to Mr. Whitlock.

"It's money," Sam said.

"Money?" He said it like it was a new word, one he had rarely had cause to speak. He slowly reached for the bag.

"It was for our trip," Sam said. "There's a lot in there. He was saving up."

Mr. Whitlock peered into the bag for a long time. The way he stared at it, the look on his face, was like a man very disappointed that some fast food worker had gotten his order so wrong. A great sadness. Sam knew that the money would pay for the casket, the service. The strange machinations of Toad's death: that he had paid for his own funeral.

• • •

He was out smoking on the step later that night, the rain falling in silver strings from the gutters. His father came out, his baseball cap obscuring his features.

"Me and a couple guys gonna go hit bottom," he said, old family slang for drinking at the Sandy Bottom. He had skipped a few trips on the boat for Toad's death but would be going out in a few days. So far, the hauls had been good; the season looked to be a promising one. His father was losing money by staying home.

"Okay," Sam said.

Gary lit a cigarette of his own and ran a hand down the rasp of his beard. "You gonna be okay?"

Sam shrugged, toed a piece of moss from the concrete stoop. His jacket creaked when he put his cigarette to his lips.

"Listen," Gary said, and then said nothing.

"Yeah?"

His father sighed, adjusted the threadbare bill of his cap. "You've had more to deal with in a year than I'd pretty much wish on anybody. I don't know if I could do it."

Wind, spatter of rain on the concrete stoop. Silence.

"What I'm saying is, I don't have the words for how proud I am. The spine you have, Sam. The kindness toward your sister. You're a good one."

"Thank you," Sam said.

"I know you wonder about Toad, if you'd have been able to do something. If things could have turned out differently. That kind of thinking will drive you crazy."

"I know."

"There's no end to it. It just circles around itself."

It was more than his father had said to him, really said to him, since his mother had died, and Gary squeezed his arm once more and then neither spoke, as if they were both afraid they would ruin it. The fragility. This was what passed for a shared intimacy, and then Gary held his cigarette out beneath the eave where a string of rain fell on it and it sputtered out. He threw the butt in the coffee can by the door.

"Listen, you want me to stay in? We can play some cards or something. Stay up and drink a couple beers? Fuck it, school doesn't start back up until next week, right?"

Sam shook his head, expansive with the compliment and a raw, fierce gratitude and love for his father. "It's okay, Dad." He knew that Gary had his own weights, was navigating his own loss in whatever way afforded him. "We'll be alright."

"You sure?"

Sam nodded, held his own cigarette out in the rain.

NICK HAYSLIP

The Sandy Bottom, full of thunder at ten o'clock on a Saturday night.

The constants: the stutter of pool balls against each other, the front windows running with condensation, the floor thrumming with jukebox bass. Smoke blanketed the ceiling. Neon beer signs buzzed on the walls. The cavelike howl of people yelling at each other in close quarters. As busy as the place ever got.

Hayslip took one of the last seats at the bar, tried to catch Ron's eyes. He was wearing his rain jacket and a pair of black Carhartt overalls, his backpack resting at his feet. A beer here and he would go out on the beach again. Things had reached a velocity; there was a certainty to the next stretch of days. Would it happen tonight? Tomorrow? It wouldn't be long. (This might be his last beer! Imagine it! How many of the goddamned things he had quaffed throughout his life and this might be the *last one!*) He could no more imagine life like this—the days stretching wide and unbroken before him with fatigue and sleeplessness, the nights fractured with looming dreams and trips down to the beach in the dark to wait for some ungodly thing to seek him out—than he could imagine life going back to the way it had been before. Lyley was right in his way: the end was coming. Shit, the end was *here.*

He ordered and drank and took a small measure of comfort in the noise and closeness of the people around him. The feeling of the chilled glass around his hand, the way the stomps and footfalls from the dance floor reverberated up the stool and along his spine. It was enough to be there among people. The simple intimacy of it.

And then, in the warped barroom mirror above the columns of bottles, he saw Fitzhugh stagger from the bathroom, still cinching his belt. He wore the concentrating frown of the very drunk, a look parked somewhere between vacuousness and a feral antagonism. One tail of his shirt hung from his pants. Through the crowd, their eyes met in the mirror and Fitzhugh immediately veered toward him, his hands steadying his passage on tables along the way. His neck and face were blotched red from alcohol. His hand thudded on Hayslip's shoulder and then found sweaty purchase on the back of his neck. Hayslip turned to face him, his pint glass in his hand. Acutely aware of his backpack on the floor at his feet.

"Hey, Fitzy."

"Goddamn," Fitzhugh crowed over the noise, pulling his hand away. Leaning back and frowning, he yelled, "You look like pounded dog shit, son. You look like a runner-up in the Dachau Olympics." His breath was moist, fetid, reeked of booze. "Being shitcanned does not agree with you."

"Good to see you too." Hayslip's smile touched nothing, so meaningless it was easy for both of them to ignore it. Fitzhugh tried to stand in place and teetered, zombie-stomped to stay upright.

Hayslip reached out to steady him. "Been tilting them back pretty good tonight, huh, Fitz?"

Some insinuation of judgment to his words, or maybe—probably—Fitzhugh was just feeling drunk and mean, but he stepped toward Hayslip and pressed two fingers against his breastbone. "Fuck. You." Pockmarks cratered Fitzhugh's nose; Hayslip felt adrenaline dump in his veins, recognized that he was yet again seeing things with a bright, strange clarity.

"Fuck me, huh? Fuck me." Hayslip said. "I've been on your shitlist since the press conference, if not before. You were cold-shouldering me then, and now this. What's your deal with me, Fitz?"

"You're kidding me, right?" Fitzhugh let out a bitter laugh and shook his head. "You that fucking dumb, Nick?"

"Yeah, I guess so."

He hooked a hand around his neck again and leaned in close. "I fucking lied for you," he yelled, stressing each syllable, dotting Hayslip's face with spit, his pale scalp gleaming beneath the red bristles. "I lied to *Dave Dobbs* for you. I put it on paper. You're lucky that shit didn't go to IA, you stupid cocksucker."

"I know it," Hayslip yelled back. "I'm grateful. How many times do I have to say it?"

The hand squeezed his neck again and Fitzhugh searched his face with his glassy eyes and seemed to find whatever he needed there because he let go and took a step back, folded his big arms across his chest. "None! None is how many, goddammit. How many times did you come see me when I'm

laid up, Nick? After I *falsified a fucking report for you?* How many times?"
Yelling it in the middle of the bar, guys on each side of them.

"One time," he admitted.

"One time," Fitzhugh agreed. "Just to get our stories straight. Just to
cover your own scrawny ass. And how many times after that?"

"None."

"None is right. Zero times, Nick." He made a zero with his thumb and
forefinger and wavered again.

"I was wrong. You saved my ass."

"I *know!* That's what I'm saying!"

In his peripheral vision he saw Gary Finster and a few other guys walk in
the front door, their shoulders hunched against the rain. His recognition of
Melissa's husband was so visceral he felt his hands flex, his eyes go wide, a pure
animal reaction. Like it was the last piece he needed. Like the world was telling
him: *Cinch closed the threads of your life. Move past your guilt. It's happening
tonight.* He yearned for quiet, for rest, and if not that, at least for something to
change. And here was the world offering change. Offering resolution. It was
an absolute. He had been looking for signs and he was finding them. Tonight
was the night. He would confess to Gary Finster, relieve himself of his guilt.

How many times in his life had he ever been certain of anything?

"Fitzy, I gotta go, man. I gotta talk to somebody." He bent down and
scooped up his backpack.

Fitzhugh scowled and flapped his hand between them. "We're still
talking, bud. Me and you are still working some shit out here."

"I have to go, Fitz. Thank you, again, for saving my ass. I owe you."

"Don't walk away from me, Nick. Worst mistake." Fitzhugh's hand
cinched around Hayslip's arm and squeezed. He had grown so wire-thin
that Fitzhugh's fingertips around his bicep nearly touched.

Hayslip motioned with his eyes down to the backpack between them;
Fitzhugh looked down and saw Hayslip had unzipped the backpack and was
gripping the .45, the barrel pointed toward Fitzhugh's stomach. Everything
matte black in the dim light of the bar; a few scant highlights on the pistol
were caught by the blue neon Hamm's sign nearby.

"I have to go, Fitz." Fitzhugh's eyes bounded back and forth between
the backpack and Hayslip's face. "You have to let go of me."

Poor drunk Fitzhugh, short-circuiting on betrayal. His mouth hanging
open, eyes bulbous with rage and shortsightedness. If anything, his grip
on Hayslip's arm tightened.

"I'll shoot you, Fitz. Without a doubt. A .45 round, point blank in the guts? At best you'll be shitting through a tube the rest of your life. Wheel-chair-bound. *Let go of me.*"

Fitzhugh let go. Hayslip could feel his heartbeat pulse in his arm, the grateful blood surging through it.

"You've lost it, Nick. There's no coming back from this."

"I keep hearing that. I need you to leave now. Do what you need to do, I don't care, but give me ten minutes."

"Or what?" Fitzhugh sneered like every schoolyard tough throughout the ages, every guy trying to hang on to some tendril of respect. Hayslip waggled the pistol and shrugged. Fitzhugh skulked across the bar, lips curled back from his teeth, glaring at him from over his shoulder, and slammed the tavern door open so hard it slammed against the outer wall. A few people turned and booed. "For fuck's sake, Fitz!" Ron cried.

The .45 was in his backpack again. He sought Gary Finster among the crowd. A calm had fallen over him; he was buoyed by that sense that things had finally begun, things that would bring him to the endpoint. Fitzhugh had been right: there was no coming back from this, and it was a relief. He saw Finster at a table near the jukebox, and as he walked toward the man and his friends, he considered what there was to say. It occurred to him then that for-giveness meant nothing if it came at the cost of someone else's pain. That was conceit and nothing more. In the months that the dreams had taken root, he had thought halfheartedly of heading to Atlanta and finding Stanley Dinkle. Asking him how he felt about it all, what he remembered, what he regretted. But he had dismissed it as idiotic—Dinkle, he was sure, regretted all of it: the man had left his legs in South Vietnam, for Christ's sake. Talking to Dinkle would be meaningless. Worse, it would do nothing more than dredge up the past for the man, and who wanted that? No. He realized he was done with the Finsters, finally. What he'd had with Melissa had been something akin to love, but not quite. Not quite, no, but enough to be transformative. But a confession here to her grieving husband would do nothing but harm. They all felt interconnected to him, all these events—Melissa to the Tumquala girl to the low walker. One had led to the other and still another. A trajectory.

He turned to leave. One more stop before the beach. One more and he would be done with it all. It would end tonight; his blood sang with the relief and joy of it.

"Son of a *bitch*," Gary Finster muttered when he saw him, and rose up from his chair so quickly that his legs smashed against the lip of the table, lifted it. All the bottles there trembled and fell to the ground with a crash. His friends traded confused looks and then Finster was on Hayslip, one fist pistoning in his face and the other searching for purchase at his collar, his throat, Hayslip's backpack with his night gear and pistol zippered and useless on one shoulder.

"Wait," Hayslip managed, his hands raised.

Starbursts of light followed, his head rattling as if on a stanchion, his mouth full of warmth and numbness. Finster dragged him down to the ground and then the inside of his head boomed with thunder when it met the floor.

FIVE

bail money • the confession • glass beneath his feet • the note • busy roads,
quiet roads • hayslip makes some noise • the low walker arrives • dobbs
with a dark heart • everyone on the beach • hayslip, finally, tired and happy
• darkness and wonder

SAM FINSTER

Later that night, the wind stepped up, howling around corners of the house, blackberry bushes scratching against the kitchen window like fingernails, a sound lonely and arrhythmic. They ate hot dogs and macaroni and cheese, and Trina ran her hot dog sections through ketchup with *The Wolf in the Basement* open before her. Sam kept checking that the lamps were on; it was one of those nights that seemed to swallow all illumination. He didn't even play any tapes, just sat and ate and moodily listened to the moaning wind, the brambles skating against the window. There was something in the air, some strange current that set his teeth on edge. An uncertainty.

Isn't that book late? Sam asked.

This isn't a library book. I turned that one in a long time ago.

Oh.

This is one of my Christmas books.

Oh. Okay.

He got Trina ready for bed, trying to ignore a worm of unease as she quizzed him, standing before the bathroom sink in her *A-Team* pajamas. Her toothbrush sat parked in her mouth as her hands fluttered their questions.

Where's Dad?

"I already told you. He's at the Sandy Bottom with some of the guys from the boat."

Is he getting drunk?

Sam leaned against the doorframe, smiling, a little sad. Since their mother's death, Trina had become preternaturally concerned with alcohol: who drank it to excess, who partook responsibly. She had asked him a few days earlier if Toad had been drunk when he died and Sam had lied and said no. "I don't know," he said now. "He's having a few beers, Trina. I think they're going out crabbing tomorrow, so I bet they won't be getting too messed up."

He'll have a hangover. She looked up at him in front of the sink as if this was a problem he could solve.

"You don't need to worry about it."

She turned back to the mirror. He saw her neck, thin and pale, this tiny girl with her chipped fingernail polish, Face and Hannibal and B.A. and Murdock scattered on the blue sea of her faded pajama top. Her socks were two different colors and, seeing this, Sam again felt that fierce starburst of loyalty. The loyalty and love he felt was the only thing that dispelled the uncertainty, that sense of continual unease they lived in, the unease that faded and flared but never seemed to go away entirely. Sam was struck with these moments more and more, the reminders of his world's frailty, how tender the grasp was on those he loved. He felt his heart lurch for her, clumsy and battered, and recognized how fierce her will was, fierce against the brutal and relentless machinations of the world. She spit in the sink—holding her hair against her shoulder in a somehow womanly, adult gesture—then turned to him. Her face was set in some resolution of her own.

I want to watch the news.

Sam was doubtful. There had been more and more talk. All the networks were promoting extra coverage of the crisis. *20/20* was airing a special tomorrow about the tensions, and various pundits were constantly interviewing all manner of military personnel, be they Soviet, German or U.S. A bunch of talking heads ceaselessly opining about what *could* happen—which was, he knew, the last thing Trina needed. UN Peacekeepers had amassed on the Lithuanian border as protesters gathered in large rallies on both sides. Sam had seen the pictures: the Peacekeepers and the riot police looked exactly the same to him, and the protesters looked the way protesters had always looked: enraged and scared and small against the men with the guns and armor. She did not need to see these news anchors plumb the depths of the worst possible variables for the sake of ratings.

"We'll see," he said.

Instead, he managed to talk her into a game of Old Maid, and soon enough, her head was dipping down, her eyelids fluttering. She asked him one more time if Dad was okay.

"Yeah," Sam said, leading her to bed. "Of course he is."

I have a bad feeling, Sam. I don't feel good.

I know what you mean, he nearly said. He tucked her in bed and she pulled her bedspread up to her nose as a gust of wind howled and the little house creaked as if buckling down against it.

"Just get some sleep. Dad'll be home soon. We can leave your door open tonight and let the light in, okay? Love you."

Love you too.

But it was twelve-thirty at night and his father was still not home when Sam finally picked up the phone in the kitchen. The house was silent, the wind having died down. The phone rang four times at the other end of the line before someone picked up, the clatter of voices brittle and raucous in the background. "Sandy Bottom."

Sam curled the telephone cord around his finger and paced the kitchen. "Yeah, I was looking for my dad. He was supposed to be having a few beers there?"

"Shit, we got any number of wayward fathers here, kid." The man let out a raspy laugh, like a barking dog. "What's his name?"

I have a bad feeling, Sam. I don't feel good.

"Uh, Gary Finster? He went there with some other guys from his crew. His crab boat."

There was a beat, an extended moment of time that pulled on his heart with the reluctant give of taffy. That sense of doom deepened and crystallized inside him. Sam heard the muted rhythm of a jukebox tat-tooing the air at the other end of the line, and through the static of the crowd, a woman's laughter pealed bright and knife-like on top of it all. Sam's knees felt loose and wobbly. He leaned his head against the cool metal of the refrigerator.

The bartender sucked his teeth and said, "Ah, man. Your dad's got a tem-per on him, bud. We had a spot of trouble with your dad tonight, actually."

"Yeah?" Sam said, his voice sounding far away to his own ears. "What . . . what happened?"

"He started some shit is what happened. You're gonna want to call the jail. The cops came and arrested him, sorry to say. He knocked a guy's teeth out."

"Thank you," Sam said, his voice still seeming to belong to someone else, amazed and infuriated at his own politeness. Somehow he was not surprised to hear any of this—the night had that feeling about it, that weight.

He stared at the phone for a minute and then called Belinda. She sounded irritated when she answered, her voice coarse with sleep. He told her what happened, asked if she could come over. "I have to go bail him out but I can't leave Trina. I don't want to wake her up."

She'd come awake as soon as she heard who it was and spoke clearly now, fully present. "Christ. Yeah, I'll be over, hon. But you're gonna need somebody to go with you."

"I know. I was gonna call Mr. Whitlock."

"Okay. You sure? Okay. I'll be there in fifteen minutes, honey."

Mr. Whitlock answered on the second ring; Sam could imagine he wasn't sleeping much. He told him what had happened.

"I'll be there in a second, Sam."

It took Sam a minute to figure out the tone of Mr. Whitlock's voice and then realized after they had hung up that the man had sounded almost relieved. Almost grateful for the distraction.

• • •

They stepped out of the glass doors, Mr. Whitlock and his father, and stood smoking on the sidewalk. Mr. Whitlock gently punched his father on the shoulder, some admonition or another, both of their faces dour and drawn mostly with shadows. Sam, from his seat in Mr. Whitlock's truck, saw his father's form limned in the light of the police station entranceway; when he turned, Sam saw the curve of flesh at his throat starting to grow soft with age, saw the streaks of gray in his beard. His father lifted his cigarette to his mouth, and Sam could see that there were scrapes on his father's knuckles, one of his eyes was nearly swollen shut, and a raw, angry scrape ran down his other cheek. He had lost his hat. He looked alien and fragile and tired, and Sam felt something catch in his chest with the look of it—a simple, clattering fear that ran in tandem with the understanding that his father was, yes, a man, just some guy. A man of flesh who could be, would be, laid permanently to rest someday, like any other. A man not impervious to harm. Someone had hit him, after all. Had hurt him. It was a feeling inside Sam like someone had pulled the ground from beneath his feet and what was under that was darkness, a chasm of unknowable depths. If this could happen to Gary Finster, it seemed, anything bad could happen to anyone. Christ, after all that had happened to Sam—his mother, Toad—how could he not understand this by now? How could he not be punch-drunk with the knowledge?

He stepped out of the truck and his father turned and looked at him, then looked away. The town was still, quiet. The night air smelled of iron and salt.

"How much was it?" Sam asked.

Mr. Whitlock turned and spit a shred of tobacco from his lips. "Don't worry about it, Sam."

"For real, though. It's not a big deal."

"If he finishes court, I'll get it back, bud."

"I'd like to do it this way," Sam said.

"Okay."

Mr. Whitlock probed a tooth with his tongue and nodded. "It was five hundred."

Sam peeled a clutch of twenties and fifties from his trip money. "Ah, goddamn it, Sam," his father muttered sadly. He pitched his cigarette on the ground and dragged his boot angrily over it. Sam's money roll was greatly diminished; it would have hardly made a dent in Toad's. But something in Sam found some measure of hope in spending the money this way. When I'm older, he thought, maybe this is something we can laugh about. Stacy Whitlock and I bailing my father out of jail after a bar fight. Some real manly shit right there.

"Bank opens on Monday," Gary said, looking out at the street. "I'll be able to pay you back then."

"It's not a big deal," Sam said again, and his father just shook his head.

Mr. Whitlock offered them a ride, but Gary said they would walk. "I been sitting in that station the past couple hours," he offered by way of explanation. They shook hands and it seemed again that Mr. Whitlock seemed comforted by it all. Sam and his father stood in front of the station and watched the truck's taillights flare and dim as he turned onto 101.

They walked back to the Sandy Bottom. If nowhere else, it was busy on the bayfront, the streets thronged with cars, music low and pulsing from the streetside bars, all the quaint tourist shops shuttered and dark. Boats rocked in their dockside moorings, and the moon shimmered like fractured glass atop the oily expanse of the water. They walked along the bayfront road, the cones of streetlight above them turning them from shape to shadow to tangible shape again, their shadows drawing long before and then behind them. At some point Gary reached out and grasped Sam's shoulder and squeezed.

"Thank you."

"Sure," Sam said, looking down at the ground as they walked.

"We're going out tomorrow. Money'll start coming in again soon. I'll get you back."

"It's no big thing, Dad."

"It was the cop," his father said, and Sam's mouth went dry. "The one from Todd's funeral."

"Did he start shit?"

Gary gave a weary, embarrassed laugh. The profile of his face was misshapen and alien with his bulbed, swollen eye. "No. I jumped him. He was just walking by, but . . . I just remembered him from the funeral. How he's been, I don't know, dogging us. Pictured him yelling all that bullshit about Todd and I just . . . I got in a few good ones and the guys pulled me off him. He ran out."

"What happened here?" Sam asked, motioning toward his own eye.

Gary laughed and lit another cigarette. "From one of the cops that arrested me. Out in the parking lot. In handcuffs. He was real matter-of-fact about it. 'That cop you got into it with? He's not our favorite guy, okay? But it's the principle of the thing.' Got me pretty good."

They walked on, passing through a loud, drunken knot of fisherman going from one bayfront bar to another. The men parted ways for Gary and Sam, shared wordless nods, some unknown currency moving between them and his father.

"I called Belinda to watch Trina."

"I figured," said Gary. "Good job, bud."

The truck was where his father had left it. The parking lot of the Sandy Bottom was full, music so loud they could hear it from outside. A jagged line of moonlight laid a silver streak in the truck's cracked windshield. They drove home in silence, the radio off. His father sighed more than once, ran his hand down his beard.

From the driveway, it seemed that every light in the house was on. Before they could open the front door, Belinda was out in the front yard like a dervish. Gary scrambled out of the cab. The living room windows threw wide swaths of light on their mud-hewn lawn.

"Gary," she said, cinching her hands around his arms. "Oh, God."

"What happened? What is it? Is she okay?"

"What?" Belinda said, searching Gary's face. He had her hands in his now, seized and pressed against his chest.

"*Is she safe, goddamnit?*"

"It's not Trina," Belinda said in a clear, bright voice as Sam ran toward the front door, mud squelching and sucking at his shoes. "It's not that. Reagan's dead," she said. "Reagan's dead and the Russians are starting the war."

• • •

"What?" Gary said, slowly. Sam felt the edges of the world soften, strangely dreamlike. "What did you say?"

"The President's dead. The bullet in his heart? It finally came loose or something like that. Nobody knows for sure. They think the Russians might have got scared and fired a missile, maybe on accident. Or they did it on purpose. Nobody knows if it's even real."

Gary actually laughed. "How the fuck do you fire a nuclear missile on accident?"

"I don't know! It's all on the news, Gary!"

They walked into the house, Gary with an arm around Belinda's shoulders. She sagged against him, her breathing ragged, a series of stuttering hiccups, the back of her hand pressed against her mouth. Her rings shone gaudy in the fierce light of the living room. A police car raced down their dark street, trouble lights painting the air blue and red. It happened so fast Sam felt that he could have imagined it.

They stared, the three of them, at the television. Most stations were taken over with newscasts. Pick one. They were all the same. The same grainy stock footage: platformed warheads being marched amid soldiers in a Soviet parade, hammer and sickle flags festooned throughout the grounds, rounded spires of gray and brown buildings in the background. The newscasters all looked ashen-faced, petrified. Sam settled on a channel and the reporter held his papers in front of him and seemed unable to keep his eyes on the camera. "I repeat," he said, "these are all so far *unconfirmed* reports. We're told a message from the White House is forthcoming shortly. People are urged to stay in their homes. Do not give in to panic. We will continue to update you with any new information as we receive it. I repeat: The death of President Reagan is so far *unconfirmed.* And there have been no confirmed reports that *any* missiles, U.S. or Soviet, have been launched. Again, I urge you all to stay calm and stay in your homes."

"Get Trina," Gary said.

"Where are we going?"

"I don't know," Gary said. "Maybe nowhere. But we need to be together."

"She's gonna freak, Dad."

"*Sam.*" Gary's eyebrows—or at least the one above his undamaged eye—rose up. It gave him a jaunty, mischievous look, completely at odds with what was happening on the television. The world, tonight, was seemingly moored in that strangeness, that funhouse quality. "Do it."

Belinda sobbed louder and then took long, exhaling breaths. She began flapping her hands in front of her face. "Okay," she said. "Okay. We should get stuff together. Supplies. Right?"

Sam crept quietly into Trina's room. He expected to see her eyes open—was it possible she could sleep through this? That, even deaf, she could sleep through the sense of terror that had suddenly flooded the house like a gas, a narcotic?

Even before he turned the light on, he knew the bed was empty.

Through the sour-penny taste of fear in his mouth, some abstract part of him thought that this was just like her. Her books were stacked neatly on her desktop, her horses all in a line on the sill. Tidy. Her closet door closed. Everything seemed to be in its place. The only thing missing was *Trina*. He looked under the bed, opened the closet. Just to be sure.

And then he saw the note sitting on her pillow. Sam picked it up.

"Dad," he called out, his voice cracking.

DAVE DOBBS

His world was a pure unbroken dark when the phone began ringing in the kitchen. He started to rise, his brain fogged and sleep-heavy until he saw a shape on the far wall, beneath the window. Enough moonlight to catch an outlined curve of a man's head, his shoulders, the back of the chair rising on each side like shunted wings: someone sitting in one of June's big wicker chairs.

Dobbs rose on his elbows, his heart a blunted engine misfiring beneath the meat of his chest. He smelled cigarettes, the sharp, fruity tang of alcohol and a close-pressed scent of sweat and blood. In his fear, the sheet that lay tangled around his legs felt coarse and unclean, something clutching at him. Lea next to him snuffled in her sleep on top of the blankets, her body heavy and warm.

His first thought was that it was June come back to him, June somehow dredged from death and now upright, and the feeling that came with that was not relief but a dread so galvanic that he cried out. He felt Lea stir, if only marginally, and his next thought was of the dog's goddamned uselessness as a protector, and his own fierce loyalty to protect her because of it.

"Dave," the man said, and there was something wrong with his voice, how both husky and stunted it sounded. Like someone with a cold, or a mouth packed full of gauze.

Dobbs reached for the lamp at his bedside, his head still clotted with sleep and swimming now with a curious infusion of emotions; fear had been traded for confusion and a kind of stubborn wonder. If this wasn't a dream, then whoever in the blue fuck *dared* to come into his home was going to have one hell of a—

"I got a piece aimed right at you, Dave. Let's keep it dark for now."

In the kitchen the phone rang and rang.

The man stirred in his chair and Dobbs could hear the wicker squeak in mild protest. Some mild, distant part of him wanted to tell the man that it was an antique, and one of June's few instances of possessiveness, and to get the hell off of it before the fucking thing broke.

It dawned on him then, the owner of the voice, and Dobbs's anger got a foothold.

"Nick," he said, his voice cracking. "Goddamn you."

The answering machine finally clicked on. Dobbs heard June's voice urging callers to leave their name and number (yet another way her ghost still walked the hallways of this house, that he had never changed their outgoing message) and he listened with a profound lack of surprise as Mark Fitzhugh's voice came on after the beep. "Sheriff,"—so loud he could feel Lea's ears twitching near his hand—"Nick Hayslip's just fully lost it, sir. Just pure batshit. Came at me in the Sandy Bottom with a pistol. I don't know all the details, but he's gone at this point. Told me to get out and then some guy jumps him in the bar and he runs off. Who knows where he is now. But Lonnie arrested this guy down at the Sandy, this fisherman, the guy that was knocking Hayslip around. Personally, you ask me I think the guy should be getting a fucking medal. We're still working it all out. I don't know, Dave. Sorry to call this late, but things are a clusterfuck here, boss. Hayslip's cracked. Now I'm back down at the Sandy taking statements and the fucking TV's saying the President's croaked? Are you hearing this? Hopefully you're on your way to the station, boss. We need you, you know? I'm heading—"

The machine beeped.

After that, they sat there in the dark for a while, the two of them.

Finally Dobbs cleared his throat and lay back, propped up on his elbows. Almost affably, almost like a friend, he said, "I can't see you too well, Nick, but you sound like you got a mouthful of marbles going on. That fisherman Fitzhugh talked about get some licks in?"

Hayslip chuckled, a dry, loveless sound like stones rattling in a cup. "He did manage that, Dave."

"Well, what's happening here?" His voice now was measured and calm. Lea still slept at his side. "Why are we sitting here like this?"

Hayslip's head seemed to droop at that. A man deep in prayer or some modicum of thought. "You know I been having these dreams, Dave? These real bad dreams?"

"Nam?"

Hayslip shrugged. A wicked gleam of moonlight from the window behind him lit, briefly, the pistol in his lap. "Yeah, that. Partly. This guy in my platoon that lost his legs when some kid hugged him with a grenade. I wonder sometimes why I never dream about the kid, you know? Why always Dinkle—this guy with no legs? Why's that the important part? Why not the kid? Why Vietnam at all?"

"I don't know, Nick."

Hayslip sighed, sounding almost wistful. "Finster knocked my teeth right out of my fucking mouth. Hurts like a beast."

Dobbs thought of his revolver in the drawer of the bedside table next to him. The two of them shooting it out in the dark, fifteen feet of distance between them. His very few episodes of gunplay since basic training nearly forty years before had taught him that pistols were fickle things. Things that served more simply and effectively as deterrents after a certain distance. Anything beyond a handful of paces and you could rely only on the unreliable. But this close? In a space this small? If either of their guns went off, much less both, it seemed inevitable that someone would die in this room.

"I don't know what it is you have to tell me, Nick. But this is a piss poor way to do it."

Another protest from the chair as Hayslip leaned back. "The thing that killed the Whitlock kid, Dave, it's not a person. It's not. I know you don't believe me. I'm going down to the beach, and I'm settling things. I've been preparing. That's why I came here. That's all I want. I don't even want your forgiveness, you know? But I need to tell the truth. Like, settle my affairs. With the Finsters, it'd do more harm than good, and that's selfishness. That's wrong. But with you? It'll come as a gift, I think." He gave another little laugh. "Give you someone to get pissed at. You know?"

Dobbs's voice softened. His anger, almost in spite of himself, shifting into something else. He struggled to find the man's eyes within the dark shape against the window glass. "Nick, I've got to tell you, you're not making much sense."

"It's my fault," Hayslip said, and for a moment, there was such earnestness in his voice that Dobbs was silenced. The quiet hung deep in the dark between them; so quiet he could hear Lea breathing, her body like a stolid little engine next to him.

"What's your fault?" Dobbs said quietly, though of course he knew.

Hayslip sighed again, and when he spoke his voice trembled, rose and fell like an animal moving furtively from shadow to shadow. "I killed them," he finally said. "It was an accident. But I killed them both. There's no other way around it. I didn't mean to, but I did."

"Who?" Dobbs asked, though of course he knew this, too.

Hayslip took in a single breath. Held it.

"Melissa Finster, man. And your wife."

NICK HAYSLIP

Had it been a dry night, things probably would have ended the same.

Probably. Almost surely. But that night the wind was so fierce that the rain flew sideways and made a sound like some ancient piece of machinery doing measured, relentless work against the side of Melissa's Buick. The clock on the dashboard said it was five minutes to eleven and both of them were soaked just from the run from the Lincoln City bar's front door out to the parking lot. The heater roared, and once they had gotten back to Riptide, they'd taken the back streets and avoided 101. Perhaps it was carelessness on his part or something destructive on hers but they had stopped hiding the affair all that much. They frequented bars outside of Riptide often enough, yes—they'd been to this Lincoln City dive enough times that the bartender knew their drinks—but when they drank in town, they drank together and made no real show of hiding it. Taking back roads was sloppy, the traffic more obvious. It was something that lay unspoken between them, their brazenness. Mostly a matter of Hayslip following her lead. He wondered what would happen when they were discovered and then wondered if that was what she wanted. It seemed likely and eventual that someone, some fishing buddy of her husband's, would see them together some night, but so far they had avoided it.

They were both drunk—of course they were!—and he was driving.

He loved the sense of momentum on these nights as they drove back to his place, the inevitability. The sense of the two of them hurtling through space, the big car taking those lumbering curves as it gathered speed. The certainty of what would happen next, at Hayslip's house, his bed. Her hand lay on his thigh, squeezing as she laughed and he hurtled through darkness, the few houses on those roads shuttered dark against the night. They blew past a rare stoplight. Melissa laughed again, her voice raspy and full of smoke and whiskey, and he was looking forward to fucking her when they got back to his place—he ached with it, was *thrumming* with that sense of inevitability. They had perhaps an hour before she would need to leave and he drove with the sure and easy looseness that comes to people when they believe they have had just enough to drink but not too much, when the world's gifts are bending toward and not away from them. That perfect mixture, Hayslip mused at the time, of alcohol and awareness, that fluidity. That perfect, even leveling. Her hand on the wet denim of his jeans. She rolled the window down and lit a cigarette and the Buick was suffused with rain and smoke: the two scents that would come to define her.

"If you saw you right now," she called out, smoke jetting in a ragged curl from her mouth to the open window, her hair a whirling cloud, "would you pull you over?"

He laughed. "Fuck yeah. We're going"—and here he squinted down at the speedometer, even as he began banking around another curve in the road—"sixty-five in a thirty. I'd probably haul me off in cuffs."

"And you're intoxicated," she offered.

"Drunker than hell," he agreed. "Absolutely."

"On residential streets!" she cried and squeezed his leg again. "You're speeding, deputy. While under the influence. Jesus."

"God have mercy," he agreed. He realized dimly that he had pulled her over that first time less than a mile from here, on the same road, and his heart felt oddly gladdened for it.

"You don't do *everything* this fast, do you?" she asked and moved her hand further up the wet denim of his thigh. They both laughed—Hayslip, even then, a little shyly—then he turned and grinned at her, was going to make some joke about how the best two and a half minutes of her life awaited her once they got back to his place, something idiotic and self-effacing, but she interrupted this with a girlish, strained sound, a *screech* really. Hard to call it anything else. A sound unlike any he had ever heard come from her mouth. Even before he could turn his head he knew what was happening.

The inside of the Buick had become morgue-bright with the headlights of an oncoming car.

He had veered into the other lane. Going sixty-five in a thirty, drunk. Drunk enough, at least.

Melissa's '77 Buick was almost two tons of old Detroit steel.

The collision was significant. He remembered very little of it.

As a police deputy who had worked the scene of any number of vehic-
ular accidents, Hayslip was long inured to wearing his seatbelt. Melissa,
in the passenger seat, was not. There was a cacophony of metal exploding,
the shockingly loud symphony of steel and glass meeting at great velocity,
the furious cough of strangled momentum that seemed to last, as Hayslip
dimly remembered it, roughly days, weeks, but was really only moments.
A few seconds. His head snapping forward, the great painful whoosh of his
breath leaving him. Then, the drawn out silence afterward; the music box
tinkling of safety glass on the roadside, the pinging of relaxing metal. The
sound of dripping fluids on the asphalt.

The world around him, he realized, was silent because of his newfound
singularity in the Buick; he knew immediately that Melissa was dead. He
had cinched his eyes shut and slowly opened them and saw her leaning with
her head lolling back on the headrest. There was a buckled blue crater in the
windshield where skull and glass had met. Her face was not purely a face
anymore. She was a great absence beside him and he saw—with a strange
and growing clarity that was quickly unraveling into terror, a clarity that
he would come to revisit later, in that squalid house with Fitzhugh—the
way her hands lay demurely in her own lap. The strangely delicate filigree
of blood that ran from her ear and down her neck and into her collar. A
tooth lay embedded in the vinyl of the dashboard.

He would never know for sure how long he'd sat there, but it was the
tooth that finally did it: he loosed a small, childish cry, unbuckled his
seatbelt, opened the driver's side door and tumbled out onto the road in a
panic to be away from her. He took big, tearing gasps of air that scorched
his lungs with their chill, their freshness, and he ran his hands along the
length of his body. He realized that, against all logic and likelihood and
chance, he was unharmed. Perhaps once shock retreated he would find
injuries, but as far as he could tell now, with that panic still fluttering on
the outer edges of his vision, he was fine. The other vehicle still had one
working headlight and it lit him up, lit up the interior of the Buick in
garish, horrible relief. He put his hands on the roof of the car and peered
down and saw the pebbles of glass on the front seat, the small clay horse-
charm that hung seemingly untouched from the rearview mirror. A gift
from Melissa's daughter that had always looked to Hayslip more like a
monkey than anything else, and now it hung from the mirror which hung
tentative and crazed behind the webbed blue glass of the windshield. And
also: Melissa's spread thighs, those wonderfully tight jeans, her hands

cupped delicately in her lap. If he leaned down and looked inside the car he would see the rest of her. Would see her face again.

His thoughts veered darkly and he thought of Dobbs arriving on the scene, his disappointment obvious on his face in the roving blue and red lights, and Fitzhugh smirking because he would know no other way to be, and the brisk professionalism of the EMTs as they gave him a Breathalyzer. He would be arrested, taken away gently by Fitzy, or Dobbs himself, someone's hand warm and guiding on the back of his skull as he was led into the backseat of a cruiser. The court case. His badge turned in. Lucky to get out with manslaughter; lucky to be working a mall security job, *at best*, when he finished up his little stretch of state time. When he thought of this last part, the panic rose again and he did what he did hardly without thinking: he reached in and grabbed Melissa by the collar of her jacket and pulled her into the driver's seat. He gave a strangled little cough when her head lolled, leaning her cheek against his hand as if she was taking some measure of comfort in his touch. Her cheek was still warm and he gagged and began taking long, wracking sobs of air. He leaned into the car and closed his eyes as he reached for her thighs and arranged her legs beneath the steering wheel. Blood on the cuff of his jacket. Her legs too still warm beneath his hands. Still warm! The occasional nugget of glass tinkled to the ground. The lone headlight of the other car lit everything in a cold light, lit it so well that he could see mist hovering in the air. What else? Would there be an investigation? Would they suspect anything? He started to walk away, pebbled glass gritty underfoot, deciding not to even go near the other car, the panic in him fierce as a squeezing hand.

He realized his mistake and turned back. He got in the passenger seat of the Buick and hiked his legs up and kicked the windshield out until it fell in two great blued chunks on the hood. The charm and mirror fell onto the floorboards. He got out and used the sleeve of his jacket to push the larger pieces of glass off the hood and then scattered them with his boots.

"Can you . . . can you help me, please?"

The voice was quavering and wet, a clotted whisper. (Like someone talking in a library, Hayslip would occasionally think later, usually at great cost.)

The driver of the other car.

It was true, he did not recognize her. Not then. She was just an old lady hunched over and dying. An old woman with a steering wheel embedded in her chest. Pressed tight between wheel and seat, her torso hunched over and sickeningly compressed. A face masked in blood, eyes a light and shining blue, the eyes of a young girl. Each hand lay curled loosely around the steering wheel. "Please," she rasped again and then rested her chin on the wheel as if she was very tired—which was when Hayslip realized all was lost. Because how bad did it have to be for someone when they could rest their *chin* on the top of the steering wheel?

"I can't . . . I can't help you," he stuttered, but the lady in the car gave no notice that she heard him, and the panic was tidal now, the panic was eternal, this was terror ten feet tall and insatiable. This terror ate everything else up like a monster, and he turned on a heel, the squeal of safety glass beneath one boot, and he ran. Oh God, he ran. He would see the article in the *Observer* the next morning and a sense of desolation, an expansive, unfurling loneliness that would prove to be the kernel of a terrible guilt, started in his throat and expanded throughout his whole body the morning he saw June Dobbs's picture in the paper next to Melissa's. And he knew it was a thing he could never tell, that he could never tell a soul, that the guilt would threaten to strangle him and yet never would, that the heart would beat relentlessly, worrying only for itself, even in spite, sometimes, of his most fervent wishes; and the guilt would keep him quiet, and—

—and as Hayslip spoke the words in Dave Dobbs's darkened bedroom, lost finally in his confession, lost in the sorrow of it, the relief of it like a balm, he heard Dobbs *move* across the room but he was too slow, much too slow, and there was a flashpoint—once, twice, the world becoming still and bright as a photograph in the muzzle flash. The shots deafening in the small room. Cordite-stink rich as an animal's spore, as savage and immediate, and Dobbs was upright in his bed now firing at Hayslip from twelve, fifteen feet away, and Hayslip was screaming and firing back blindly, pure instinct; and somewhere in all that noise, he could still hear the dog barking. In the funhouse strobes of their gunfire, Dobbs looked maddened and insane, his lips drawn back from his teeth, tears lit like traceries down his cheeks; and then Hayslip felt a hammer strike him to numbness in his side—a blow against his ribcage that spun him out of the chair and onto the floor—and then he was out of the room and down the hallway and running through the darkness of this unfamiliar house with his hand to his ribs and the old man's anguished howls chasing after him like some errant ghost.

TRINA FINSTER

In the darkness, she dreamt that the world was like a body.

The bad feeling she had felt all day followed her in her dreams. She saw the body from above, from a great height. The topography of the land like plaits of skin plied and bunched, and here lay wending rivers like arteries, and lakes like eyes, like concavities pooled with blood. Great forests like tumbles of hair. The ceaseless tide of the sea like a heartbeat. And then she saw the warhead, a single one arcing like a bullet for the body, a thing built for one sole intent. She knew she was asleep but the realization helped nothing. Trina felt a savage moment of recognition—*I told you this would happen!*—and then a great white flash flared and snapped and expanded across the surface of the world. The body rippling, the body in flames. A great explosion, a vacuum and expansion of heat and pressure, and following behind it, mountains were leveled to a warped and smoking floor of glass and sand. Valleys filled with the mountains' effluvia. In moments, the world became little more than a riddled, lunar orb choked in dust. Otherworldly in its ruination. A devastated, alien place where the old one had been.

She spent some time blinking sleep away and looked at the red digits of her clock and knew that something had changed. A bright swath of light from the living room fell along the floor and across a corner of her comforter, which was strange because it was late and normally her dad was in bed by now and Sam was in his room listening to his tapes, and all the lights should be off but were not.

She had to pee. She sat up in bed for a moment, the image of the boiling seas and the land suddenly gone liquid as molten glass fading from her, sepia-toned and not as fearsome now that she was awake. Just the phantom of it, the vestiges like something snagged in her clothes, her hair. She stood up and stopped in front of her doorway. She rubbed her eyes, her hair sleep-knotted, full of tangle-rats. Trina's bedroom faced the television and the back of the couch, and she immediately recognized Belinda's silhouette, that bright bottle-red hair. Beyond the couch she saw the television screen. A jittery image that meant the cameraman was running while he filmed. What was it? A city somewhere, a wobbling nighttime shot of buildings. Words ran in the ticker beneath the image and she squinted to read them, still thumbing the sleep-dust from her eyes:

PRESIDENT'S WHEREABOUTS UNKNOWN, POSSIBLY DECEASED FROM MEDICAL COMPLICATIONS OF 1980 ASSAS-SINATION ATTEMPT.

She touched the doorknob of her door, ran her fingertips along the key-plate just to feel something, to make sure, *for certain,* that she wasn't still dreaming. And then:

POSSIBLE SOVIET MISSILE ATTACK EN ROUTE TO U.S., GER-MANY. CITIZENS URGED TO STAY INDOORS AND AWAIT EMERGENCY INSTRUCTONS.

It was the misspelled word—*INSTRUCTONS*—that solidified it for her, that somehow cemented the reality of it. She was surprised at her sense of relief. *Finally,* some dim part of her thought. Some shameful part. At least the end was moving toward them now. There was little they could do but try in whatever way they could to save themselves. If they were to perish, how would it happen? She had read all of the scenarios in *The Looming Error,* committed them to memory the way she would entire passages of *The Wolf in the Basement.* A pulsed white flash that seared through the eyelids? A thunder so strong she felt it, for a split second, thrumming in her bones? A single heartbeat of indescribable heat, and then nothing? A vast quiet? Or would she and her family perish more slowly, through radiation sickness? Starvation? She could see Belinda there on the couch, could recognize now that her mother's friend was weeping, her shoulders rising and falling, but where was her father? Where was Sam?

Belinda must have sensed her. She whirled around, her eyes ringed with smeared mascara. A clot of tissues was pressed beneath her chapped nose.

"Go back to bed!" Belinda screamed frantically—even Trina could tell she'd screamed it. Belinda took a ragged breath and pressed the heel of her palm flat against her mouth, her eyes glimmering with tears, and then took her hand away so Trina could read her lips. More measured, she said, "Go back to bed, Trina. Your dad and brother had to run an errand. Go to bed."

"We have to go," Trina said. "Is it really happening? It's not safe here."

"It's just rumors, baby. Everything's fine."

"I knew this was going to happen," Trina said, and at this, Belinda began crying in earnest and stood up and went to the telephone in the kitchen, pulling the cord taut so she could stand in the living room and watch the television and Trina both. "We should get near the water first," Trina said, "and then go underground. It's better to be near water when they explode. It doesn't dissipate as well." She wasn't sure if she'd pronounced all the words correctly; they felt clumsy in her mouth.

Belinda spoke into the receiver of the telephone and only when she took it away from her mouth did Trina realize she had been speaking to her. "We're safe," she said. "We're safe, Trina. Go back to bed. I'm calling your dad, he'll be here any minute."

There was more Trina could say, *should* say, but she didn't. Adults in their way could be as deaf as she was, but it was a willful deafness. She wondered about the President—if the bullet had finally tumbled into his heart, if that was what had killed him. If he was really dead. People would sit and wonder what they should do until there was no option to do anything at all.

She *wanted* to go back to bed, pull the covers up over her eyes and wait for her father to come home. But then the image returned: pulsing, interlocking rings of expanding devastation checkering the globe. *The death of the world.*

"Go back to bed," Belinda said, biting a thumbnail as she continued to hold the receiver pressed to her ear. "I mean it."

Trina gently shut her bedroom door and turned on her bedside lamp. Even before she walked to her desk and ripped out a piece of paper from her notebook, she had dumped her backpack out onto her bed. If there was anything that her mother's and Toad's deaths had taught her, it was that no one was going to wait for you. You had to help yourself. The people in charge were the ones who had done this. She grimly pictured Toad asking for a timeout there on the beach, a do-over as he was attacked and eaten by a bear, or a crazy man and his dog, or whatever rabid animal that had hurt him so badly they'd had to keep the lid of his coffin closed at the funeral. No one would save them. She had to do it herself.

She sat at her desk, the world outside her window etched with the crystalline brightness of moonlight, and she took one of her favorite pencils from her pencil box and began a note, trying not to imagine that this would be the last time she would see this room, their house. Again, that ceaseless biting fear that it would all simply be a moment of heat-death, a brutal, momentary glare, and then nothing. The seconds rushing like a waterfall, irretrievable. If she thought too hard about it, she would freeze up. All the times that her parents and teachers had told her how smart she was, but here was where it mattered—staring at this blank white page.

It was a short note. She put it on her pillow and began getting dressed, quickly and carefully. She still had to pee, and there was a brief moment of doubt when she thought of Belinda finding the note when she was alone, and how that would terrify her, but her resolve stayed. No one else was going to save them. She put clothes and the little money she had in her backpack, along with a pair of Twix bars that had been on her windowsill forever because her dad bought them for her, sometimes, even though she didn't really like them. Next, one single horse from her windowsill—the brown one with the white spot and the gold mane. *The Looming Error* was the last thing she put in there, on the very top, a weighted and solemn thing. She zipped up her jacket and turned off her light and then, as quietly as she could, pushed up her window and climbed out, the dew-heavy air cool on her cheeks.

She knew where she had to go. She began crying as she crept along the side of the house, hoisting her pack on her shoulders. There was only one place where they would all be safe. She just had to hope that she could lead them there. That they would follow her.

SAM FINSTER

It was her handwriting that just killed him.

The looping cursive, her *E*s slightly larger than all of the other letters, the dots of her *I*s made of actual circles. The pained penmanship of it threatened to undo him. The nine-year-old who read romance novels and books about nuclear proliferation and loved *The A-Team*. The one who was probably a genius and still misspelled words because she was *nine fucking years old*; surely nothing bad could happen to a sister like that. Surely the world had taken enough.

Maybe it was just a mistake, he thought. Maybe people were confused. An accident. A man like Reagan, with his swagger and bravado and seamed face; a man like that just seemed deathless, didn't he? Surely it was all just . . . confusion. A fuck up.

The three of them had walked out into the front yard in a daze, the wind clacking the tree branches together, throwing a fine mist on their faces, the sound oddly musical. Gary had gone to his truck and Sam had said, gently, like speaking to a small boy, "Dad. There's not enough room," meaning there wouldn't be enough room for the four of them if—*when*—they found Trina, and his father had stared at him over the hood with a lost look, a look of raw, naked gratitude, and Belinda had sobbed, just once, and handed his father the keys to her car. "Here," she said, "I can't see for shit right now." Gary had peeled out so hard they heard gravel clanging against the undercarriage.

They drove toward Wolf Point as Belinda leaned her head against the passenger side window. "I'm sorry, I'm so sorry. I told her to get back to bed." In the side view mirror, as they passed beneath streetlights, Sam from the back seat would watch her face smooth into some measure of normalcy and then crumple in on itself again. He held Trina's letter in his lap and smoothed it flat against his thighs as if it were some kind of piss poor talisman.

"It's okay," Sam told her, because Gary was not going to.

"I didn't think she'd l-l-leave," Belinda gasped.

His father slammed his hands against the steering wheel. His swollen eye like something half-formed, some new feature only halfway finished and left there. The streets were empty. Gary spun the radio dial and all the stations full of the same vacuous nothingness, the same smoky tendrils of information: the President had gone into emergency surgery that day after collapsing, but it was still unconfirmed whether or not the bullet had tumbled into his heart and blocked a valve. "He's not a young man," they heard one pundit say, and then, after another spin of the dial, they heard one DJ, with the mellow, languorous tones of a bluesman, say, "Hey, how long's it take a Russian ICBM to hit Anchorage, Pete? Or New York? D.C.? They have the range, right? They'd tell us West Coasters, right? They wouldn't keep us in the dark, right?"

KRPT was playing the Everly Brothers.

"Oh for sweet *fuck*," Gary hissed.

Sam kept looking toward the sky, as if he would see the actual criss-crossed arcs of missiles heading to their targets. The moon hung like junk jewelry on velvet. A cloudless night sky. When was the last time that had happened? When was the last time he had *looked*, really? Gary turned back to the bluesman; on second listen the man's terror was woefully apparent, running jagged and brash beneath the bravado. "We're getting messages from some East Coasters, folks, who are saying the missiles are definitely up in the air, baby. This shit's for real. Someone's told us Manhattan's been hit, Philly's been hit. Boston. What kinda timeline you folks think we're looking at before the whole motherfucker goes all dark and hot on us?" There was a pause and the man let out a shrill laugh that went on for much too long. "My producer just got on my case for swearing, folks. Pete, I don't think the FCC's gonna be too worried about my language for much longer. I don't think we're gonna be worried about *anything* for too much longer."

"Turn it off, Dad. Please."

The voice on the radio continued: "So let's go out in style, folks. I got half an ounce of Jamaican Red here, and me and Pete are gonna play *all* the love songs, all them panty-droppers and heart-stoppers, 'til Boris goes and shuts out all the lights on us for good. It's been a hell of a run, baby. This one goes out to all you lovely people, and our dead dumb cowboy of a President, and hell, even you Red commie cock-knockers. I'll miss you all quite terrible."

Gary turned the radio off.

Sam smoothed out the note again. In that looping, labored cursive of hers, the words there and gone and there again beneath the passing streetlights:

> *HURRY! It won't be as bad if we're all at the beach. I learned about it! It's not as concintrated an explosion. We'll be safe. I didn't know how else to leave except run away. Meet me at wolf point! I love you so much please don't be mad at Bilinda because I snuck out. Meet me there! Hurry! Love TRINA*

Hastings Street was gilded in silvery moonlight and all three of them were smoking, the wind tearing through the interior of the car. After Gary took a long curve in the road that offered them an unbroken view of the beach below the cliffs, a pulsing red light filled the inside of the car and Sam, for a moment—he couldn't help it—thought of the missiles, thought one was *behind* them, but then he turned and saw a pickup looming up fast, a rotating bubble-light on its dashboard.

"I'm not fucking pulling over," Gary said to the rearview mirror, his voice tight. "You can forget that." His lips pulled back from his mouth like an animal stuck in a trap.

The truck swerved into the other lane and blew right past them, the red light throwing long curling afterimages in the darkness.

NICK HAYSLIP

Hayslip sat in his Datsun kicking out tiny little gasps of air, little harsh ones, his hands pressed to his belly. He sounded like a pregnant woman practicing her Lamaze techniques. Hayslip had never been one to appreciate irony. He just hadn't been built for it. But it was impossible at this juncture in time *not* to draw correlations between Hayslip and Atlanta's favorite son, Private Stanley Dinkle, the Grenade Magnet, the Dope-Smoking Legless Wonder: Hayslip's car smelled like spools of copper wire, like a cupful of new pennies, and blood ran freely through his cinched fingers. His hands were black with it under the moonlight; he was gloved in it up to his fore-arms. He and Stanley Dinkle, at last united in their damage. The pain was there, but in a distant, throbbing way, like he'd taken a decent punch to the kidneys. But the bullet was in his side, had entered under the curl of his ribcage, and there was no exit wound as far as he could tell, though even through the numbness it had hurt like living shit to try and reach behind his back to check. God knew what kind of ricocheting had gone on in there. Any way you looked at it, it was stuck in there, and that was bad. Any blood from his mouth and he'd know a lung had, at the least, been grazed. But for now, as long as he sat relatively still and practiced his Lamaze, the pain was like someone else's toothache, pain that belonged in another room somewhere. He'd run out of Dobbs's house and then half-galloped in a ludicrous, lurching gait back to his hatchback parked a quarter-mile down the sheriff's meandering forested driveway. He turned the ignition on and drove one-handed, south down 101.

He surprised himself with his lack of regret toward telling Dobbs. Unlike Gary Finster, he still believed telling Dobbs had been the right thing to do. He had done the man wrong, had done June Dobbs wrong. He should have stayed and tried to help. There was no walking away from that. It was doubtful he could have saved her, she had been too far gone, but he could have stayed with her. He owed Dobbs the rage the man felt now. He owed Dobbs a body to direct it at. Better that than to simply curse the world, wrestle for the rest of his life with some dipshit idea of fate or circumstance or God's will at work. It had been none of those things—it had been Hayslip driving drunk and trying to hide what he had done.

"Sometimes all you can be is an excellent shitty example," he said, and his voice was so gravelly and worn that it frightened him and then sent him into a gale of hysterics, which frightened him even more, and he clamped his mouth shut so hard his teeth clacked together. He drove with one hand pressed to his side and, with the other, felt the dull pulse of warm blood against his palm. Slowly, the woods gave way to the scattered outbuildings and silos and salvage yards that made up the outskirts of town.

The Whitlock kid had been discovered eviscerated at that small inland spit just past Wolf Point. A spot normally reserved for high school bonfires, the occasional fistfight and, for those kids truly adventurous or desperate, maybe some awkward, uncomfortable sex amid a scattering of blackened driftwood and empty bottles. But after Whitlock's death, and the Tumquala girl's bones being discovered nearby, it had become a marked place now. And who else, before the girl, might have died there? Who could know that? If Leon Davies was to be believed, the *tah-kee-na-teh* had been around for a long time. The little cove was now an abattoir, heavy with the dead. That's where he was called, that's where he needed to go.

It's a muscle flexing, Davies had insisted. *It's idiotic. There's no purpose to it.*

"All the more fucking reason, right?" Hayslip rasped, folded nearly in half, squinting at the windshield.

The parking lot of the turnaround was empty. The beach beyond the ramp was dim but visible enough, a lighter expanse against the dark wash of the sea. The moon hung in the sky above him and he stepped out of his car, his .45 clutched in a bloodied hand.

He looked down and saw in the unforgiving light that he was blood-soaked from ribs to thigh. The blood shone a garish funhouse red at his t-shirt, but was black at his jeans and jacket. The disparity surprised him; it was almost pretty. The red clay scree bracing the parking lot was pooled in shadow, and the dunes—with their dottings of crabgrass hackles—shirred in the breeze.

Hayslip walked down the ramp, carefully stepping over the sagging yellow caution tape Fish and Wildlife had laid down after the death of Todd

Whitlock. It was colder down here on the sand, the air heavy with mist, and he walked leaning over, his fist pressed against his poor divided guts. Everything felt hot now save his hands and feet, which felt stone-like with cold. It felt like there was blood in his boot but it didn't look like there was. I should ask Dinkle if he ever thought about his legs. Or if he could ever feel his legs get up and do ghost-laps around the room. Did he dream about them? Did Dinkle ever dream about *me?* Hayslip's thoughts were becoming loose, slippery things, difficult to hold onto.

He walked. No one was out. No children had defied the yellow tape that night, taken the chance. Was he far enough away from the lights of the parking lot? Did a thing like the low walker even care about shit like that? About being seen? Or was it like any other animal, prowling under the canopy of darkness?

The Whitlock boy's body had been found not fifty yards away from where Hayslip stood now, as he leaned over and gasped the way he used to after a particularly hard run. Just around that outcropping of stone right there. He coughed and spit up a clot of dark blood onto the sand. It had hit a lung, after all.

He cursed and began walking toward the cove. The tide was coming in, and foam played at the heels of his boots.

He turned past the wedge of cliff and saw nothing in the cove save the normal detritus: the blackened bones of a few small fires, bottle caps that gleamed like worn coins beneath the moon. No monster, no beast culled from a book of nightmares. Hayslip lowered himself gingerly onto a large log laid before a charred fire in its ring of stones, hissing in pain as he did. He spit again, wiped his mouth and stared for a moment at the dark blood creased into the back of his hand. It wasn't sadness that was playing tug-of-war inside him with his flitting thoughts and his fatigue, but a profound sense of waste. The images came unbidden: Sherry in his bathroom, one pant leg on the floor as she curled her hands around her head and pressed herself against the cabinets, the door halved behind him. The frightened, searching eyes of June Dobbs as he turned and ran away from her. Kicking the windshield out of the car to throw off the forensics team and hide the impact point where Melissa had died—the gross, brilliant, piece of shit *cunning* in that. All these things rose up in him, all these and more, a cavalcade. "I'm so sorry," he said, sobbing. His voice high and pinched, a little boy's voice as he buried his face in his bloody hands. "I'm so sorry, everybody, Christ."

The wind howled in the little cove. Eddies of sand scudded along his boots.

He rose on unsteady feet and staggered, wheeling around to face the cliffs looming above him, his back to the sea. "Come on," he screamed, his voice cracking, his vision flaring dark at the corners. "Let's go!" He spread his arms wide and then hunched over in pain. His clothes tented in a gust of wind, a scarecrow come to life.

Nothing. Just the howling wind in that sad, hollow pocket of land, the age-old susurration of the sea at his back. He screamed so hard something vital in his throat threatened to come undone and still the wind took his voice like it was nothing; the tender scab on his lip broke and welled with blood. The notion of dropping to his knees and *resting* seemed like a good one, one worth considering. Then, as if in some wretched call and response, around the edge of the cove, back near the turnaround, he heard it: a scream.

He turned and staggered that way, kicking up fans of sand before him, half bent at the waist, arms wrapped around his sides. *I call this the zombie-stomp,* he thought, feeling for certain now the slickness of blood in his boot.

He passed around the cove's edge and saw the little girl standing half-way down the ramp to the beach, just visible in the reach of the parking lot lights. Melissa's daughter, Trina. Some part of him was unsurprised; their lives were intertwined, incalculably, as woven braids. Some things were left up to you, but others? Try turning away from fate and fate greets you in some other doorway. Fate hunts you down. He broke out in a smile, his teeth rimed in blood.

And then he saw something moving between him and the girl, something at the bottom of the ramp.

The girl was stock-still with her hands at her sides. She screamed again, high and wavering, the sound louder now that he was out of the cove.

In the parking lot above, a truck, its red trouble light spinning, skidded to a stop behind his car. The thing crept closer to the girl, and Hayslip stood there dumbly enrapt. Even with its back turned to him there was something intrinsically *wrong* with its shape, the way it moved. How its curving lines seemed broken up here and there with distended knuckles of cartilage. The eye struggled to settle on it. It took another low-slung step toward her, eating the distance. The girl stood frozen. He was seeing the low walker, the *tah-kee-na-teh.* What had it said in the story, after the man had asked why it wore the face of his wife?

Because you are in mourning, and I am hungry.

With an arm seemingly weighted by stones, Hayslip raised his .45 into the sky and fired. Even the gunshot seemed puny, swallowed by the night, but the low walker's head whipped around. It saw him and let out a cry that sounded human—some dim part of him insisting it sounded much like Stanley fucking Dinkle—it might as well have arrived directly from his nightmares.

But it turned his way—turning from the girl—and settled its claws into the earth, adjusting.

And then, in a burst of sand, rocketed toward him.

TRINA FINSTER

She went first to Tumquala Park, skirting 101 and sticking to the tree line along Hastings Street, skulking along in the ditches or the brush when she saw the headlights of an approaching car. Maybe the route to the destination was simply from habit, because she went there so often. The park made her think of Toad, Mr. Whitlock and their orange cat and their little leaning house just over the hill and down the gravel road. She thought of all the times Toad and Sam, smoking cigarettes and laughing, had watched her slide down the hill—these two boys who everyone thought were bad but were not. She started to cry for real then and, after swinging her arms in the dark, clearing the cobwebs, sat in the dark shadows of the wooden bullet. The hillside, once sharply and precisely carved, was becoming worn smooth again. Now, it was little more than a slope, and soon it would be hard to tell people had ever done anything to it at all. She thought about taking *The Looming Error* from her backpack and reading some of it, but she hated it at that moment; after all of that time she had spent reading it, obsessing over it, memorizing entire passages—how had it helped her? As if *knowing* about something terrible could keep it from happening.

She rose and rubbed her face and settled her backpack on her shoulders again. She started toward the turnaround at a trot; if her note said she was going to Wolf Point, she needed to go to Wolf Point. What would happen if they got there first, Sam and her father and Belinda, and she wasn't there? They'd be freaked out, for one. And then they'd go somewhere else to look for her, probably somewhere in town, and the whole thing would have been for nothing.

She remembered a passage in *The Looming Error*—had committed one specific line to memory the same way she could remember the dialogue for entire scenes of *The A-Team*, or the really good parts in the romance novels she got from the library. The General had written about how a group of Army scientists and engineers had gotten a hold of a bunch of Japanese ships after the war—huge ones, warships and aircraft carriers and everything—and put them in the ocean and dropped a bomb on them to study what would happen. And what happened was hardly anything. Only two of the forty-five ships sank. There were tons of problems with the detonations, and some of them didn't even suffer damage. The scientists, according to the general, said that the bombs worked best in highly concentrated urban areas. Cities and towns. But oceans? Even beaches? Not so well.

It is as if we are at the grace and mercy of the tide, the general had written. That was the line, and forty years later she just hoped it still counted for something.

There was no good answer here—even after surviving the blasts, they had radiation to consider, not even counting what all else the coming days would bring—and yet she still found herself hoping, just a little, and immediately chastised herself for being stupid. For the millionth time she raged at her deafness, the pure, animal *brokenness* of it; she could be listening to the radio on Sam's Walkman right now, listening to the news, finding out what was happening.

The parking lot of the turnaround was empty aside from a red, rust-battered Datsun hatchback. Crosshatches of yellow tape sagged across the ramp entrance and fluttered limply in the breeze.

What now? What else was there to do but wait? Wait for her family to find her or for the missiles to explode. One or the other. She started crying again—that these were her only choices!—as mist drifted like brightened halos around the streetlights. She should have stayed with Belinda and waited for her father, for Sam. Being with them would have been better than this. It's not like Riptide would even be near any major cities, what the book called "built up targets." Portland? Seattle? No, radiation would be their concern. She should have stayed home. She'd run away and now they would come looking for her. She should get down into the darkness a little bit more. She would watch the entrance of the ramp; if she saw her father's truck, or Belinda's car, she would run back up. But if a police car came, they would just take her back home. Or take her somewhere else, and then Sam and her father would never find her.

She walked down the ramp, her head hung low, to where the cement gave way to hard-packed sand, fighting back her tears. When she looked up, there was something in front of her that seemed to have been pulled from a nightmare, somehow. She caught a scent of rot, like the time a mouse had died in the walls of the laundry room, but a million times worse, and her throat cinched closed like someone had pinched the end of a balloon. It took a step toward her and she saw its face, and finally, a scream ripped loose from her mouth.

She chanced a desperate look back at the parking lot and saw a blue pickup with a flashing red light skid to a stop behind the hatchback, and when she looked toward the thing again, it had taken another step toward her, creeping with its belly in the sand like a cat, its eyes unblinking. It seemed *mostly* like a cat, but a cat with its jaws unhinged beyond all possibility, and a mouth hung busy with strips of dead flesh, a mouth filled with rows of teeth that bent every which way. It shook its head and she watched as muscles rippled along its back.

Hunched and low, it kept coming toward her.

Then, further down on the beach, a single gunshot rang out.

DAVE DOBBS

I'm going down to the beach and I'm settling things.

They had found the Whitlock boy at Wolf Point, and Dobbs was sure that's where Hayslip had gone. He'd thought that, perhaps, he'd heard the phone ringing once, twice, its shrill whine through the glass as he'd slammed the front door, but it didn't matter. He got in his truck, slapped the red trouble light on the dashboard—something he had not done since he'd gotten the call about June's accident, and not once in his entire life before that—and went to find the man. There was blood on June's wicker chair and stippling the wall behind it, scattered drops that led out the front door. He had locked Lea in, the dog barking and pissing everywhere, terrified, springing to life on the bed once the gunfire had started. He was amazed that Hayslip had missed both him and the dog, and some dim part of him wondered if it had been intentional.

That thought, however, resolved nothing. Changed absolutely nothing at all.

He looked at the radio mounted on his dash, considered raising someone at the station, getting backup. Houses flickered past, his wipers shearing a light rain from the glass. He was driving too fast. These night roads, even 101, would always be deathly quiet here in the witching hours—until a dog or a drunk inexplicably stumbled out in front of the headlights. He should get someone to back him up, but—even as he thought of June and called it love, he knew he wanted Hayslip for something else, something uglier and crafted from hurt and vengeance. He wanted Hayslip for himself. Forget whatever else Fitzhugh had said about Reagan, about whatever else might be going on: it was all moot once he pictured June crumpled against the steering wheel, imagined her poor body twisted and broken as she had *begged him for help*—

He skidded over to the shoulder and stumbled out of the truck and vomited on the sparse gravel next to the road. Asphalt glittered in the moonlight.

His heart like a fist. He wiped his mouth with the back of his hand, then ripped the antenna from his truck and whipped the side panel of it like a petulant child as strange animal keenings worked their way from his throat. He sagged against the door and dropped the antenna as the wind continued its stupid mindless ministrations among the thin woods surrounding him. Somewhere beyond the trees, he could see the black expanse of the sea and he got back in the truck and tried willing his heart to slow, some part of him abstractly considering the possibility of a heart attack. It seemed possible. On the one hand, the entire fucking mess would be over, wouldn't it? On the other—there was still Hayslip to consider. He didn't know what he would do when he found the man. He hoped it wouldn't be murder. But at that moment, he was unwilling to deny the possibility entirely. His blood was too heated, his heart too sick and heavy with this new knowledge.

He drove slower now, his tires no longer kicking loose roadside scrabble as he curved around corners. An ugly blast of validation ripped through him when he drove south through town and finally saw Hayslip's car parked at the bottom of the turnaround. He pulled to a stop behind it and stepped out, his revolver in his hand, the truck's interior and the night beyond spinning from red to black to red again beneath the bubble light. He started toward Hayslip's car when he heard someone cry out across the parking lot near the ramp leading down to the beach, the sound thinned by the wind and distance but recognizable enough for the simple fact it was heavy with terror.

That, and it sounded like a child.

And then further away, unmistakable above the ceaseless waves: the sharp report of a gunshot.

SAM FINSTER

"Ah, what the sweet fuck is this?" Gary hissed. Down at the bottom of the turnaround sat a pair of vehicles, a rotating red light on one of them flaring and fading, idiotic in its insistence. His father accelerated, the engine groaning with its own seeming fury, the dark sea and the pale concrete abutments of the parking lot looming toward them, and then Gary slammed the brakes and wrenched the wheel and they skidded to a stop behind the other vehicles, amid a rasp of burnt rubber. Sam's head bounced off the headrest of the front seat.

Through the rain-dotted glass he saw an old man trotting down the ramp to the beach. When the man looked back at them, Sam saw that it was Dave Dobbs, the sheriff, but he seemed fundamentally changed. The measured, careful man he remembered—from when they had discovered the bones—was gone: this man looked terrified. He was carrying a revolver and seemed ancient and panic-stricken. Everything fiercely bright under those parking lot lights.

"Dad," he said.

"I see him," Gary said. Even as he said it, he was out of the car and tearing after Dobbs in the darkness, his father all pumping elbows and legs in a way that Sam had never seen. *"We don't even know that she's here,"* Belinda cried out, clambering from her side of the Buick, but of course they did. The surety of it was in the air. The world was electric with it.

Sam opened his door; the night was rich with the brine of the sea and his own dry-mouthed fear. The sound of the waves crashing was so familiar and constant as to hardly be there. Gusts of wind flattened his jeans against his legs. He started running toward the ramp, his jacket so heavy it felt like something pulling him down. He peeled it off and dropped it to the pavement, the bark of chilled air sharp against his skin. It seemed to revive him, awaken him in some vital way. He kept running.

Down the ramp and beyond the ring of parking lot lights, where there was only moonlight and the pocked, lunar surface of the beach, driftwood lay in tumbles, pale as castaway bones. The moonlight painted the caps of seafoam with a glowing luminance and he was surprised to see a number of people down on the beach; the closest was his father, who was on his knees clutching Trina, burying her in the folds of his coat, wrapping her in his arms, and beyond them was Dobbs, on one knee in a shooter's stance, his white hair bright in the gloom. He fired once, the sound of the gunshot flat, swallowed by the night. Sam ran to his father and touched his shoulder and Gary, without turning, reached over and grasped Sam's hand in his work-roughened one. Gripped it so tightly the bones nearly ground together. "It's okay," his father kept saying. "It's okay. We're good."

Beyond Dobbs, thirty or forty yards down the beach, lay a man on the sand. He was being attacked by some animal, some kind of cat, a writhing, black, long-legged thing. He thought of the cop at Toad's funeral, skeleton-thin and crazed, asking Stacy Whitlock if Toad had gotten into anything regarding dark magic, if he had talked about something on the beach—and then the world suddenly threatened to tilt beyond Sam's vision, and he looked down at his sister, instead. He knew absolutely the animal that had killed Toad was right there on the beach, and as if an affirmation, a man's watery scream drifted toward them. Sam chanced a look. The man—he saw that it was, in fact, the cop from Todd's funeral, the cop that had been strangely immersed in their lives lately—kicked his feet in the sand as if he might push himself away, but the thing cloaked him like a shadow, had fallen on him like a draped overcoat. Dobbs, meanwhile, rose up and fired his pistol again while slowly walking further down the beach. They were paced, even shots, the sound of them pealing off the low ceiling of the sky, flat and hollow-sounding.

His father clutched Trina, one hand enveloping the delicate bowl of her skull, pressing her to the dark cave between his shoulder and heart as she wept. Gary still held Sam's hand with his other one. "It's okay," he kept saying. "We're safe. We're safe."

NICK HAYSLIP

The *tah-kee-na teh* had at least gone straight for him, its interest in the child seemingly forgotten.

He fired once and the creature pivoted in the sand, a crazed flexing of joints that sent it swerving out of the bullet's path. *It runs like a fucking greyhound*, he thought. Seeing the thing, its impossible fluidity—its impossibility at all—was probably the most singular moment of vindication he had ever experienced in his life. It was a savage, coin-bright feeling that tore through him like a baptism and he walked toward the *tah-kee-na-teh* with his pistol raised in both trembling hands, his guts a roiling fire.

As if sensing this, it stopped and stood stock-still, only its tail whipping divots in the sand. A low growl like the muted thunder of a diesel engine rumbled from low in its chest. The wind changed and he caught a whiff of rot, the sugar-sweet fug of spoiled meat. More thoughts came to him like a startling of birds. He was reminded again that he'd done more than end two lives the night of the accident: he'd been the catalyst of irreparable heartbreak for countless others. His life before the accident had been spent in a kind of wretched half-life—a strange, *dim* life, one mostly misspent. Mostly wasted. He'd squandered his time, really, and yet caused pain for so many. He'd been selfish, blind. These lofty realizations were very different from the stasis that had enveloped him in the house with Fitzhugh. Here, now, the world seemed to open up. He kept walking toward the *tah-kee-na-teh*.

Beyond the creature, he saw Dobbs running down the ramp, seconds before the low walker slammed into his ribs with its seething black mass of rippling muscle and bone and bristling teeth. It felt like he'd been hit by a car. He had time to think—*This is your purposeless thing, Davies? Your pointless vanguard?*—before he was thrown breathless onto the cold sand, and even before he landed, the thing was already biting at his arms, at the pale meat of his upturned hands. He wrapped one hand around its ribs and felt a ladder of muscle walk up its spine as it settled on top of him. The jointed, flexing things that settled on either side of his face were almost hands. Clots of hair hung from its skull and pooled in dank coils in the sand around his head and it smelled like every flyblown carcass on every road he'd ever driven down, and it had his left hand in its mouth and shook it like a dog playing with a toy. Hayslip screamed. He felt hot blood stipple his face. Dimly he heard a gunshot—Dobbs—and realized he still held the .45 in his other hand. He pressed it to the bone of the thing's misshapen skull and pulled the trigger. The head hardly recoiled, but it let go of his hand, a number of jagged teeth breaking off like yellow quills in his palm, between his knuckles. One of its eyes—a glimmering, baleful green only moments before—winked out like someone snuffing a wick. He dug his feet in the sand and tried to push himself away and it settled one hand on his chest, pinning him, claws effortlessly puncturing fabric and then flesh, hooking into his collarbones in a bright frieze of pain. With its other hand it swiped its claws down his torso from neck to thigh. Hayslip felt his guts unspool in one hot dark splash. The pain was galvanic and he screamed again.

Dobbs's pistol shots echoed down the beach and the low walker's head shifted like moving water toward the sound. Hayslip saw a bullet kick up a clot of sand near his own ruined hand. His lifted his head—easily as difficult as any run he had ever done, easily as difficult as the entire eleven months he'd spent in Vietnam—and saw more people gathered at the bottom of the ramp. Things were darkening, growing quiet. The Finsters were gathered together, and Christ, was that Melissa's friend, the redhead? It was! It was a goddamned family reunion down at Wolf Point tonight. Dimly he saw the low walker give him one last glance and then begin its low loping run away from the turnaround as Dobbs fired another shot. Hayslip dropped his head back in the sand, so warm now, like it somehow still held all the day's meager sunlight, gathered it and saved it for him, for this express purpose—to keep him warm. He was glad that people had come in time, glad that Melissa's daughter was safe. After all of his grievous missteps, it was good that he had gotten this one thing right. He turned his head and saw the ocean and the moon, and he was tired and happy, and he realized, finally, Christ—he was *finally* ready to sleep.

SAM FINSTER

Trina was a shape tucked against his father's kneeling body, her tiny hand curled around his neck. His father did not seem interested in letting go of her any time soon.

"We have to go somewhere safe," Belinda said.

"Trina thinks the beach is the safest place," Sam said, and then almost laughed for how insane that sounded, how clearly that bright idea had been disproven.

Sheriff Dobbs turned and looked at them, his mouth opening and closing. He looked pale and tired and old—fragile in his civilian clothes, his face wide and seamed. "I have to go look after that man," he said. "Please go back to your vehicles." He saw that they had no intention of doing what he asked and shook his head. As he walked toward the man's body down the beach, he opened the cylinder of his revolver and dumped the spent cartridges in his palm and put them in his pocket in one smooth motion, and began quickly putting fresh cartridges into their chambers. As smoothly as any western. Sam gazed at him, stunned at the ease of motion, the muscle memory of such a thing, in spite of what they'd just witnessed.

"Did you . . . did you see that thing, Dad?"

Gary let go of his hand. "I saw it," he said into Trina's hair. "I didn't get a good look at it."

Even in the dim light and with the wind tearing at his father's words, Sam knew a lie when he heard one.

"It wasn't an animal," Sam said. "I mean, it was *kind of,* but . . . Jesus, man. Jesus Christ."

His father said nothing, might as well have been deaf himself, and Sam was about to say something else, something about how poor fucking Toad, tough as he was, had never stood a chance against that thing. And how something about that idea almost helped; made it like it wasn't Toad's fault at all. There was nothing he could have done. That thing had been a monster. Like, a real one. Again, Sam's world threatened to upend itself, that leaning kind of internal vertigo that was probably just his head telling him enough was enough, no more, please, boss, the inn is full, and his jaw clacked shut.

"So, what," Belinda said, "are we supposed to—"

From somewhere deep in town came a sudden wailing that rose from high to low, a sound so brash and robotic and *loud* that, even there on the beach, Sam could nearly feel it vibrate in his ribs. Probably feeling it as well, Trina pulled her head from Gary's chest and looked wildly around the beach.

"It's happening," Gary yelled. He looked absolutely lost, in a way that even his wife's death hadn't brought him to.

"Not for sure," Sam yelled back. "We don't know for sure, right?"

Belinda grasped his arm and leaned close. "We have to get inside."

Dobbs came trotting back to them, his gun still in his hand. He put it in his pocket and then put his hands on Sam's and Gary's shoulders. The five of them formed a loose circle, a huddle, as Dobbs leaned forward. "Emergency siren. That's from the hospital, Jesus, a mile and a half away? Two miles?"

"That's loud," Sam said. "I didn't think anything could be so *loud*."

Dobbs nodded. He looked like somebody's grandfather out here, with his paunch and his silver hairs curling out from the collar of his shirt. But then Sam remembered the smooth, practiced motion when he'd emptied the revolver. "I don't know what in Christ's name is going on," Dobbs said, "but we all need to head to the station, just to be safe."

"The President's dead," Belinda said.

"We don't know that for sure," Gary said.

"I know it," Belinda said.

"It's dangerous out here right now," said Dobbs. "We'll see how serious things are once we get to the station. We'll get organized, figure out what happened. Figure out what we can do."

"Did you see that thing?" Sam asked.

Dobbs nodded, and Sam was grateful that at least this man made no bones about what they'd witnessed. "I did. I don't know what it was, but I saw it. I don't know what the hell is going on."

Trina signed something to Dobbs then, solemn and unsmiling, and Dobbs smiled at her. It took years off his face, that smile. He was grateful, probably, that she was safe. That she was speaking to him in whatever manner she was able. "What'd she say?" he asked Sam.

"Nothing," Sam yelled back. The wind was at his back and he felt the chill, thought about that moment when he'd discarded his jacket, the lightness he'd felt. The siren stopped and, within a moment, began another one of its drawn out, piercing cycles. "We should get going. We don't need to go home. We can follow you."

"Sam," Gary said.

"Dad, we need to go. He's right. We need to go *somewhere*."

Dobbs nodded.

Sam spared a last glance at the body on the beach. His heart was an amalgam of many different things at war with each other as he gazed at it. The body itself, from this distance, looked like nothing. A gathering of sticks, dark fabric. *That's a man*, he thought. *That's a person. Whatever happens to you, don't forget this. Don't forget what you saw, and how that guy looks now. Shit, he looks like laundry, like flung bones. Don't forget how final this is. That's a person.*

They began walking quickly back toward the ramp, up toward the parking lot where Dobbs's trouble light still spun, where it still roved red along the concrete and the sand, along the panels of their vehicles, where it illuminated the inside of the sheriff's truck, bright as a crime scene.

What Trina had signed to Dobbs, what Sam hoped wasn't true: *It's the end of the world.*

That he could still hope, though, that was something. After all of this, and whatever would happen to them next—through all of this, that he could still hold onto some vestige of hope at all. That counted for something, didn't it?

They walked up the ramp, the five of them, and Trina took his hand in hers.

Acknowledgments

Huge thanks to Tricia Reeks and Meerkat Press. This is a weird book, and you took a gamble. I'm indebted. My agent, Christopher Schelling of Selectric Artists, is a hilarious, fierce advocate for the writers he works with. I'm lucky.

Writing friends, who have provided me throughout the years with both thoughtful critiques of my work and a much-needed sense of fellowship: James Mapes, Ryan Sotomayor, Hannah Pass, C. Christopher Hart, Sheila Ashdown, Jeanie Gosline, Amy Lam, Alan Dubinsky, Christen McCurdy, Ron Austin, Mike Huguenor.

And tons of folks who've helped simply by being themselves: Robin Corbo, Darlene Morey, Jeffrey Arnsdorf, Lyndsay Hogland, Scott and Cat Bice, Lorene Morey, Sami Hensel, Tres Burns, Heather May Radetzke, Shawn Porter, Josie Corby.

And to anyone I've forgotten, let's hope there's another acknowledgments page in the future. I'll get you then, okay?

About the Author

Keith Rosson's fiction has appeared in *Redivider, Cream City Review, PANK, The Nervous Breakdown*, and more. He is the author of *The Best of Intentions: The Avow Anthology*, an omnibus collection of his long-running punk fanzine, *Avow*, as well as an illustrator and graphic designer, with clients that include Green Day, Against Me, the Goo Goo Dolls, and others. An advocate of both public libraries and non-ironic adulation of the cassette tape, he can be found at keithrosson.com.

an excerpt from

Smoke City
by Keith Rosson

Vale turned the dial on the radio, and we started drifting towards the shoulder. He settled on the Kinks—"Lola"—and absently put his hands back on the wheel.

One of my Five Rules: *Look for portents and signs.* Lola, I thought, close enough to Tyla? I was reaching.

Vale, meanwhile, was oblivious. Trying to light his cigarette going eighty with the window rolled down. "What brings you out on the road, Marvin?" His cigarette wagged as he spoke.

"I'm heading down south to visit a friend."

"Yeah? I'm heading down for a funeral, unfortunately."

"Sorry to hear that," I said. "How far south do you think you'll be going?"

"The funeral's in LA. I'm just doing a straight shot down there."

My heart did a clumsy stutter. *Portents and signs.* "So you're going straight to Los Angeles?"

Beyond the ceaseless repetition of my death and rebirths, I'd quit searching for any *meaning* a while back. How does one find meaning in a maelstrom? Order in a cyclone? The parameters of the Curse had made themselves clear long ago. It was like a palindrome, the repetition of it. But I believed in coincidence no more than I believed in benevolence. This was the problem with searching for portents and signs—once you found them, once they revealed themselves, what did you *do* with the goddamn things? How did you read them?

What were the odds that the man who picked me up in Portland would be taking a straight shot to Los Angeles, where Lyla was?

Vale finally got part of his cigarette lit, an inch-long section of ash running down one side of it. "Indeedy, straight there. I am heading to Los Angeles like a fucking bullet train, Marvin."

"Wow," I said, my voice heavy and strange in my own ears. "That's crazy. That's where I'm going, too."

Vale turned and looked at me—much longer than he should have, we started veering again—and said, "You should ride with me, Marvin. I could use the company." He sounded joyous, happy. A dark coin of blood had seeped through the gauze wrapped around his head. "To be honest, it's been a rough day."